THE GIRL WHO COULDN'T BE FOUND

FOUND

The Salazar Redwood Forest Thrillers
Book 3

LAUREN STREET

STERLING & STONE

Chapter One

Chapter One

TWO

Kody

TEN DAYS AGO...

"HERE WE GO. FINALLY."

Kody pulled her Subaru off the road and into the apparent parking lot hidden in the trees just off the narrow lane she'd been driving up and down for what felt like hours.

Leave it to Rip to get his directions completely mixed up.

Not even mixed up; they were just shit.

Kody had followed the frontage road past the cemetery, just like the man had told her. After that, his sense of distances and memory of what the parking spot actually looked like had ceased to be helpful to her.

As it turned out, she was more like twenty miles from Rip's farm after having passed the cemetery almost immediately. And when she'd first reached the end of the road, which didn't actually contain the shady parking spot Rip

3

had described at the head of the trail, she'd had to take a better look around before finally finding it.

This *had* to be it. There was nothing else here.

When she pulled her vehicle to a crunching stop on the gravel beneath layers of dry pinecones and small seeds popping under the rubber, Kody was certain this was it.

It better be. Or we're gonna have a serious problem.

But when she opened the driver's side door, stepped out, and deeply inhaled the crisp mountain air amidst the brightening sky just after dawn, her frustration subsided. Sure, she'd wanted to get a head start as early as possible, but even with backtracking so much to find the spot, it was still just past sunrise.

Now she was out here in the mountains at the head of a trail she meant to follow only for a little while until breaking off on her own, surrounded by nothing but the California wilderness once she left this spot at the end of the road.

With her motivation and excitement to get moving growing by the second, Kody pulled her trekking pack toward her from its place on the passenger seat and propped it up to look through her equipment and supplies one more time.

Two full bottles of water bottle plus iodine tablets for later. A whole pack of protein bars. Her survival blanket. The pink Hello Kitty whistle her mom Denise had bought her ten years ago but which still worked like a shrill charm when needed. Bear spray. Matches in a waterproof bag. Homemade granola. Fully charged phone. Map. Compass. Extra windbreaker. Twenty feet of coiled climbing rope. The utility knife she'd bought brand new online just two days ago for an epic steal.

Once she'd double-checked her list to make sure

everything was accounted for, she stretched across the front of the car to open the glovebox and drew out the unsealed envelope on which she'd written today's date. Then she pulled out a pen, checked her watch before scribbling down the time below the date, and set the envelope down on the driver's seat. It had to be clearly visible from the driver's-side window and through the front windshield, just in case.

"Prepare for anything."

That had been one of her dad's standing laws of life, as he called it, and Kody took it to heart now. Especially when she was heading out on a trail like this and then off-trail to cruise through the wilderness on her own.

That envelope contained everything someone else might need, should the worst-case scenario actually play out.

That wasn't likely, of course. The worst case was never likely, but it still existed for a reason, which was why Kody had written out her entire hiking plan, after weeks of studying maps and the layout of this particular range of mountains.

On multiple sheets of paper inside that envelope, she'd also written a date range of the forty-eight hours in which she intended to return to her car and then head back into town. At the end of it all, she'd signed her name, offered emergency contact information, and specified clear-cut instructions for anyone who found this letter to contact the authorities if Kody hadn't returned by her specified date within the allotted forty-eight-hour window.

"Prepared for everything."

With a flickering smile as her pulse quickened with the excitement of finally heading out for this, her longest solo overnight trek yet, Kody strapped on her pack, situated all her gear so it remained within easy reach, tightened the straps, and shut the driver's-side door.

Even after the last three years and hundreds of miles of backwoods hiking under her belt, the worst thing Kody could possibly do was act like her experience and proficiency levels were enough to protect her from unforeseen events.

With a deep breath and a firm nod at her car in farewell, she headed off into the thick forest that began literally right in front of where she'd parked.

Once Kody got about two miles in and was certain she was far enough from anything remotely resembling civilization, she took out her phone and started photographing her progress along the way.

Unfortunately, she'd missed the sunrise on this hike, thanks to Rip's unhelpfully inaccurate directions. But there were plenty more sunrises and sunsets ahead of her in the coming days, and it was always better to catch them in the middle of nature than from the front seat of her car.

Or standing on a path or beside a road.

Kody moved at a brisk but sustainable pace. She wanted to make it down the first five miles of the trail before she branched off on her own to follow the route she'd previously mapped out for herself. Once her watch beeped at the five-mile mark, she paused for a quick rest and a drink of water and surveyed her surroundings.

It was gorgeous up here. How anyone could live in a place like Rush and not spend all their free time out here in the mountains, amidst the redwoods and the stubby pine trees and all the local wildlife, was completely beyond her.

Still, she knew that kind of thing wasn't for everyone. Other people could do what they wanted with their own time, and she had her own trail to blaze.

Two miles later, she stopped again for her first protein bar of the day. Already, the energy from the giant breakfast she'd had before setting off this morning had worn out, which was fine. Kody knew exactly how to keep up her energy, when to stop before she completely burnt herself out, and what it felt like to burn out far sooner than she'd expected.

Not today.

Just as she finished her snack with another quick drink of water, gazing around at all the early-morning beauty at the very beginning of this next adventure, a crack and snap rose from behind her.

Kody paused.

That wasn't a normal sound, even for out here this far off the trail.

It sounded like footsteps crunching on twigs.

She slowly turned around, searching the trees stretching out in front of her. "Hello? Is anyone there?"

No reply.

If it had been another hiker out here, they definitely would have been close enough to hear her.

Wanting to make sure, Kody headed toward where she'd heard the sound. Before she reached it, a violent rustle of leaves made her stop again before two enormous crows surged from the trees in front of her.

Kody was quick enough to raise her phone and snap a picture of two fleeing crows against the bright azure backdrop before they disappeared. Smiling, she studied the photo, nodded, and continued scanning the area.

Then she found the huge dead branch that had newly fallen off the tree from somewhere yards above the forest floor. It had caught in the net-like branches of a thick manzanita bush stretching beneath the stand of trees. The branch was heavy enough to have fallen halfway through the bushes before finally being caught.

Not another hiker after all.

Situating her pack on her shoulders again, Kody took off along her pre-planned route once more, though now she found herself far more alert and aware of everything around her than she had been previously.

When her watch beeped again after another two miles, Kody couldn't help the feeling that something was a little off.

She'd studied this area of the mountains day after day for the last three weeks. Sure, Rip had given her a slightly different destination, but she'd memorized *that* route too in the last two days, committing to memory every natural checkpoint she intended to reach during the day. A little over ten miles already this morning, and she should have been standing in front of the low ridge dipping into an enormous valley on the other side.

There was no sign of the ridge or the valley.

Had she miscalculated?

That was always a possibility, though it would have been one hell of a rookie mistake for someone who'd been doing this for as long as Kody had.

So she stopped again to pull out the map Rip had given her when she'd decided she'd come take a look at this area of the mountain after all.

It wasn't *her* map. She'd figured someone who lived and worked so much closer to this area of the woods would have shared more detailed directions.

Then a surprisingly disturbing thought hit her.

What if Rip's map was as accurate as his verbal directions for finding the parking spot off the narrow dirt lane up here?

Don't be stupid. The guy didn't draw the map himself.

It didn't take her long to find the nine-mile point on her map from where she'd started. Sure enough, the map had the same ridge as the one she'd studied, just her own map marked with her pre-selected route, which she'd left behind.

By all rights, she should have been at that ridge right now. Or possibly in the next fifth of a mile at most, seeing as her starting point hadn't been exactly where she'd thought it would be.

Kody turned, surveying her surroundings.

Another crackling snap rose to her left. This one was louder and sounded closer.

But there was still no one there.

She stood perfectly still, focusing on catching any movement in her periphery instead of actively looking.

There were no crows this time. No signs of falling branches. No other rustling sounds that might have indicated a fox or rabbit or ground squirrel.

With a quick frown, Kody glanced at the map again, then reoriented herself with her compass and decided she'd keep going another mile or so before she might have to take another hard look at her route.

Five minutes later, she found herself climbing an outcropping of boulders rising at a steady incline. From an opening in the trees, the bright blue sky stretched out forever above her. Whatever concern had been growing inside her dissipated with the feel of moss-covered rocks beneath her fingers and the solid support of footholds in the boulders beneath her boots.

Kody loved climbing too, pushing the boundaries of her strength and determination to make it to the top of something. Not every hike included literal rock climbing. But when it did, she was always happy to brush up on her technical skills — not just for show but for practicality, useful in situations like today's.

Almost at the summit, she was certain this was the ridge she'd been looking for. It would dip down onto the other side into a wide, sprawling valley with a small lake a few kilometers across, where she could take another break and refill her extra water bottle before filtering it with the iodine.

When she reached the top, though, a tight, heavy knot sank in the pit of her stomach.

There was no sign of the lake.

This was definitely a ridge with a somewhat steep but passable descent along even more boulders on the other side. Just no lake.

No sprawling valley, either.

"Seriously?" she murmured.

Scrunching up her face, Kody turned on the top of the boulders to look back the way she'd come. Even from this vantage point, she didn't see any sign of where the lake might have been within the valley. Frankly, she hadn't seen anything else she was supposed to have recognized by now.

This hadn't happened in a long time. Not since her second solo hike.

It had to be because of Rip's damn directions.

She should have recalibrated from that parking spot instead of just chalking it up to the man's muddled memory.

She stopped at the top of the boulders and turned to her cellphone again, this time to pull up her GPS instead of the camera.

But even at this elevated spot among the rolling hills and steep drops of the mountain range, cell service was nonexistent. Not even enough for the GPS to pull up her location, let alone a digital map of her current surroundings.

"Damn."

Slipping her phone back into the pocket of her windbreaker, Kody figured she should turn around and retrace her steps, no matter how disappointing that might be.

Better yet, she might even go all the way back to her car, recalculate her route, and, worst-case scenario, start over early tomorrow morning now that she knew exactly where she'd be starting from.

That small fluttering of defeat and disappointment she hadn't felt in years, however, kept her from acting on her first gut instinct.

She wasn't some beginner. Her dad had taught her exactly how to do this. She just had to find one of the landmarks and reorient herself from there.

Even if Rip had given her shitty directions and she'd started somewhere completely different than her planned route, it wasn't like the man could just snap his fingers and change the cardinal directions. Kody still had a compass, she had plenty of daylight left, and it wasn't even 10:00 a.m. yet.

So she descended the other side of the boulders instead, determined to make this work.

Halfway to the bottom of a valley much smaller than the one she was supposed to have reached by now, she spotted a cave about half a mile to the northwest.

That could be something. It was a major landmark, at least.

Kody descended diagonally the rest of the way toward that cave. When she finally reached the bottom of the boulders' incline, she found a new surprise waiting for her.

Something she preferred not to see while trekking through the wilderness, especially on this particular trip.

Another hiker.

It was impossible to tell his age from this distance, though he carried himself like a man in his late twenties or early thirties. He wore jeans, a hoodie, and sneakers, of all things.

She fought back a laugh. Some people just really liked their sneakers.

Kody moved toward the cave. Once she thought the other hiker could see her from that distance, she lifted a hand in greeting and offered a quick wave.

He tilted his head and returned the wave, then stuck both hands into the front pockets of his hoodie and just stood there, watching her.

Well, at least he's not trying to follow me, I guess.

She headed toward him until they were close enough Kody was relatively certain they could hear each other without screaming at the top of their lungs. The guy was still watching her, so she briefly lifted her hand again and called out, "Hey, there. Maybe *you* can help me. I'm supposed to be at a lake right now. Do you know if there's one close by?"

The other hiker slowly shook his head and shifted his weight onto one foot. He gazed out over the smaller valley around them, squinting against the sunlight. "No lakes this way. You lost?"

"As much as I hate to say it, yeah. I think I just might be."

Sounds like he *knows his way around the area, though.*

One more loud, startling crack rose behind her — so loud and so close Kody flinched and instantly spun around, preparing to leap out of the way or duck to avoid more falling branches.

But she found herself standing face to face with Rip Graham.

No. It wasn't Rip.

It absolutely looked like him. Same height, same build, same scrutinizing gaze without any other display of emotion. They even had the same slight crookedness at the tip of their noses. But this guy standing in front of her looked quite a bit older than Rip, at least a decade. He'd grown his hair out long past his shoulders, and it was a light gray bordering on white instead of Rip's dark brown going salt-and-pepper at the temples.

"Whoa." Kody flashed him a quick smile. "You snuck up on me. Nice day, huh?"

The man said nothing as he took three more easy steps toward her. His long walking stick — quite a bit thicker than Kody would have picked out for herself — thumped onto the ground beside him as he looked her up and down.

"That's a hell of a walking stick," she added. When he didn't respond, she figured she might as well take advantage of speaking to another human. "Uh … this is a little embarrassing, actually. I'm looking for a lake on this mountain. I had mapped it out on my route, but apparently, I made a few miscalculations. You think you could show me where we are on a map?"

The man stopped just in front of her and lifted his chin. "Lake, huh?"

"Do you know where it is?"

He stared at her.

Kody took it as assent, though, and slid one strap of her pack off her shoulder so she could get to said map. "Once I know where I am now, I'm sure I can make it to where I'm supposed to be. Guess it serves me right for asking the wrong person for directions, but now I've learned my lesson."

The second Kody pulled her map from her pack and

looked back up at the man, he moved faster than she could have possibly anticipated.

The next thing she knew, he'd lifted his enormous walking stick in both hands to swing it back and high over his shoulder.

It whistled through the air as it swung toward her head.

Kody didn't even have enough time to shout in surprise before the whole world went dark.

THREE

Sam

"WHAT DID I DO TO DESERVE SUCH A SHITTY DAY?"

Sam parked her Jeep in the lot of the old bus station in downtown Rush, which had closed down just before she'd rolled into town almost two and a half years ago. Now the place was little more than an abandoned building of what had once been the station, and free parking for anybody who wanted to use it.

Sam definitely did. She wasn't going to pay for parking if she could help it, especially because she was already paying for what she was about to do and would pay some more before it was all said and done.

Gritting her teeth, she stared through the front windshield at nothing in particular, then slapped a hand down on the steering wheel and finally turned off the engine.

Come on, Sam. Show a little backbone, huh? Get out.

That little personal pep-talk got her as far as slipping out of her Jeep and making the half-mile walk from the old bus station to a squat brick building right there on Rush's main center drag. When she reached the front doors, she briefly scanned the brass plaque tacked to the brick beside the door, touting this particular edifice as one of the very oldest in Rush and protected by the county's Historical Preservation Society.

And here she was, about to step inside to do one of the things she absolutely hated more than almost anything else in this world.

Something she'd sworn she would never let herself do again after the last time. That had been nightmare enough.

Standing at the building's entrance, Sam quickly scanned the sidewalk on the side of Main Street in both directions. There weren't many people out this early in the morning on a Wednesday. Sam usually wasn't up this early, either, but she'd forced herself out of bed anyway.

It just had to be done.

You fucking coward, she thought, staring at the door handle. *Quit trying to talk yourself out of this. You're the one who stepped in it, and now you gotta clean up the mess. Let's go.*

With a pained grimace, she pushed down on the handle much harder than necessary and practically flung the door open to enter the building.

A loud bang of the weighted door hitting the interior wall echoed within the bare lobby serving as a central point for all the signs directing visitors to different offices and destinations inside.

Sam headed straight for the staircase off the right-hand side of the lobby. The door into the stairwell banged open just as violently before she slipped through and stomped up the stairs to the second floor.

Sure, she made a hell of a lot of noise, but it felt like the only way she was going to push herself through to the very end and get this done.

She'd been putting it off for far too long after one excuse or another, and now she was paying the price for it.

Including having to be here first thing in the morning in the middle of the week.

There were only two doors at the top of the staircase, one of them marked as a janitor's closet and the other propped wide open, as if that would encourage anyone to come right on in at their own leisure.

Yeah ... step right on into hell.

She almost turned around to bolt back down the stairs, but her feet moved her forward anyway. Then she'd entered the reception area of the last place on earth she wanted to be.

Even the lobby had a sterile, slightly sweet, minty odor to it. All over the country, it was the same. The smell she'd quickly come to associate with agony and torture.

Sam paused briefly to eye the six-foot-wide aquarium propped on a large dresser at the side of the reception area. The fish in there flittered around between bits of fake coral and a tiny plastic skeleton in a pirate hat beside an equally fake treasure chest that rocked open every twenty seconds to let out a burst of bubbles before it closed again.

Wouldn't wish a cage like that on anyone. But right now, those fish have it better than I do.

She wrinkled her nose and headed for the desk on the other side of the room.

The receptionist looked friendly enough, but of course that was all just a ruse. All the smiles and welcomes and posturing of care and empathy were just a fake front for the real horrors that took place on the other side of this lobby.

Sam knew it. Everyone who worked here knew it. They had to.

"Good morning," the receptionist said. "Checking in?"

"Yeah."

"Go ahead and sign in right here. Someone will call

you back when he's ready for you." The woman slid a clipboard with sheets of lined paper and a pen across the desk toward Sam.

Both the pen and the top of the clipboard had been marked with the credentials of this place: Dr. Turner, DDO.

It looked official as hell, and that still didn't make Sam feel any better about what she was walking into.

She filled out her personal details according to the sign-in sheet, then slid the clipboard back toward the receptionist and turned away before the woman could strike up any further conversation.

This wasn't a place for small talk and making new friends.

This was a place where the unfortunate souls who skimped on certain requirements of daily adult life came to be punished for their transgressions.

Sam eyed the chair closest to the open front door of the office and fully intended to sit in it. That way, if she lost her nerve, she could jump through that open door and bolt down the staircase again without anything getting in her way.

Before she even crossed half the lobby again, her phone buzzed in her back pocket. She pulled it out to see who was calling.

It was Meredith.

That's a surprise.

Meredith. She was hot and cold toward Sam, even when they were together in person. But the woman was well-known within certain circles for running the town's only available Twelve-Step meetings at the Community Center, so getting a call from her was particularly odd.

Sam wouldn't have had time to answer even if she'd wanted to.

A woman's voice called across the entirely empty lobby. "Samantha Salazar?"

Shit.

Sam thrust her phone into the back pocket of her jeans again and turned around with wide eyes.

The receptionist smiled at her with a little beckoning wave. "Right this way, Samantha. I'll bring you on back. We've got a room waiting for you."

"It's Sam," she corrected.

The other woman's smile widened as she waited for Sam to catch up.

As they moved through the hallway shooting straight back across the building, Sam rolled her shoulders back and held her head high. The hall looked fairly benign, walls painted in an allegedly calming pale-mint green, which was honestly a color that made her start to feel nauseous.

But when the receptionist let her into the first patient room they reached and gestured for Sam to take a seat, Sam knew this was where the real horror began.

"Dr. Turner will be right with you," the woman said, then slipped out of the room altogether, pulling the door shut behind her.

Sam wouldn't have been surprised if she heard a lock turning from the outside even though, so far in her life, she'd never witnessed that actually happening.

Now it was just her in this room, among the cabinets of grotesque figurines and diagrams and all manner of tools and molds she really could have done without having to look at today.

Of particularly morbid curiosity was the tall glass display cabinet against a wall to her left filled with dental molds, some of which boasted real teeth placed within the mold setting instead of the dried plaster knock-off. She could tell they were real teeth because all the rest of the molds were of either a dark-gray or light-blue plaster.

The real teeth looked like real fucking teeth.

Some of them were cracked and split. Some had turned almost entirely black. One was gold-plated, winking at her — a macabre mockery of the horrifying circumstances in which she now found herself.

On the top shelf were a number of old, shiny metal instruments that looked more like torture devices than something that had any business in the vicinity of a living human's mouth.

Like Sam's, for instance.

Which had suddenly gone quite dry.

A brisk knock came from the other side of the door, which opened slowly before a man who couldn't have been older than thirty-seven or thirty-eight at most stepped into the room, wearing that damned white medical coat with light-purple stitching over the left breast pocket to spell out the same name that was all over this place's branded office supplies: Doctor Zach Turner, DDO.

"You must be Sam," he said, flashing her a beaming grin as he turned to gently shut the door behind him.

Sam's eyebrows shot straight up.

Guess the receptionist was listening, after all.

"I'm Dr. Turner," he said, turning back toward her. "Haven't seen you in here before."

He extended a hand toward her, and she stood to take it.

"I try to stay away as much as possible," she said.

He laughed. "You and everyone else in this town, it seems. I'm the man *no one* wants to see, but when it comes right down to it, I'm the only man for the job."

"Lucky you."

"Ditto," he replied with a flickering smile. "You've come to the best of the best."

"I could definitely do without the front-row seat to the horror show over there." Sam nodded toward the curio cabinet full of teeth molds and torture devices. "Is that a trophy case or something?"

Dr. Turner chuckled. "Most of that stuff my dad collected. He's retired now, and I'm the lucky guy who inherited the practice afterward. Definitely a whole-family affair, though. My mom used to buy him a new mold or antique dental instrument or fossil, like some of those, every year for their wedding anniversary."

"Nothing says true love like someone else's teeth," Sam quipped.

"Well, I just couldn't bring myself to toss any of it out. Quite a history in these cases, you know? Every one of our patient rooms has one. Sure, I inherited the practice and kept the family business going, but I have to admit my dad's the one with the real love of teeth and what they can say about the person they once belonged to."

Sam snorted and folded her arms. "Where the hell does she even *get* stuff like that?"

"eBay, mostly."

They shared a laugh at that. Dr. Turner's was light and easygoing, while Sam's felt like a crab shell covered in spikes was trying to work its way back up her throat.

Against her better judgment, she stepped closer to the cabinet and pointed at one of the aforementioned "fossils," which was an entire jaw mounted on display. "What would these teeth tell you about the person they belonged to?"

Dr. Turner tilted his head to study the item in question and raised an eyebrow. "First and foremost, they tell me that person was a dog."

She couldn't help it. Sam laughed again, and it was

genuine, and it made her feel like a traitor to all poor lost souls who found a trip to the dentist just as excruciatingly agonizing as she did.

Dr. Turner's gray eyes glinted at her above a widening grin. "Why don't you come on over here, Sam, and take a seat. We can get a good look at that cavity. See what needs to be done. And if all goes well, we'll have you out of here in no time."

"If?" Sam plunked herself down into the dentist's chair and wriggled around, trying to get comfortable and unable to decide whether that included her arms slumped over the armrests or not. "What happens when all *doesn't* go well?"

Dr. Turner rounded the chair and stopped just beside her as he wheeled a metal cart toward him before reaching for the overhead light on a swivel. "Let's just hope it doesn't come to that."

She gaped up at him and almost leapt out of the chair again before he chuckled.

"I'm kidding, Sam. Only kidding. Can't help but play into the stereotype every once in a while. You'll be fine. I promise."

"I'm gonna hold you to that," she said, facing forward again and tightly clamping down on the chair's armrests, her fingers digging into the upholstery with barely audible squeaks.

"Comes with the territory."

Then his dental assistant entered the room and, in a flurry of hurried activity, got Sam all dressed up and ready to go — little paper napkins strapped around her neck, all the tools and implements on the tray prepped and waiting, and a bunch of dental-jargon bullshit Sam wished she could understand so she would at least know what to expect.

Neither of them bothered to explain any of the more confounding words and phrases.

But Dr. Turner was incredibly gentle from the get-go. While he talked at her as he worked, asking questions Sam didn't bother to answer, she stared at that cabinet of morbid curiosities on the far side of the room, thinking that at least half of those jaws, frozen and eternal, were grinning back at her the whole time.

FOUR

Sam

SAM HEADED STRAIGHT TO THE REDWOOD RINGS FOR HER shift behind the Back Bar, though she hadn't bothered to look at the time when she entered because everything felt like it was running on autopilot now.

Except she didn't make it across the front pub and through the swinging doors of the kitchen toward the back office, due to the constant, heavy drip of water pouring from the ceiling in at least three different places she could see and pinging into a metal mixing bowl, a trash can, and what sounded like a soup pot.

Still, she went to the bar, on a mission to head straight for the fountain gun beside the ice bucket to fill up a glass of ice water. Her mouth still felt funny as hell and partially numb, though partially in this scenario was more like eighty percent. She kept touching the right side of her lower lip to make sure it still felt like a lip from the outside and not some garish experimental thing the dentist had gotten away with when adding onto her cavity filling.

Sam almost lifted the cup to her mouth, then opted for

25

a straw and tried taking tiny sips to help her parched throat.

The swinging doors from the kitchen squealed a little behind her. Footsteps headed her way, then stopped abruptly.

"Holy shit. Look who showed up on time today."

"Did I really?" Sam asked.

"Yeah, and unfortunately for us, it might as well not have happened." Chris headed toward her and nodded at the leaks pouring down through the ceiling. "Upstairs plumbing sprang a leak. Haven't quite figured out exactly where it's coming from yet. Still working on it."

"Doesn't sound like something that normally takes you more than an hour or two." Sam tried not to frown at her own words, which sounded as stuffy and muffled as they felt while practically tumbling from between her numbly swollen lips.

Chris shrugged. "It's not normally something that makes me all that suspicious, either, but I'm still not convinced this is entirely accidental."

She turned to look at him with raised eyebrows, and Chris rolled his eyes.

"The Petes have been pressuring me to fire you, you know," he said.

"So you think they're the ones who broke your pipes?"

"Of course not." The usual certainty in his voice that filtered into statements Chris Nelson actually meant was entirely absent now. "Don't get me wrong, Sam. I'm glad you showed up in town when you did. I'm glad you're still here. But there's no denying life was a hell of a lot quieter before you did."

"And here I was, thinking I'm a quiet, pretty laid-back person."

"Looks like you get to keep being that today," he said.

"Bar's closed until this plumbing situation gets fixed. However long that's gonna take."

"You don't sound all that upset about it."

He studied her face, and the corners of his mouth flickered in a joking smile. "Honestly, I'm just thinking it's a good thing we're closing up. With all the drool on your chin right now, you're bound to scare off customers anyway. Might as well keep them outside."

"Shit." Sam dabbed at lips she couldn't feel with the back of a hand. Sure enough, she'd been drooling all over herself and probably hadn't even gotten half the ice water into her mouth the way she'd intended. "It's temporary."

"Christ, I hope so. What'd you do? Walk face first into a brick wall on your way over?"

Sam glared at him. "Brick wall sounds like a walk in the park compared to this. Had a cavity filled."

Chris grimaced. "Ouch."

"Don't even." She wiped again at her chin and the corners of her mouth before wiping the back of her hand off on her pant legs. Sam looked across the front pub and nodded at a table in the corner where Christian, Levi, and Eddie sat nursing their drinks. "What's up with them?"

"Looks pretty normal to me," he said.

"They're never here this early on a Wednesday," she told him. "Other days, sure. But didn't you just say the bars were closed until the ceiling stopped dripping?"

"Yeah, but I can't get rid of 'em." Chris shrugged. "As far as it being Wednesday, apparently, the sawmill's been cutting back again. This is what happens when hard-working men get laid off."

Sam glanced again at the guys huddled in their corner table. "You're letting them stay?"

"It's not like they were gonna pay me anyway," Chris

said, raising his voice so the guys would hear him. "It's the least I can do."

The fellas all raised their half-empty pint glasses one by one in a silent, morose toast toward the bar.

Sam jerked her chin up at them. "So what are you guys gonna do now?"

"Question of the century, Sam," Levi said before tipping back his beer.

"That's why we're here," Eddie added. "Brainstorming session, you know?"

Christian drained his glass, slapped it down on the table, and turned toward her with a grin. "You know what? I'm thinking I might take up gold panning."

All three of them cracked up laughing, and Sam couldn't hold back a small smile.

Leave it to hardworking men to make jokes about a few tough hits on a run of bad luck. At least when they had a drink during the process, anyway.

"As proud as I am to see you finally in here on time," Chris added, "you can split whenever you want."

"You sure there's nothing I can do to help with the plumbing?"

"Not unless you've got a plumber's certification I don't know about and a whole lot of tools I don't know where to begin finding." He stuck his hands on his hips and shrugged. "Something tells me that's a shot in the dark."

She smirked at him. "Don't count it out. There's still plenty about me you don't know."

Chris cocked his head and raised his eyebrows. "Are you really gonna tell me what to do here?"

"No way in hell." Sam nodded at the ceiling. "Not with *these* pipes."

He snorted and waved her away with a bar rag. "Get outta here. I'll let you know when we're back in business."

"Let me know if we're *not*, too, huh? I've still got my shifts on the schedule."

"I'll be in touch, Sam." He grinned at her, and she figured it was better to get out of the Redwood and out of Chris' way to let him focus on repairs.

No point in her being here during the day if she wasn't working, because she certainly wouldn't stay at the Redwood for a drink.

When Sam walked back out to her Jeep, she wondered what she was supposed to do with all this newfound free time that had suddenly sprung up in her schedule. Leaky pipes weren't that big of a deal, but they'd also sprung a leak in her routine, and that could potentially turn into an even bigger problem for her personally.

Sam Salazar — at loose ends with nothing to keep her busy and nothing to take her mind off the boredom — and the fun-but-deadly things she used to do to alleviate that boredom were not a good combination.

Maybe she should get out of town for a while, take some unplanned time off now that it had been given to her anyway. Maybe go find some other town, see the sights, entertain herself somehow...

No, if she left, there was a good chance Sam might never come back to Rush, California. As much as she didn't want to admit it, there was enough in this town to keep her here a little longer. For now.

Instead, she drove out of the town center and down the frontage road through the middle of nowhere back to Birdsong Park and the trailer she called home.

Syc was out in his usual lawn chair by the firepit when she arrived, with trusty Dog lying in the grass beside him like just about every morning.

Sam disappeared inside the Deville to grab a can of Coke from the mini fridge. Then the park filled with the sharp clack of her trailer's door smacking shut, followed by the bright, refreshing hiss and snap of opening the only thing she ever drank out of a can these days — non-alcoholic, loaded with sugar, but still with plenty of kick to get the job done.

Caffeine and cigarettes would have to do.

Sam plopped down into the lawn chair that had unofficially become hers over the last two and a half years of sitting in it next to Syc almost every morning and evening. She chugged half the Coke at once, then pulled out her smokes and lit one to add another thick gray cloud to the puffs of white in the air rising from Syc's joint.

He stared into the crackling fire without looking at her. "What're you doing back so soon?"

"Temporarily out of work, apparently."

"You don't work at the sawmill."

She snorted. "No shit. Guess the cutbacks are making their rounds through everything right now."

"And how long is 'temporary' supposed to last?"

"As long as it takes for Chris to fix some leaky pipes. From the look of things, my guess is a week. Maybe two."

Syc tapped the ash off the end of his joint without moving any other part of his body. "That bad, huh?"

"Come on, man, I'm really trying to look on the bright side here."

"Uh-huh. Ain't you always."

They sat by the fire with nothing but Dog and silence between them for a moment longer. The mutt let out a squealing yawn, then rolled over in the grass to wiggle around and for a good back scratch.

Sam couldn't help but smile as she watched him. "And this guy doesn't have a care in the world, does he?"

"I gave up trying to read his mind ages ago," Syc said.

"Speaking of, some guy showed up here today asking for you."

Sam looked sharply up at Syc. "Does this guy have a name?"

"Sure. Didn't give it, though. But I took a picture, just in case. Figured I'd hold onto it and let you take a look when it came up."

"Let's see it, then." Sam extended her hand toward Syc's lawn chair, and he slowly rummaged around in his pockets, between his legs, and then in the folds of his long-sleeve flannel shirt before finally producing a ridiculously outdated flip phone.

He took his sweet time clicking through that technological dinosaur just to find said picture.

If Sam had been on a time crunch for anything, she would have lost her patience with him after about twenty seconds. Instead, she bit back a laugh, forcing herself not to bombard the guy with smart-ass comments about his phone being almost as old as he was.

"Here." Syc finally handed over his flip phone, and Sam peered at the tiny square picture captured in grainy non-detail with only a little color.

She snorted. "Oh yeah. Back of this dude's head is *real* defined. Thanks for this, Syc. I bet I could pick him out in a crowd anywhere."

"Piss off," he grumbled, but a smirk flashed across his lips before he puffed on his joint again.

"I appreciate the heads-up, though." Sam handed back his phone.

"Don't mention it. And no, I didn't tell him a goddamn thing."

"Never even crossed my mind."

Syc tucked his phone away again somewhere within his clothes, then cleared his throat but said nothing.

It wasn't exactly the kind of news Sam enjoyed getting — that some dude without a name and only the back of his head captured on camera had found where she lived and come to question her landlord-neighbor-friend about her.

She downed the rest of her Coke, leaned back in the lawn chair with a sigh, then took another long drag of her cigarette before flopping both arms down on the canvas armrests. "Can't really put it off much longer after this, though."

"What's that?" Syc asked, still staring at the low flames in the firepit.

"Getting a firearm. Been thinking about it for a while, but nothing ever really felt like the right time until now."

Silence was the only response she got before Syc grunted and pushed himself to his feet.

"Where are you going?" Sam asked.

"You stay right where you are." With that, Syc ambled off toward his own trailer.

Dog remained stretched out on his back in the grass, though he slightly lifted his head to look at Sam and let his tongue flop over the side of his mouth.

Then the clack of Syc's trailer door echoed across the park.

He wasn't gone very long, and when he came back, Syc stopped beside Sam's chair instead of returning directly to his own like usual.

Next thing she knew, Sam was staring at the polished wooden grip of an old Smith & Wesson Model 629 revolver shoved right under her nose.

She looked up at him. "I didn't mean I was trying to take one of yours."

"I ain't using it." Syc wiggled the revolver at her, and she took the heavy but smooth wooden grip in one hand before holding the weapon across her lap to give it a good once-over.

Syc returned to his lawn chair with a heavy sigh. "Was my dad's. Never much liked the thing myself, but you're welcome to it."

"And leave you unprotected all the way out here?" She shot him a sidelong glance.

He crossed one leg over the other and leaned back in his chair. "You and I both know that's a load of shit."

No, she didn't expect Syc to only own one firearm for personal protection. Not with what little she knew about Syc, which was more than enough for her. To date, he hadn't once let her down.

Sam deftly opened the pistol's cylinder, her smile widening at the telltale click of it spinning slowly in her fingers. "This thing's been well taken care of."

"Of course it has."

"And it's fully loaded."

"Of course it is. Don't expect me to shell out for more ammo, though, Sam. That's on you."

Chuckling, Sam clicked the cylinder back into place and hefted the revolver in her hand, testing its weight.

She didn't *want* to have to use this thing, and she didn't particularly plan of having to use it for any reason. No one ever did.

But she felt a hell of a lot better knowing she could, if necessary, and that was what mattered.

It had been a long time since she'd felt the solid weight of a firearm in her grip. Though it hadn't occurred to her before now, she knew she wouldn't have been ready to hold one again before this very moment.

That, in turn, inevitably made her wonder what else she might be ready for that she hadn't even let herself consider until it showed up right in her lap.

FIVE

Sam

SAM WOKE UP TEN MINUTES BEFORE SUNRISE THE NEXT morning with an honest-to-god smile on her face. By the time she was out of the park's community showers, the sun was up, and she actually felt like sitting down for a breakfast of Apple Jacks cereal and milk to kickstart the day spreading out wide open in front of her.

She couldn't remember the last time she'd gone to bed as early as she had last night. She couldn't remember the last time she'd slept this well, either.

After washing up her breakfast dishes, Sam stopped at the kitchen counter as her gaze fell on the pistol Syc had given her. No, it wasn't the best idea to leave something like this lying out on the kitchen counter, but she hadn't quite known what to do with it last night.

Now, she wondered whether it was a good idea to start carrying again, too.

With Sam's luck, there was always something just around the corner that needed running from or facing or fighting off. In some ways, it was a damn miracle she'd lasted this long without personal protection — either before or after she'd had her taser confiscated.

She didn't feel like she was in any immediate danger, but now she had Chris telling her that the Petes wanted her fully out of a job at the Redwood Rings, plus Syc telling her that some strange dude with a funny-looking back of his head had shown up at her home, asking about her.

Maybe carrying again was called for these days.

Maybe she was overreacting and jumping the gun too quickly, as it were.

Probably for the best she left the revolver at home for now.

Instead of leaving it out on the kitchen counter like an idiot who didn't know how to care for, conceal, or even handle a weapon like this, she tucked it into the narrow drawer of the only small side table that fit in the Deville's tiny-ass living room and called it good.

If she needed the thing later, she knew where it was.

With no work today and no other plans, Sam hopped into her Jeep to head to today's morning NA meeting, which she would have gone to anyway before work.

No more than a quarter mile past the entrance to Birdsong Park, Sam came upon a dark SUV parked on the side of the dirt road that only led to Birdsong Park in the first place. The vehicle's windows were so darkly tinted, she couldn't even tell if the SUV was occupied.

Pretty strange when she'd never seen this car before and there was no reason for anyone else to be parked here on the dirt shoulder unless they were having car troubles.

She might have stopped to help with those, but there was no sign of anyone in or around the SUV, so she just kept going.

The long dirt road curved back and forth through the woods on its way to the wider, more frequently used frontage road crossing the highway into Rush's center. Sam found herself enjoying the drive for as much as she could enjoy something she did multiple times every day and could probably do with her eyes closed if it came to it.

When the road finally straightened out, she looked up in her rearview mirror to see the same dark SUV pulling around the last bend and quickly coming up right on her ass.

"What the hell?"

Sam stepped on the gas, frowning at the rearview mirror and now going fifteen over the speed limit. The roads here weren't frequently patrolled by local Rush police or even state troopers. Not out here in the middle of nowhere, so high speeds didn't mean much.

Apparently, they didn't mean much to the driver behind the SUV's ridiculously tinted windows, either.

The other vehicle kept pace with her, the sound its engine rising above the otherwise fairly loud growl of the engine of the Jeep that had gotten her through so many other tight spots over the years. When Sam put on another burst of speed, so did the SUV.

Then it started flashing its lights at her.

"Oh fuck no," she muttered, scowling at the front of the vehicle in the rearview mirror.

And of course, she'd left the damn pistol in her trailer.

Sam wasn't an idiot, though. She didn't slow down, and she didn't go to her original destination at Rush's Community Center off the frontage road, also surrounded by nothing but dirt road and thick woods. Instead, she went all the way into town down Rush's main drag. This time, she drove at exactly the speed limit, thinking maybe the other driver would see this as an opportunity and screw up by driving like a lunatic in a thirty-five zone.

The driver slowed down too and stayed on her the

whole way, though he'd stopped flashing his lights now that there were potential witnesses around.

Sam kept her cool. Being tailed was one thing. Being overly paranoid was something else entirely, and she wasn't about to cross that line just yet.

So she changed her plans slightly and headed for the police station instead.

The SUV followed all the way to the point where Sam deliberately engaged her turn signal like a good, law-abiding citizen before slowing down and turning into the station's parking lot.

The dark SUV slowed down with her.

She started to wonder if maybe the driver had the same idea all along of going straight to the Rush PD anyway. Then the SUV kept going straight, putting on one more small burst of speed to pass the station but still remaining within the legal speed limit.

Sam pulled her Jeep into an available parking space just in case and let out a long, slow breath.

That was weird as hell.

There was a good chance the driver of that SUV was the same weird-headed stranger who'd questioned Syc about her yesterday, which meant Sam definitely needed to start carrying. Also thanks to Syc, she now had a weapon of her own again.

Not that it did her any good when it was in the side table at home and Sam was out here.

A brisk knock on her driver's-side window startled her away from her search of the town's main street behind her through the rearview mirror. Blinking quickly, she jerked her head forward, forced herself not to laugh, and rolled down the window even before Chief Ralph Colton motioned for her to do so.

"Can I help you with something, Salazar?" he asked

gruffly, gracing her with his perpetual scowl that never changed. At least not in Sam's presence.

"Morning, Chief." She flashed him a smile they both knew was completely fake at this point. "Thanks for offering, but no, I'm good. Thanks."

"What the hell are you doing here?"

"Oh, just visiting. Really sets the mind at ease knowing the station's here, you know? Still intact. Still full of Rush's finest men and women in blue. You have yourself a good morning, Chief."

"Uh-huh." Colton studied her a minute longer, chewing on his bottom lip with both thumbs thrust through the loops of his belt. "Get a move on."

Then he walked away.

Sam rolled up her window and got ready to pull back out of the station parking lot, but not before her gaze fell on the giant bulletin board posted outside the station's front doors. This one was covered in old missing-persons posters, ninety-nine percent of which contained photos, descriptions, and last known whereabouts of girls and women between the ages of seven and seventy-eight.

The sight left a deep, dark, gnawing pit in the depths of Sam's stomach.

She swallowed, tore her gaze away from the bulletin board, and backed out of the parking space.

SIX

Kody

TEN DAYS AGO...

KODY'S HEAD felt like someone had split it open with an axe.

The pain of it when she first regained consciousness was nothing compared to the spinning dizziness in the complete darkness when she pushed herself up on the cold, hard ground.

Not ground, exactly. It felt more like solid stone beneath her hands, but she didn't have much longer to grope around with her fingers before the dizziness overwhelmed her and she lurched forward on hands and knees.

The sound of her own vomiting echoed around her, louder than it should have been. When she finally stopped, she wiped her mouth with the back of her light jacket sleeve and swallowed, trying to catch her breath.

Then she remembered what had happened.

It hadn't been an axe to the head after all. Just a giant walking stick. Kody knew enough about what she was feeling now to safely assume she was the proud new owner of a slightly-more-than-mild concussion.

She sat perfectly still for a few minutes, trying to let her vision adjust to the darkness. It almost always did, as long as she gave herself enough time, but it just wasn't happening now. Not here.

Gingerly, she patted down her sides and found her phone still in her jacket pocket, where she'd kept it within easy reach for all her photography endeavors during her hike.

The light blazing from the screen when she turned it on almost blinded her, sending another spear of agonizing pain through her head.

Kody instantly clenched her eyes shut against the glare. It took another minute before she could open her eyes without thinking she might vomit again, then she turned on her phone's flashlight app and used it to investigate her new surroundings.

No wonder it was pitch-dark in here without her phone.

She was sitting inside some kind of pit with a mostly smooth bottom in a rough circle about eight feet in diameter, surrounded by crudely cut circular walls of stone and packed earth. When she shone the light up above her, all she saw was more stone and more barely illuminated darkness. The ceiling had to be at least twenty feet above her, if not more, but it did seem like the walls of this pit ended about twelve feet off the floor.

Was she in that same cave she'd seen before being attacked by a man with a big stick?

A shiver raced through her, and she zipped up her light jacket with trembling fingers, hoping it would be enough to ward off the chill.

Definitely in a cave, then.

With absolutely no way to get out of this pit and no one around to help her.

Or at least the two men who found her out in the wilderness wouldn't help her. Clearly, it hadn't been their intention after knocking her senseless and tossing her down here.

Despite her best efforts to maintain a grip on her reason and sanity, Kody couldn't help the swell of panic rising up her throat.

This hadn't been part of the plan. It wasn't like she hadn't prepared for every eventuality, but when she checked her phone again, there was no service whatsoever. The date was the same, though, and the time showed only about half an hour had passed since she'd last checked it, which meant she hadn't been down here very long.

Somehow, that just wasn't very reassuring.

With her phone's flashlight beam, she searched the floor of the pit around her, and her panic only intensified when there was no sign of her pack.

"Hello?" she called, her voice echoing over and over, up and away from her. "Hello? Is anyone up there? Please help. I'm down here!"

She hadn't really expected a reply, but she'd had to try.

With her heart racing and her hands trembling, Kody patted herself down to take inventory of what was available to her. Her pack was gone, and that was a major loss, but she did still have her phone, along with one smaller water bottle and two protein bars tucked into the other pocket of her jacket.

That was something.

After that, she took inventory of herself, gently prodding the sorest spots of her head and wincing at the brief flashes of pain shooting through her at the pressure. But she didn't feel any wetness. If that crack to the head had split her open, at least the bleeding had stopped or she wasn't bleeding at all.

Everything else just felt sore and tender and heavy. Her left shoulder and hip ached furiously, and she found her arms and legs covered in bruises when she shined the light on them.

So she hadn't been gently escorted down into this pit after all.

More like she'd been rolled over the side for a twelve-foot drop onto the hard stone.

Maybe they'd thought it would kill her.

But then why knock her unconscious and drag her all this way, hoping the fall in a pit would do the job for them? There had to be easier ways. That just didn't make sense.

Kody opened her mouth and almost shouted again in case the men she'd seen were still here. In case anyone was here.

But she stopped herself when a new sound broke through the all-encompassing silence of her new surroundings.

At first, it was just a muddled echo of a single male voice. Then another, lower and deeper, joined it.

Kody strained to make out what they were saying.

It was one of the hardest things she remembered doing in a long time.

The acoustics in this pit, or cave, or whatever she was made it impossible to pick out words. Moments later, the timbre of conversation quickly changed. She realized she could pick out one voice from the other, and the lower, gruffer, louder voice seemed to do most of the talking.

Whoever it belonged to sounded pretty damn angry, too.

"...to *do* something about her."

Those words were loud and clear. She picked them out a few times again after that — the mention of her, about doing something, about getting it out of the way.

Every time the tamer male voice started up, it was cut off again by a brusque, growling protest over and over.

It didn't take Kody long to realize these men were arguing, nor was she ignorant to the fact that they were arguing about her.

These had to be the men she'd seen outside the cave. The guy in a hoodie and jeans, and then the man she could have sworn was Rip Graham's twin if it weren't for the scraggly white hair and the extra years he carried.

The voices rose louder, accompanied by shuffling footsteps whispering across what sounded like stone from up above.

Still sore with her head throbbing and admittedly unable to think at her clearest, Kody acted on instinct.

"Hey!" Again, her voice bounced around the dirt walls encircling her before echoing against the stone ceiling twenty feet above. "Hey! Whatever you're doing here, whatever I stumbled onto that I wasn't supposed to see, you can let me go. Whatever it is, I don't care. Help me out of this hole, let me go, and I'll walk away. I'll head off the mountain like this whole thing never even happened, and I won't tell anyone, I swear. I know it was an accident. Please help me out of here."

She wasn't sure what she expected in response, but it hadn't quite occurred to her until now that she wouldn't actually get one.

Neither of the men above her said a thing.

Damn. Did they leave, or did I scare them off?

The longer she listened, hoping for the sound of approaching footsteps and then the presence of anyone so she could have an actual conversation, the harder it was to believe what was happening. Again, the silence in the cave was overwhelming, and this time it felt even thicker and heavier now than when she'd first regained consciousness.

No more footsteps. No more arguing voices. She couldn't even hear breathing.

No sign at all that anyone had been here.

If she'd hit her head hard enough, she might have been hallucinating the sounds.

But someone had to have thrown her in here. She hadn't just stumbled across this pit on her own while investigating caves. She'd never even made it that far on her own.

When it was clear no one was coming to save her or even speak to her, Kody took inventory of her things one more time. She had little food, some little water, and her jacket at the very least, which was something. She also had a phone, but the battery wouldn't last forever, and the lack of cell service was even more concerning.

That didn't stop her from opening up a text to her dad anyway, just in case.

HELP.

SHE SENT IT, but of course it didn't actually make its way from her phone at the bottom of a mountain-cave pit to wherever her dad's cell happened to be right now. Maybe, though, if she was lucky, she'd get a bar or two, and that text would seep out. Then he'd know something was wrong.

For now, all she could think to do was find a way to stay calm.

So she opened the Notes app on her phone and started

cataloging everything she remembered about where she was on this mountain and what she'd seen of the two men who had to also be the ones keeping her down here.

If it came to it, she might be able to identify them later.

A task like this kept her focused. The last thing Kody needed right now was to start panicking before she had any idea what was really going on.

SEVEN

Sam

DESPITE DRIVING AS FAST AS SHE DARED BACK OUT OF town after leaving the police station, Sam still made it to the meeting room at Rush's Community Center twelve minutes after the morning meeting had already begun.

She tried not to bring too much attention to herself, but showing up late, slipping through the double doors, and all but tiptoeing across the room to drop into an empty seat wasn't particularly inconspicuous.

Today, she found her seat right next to Hector, who jerked his chin up at her with a crooked half-smile as he eyed her up and down and said nothing.

At the table across the room, Meredith sat as the meeting head. The woman finished going through whatever Twelve-Step literature she'd chosen for the day, then opened the floor for anyone who wanted to share.

Sam only half-listened. The other half of her focus centered on Meredith. The woman didn't look at her worst today. In fact, she'd markedly improved from a few months ago, when Sam had returned to these meetings after Beth Garrick's death. Normally, Sam wouldn't have scrutinized the woman so much, but she was still curious as to why she'd gotten a call from Meredith, especially so early in the morning.

When the meeting finally wrapped up, Sam would have been the first out of her seat if Hector hadn't stopped her immediately with a dip of his head in her direction.

"Sam, hold up a second."

She dropped the rest of her weight back into the chair and looked fully up at him. "What's up?"

"I know it's really none of my business, but I figured you oughta know about it all the same. Some man stopped by before the meeting yesterday. He was looking for you."

"You don't say." Sam narrowed her eyes. "What did he ask about specifically?"

Hector shook his head. "Not sure. Didn't ask me. He went straight for Meredith to question her about where you were. Where he could find you. I just happened to be here early and overheard the whole thing."

That must've been why she called me yesterday.

A dark chuckle escaped her. "Let me guess. It was around eight o'clock in the morning."

Hector's eyes widened slightly. "Uh-huh."

"What were you doing here three hours before the meeting yesterday?"

He shrugged and gazed across the room. "I've had a lot of free time on my hands lately. Came by to offer Meredith my skills as a handyman. She found herself in need of them."

"Doing what?"

"Whatever she needs."

"Thanks for letting me know, Hector."

"Yep." He scratched his head, then studied her face sideways. "Something going on I should know about?"

"As my sponsor, or as a friend?"

"Either. Both."

Sam sighed. "Not as far as I know. Any chance you got a better look at the guy than the back of his head on the way out?"

He shot her a confused frown but didn't bother asking for clarity about a joke he wasn't in on in the first place. "Nothing all that unusual. Or specific. Average-looking fella, if you ask me. Little on the taller side. Short-cropped hair. That's about it."

That didn't narrow it down at all, nor did it help Sam pinpoint who this new mystery stalker of hers was.

With a nod, she stood and folded up the metal chair to stack it against the wall with all the others. "I'll keep an eye out, then."

"All right."

She didn't stop to question Meredith about this stranger questioning everyone else about Sam. Meredith hadn't left a message on Sam's phone after calling, so the woman clearly didn't think it was important enough to tell Sam herself.

For her part, Sam didn't particularly enjoy engaging Meredith Graham in conversation, casual or otherwise. The woman had taken a few too many liberties with their shared fellowship in NA and had crossed a few too many lines trying to insert herself into Sam's personal life in the past.

Today, Sam figured she'd just avoid all of it. If something important came up, the other woman would make it a priority to let her know.

Like usual, Sam was the first person out of the Community Center and heading across the parking lot to continue the rest of her day. She scanned the cars out here but didn't see the dark SUV, so at least this asshole hadn't followed her from the station.

Time to head back into town again for a few errands before trying to figure out what the hell to do with the rest of her suddenly free day.

Sam left the Community Center and headed back toward Rush's town center. Just when she started to feel comfortable about a lack of a tail, she caught a glimpse of another car behind her in the rearview mirror.

That damn dark SUV again in the same shade of slate-gray so dark it was almost black, unless the sun shone directly on it.

"Jesus Christ," she murmured. "Where the hell did he come from?"

While Sam drove like a normal human, the SUV gained on her by the second.

She stepped on the gas a bit, and of course the SUV responded in kind, staying on her ass by half a dozen yards at most.

When the driver started flashing his lights at her all over again, Sam had had enough.

"All right, fuck this."

It wasn't like this stretch of road from the Community Center to downtown Rush was as remote as anything up closer to Birdsong Park. If she found trouble here and now, there were sure to be more people driving back and forth on this road, potential witnesses all. She felt confident enough in her ability to handle herself that she made her move now, armed or not.

She didn't bother with a turn signal or emergency flashers. Stomping on the brake and veering partially onto the shoulder without warning was her last-minute attempt to keep her pursuer on his toes. If he rammed into her from behind, that'd be his fault for tailgating.

Besides, her Jeep could handle it.

With a short screech of her brakes and the grumbling

crunch of the Jeep's tires across the dirt shoulder, Sam came to a complete stop in a cloud of red-brown dust. It billowed up behind her, and a breeze carried it forward past her Jeep, momentarily enshrouding her and cutting out all visibility.

She didn't give a shit.

Sam left her engine running, threw open the driver's-side door, and hopped out of the Jeep.

The SUV — scratch that, the SUV's driver — had decent reflexes. He had stopped in time to avoid ramming into the back of her Jeep. There was still plenty of space between their vehicles where he too had parked on the shoulder. Sam stormed toward the SUV's driver's side anyway, squinting against a flare of sunlight reflected off his ridiculously dark tinted windows.

Then she reached the SUV and knocked briskly on a window through which she could see absolutely nothing.

For all his following her, the driver had enough sense to know what that meant, or at least to know that Sam Salazar wasn't playing any fucking games anymore.

The window instantly rolled down, and Sam was greeted by a glistening white smile and familiar light-brown eyes.

"Hey there, Salazar."

She gaped at the guy.

EIGHT

Kody

NINE DAYS AGO...

KODY DIDN'T THINK she could get any colder after waking up at the bottom of this pit, but a few hours later, she was proven wrong.

The rest of the cave was damp and dank. She could hear water dripping somewhere, some of which came right down from the cave ceiling so far overhead to patter down into the pit with her. Her light windbreaker, which was only an outer waterproof shell, wasn't enough to keep out the chill of steadily decreasing temperatures or the dampness of the cave.

When she first regained consciousness, she thought it had been entirely dark in here. Now though, she realized just how dark pitch-black truly was. The light had definitely changed in the last ten hours. Even if she hadn't had her cell phone to help gauge the passage of time, she would have figured a decent approximation based on the complete lack of light now.

It was dark outside, she knew. All the way up here in these mountains, away from any form of civilization — even small towns like Rush — there was zero ambient light available to spill through the cave entrance.

She couldn't even see her hands in front of her face unless she turned her phone on from sleep mode, in which case the pit lit up with a flare of electronic backlighting, momentarily blinding her and triggering her concussion headache every time she checked it.

Three times now, she'd seriously considered turning her phone off completely to conserve battery life, but she just couldn't bring herself to do it. She told herself it was because there was still a chance some sort of service might reach her when she least expected it, that the emergency text to her dad would finally make it through.

Deep down, though, Kody just didn't want to be left alone at the bottom of a pit in this cave, in the cold and damp, with absolutely no light. She worried that if she turned off her phone now, she might not be able to find it again, either for light, to check for bars, or to reassure herself with the occasional glance at the time.

Now that she'd had more than enough time to think about it, she was barely certain she'd been left inside the cave she'd first seen. When she realized she'd crested the wrong hill into the wrong valley, it was the only thing that made sense when only thirty minutes had passed between being clocked on the head with a giant stick and waking up in the bottom of this pit.

What didn't make sense was why the men she'd seen, who she thought were the same men as the owners of those voices, had felt the need to put her down here. She hadn't recognized either of them. She didn't even really know anyone in the area. She certainly wasn't from here. All she'd asked was for directions to a lake.

Kody couldn't think of a single thing she'd done that might have pissed someone off enough to incapacitate her and effectively kidnap her out here in the middle of nowhere.

In the last ten hours, she hadn't heard the men's voices again.

Had they done this just to get her out of the way? Or were they trying to leave her down here on her own long enough that it broke her so they could do whatever they wanted to her after that without resistance?

Or had it really somehow just been an accident after all, and they'd panicked instead of trying to talk it out?

She was tired of sitting here in the bottom of the pit. She was cold. Her whole body hurt. She knew she needed to get dry. And she was done waiting.

"Hello?" she shouted again. Her voice echoed everywhere, and she hoped that echo was loud enough to at least make it out of the cave's entrance.

Not that anyone was likely to be out and about on the mountainside and off the hiking trails at nine o'clock at night.

Then again, she hadn't expected any of this, either.

"Hello?" she tried again, louder. "Is anyone there? Help! Can anyone hear me? Is anybody out there? I'm in the cave! I'm down here!"

She shouted over and over until her throat was raw and her voice hoarse.

Then she stopped.

She needed to preserve her energy. Screaming from the bottom of a pit without at least attempting anything else first clearly wasn't going to cut it.

She took the tiniest sip of water from her smaller water bottle in her jacket pocket, preparing to save it. She didn't want to spend all night coughing with a raw throat, either.

Kody pushed herself to her feet, double-checked that her phone and protein bars were also back in her jacket pockets, then felt around in the dark for the walls of the pit.

Her previous investigation of them with only her phone's flashlight app had made her think these were mostly stone walls around her, but she'd been wrong. Feeling them gave her an entirely different answer.

There were some stones down here, sure, but they were embedded in the densely packed earth that crumbled away at her fingertips. Damp. Lots of dirt.

It felt like this hole had been relatively freshly dug at the bottom of the cave, which only confused her more.

Kody took her phone out to briefly shine its light up at the walls of the pit and the rest of the cave above her. Definitely twelve feet, maybe more, but she might be able to climb her way out.

She chided herself for not having tried this earlier, but her pounding headache had lasted far longer than she'd expected. Now it was more of a dull nuisance around her skull, but she could finally focus enough to try something a bit more physical.

Kody spent the next five minutes listening for footsteps or those voices again, and really any sound at all. There was absolutely nothing in here but the occasional drop of water falling into a small pool or splattering on the cave stone floor. Not even chirping crickets or the rest of the wildlife moving around outside the cave.

She was entirely alone.

Might as well start now.

Kody kicked the toes of her hiking boots into the pit wall. It gave with surprising ease under the pressure. She thought she had a decent foothold, but when she reached up to do the same with her hands, huge chunks of damp earth crumbled away beneath her.

She slid back down again, coating the front of her light jacket with soggy grit, then shook off her hands and tried again.

Another half dozen times, she tried to climb the earthen walls, each of them at a different location around the pit's perimeter. Half a dozen times, the walls broke away beneath her, and she never got more than two feet off the ground.

That only led to frustration, which she knew would eventually turn to panic when her perseverance didn't get her any farther than this.

Beyond that, she was exhausted. She hadn't eaten nearly enough food or water for the kind of energy required to keep this up all night. It occurred to her that she'd probably end up hurting herself even further somehow and wasting the precious energy she had left on something so obviously futile.

With a disappointed huff, Kody brushed off as much of the slick, grimy muck from her hands and chest and thighs as possible, then slowly lowered herself back to the ground and rested her against the pit's wall.

Best thing to do now is just try to stay warm. Maybe get some sleep, if possible. In the morning, I can try again as soon as a little light comes into the cave.

It was a horrifying prospect, but she did her best to stay positive about the situation. Maybe with a little more light in the morning, and her vision now almost fully adjusted to complete darkness, she'd discover a more viable escape route.

Besides, someone was bound to find her car up there on the tiny turnoff in the trees past the cemetery. Though it was out in the middle of nowhere, there were still plenty of people driving up and down that highway past Rip's farm.

Yeah, someone would definitely see her car and notice it had been there for a while. Someone would check around, find her detailed hike plan in the envelope inside, and realize the owner of that car and that envelope hadn't made it back.

That was the whole point of leaving it there in the first place. Safeguards against just this kind of thing. Situations in which she never imagined she'd find herself — kidnapped and stuck at the bottom of a hole in a cave she wasn't even supposed to have reached in the first place.

If no one bothered to search her car for days, her absence would still sound the alarm at the bed and breakfast in town where she was staying. She'd told the owner she was going out for a long hike today, possibly even overnight, but that she'd be back tomorrow night at the latest.

Worst-case scenario, Kody would have to spend another twenty-four to thirty-six hours down here on her own before the B&B's owner went to the police about a missing guest, and then she'd have help. She knew it.

With three protein bars and just under twenty ounces of water, Kody could make it work for another twenty-four to thirty-six hours. In the scheme of things, as far as missing hikers were concerned, that was nothing.

When she thought about it, she was one of the lucky ones. She hadn't gotten stuck. She wouldn't have to cut off one of her limbs. She wasn't hurt so badly that she couldn't move. She just couldn't climb out of this stupid hole.

So what she had to do was stay put, stay warm, stay calm, and help would be here before she knew it.

After all, she'd gone into this as prepared as a person could be.

NINE

Sam

SAM GAPED AT THE MAN. SHE HONESTLY HAD NEVER expected to see him again. But here he was, years later, grinning like a stuck-up asshole at her from inside a dark SUV on the side of the road.

"What's the matter, huh?" he asked, his grin unwavering. "You don't look all that happy to see me."

She couldn't immediately think of anything to say. Instead, she acted on impulse, jabbing out with her left fist to punch the guy in the shoulder.

With a grunt, he lurched back in the driver's seat. Then with a grimace, he grabbed his shoulder to rub out the unexpected pain before he chuckled. "There's the Sam I know. Damn."

"Don't act like you didn't have it coming, asshole," she hissed. "You scared the shit out of me."

"Really?" He stopped rubbing his shoulder, then wrinkled his nose. "I don't remember you scaring easy."

"Well when some douchebag in an SUV with tinted windows starts popping up all over my life and asking about me and I can't see his face, yeah. It puts me a little on edge."

She knew she sounded angry, partially because she was.

Most of it, though, was plain relief.

Now that she knew it was Brad Anderson following her around Rush with his souped-up vehicle, she could stop worrying over the mystery factor. Now she just wondered why the hell he was here.

"All right, I definitely deserved that," he said with another chuckle, his smile more sheepish than self-centered now. "Sorry for that."

"What the hell are you doing here, anyway?" she asked.

"That's what I've been trying to get to. I would've told you already, but you're a hard woman to get to, even when I'm riding your ass on the highway."

Sam snorted and narrowed her eyes at him. "Well, I'm here now. So start talking."

"Sure, I could do that. Though it might be a little more comfortable if you let me buy you a cup of coffee first."

Clicking her tongue, Sam almost shot back with her normal biting wit, but she didn't have a chance.

The sound of another large vehicle slowing down on the road behind them filled the air. The huge engine growled before a squeal of brakes joined it. Sam and Brad both faced the newcomer, and Sam almost laughed when she recognized Hector's truck.

The passenger-side window rolled down, and the man behind the wheel nodded in their direction. "Hey, Sam. Everything all right over here?"

"For now, yeah," she replied.

"Uh-huh." Hector leaned slightly forward to peer past

her and directly mean-mug Brad while his engine idled loudly. "Anything I can help with?"

"Hector, this is Brad," Sam said, gesturing between them. "Old Army buddy of mine."

"If you say so." Hector sniffed and finally stopped his staring contest with Brad. "Guess there's no need for me to stick around, then."

"We're all good here. Thanks, though."

Hector nodded, but he didn't take his eyes off Brad until he pulled his truck too far forward to keep staring at the man instead of watching the road as he headed back toward town.

"Just an old Army buddy, huh?" Brad said. "Honestly, Sam, I thought you and I were a little more than that to each other."

"That was back when you failed to tell me you were married," she said blandly. "So yeah, you get relegated to friend status. And that's all this is."

"You sure?" He eyed her up and down with a smile that looked exactly the same as when she'd actually thought she was a fan of it. "It's been a long time."

"Not long enough. What do you want?"

"Oh, come on, don't be like that," he said. "Listen, I know I was a serious shit back then—"

"And then some."

"And I should've told you about Denise before you and I got close the way we did. I'm sorry about that."

She glowered at him. "Yeah, well, you can't take a hundred percent of the blame. I was a shit back then too. Just wish I really could've done without adding home-wrecker to the list."

"Nah, that's not on you."

Sam scanned the road back the way she'd come from the Community Center and tried not to look as curious as she felt. This was one of those surprises she never expected to catch up with her in a place like Rush.

"Really, though," she continued, "what are you doing here? You didn't correct me when I pegged you as the out-of-towner stalking me all over the place. That *was* you, right?"

His brilliant grin flashed again. "I mean, I wouldn't necessarily call it stalking…"

"Then maybe keep one of these stupid windows rolled down next time so people can see your face."

"Sure, all right." Lifting both hands in concession, Brad nodded. "I can see where that might have sent a bit of a mixed message. Listen, Sam, I'd love to catch up, but it feels a little awkward just parked here on the side of the road."

"I remember awkward being your middle name."

"That was a long time ago too." He grimaced. "Obviously, you know I came out here looking for you. I wasn't kidding about that coffee, though. Is there somewhere we can go to talk? Sit down face to face so you don't have to stand outside my window like you're still on duty?"

She rolled her eyes, glancing down the road in the other direction toward the heart of town. "Yeah, we can go somewhere else."

"How about your place?"

She glared at him. "Fat fucking chance, Anderson."

His laugh rolled through the SUV's open window. "Oh, come on. I've already seen the outside of your trailer. Might as well show me the inside. My guess is it doesn't get any more private and cozy than that."

"Little too cozy, if you ask me. Nah, my place's no good, and I'm not exactly set up for visitors."

That was the excuse she gave him, anyway, but the real reason was that Sam just didn't want the guy to see how far she'd fallen since their Army days together. A lot of shit had changed. Not much of it for the better.

"There's a café attached to the first hotel just on this side of downtown," she said. "Coffee's decent, and it's usually pretty empty."

"Oh yeah? Coffee can't be *that* good, then."

"I said it's decent. You can follow me."

He did, but this time, Brad managed to keep a respectable distance behind her Jeep instead of barreling up on her from behind. He didn't flash his lights at her, either.

That made her feel only a little more secure, because she still had no idea why he'd come all the way out to Rush looking for her specifically. After the way he'd avoided actually telling her why on the side of the road, she had a feeling it wasn't for anything good.

Especially since the last time they'd seen each other — the night they'd parted ways for good, in fact — she'd hurried out of his hotel room halfway across the country because his wife had walked in on them together.

She'd had no desire to stick around long enough to see how the rest of that one played out.

When Sam pulled into the parking lot of the dingy hotel with the attached twenty-four-hour café, Brad's SUV pulled up in the spot beside her. He'd rolled his window up again, but when he stepped out of the vehicle, he was still grinning.

She really didn't remember him being this full of himself, but time tended to warp a lot of memories, didn't it?

They walked into the hotel side by side, across the poor excuse for a lobby, and into the café diner, where they were invited to seat themselves before the waitress came to take their coffee orders.

While they waited, Sam folded her arms and stared at Brad across the table.

Brad tilted one knee, bouncing it up and down beneath the table. He smiled at her, looked away for a few seconds as if taking in their surroundings, then inevitably looked back at Sam and laughed a little each time.

If he was trying to flirt with her again, this sure as hell wasn't the way to do it.

Whatever had been there between them was better left in the past. Sam already knew everything from her life before Rush was better off behind her where it belonged. This wouldn't be any different.

The waitress finally brought them their coffee, and Brad dumped a startling amount of sugar into his while Sam just went with plain old black. When he finished stirring it all up, tested it with a sip, and looked pleasantly surprised by the results, Sam didn't even give him a chance to comment on the quality of the coffee.

"So, we're here," she said. "We've got our coffee. I'll even let you buy it for me. Now this is the part where you tell me what you're doing here."

"What? No 'Hi, how you been? Good to see you'?" he asked with another laugh. "Come on, Sam. How long *has* it been?"

"Long enough to forget and wanna keep it that way," she retorted but couldn't help cracking a tiny smile at that and shake her head. "Such an idiot. Following me around like that."

"Eh, I honestly thought you would've figured it out sooner," he said. "That's my bad. How you been, though? Really."

She looked around the café and shrugged. "Fine. I mean, I'm here. Taking it day by day."

"How long have you been here? In this town, I mean. Specifically. Rush."

"About two and a half years."

Nodding slowly, Brad dipped his head over the rim of his coffee mug, lifted it halfway to his lips, then set it down on the table again without taking a sip. "A while, then. I wish I'd tried to get in touch sooner. For what it's worth, I'm sorry to hear about your daughter, Sam."

Whatever casual ease she might have adopted in his presence disappeared the second he'd mentioned Sophie.

The topic always put her on alert, always made her tense, and now she wondered how someone like Brad, someone she hadn't talked to in far longer than just two and a half years, had found out about her daughter in the first place.

Historically, that was a giant red flag.

"Thanks," she murmured. "But there's no way in hell I believe you came all this way just to offer your condolences in person. You would've been several years too late, anyway."

His gaze flicked quickly up toward her, his eyebrows flickering as well, like he couldn't figure out if she was serious or joking or both. Then he puffed out a sigh and took another sip of coffee. "No. I didn't."

TEN

Sam

"IT TOOK ME A LITTLE LONGER TO FIND YOU THAN I thought it would," Brad continued. "I mean, I still know people who know how to find people."

"We both do," Sam said flatly.

"Sure, but I still stay in touch."

When her scowl only deepened, Brad laughed and exaggerated a sheepish shrug. "Kidding. I'm kidding, Sam. Mostly. I mean, it was easy enough to figure out you were up here in this neck of the woods. You still get mail, but a P.O. box doesn't exactly provide a whole lot of detail. So I had to resort to asking around personally. I did eventually find out you were staying at that trailer park outside town, which was a little surprising—"

"I like it," Sam cut in.

She didn't know why she felt she had to defend herself to this guy. They hadn't spoken in years, and she certainly hadn't wasted any of her own time thinking about him.

Yet here they were.

"Hey, I'm not here to judge," Brad quickly replied.

71

"Just saying. You're a hard person to find, when you wanna be."

"I never said I wanted to be."

He studied her for a moment, then nodded. "You're right. That's me making assumptions. Anyway, yeah, I paid a visit to the trailer park first. That guy there with the dog? He's something else."

"Syc."

"He's what?"

"That's his name," Sam said. "Sycamore."

Brad raised his eyebrows. "There's no way that's his real name."

"Oh, I know. But it suits him."

"You're telling me. That guy was as tight-lipped as they come. Wouldn't tell me shit about you. So I figured I'd stop by the Community Center. Did a quick search online of local NA meetings. Looked like that was the only one. Thought maybe someone there might know something."

"What did Meredith tell you?" she asked, casually sipping her coffee and trying not to look too engrossed in the answer.

"Not a whole lot more than this Sycamore dude. Then I figured I might catch you on the road somewhere in between. And that worked out."

"You still haven't told me why you came looking for me in the first place though."

"Right." Brad's smile disappeared, and there was real concern behind his eyes when he cleared his throat again. "My daughter. It's my daughter. Kody. She came out here to Rush a couple weeks ago. Maybe three. She's been doing some field research for her Master's."

Sam gaped at him. "*You* have a daughter."

She said it, though it definitely sounded more like a question.

"I have a daughter."

"How old is she?"

"Twenty-five."

Sam almost choked on her coffee. "Holy shit. How is that even possible? You're not that much older than me."

"Denise and I were real young. That's how. I never mentioned her to you?"

"No, Brad. You know, somehow, during all our time together, you never said a goddamn thing about having a kid."

"Damn. That's my bad too," he murmured, avoiding her gaze now.

"Yep. You can take all the credit for that one." Now, it felt like she finally smiled at him for the first time.

Brad returned the smile and scratched the side of his head. He kept his hair cut neat and close in true Army fashion, though Sam had no idea if he was still on active duty or Reserves or what the hell the guy had done with his life since they'd last seen each other.

Now that she watched him, his nervousness seemed to take off all the years that had passed since they'd worked together. He suddenly looked a hell of a lot younger.

Sam wondered if that ever happened to her when *she* was caught off guard like that.

"Anyway," Brad continued. "She's earning her Master's in Environmental Studies. Kody. Apparently, she picked Rush as one of the best places to conduct the rest of her research for her thesis. She told me a little bit about it, what she'd been looking into up here. Did you know that cultivating pot uses up twenty-two liters of water per plant per day during the growing season?"

73

"No, I didn't." Sam huffed out a laugh. "Never occurred to me to look it up."

"Right? But Kody's fascinated by that kinda thing. She sent me a few texts when she first got here, describing the town and some of the work she was already doing. So, like I said, she came out here maybe a little over three weeks ago now. And we were in constant daily contact since even before she headed out this way. To be clear, we weren't talking on the phone every day, but she still texted me otherwise. Said she was getting too busy to step away for long chats, and that the cell service was pretty shit up here."

Sam sipped her coffee. "Depends on where you are."

"I figured. But I still *got* her texts. Then about nine or ten days ago, she just stopped. Just like that. No reason, no word. The phone goes right to voicemail, and I haven't heard a thing from her since."

"Maybe she just got extra busy," Sam suggested.

"No, that's not like her. If that were the case, she would've told me she'd be out of contact for a while. That's just how we communicate. She doesn't fall off the face of the planet like that. And ... honestly, Sam, I'm worried. Ten days might not seem like a long time, but it is when I haven't gone more than twenty-four hours without hearing *something* from her."

"And you decided to come find *me* about it?" Sam asked. She was well aware of the skepticism in her voice, but she just couldn't quite bring herself to believe that she was the first option that sprang to mind when Brad started to worry about his noncommunicative daughter. Especially since they hadn't spoken in such a long time.

"Well, no." He forced out a cough this time. "I didn't come *straight* to you first. I contacted the police here, asking about Kody. Honestly, they didn't seem to take me all that seriously, which was weird."

"Not really," Sam muttered. "Not here, anyway."

That made him frown, but he continued without asking for further explanation.

"When it looked like I wasn't gonna get much help from law enforcement, I started digging a little more on my own. Got in touch with the owner of the bed and breakfast where Kody's been staying. Talked to the woman who owns the place. Real nice-sounding lady. But she hadn't heard from Kody in the last ten days, either. She said Kody had checked out earlier than planned, and that was it. She couldn't tell me anything else."

"All right." Sam nodded. With another sip of coffee, she waited for him to continue.

The Brad Anderson she'd known hadn't needed much prompting to get to the point. Then again, they'd known each other a long time ago. He'd probably changed a bit since then.

Sam sure as hell had, whether or not anyone else from her past could pick up on it.

At least she hoped she had.

When he didn't say anything else, her curiosity compelled her to push for something more.

"And that was all just over the phone?" she asked. "Calling the bed and breakfast?"

"Yeah, and the police. Nobody had any other information for me, so I figured my next step would be to come out here personally and see if I could figure out what the hell was going on up close. Whoever I talked to at the station when I called didn't remember shit about our previous conversation. Or maybe I talked to someone else. I can't remember... But I did file a missing person's report."

"And they accepted it?"

Brad's frown deepened, and he cocked his head. "Well yeah. That's how filing a missing person's report works."

She pressed her lips together and nodded for him to keep going.

"That was a few days ago now. Obviously, I'm past the forty-eight-hour window, so I don't know how much help the police here are gonna be this long after the fact. But I'm not leaving until I find her, Sam. No matter what happened. I can't just give up. I have to know. I have to make sure she's okay. I gotta figure this out."

"And how exactly did you figure out that I was up here too?" she asked.

He stared at her with that deer-in-the-headlights look.

"Listen, Brad," she continued, "I get it. This is a tough situation. You're stressed. You're worried about your kid. All fair. But I've already had my fair share of people not telling me the full story before I decided to get involved, and it didn't turn out very well. Wasted a whole lot of everyone's time and mine. If there's something you're not telling me, now would be a good time to spit it the hell out."

He cleared his throat and looked nervously around the café as if he thought someone might be listening in or would show up to recognize one or both of them and ruin their private talk. He took another quick sip of coffee, then nodded. "Yeah. Well, I mean, you and I fell out of contact. For various reasons. Which I completely understand, and I don't blame you for them. We've been over that."

"Uh-huh…"

"I did still keep in touch with other people from back in the day. Bunch of the guys. The rest of our platoon. And then, um … I'd actually called Ian up. Just to talk, like we do sometimes. And he mentioned you were up this way."

Sam sat up straighter in the booth, her face expressionless despite the flare of resentment and anger and grief rising up in her at the mention of Ian and everything that bastard represented in her life, past and present. "You still talk to Ian."

This time, it didn't sound at all like a question.

"From time to time." Brad pressed his lips together, then spread his arms. "And that's when I found out *you* were up here. Hell of a coincidence, if you ask me."

"Sure is."

Everything about Brad's presence here sounded like a coincidence.

If he'd given her some other explanation, she would have instantly called bullshit. But the concern in his voice and the way he spoke about his daughter and wanting to find her couldn't be faked. She knew that much.

Whatever other secrets Brad Anderson was keeping in his life right now, this wasn't one of them.

"All right," she said, wanting to quickly move on from the topic of Ian because she just couldn't with that shit right now. "You did your due diligence. Filed a Missing Persons. Called around. Asked as many questions of as many people as you could, and then you found out your daughter disappeared from the same town where I live now, huh?"

"In a nutshell," he slowly replied, gauging her reaction. "And after what I've seen of the local law enforcement here, I really don't trust them to do their jobs the way they need to to help me find my daughter."

"Now *there's* something you and I can agree on."

An attempted smile flickered then quickly died on his lips. "Why do I have the feeling you don't get along very well with the Rush PD?"

"Feel free to keep your feelings to yourself, Brad," she quipped.

"Fair enough. So, here's the deal, Sam. This is why I've been trying to get in touch with you to have this conversation. I know Kody's out there. I know something's wrong. Honestly, I don't trust anyone else to find her, protect her, help her out the way I know in my gut she needs right now. So I'm gonna do it myself. And I was hoping you'd be willing to help."

He huffed out a wry laugh and sat back against the booth before adding, "Honestly, right now, I'm also hoping you won't just tell me to fuck off."

Sam lifted her coffee mug to her lips and shrugged. "You always did have high expectations, Anderson."

ELEVEN

Charles

SIX YEARS AGO...

CHARLES PUTNAM PUSHED himself backward away from his desk and scratched his chin, removing his fingers instantly from the keyboard the second his alarm went off at noon on the dot.

That was the deal now. It had always been the deal since he'd held his position here as *The Daily Rush*'s senior editor. Because it wasn't just him anymore.

Charles wasn't alone, and the promises he made were to more people these days than merely himself.

With a quick swipe, he shut off the alarm on his phone, switched his computer screen to sleep mode, then gazed at the only framed photograph he kept on his desk because it was his all-time favorite.

Him, Rose, and Frankie all together, when Frankie was a little over two years old, he and his mother laughing at each other while she held him and Charles gazing at his family as if nothing else in the world existed.

Sometimes, nothing else did.

But today was Friday, and *The Daily Rush* had quite a bit of work to finish up for the Saturday editorial issue to be printed and prepared to ship out all across town bright and early tomorrow morning — or before midnight tonight, if they were lucky.

But that was still hours away, and Charles had somewhere else to be.

He left the newspaper's building like he did every day at the same time and walked across the street to The Toffee Shoppe.

Even after all these years of living and working and raising his little family in Rush, Charles still got a kick out of the place. Of course, small towns like this always had their so-called gems, little standout pieces of history or entertainment that catered directly and almost exclusively to tourists. The Toffee Shoppe was one of them.

Not only did the folks there create their signature candies in almost every flavor imaginable, they also carried what Charles thought was a ridiculous number of postcards and traveler's knickknacks and touristy tchotchkes one could only buy from The Toffee Shoppe, specifically in Rush, California, and nowhere else.

Charles had always thought it was ridiculous. Rose, however, still thought it was cute, which was why she was the one who stopped into The Toffee Shoppe every day at noon to pick up her regular batch of six different toffee flavors to-go, in a rolled-up paper bag, before stepping through the front doors to meet Charles out on the sidewalk like she did every day at six minutes past noon.

For a relatively young married couple with a four-year-old and an entire newspaper to run, it was amazing how Charles and Rose could remain so punctual about even these small daily interactions. It was the little things that counted, the little things that added up to the bigger picture. If he had his way, Charles would have run stories about the little things every single day.

The rest of the town, though, had gotten over it pretty quickly when he'd taken on the editor position.

There was also quite a bit to be said for the ability to adapt and be flexible.

Rose met him on the sidewalk outside The Toffee Shoppe, staring down at her paper bag of toffee and biting her lower lip in an attempt to stave off her astoundingly perseverant sweet tooth.

Charles chuckled. "I seem to remember something about dessert coming *after* the meal."

His wife didn't even look up from the open top of the brown paper bag in her hands. "There aren't any rules about *looking* before a meal. Don't try to convince me there are now."

He waited for her to roll up the paper bag, which she quickly deposited into her purse before Rose linked her arm through her husband's and they took off down the sidewalk along Main Street.

"Anywhere specific today?" Charles asked.

"We haven't been to that little café on the corner in a while," Rose suggested. "You know, just two blocks up. The one with the really good tomato bisque. How does that sound?"

"Sounds like my wife wants tomato bisque. I can't in good conscience deny her that. Mrs. Putnam gets what Mrs. Putnam wants. End of story."

"You know, a girl could really get used to this." She leaned into his arm, gripping it with both hands now.

Charles grinned. "I'm counting on it, actually."

The café on the corner seemed to have just the right number of tables to sit just the right number of lunchtime guests, most of whom worked right here in town and all came in for the same reasons. The place was close, was open during their hour-long lunch break, and it wasn't the rowdier of available options in town. Plus the food was decent, and Rose was right.

The tomato bisque was excellent.

Over lunch, Charles and his wife discussed what had been on their minds for several weeks now, but the topic still hadn't been settled.

"I was just thinking about this earlier this morning," she said. "I think we should do San Francisco."

"Really?" Charles bit off a piece of focaccia bread he didn't know how to get his hands on anywhere but at this specific café, then raised his eyebrows, speaking around his mouthful. "We've already done San Francisco."

"That was three years ago."

"Right. But I thought the whole idea was to make *new* family memories. And Frankie's already been to San Francisco."

"He was barely even a year old then, Chuck." She offered him a playful frown. "I promise you our son doesn't remember San Francisco. It'll be a brand-new experience for him all over again, and we already know we like it."

"You don't think we should try getting out of the state this time around? Try something adventurous?" It took him a few seconds longer than he would have liked to work up the courage to look her in the eye, though he already knew whatever he found there in his wife's expression would be automatically tinged with lightheartedness and her playful nature, because that was just the way she was.

The sight of her trying to scowl at him with pursed lips

82

and a deepening frown, though, almost made him choke on his focaccia before he let out a surprised snort.

"San Francisco's adventurous," Rose said.

"I never said it wasn't." Charles swallowed and had to wash it down with more iced tea.

"*I* can be adventurous," she added. "There's loads to do in San Francisco, and it's only about a day's drive. Plus, we won't have to buy plane tickets. It's that much more expensive now that Frankie's over two."

"A fantastic reason not to fly anywhere, for sure."

"Don't make fun of me for that, Mr. Putnam." Despite her attempts to come off as serious and commanding, Rose failed to hold back her own flickering smile. "The only reason we're able to take family trips like this the way we do is because we don't have to dish out everything in the bank just to *get* to those family trips."

"Absolutely," Charles replied. "And you get all the credit for that. You manage things with a tight fist, Mrs. Putnam. Our family's a well-oiled machine. We couldn't have done it without you."

Rose scoffed, rolled her eyes, and gave up pretending she was annoyed with him before shoveling more tomato bisque into her mouth. "You're impossible."

"And you're incredibly skilled at putting up with me."

"Yeah, I think I'll keep you," she said with a playful shrug. "Maybe."

Then lunch was over, they both had to get back to work, and it was time for Rose to walk her husband back to the front doors of The Toffee Shoppe after lunch, just like she did every day. They kissed each other goodbye. Charles turned around to cross the street back toward the newspaper's office and his personal editor's office in the back, while Rose kept heading down the sidewalk, her face now all but hidden in the open top of her brown paper toffee bag as she deliberated over which of her six daily flavors to try first. Also just like every day.

This Friday, Charles found his work on this week's editorial on the growing numbers of migrant workers flooding into Rush, specifically during the trimming season, far more engrossing than he'd previously given the topic credit for. The rest of the day got away from him in what felt like no more than twenty minutes, and before he knew it, his phone was ringing.

Charles sucked in a breath through his teeth, grabbed his phone, and saw both that it was 5:30 p.m. already and that he was getting a call from Juana Aguayo.

He had to answer.

"Juana, hi. Is everything okay with Frankie?"

"*Sí, sí,*" she replied in her thick Spanish accent. "He is just fine, *Senior* Putnam. Everything is very good here, only that Frankie is still here with me. Normally, *la Señora* Rose arrives here for him at five o'clock."

Charles absently checked the time again, just to be sure, and frowned. "Yeah, she usually does."

"Did you maybe forget *you* are supposed to come get him, Señor Putnam?" Juana asked with a note of humor in her voice. "These things happen, yes? There is no problem at all, but I am sorry. Someone must pick up your boy. I think he might be sleeping if he is here for much longer."

"I'm so sorry, Juana," Charles added quickly. "You know what? I've just been so focused on work. I bet Rose got one of her migraines again and went home to sleep it off. I'll be right there to pick him up, okay? Thank you so much for calling."

The man scrambled to gather his things, then stopped to check his phone one more time.

Sure enough, there was a missed call from Rose about an hour ago.

And she'd left a message.

While he finished packing his things, Charles put his phone on speaker to listen to her voicemail.

It was definitely his wife speaking, but after the first five seconds, something was clearly very wrong.

He couldn't quite put his finger on it at first. Her words were slurred, muffled a little — not like she'd been heavily drinking, which was unusual for Rose, but as if she were trying to speak through pillows or maybe had cotton stuffed into her mouth. Even her migraine medication didn't make her sound this strange.

Most of the voicemail was difficult to interpret, but Charles did make out his wife saying something about an appointment and then about picking Frankie up from Juana's.

He tried to call her back, but her phone must have died. It went straight to voicemail.

Great. She'll never let me live this one down if Frankie and I don't get home before she does.

Puffing out a sigh, Charles slung the strap of his messenger bag over his shoulder, headed across his office, and slapped off the lights before locking up. Then he marched down the center aisle of the newspaper's main room split into dozens of cubicles for his staff, most of whom had already left for the night.

One of his writers, though — a young woman with shoulder-length chestnut hair and black-framed glasses that were actually somehow flattering — remained at her desk, diligently typing away on her laptop. She was one of Charles' few employees dedicated to consistently meeting her deadlines, even when that meant staying in the office after hours. It usually did.

"Patty?" he called as he approached her desk.

She stopped typing and turned in her chair to look up at him. "What's up?"

"I hate to do this right now. I missed a call from Rose earlier. She wanted me to pick Frankie up from daycare, and I totally dropped the ball. Thing is, she's got the car, so... Would you mind driving me to pick up my kid?"

Patty broke into a wide grin. "Are you kidding? Frankie's awesome. Let's go. I was just finishing up, anyway."

FOUR-YEAR-OLD FRANKIE REMAINED BLISSFULLY unaware of being picked up an hour later than normal from the Aguayo family property on the outskirts of town. To Juana's credit, she'd put the boy to work playing out in the grass and dirt on the property that contained three homes altogether in a massive plot of land inhabited by countless generations of the Aguayo family. Far too many for Charles to count, anyway.

He'd gotten the breakdown of the Aguayo family tree once or twice from one of Juana's sons, but he hadn't written it down, which meant he had no way of recalling it in a pinch.

When he finally knocked on the door, Juana happily handed over Frankie and his backpack, assured him there was no problem, that these things happen, that she wouldn't mention it to Rose unless Rose brought it up first, and that she looked forward to seeing Frankie again tomorrow morning.

Patty was kind enough to chauffeur them both back home as well.

The relief Charles felt when they turned the corner onto his street thickened and tightened into another knot of apprehension the second they pulled up in front of his modest home.

Their car was still gone, and there was no sign of Rose.

The vehicle squealed a little when Patty pulled it to a halt. Her smile faded when she turned to look at him. "What's wrong?"

Only then did Charles realize he'd been scowling. "Oh no. Nothing. It's … what? Almost 6:30? I just thought Rose would be home by now is all, but that's all right. Listen Patty, I really appreciate you helping us out here."

"Hey, no problem." She turned around in the driver's seat and wiggled her fingers at Frankie in his car seat in the back. "Anytime this little guy needs a professional driver, I'm totally available."

Frankie stared at her with wide eyes, then cracked a brief smile. "I'm hungry."

"It's exactly what we're going to do next, buddy," Charles replied. "See you tomorrow, Patty."

"Bright and early, boss."

Then he got his son out of the back seat before carrying Frankie inside under one arm and their car seat under the other.

It was all he could do after that to focus on making his son dinner beyond the last bit of snacks Juana fed the daycare kids at 3:30 p.m. and not a minute later. Fortunately for Charles, there were lasagna leftovers from last night, which made dinner almost as easy as making Frankie happy, which honestly didn't take much.

Three more times, Charles called Rose's phone. Each time, it went straight to voicemail again, and he didn't hear a thing from her for another two hours.

Then he really started to worry.

Somehow, he got Frankie to bed on his own when the kid was too tired to ask more than once where Mommy was. Once he was alone, though, Charles fought with his growing apprehension and thought about logical next steps for getting in touch with his wife.

He went through the contacts saved in his phone first and called their mutual friends to ask if they'd heard from her or knew anything about where she might be. If she'd been unable to get ahold of him somehow, she might have called someone else she knew Charles would contact first.

No one had heard from her since yesterday.

Then he called numbers from her phone specifically, which she'd shared with him because Rose had wanted him to reach out to one couple or another they knew in town who also had small children to get the families together. He still hadn't done any of that yet, but he had their numbers.

No one they knew personally had any information on Rose. No one had seen her today. No one could help him.

After that, Charles called first the local hospital on the outskirts of town and then the much larger regional hospital serving several counties. Nothing.

He was running out of ideas.

The last thing he wanted was to panic, but if he didn't hear from his wife soon, he'd have to go to the police. And then it would be a whole different story.

TWELVE

Sam

As distraught and off his game as Brad claimed to be, he did just fine giving Sam detailed directions to the bed and breakfast where Kody had been staying.

The place was another enormous Victorian home in almost the same mansion-esque style as the Griffith Mansion in town converted to the Kalamac Club. This home, however, boasted a much more open, grounded, down-to-earth feel from the second Brad pointed it out.

They'd gone a decent way outside downtown Rush, no farther across the other side of town than the Community Center. Sam had rarely had much of a reason to come all the way out here; she rarely passed completely through town as it was and now felt like she was seeing parts of the area she currently called home for the first time and with brand-new eyes.

This was a good thing though, because fresh eyes were exactly what Brad had said he wanted in this search for his daughter.

They walked up the neatly maintained flagstone walkway, up the freshly painted steps of the front porch, and stopped at the door complete with a bright yellow and lilac theme on the door itself and the surrounding frame, plus a hand-painted wooden sign hanging from a nail by a strip of chicken wire that simply said *Welcome Home*.

"Nice-looking place," Sam murmured.

"Pretty sure that's exactly what Kody thought," Brad said.

He knocked firmly on the front door and waited all of two seconds before knocking again with increasing urgency.

Sam practically slapped his arm away from the door. "Hey, come on. What are you doing, man? Give 'em a chance to at least get to the door before you pull out the battering ram."

He snorted but couldn't hide another sheepish smile as he clasped both hands behind his back and took a single broad step away from the door to wait.

Sam wasn't new to mediating get-togethers and conversations between parents with grown missing children and literally anyone else in town. She wasn't exactly excited to have found herself in this position for the second time in almost as many months, but all she could do now was keep moving forward.

"Knock one more time," Brad suggested.

"I'm not gonna knock one more time."

"Just in case. Maybe they didn't hear us."

"Bullshit. Everyone up and down this entire street can hear you. We're gonna wait here like normal, sufficiently patient people—"

"Come on, Sam..." His voice was urgent and jittery now as he bounced slightly on his toes, fighting to keep his hands clasped and away from either her or the front door.

"We gotta talk to someone, right? We need to get inside, take a look around, and knock again—"

"Will you just—"

The sound of footsteps heading toward the front door finally reached them.

Brad stared blankly ahead, speechless now that he'd been proven wrong.

Sam gestured toward the house in front of them and pursed her lips at the guy.

"Fine, whatever," he muttered. "Don't get a big head or anything."

Before she had a chance to snap back with some witty comment, the front door creaked open, and a woman in her late sixties with a large bun of thick, graying hair piled high on the top of her head greeted them with a smile.

"Well, hello there. Good morning. I'm so sorry, I wasn't expecting new guests today. You must be walk-ins, hmm?"

"Not really," Brad said. "We're here to talk to you about one of your most recent guests who just checked out a few days ago. You and I actually spoke on the phone earlier this week. I'm—"

"Oh yes," the woman said, her eyes widening in recognition. "You must be Kody's parents."

Brad nodded. "That's us."

Sam shot him a sidelong look but didn't bother correcting him.

Of course people were more willing to openly speak with a married couple showing up in concern for their shared offspring than some single guy who looked way too young to have a twenty-five-year-old kid and his long-time sort-of friend from back in the day who ruined his marriage and now spent her free time pretending like she was still entitled to active MP duties.

She could play along just fine, sure, but she couldn't guarantee the genuineness of the smile she tried to offer the other woman now.

"I'm Brad," he continued.

"Oh yes, yes," the older woman cut in again, nodding vehemently as she stepped aside. "I remember you. Please, come in. You've come all this way. Step inside."

"Thank you." Brad hurried past Sam to be the first one into the house, and Sam did her best not to roll her eyes at him as he gestured toward her with an open hand. "And this is—"

"Sam," she said, extending her hand.

The owner grinned, her eyes widening as she seemed to fully look at Sam now for the first time, and they shook hands. "Pleasure to meet you. I'm Susan, and this is the Home Sweet Home Bed & Breakfast." Her smile fell as she shut the front door. "If you're here, I can only imagine that means you still haven't heard from Kody."

"That's an accurate assessment," Brad muttered.

"Oh my goodness." Susan slowly shook her head, then looked quickly up toward the next room off the front entryway and gestured in that direction. "Please come inside and take a seat. We can talk some more. And I'd be happy to bring you something to drink, if you like. Lemonade. Tea. Coffee."

"Thanks," Sam said. "We just have a few questions for you, if you don't mind. Is it just you running this place all by yourself?"

"Oh no." Susan chuckled, but it was tight and strained. "Well, I'm not here by myself, at least. My husband Steven is here with me, of course. This has been our home for the last, oh, going on fifty years now. Unfortunately, though, I do find myself running this place more or less on my own these days."

Sam couldn't quite think of anything to say to that that didn't sound like she was rudely prying too far or blowing off everything the woman just told her.

Susan saved her from having to figure it out when she headed toward the living room and waved her guests along with her. "He's just in here. The living room is the best place for a comfortable seat and a little more space. The windows are lovely for natural lighting at this time of day. Follow me."

Feels like we already booked a room.

Sam looked quickly at Brad again, but the man was thoroughly engrossed in following Susan through her enormous home.

They stepped into the living room, which hadn't been done justice by Susan's description. This had to have been more of a parlor room back in the day when the home had been built up here in the late 1800s. It was enormous, the two exterior walls filled entirely with windows spilling soft natural light onto everything and making the whole place look clear and spacious and surprisingly welcoming.

In this part of the state, Sam had figured out pretty quickly that keeping large spaces clean in a town like Rush was all but impossible with the old houses and the dust and windstorms that kicked up all year round. A layer of red-brown Northern California dust made its way onto every available surface within twelve hours, if there wasn't someone there for constant upkeep.

Susan and Steven's home was immaculate.

Sam could only imagine how much time the woman spent on nothing but dusting in a place this size. No, thanks. Sam would take her Deville over this any day.

"This is my husband Steven," Susan said, gesturing to a tall, well-padded armchair placed almost directly in front of the hearth. There was no fire in it today, but the man sitting in the chair looked like he'd just come in from a long day of physical work and was now trying to keep warm in front of the nonexistent flames.

"Say hello, dear," Susan called. "This is Brad and Sam, Kody's parents. You remember Kody, don't you? The sweet young woman who'd been staying with us for a few weeks."

Steven's only response was a low grunt, which could have been of assent or apathy or even because he had phlegm stuck in his throat.

The man stared blankly at the floor in front of the fireplace, seemingly not quite capable of lifting his head enough to look into the hearth itself. His cheeks were sunken, mouth hanging partially open and slack jawed. Though he'd rested both arms on the chair's armrests casually enough, one of his legs was bent at an awkward angle, his foot in its loafer resting on its side on the hardwood floor instead of its sole.

Sam noticed two fingers on Steven's right hand tapping sporadically, but otherwise, the man hardly moved.

"Well today, I think that might be as much of a greeting as we're going to get out of him," Susan said with an apologetic smile. Turning back toward Sam and Brad, the woman lowered her voice enough to make it noticeable but not nearly enough to keep her husband from overhearing. "Steven has dementia. Going on six years now, actually. He has his good days and bad days, but even on the good days, he doesn't talk much anymore. And when he does, none of it makes much sense.

"That's part of why I decided to turn our family home into a B&B down here. He's retired, yes, but I needed something to do. Besides, bringing guests in every now and then gives me an opportunity for intelligent conversation and bright young people to talk to. Like yourselves. It gives me something to look forward to beyond the day-to-day. You understand."

Sam wouldn't necessarily have called her and Brad young, by any stretch of the imagination, but she supposed from Susan's perspective, that was exactly what they were.

"Please." Susan jumped a little as if she'd forgotten why they were here, then gestured toward the arrangement of comfy-looking couches that clearly hadn't come as a set but had been tastefully arranged to look like they belonged together. "Please come have a seat. Are you sure I can't get you something to drink?"

"We're fine," Brad said. "Really, ma'am. Thank you."

Ma'am?

His use of the formal address took her right back to their Army days and the time they'd spent working together during their shared assignments to the same unit. Sam forced an almost violent fit of coughing just to hold back the laughter wanting to burst up out of her.

When everyone was situated on the couch and Steven still hadn't moved in his armchair or shown any form of interest in their guests, Brad was understandably eager to get back to the conversation.

"I know you and I spoke a bit about this over the phone," he said, "but for my wife's sake, would you mind just covering everything you know in your own words again?"

Jesus, now I'm his wife too?

She wanted to punch him again for setting her up like that, but when she looked at him, Brad was leaning forward over his lap beside her, gazing intently at Susan without any indication that he'd misspoken or was particularly pleased with himself for playing this little practical joke on his old Army buddy.

She glared at the side of his face but said nothing, and

she finally had to pull her attention away from him when Susan started talking again.

"Absolutely," she said. "Yes, of course. Um, Kody. Let's see. Such a sweet young woman, by the way. I'm sure you two are incredibly proud. She had scheduled her stay with us before she came out here through some online portal. I know how to sign in and accept booking requests, but other than that, I couldn't tell you much more about how it works. I don't even know the name of the thing.

"Anyway, she'd booked a room with us. The real sweet mother-in-law cottage out back, all to herself for a total of six weeks. I had a handful of truly lovely conversations with her the first few days of her stay. She told me all about her fieldwork in environmental studies, what she was looking into up here in this part of the state, how it all tied into her Master's."

A self-conscious chuckle escaped the woman as she gently patted her thighs. "Now, I can't say I fully under-stood everything she told me. I'm a simple woman in comparison. But it was so nice to hear her talk about it. You can tell she's incredibly passionate about what she does and excited to make an impact in her field."

"And the last time you saw her?" Sam asked.

Susan nodded. "Yes, that was ... oh, just under two weeks ago now, I'd say. Well, no, I think it'll be two weeks on Sunday, and she told me all about her plans the night before. Sometimes, I like to make dinner for the guests, especially when we don't have many. It's the least I can do. And we all sat down right there in the kitchen when she told Steven and I all about the long hike she'd mapped out.

"Said she wouldn't be gone for too long, no more than forty-eight hours at most, if she could help it. That was what she told us, anyway. And she was gone bright and early the next morning. I'm assuming she left. I didn't see her car, and she didn't come down for breakfast. Honestly, I was a bit surprised when I found her note."

"What note?" Brad asked, shifting on the edge of the couch cushion. "She checked out?"

"Well, she did by leaving a note," Susan said, swiping some stray loose hairs away from her face. "I didn't bother going out to her room until another twenty-four hours after she said she planned to be back. Thought I would check in on the cottage if she'd happened to return, see if she needed anything, if she wanted to join us for dinner… But her room was empty, obviously, and I have duplicates of the keys to every room. So I went in just to take a peek."

"Makes sense," Sam said with a nod.

"Thank you for saying so. I'm very much of the same mind, especially in my own home. Some folks these days, though? You wouldn't believe the kind of ruckus they kick up when they think their privacy and personal space are being infringed upon. As if *they're* the ones who own this place and I'm just the hired help."

Clicking her tongue, Susan shook her head and looked thoroughly disappointed now. "But I thought—"

"The day you say she checked out?" Sam prompted.

"Oh yes. Forgive me. I opened the suite out back to check in on her, and she had already cleared out completely. Her bags were packed and gone. She'd left nothing behind. The cottage itself was cleaner than even I usually keep it."

"So your guest just disappeared, and you didn't think that was strange? Sam asked.

"No. She checked out." Susan looked surprised by the fact that Sam hadn't already put the two together. "She left a note right on the little writing desk in the corner. I'm assuming that was her way of checking out. At least, that's how her note made it seem, and she was gone.

"I assumed she packed up sometime in the middle of the night and didn't want to wake us by officially checking out. Why she couldn't wait until after breakfast the next morning, I have no idea. She stayed with us for only a fraction of the length of time that she booked, but no, everything was all accounted for. I had no reason to be suspicious. Young people these days are difficult to pin down. You know what I mean."

"What did her note say, exactly?" Brad asked.

"I can't remember it word for word. It was just a very polite and short thank you with her name at the bottom. Simple."

"Do you still have it?" Sam asked.

Susan's face folded in on itself as she searched the empty space in front of her, her frown deepening by the second. "No. I'm sorry. I'm afraid I threw it out with last week's trash. I didn't think it was important to keep around."

"That's all right," Sam said. "Sounds like you didn't have any reason to. What about the room where Kody stayed? Can we take a look at that?"

"Of course. There's no one staying there now. I usually reserve the place for extended stays or small families. Newlyweds on their honeymoon. That kind of thing. I haven't even really gone back there more than once since she left because the place looked so spotless. It's just through the back. I'll show you."

The woman stood from the couch and turned slightly toward her husband. "How are you doing, sweetheart? Can I get you anything?"

Her husband offered a soft, wordless grunt and still didn't move in his armchair.

"Well you just stay right there and relax. I'll be back. I'm just showing Sam and Brad the back cottage. We won't be long." She nodded for her guests to follow her, and they left Steven in the armchair on his own.

He didn't seem to mind.

The back cottage couldn't have been more aptly named, nestled on the back side of the property with plenty of space between it and the rear fence, plus an open patio with an elevated iron firepit on a circle of flagstone surrounded by patio furniture, all centered in the yard. Well-manicured walkways wound through the grass to different parts of the property, but Susan led them straight back to the front door of the cottage, which she unlocked with a key from one enormous set she'd pulled off a hook by the back door of the main house.

Then the cottage door swung open, and the woman gestured for them to take a look inside.

"Take as much time as you need," Susan said. "I have to get a few things into the oven for dinner. I like to keep Steven on a set schedule. At least for meals. If I'm late, sometimes it can make the dementia even worse. But when you're finished out here, please just close the door again and feel free to let yourselves back inside."

Brad marched into the cottage without a word.

Sam turned to at least acknowledge Susan with a nod. "Thanks. We shouldn't be too long."

"Like I said. As long as you like." An approving smile flickered across the woman's mouth, then she spun around and headed back to the main house.

Sam thought Susan seemed particularly at ease with letting complete strangers roam about in her back yard however they pleased. Then again, she'd converted her home into a bed and breakfast. There were strangers in and out of here now on a regular basis. Of course, she'd have grown comfortable with it by now.

SHE AND BRAD spent fifteen minutes in the back cottage, investigating every inch of the place without a single sign of foul play or hidden belongings or any additional lead to point them toward Kody's whereabouts. In fact, the place looked like it had hardly ever been touched, so at least Susan hadn't exaggerated.

"I don't think we're gonna find anything in here," Sam said as Brad finished looking under both the mattress and the box spring for the third time.

With a heavy sigh, he dropped the box spring back onto the bedframe again with a creak of wood and a much smaller puff of kicked-up dust than Sam would have expected. "I know. It doesn't make any sense."

"Why?" Sam asked. "Kody wasn't clean like this?"

"I don't know." He shook his head, then seemed to think his own response odd enough to warrant an explanation. "I mean, she hasn't lived with me in a long time. But judging by how organized she was with everything else, this level of cleanliness doesn't surprise me. I just don't understand why she left less than halfway through her six weeks here. With a *note*. That doesn't sound like something she'd do."

"But she did leave a note."

"Yeah, that's the story." Brad's eyebrows drew together in confusion, or maybe that was just the visible strain on his face brought by the act of deep thinking. Sam really didn't know anymore.

She didn't even really know *him* anymore, all things considered, but here they were.

They found Susan in the large living room again when they returned. She sat on one of the couches, flipping through a magazine, and quickly looked up at them when they entered. "Did you find anything?"

"Nothing but a clean, well-kept room," Sam said. "What did that used to be out there? A shed?"

"Good guess," Susan replied with a smile. "It was our tool shed for a long time, but then our son converted it. Now it's one of our guests' favorite suites. You know, with all the privacy."

The living room fell silent again, Sam and Brad sitting on the couch, smiling, and Susan sitting across from them. Steven remained motionless in his armchair by the currently empty fireplace.

Susan's smile seemed frozen on her face until she finally slapped her hands down on her thighs and nodded. "Well. Is there anything else I can help you with?"

"I think that about covers it for now," Brad replied as he stood. "Thank you so much for your time, Susan."

She stood as well, approached him, and grasped his outstretched hand. "Absolutely. Sorry I couldn't be more helpful."

"If you do happen to think of anything else that might help," Sam added as she joined them, "I'd like to leave you my number. Feel free to reach out with even the smallest thing—"

"Both our numbers," Brad added quickly with a firm nod. "Just in case."

Sam shot him another sideways look. It had been a long time since she'd had a ride-along, either as an MP or now that she was no longer in active service. Especially when that extra person with her spoke up about nearly everything she said to either contradict or correct her.

She hadn't liked it back in the day, and she certainly hadn't changed her opinion about it now.

Brad still acted like he had no idea, which either made him completely clueless, even after all this time, or still an asshole, even after all this time.

"Yes," Susan said as she searched the living room. "I would love to have your numbers. We've got some paper right over here. Let me grab it."

While the woman scurried across the enormous sitting room toward the antique writing desk for paper and pen, Sam and Brad stood silently beside the couch. Then they each quickly scribbled down their numbers, and Sam made sure she differentiated them by writing her name beside her own.

"Thank you so much," Susan said, grinning as she took the notebook back, like Sam had just handed her a giant wad of cash instead.

"Thank you, Susan," she said. "We really appreciate your help with this, and please don't hesitate to call if you think of anything."

"Absolutely. I hope you find your daughter soon. Such a sweet young woman. From what little I know of her, she seemed remarkably capable and able to take care of herself. My thoughts are with her, and we're hoping everything turns out all right."

"Thank you," Brad said. "So are we."

Just as Susan gestured toward the front entryway to lead them to the door, her husband stirred for the first time from his place in the armchair.

At first, it was just a little rustling and shuffle as his knees wobbled and his one crooked loafer finally righted itself after so much time. Then the armchair groaned when Steven tried to push himself up out of it and simultaneously turn around to look at their guests.

"That girl..." he grumbled, his voice harsh and gravelly with an extra little something that made Sam fight the desperate urge to clear it out of her own throat. "That girl..."

"Kody?" Sam asked him, taking a slow, gentle step toward the man. "Is that the girl you mean, Steven? Kody?"

He squinted up at her, his cheeks sunken and gaunt, his mouth hanging slackly open with bubbly puddles of drool collected in their corners. But the glittering lucidity behind his eyes was unmistakable.

At least, Sam thought it was before his next words.

"I didn't like her," he said. "That girl, Kody."

"I'm sorry," Brad said, leaning to the side to get a better look at the man around Sam.

Steven grunted and slapped a limp, slightly trembling hand down onto his chair's armrest. The only sound it produced was a soft, muffled thump with no real strength behind it. "That girl... She had a mouth full of rot."

Sam widened her eyes, and as she slowly turned to look back at Susan and Brad, the other woman let out a nervous chuckle.

"I'm so sorry. You'll have to ignore him. This is one of those days where, like I said, what does come out of his mouth doesn't make any sense at all. Sweetheart?" Susan headed toward her husband, who hadn't stopped glaring at Sam since he'd first made eye contact. "Steven? Honey? These are Kody's parents. You enjoyed our dinners with Kody when she was staying here. She told us all about her hikes. Remember?"

Steven looked almost terrified by the sight of his wife hovering there in front of him, bending over him to stick her face fully in his view. But when she gently lifted one of his hands from the armrest and patted the back of it in reassurance, her husband's entire body relaxed all at once, as if all the fight had gone out of him now that he realized his wife was still here.

"That's right," she murmured. "You just sit back and relax now. I'm going to show our guests out and—"

"There's no need, Susan," Sam interrupted with a small wave of farewell in the couple's direction. "We can see ourselves out."

THIRTEEN

Kody

EIGHT DAYS AGO...

THE FIRST THING Kody was aware of the next time she woke was the all-encompassing cold permeating her entire body from what felt like every direction. She wasn't shivering yet, but a chill still tore through her, racing across her limbs and back up through her torso again before she remembered where she was.

Despite knowing she was still in the pit, she fumbled around in the dark as if she expected there to be a light switch somewhere. It took a few more seconds for the rest of her awareness to settle in, then she reached for her cell phone tucked into her jacket pocket.

At this point, any kind of movement now brought pain of one kind or another. Her head, where she'd been hit by that giant stick, was still swollen and incredibly tender and sore when she experimentally brushed her fingers across it. That alone wasn't a good sign.

The swelling felt awful, and she could only hope it

wasn't actually as bad as it looked. She thought about trying to take a look at it with her phone's camera but didn't want to use up any more of the battery life.

Every other part of her body was stiff and tight from the constant cold and from lying on such a hard stone floor.

How long had she been out?

She woke her phone's lock screen just long enough to check the current date and time, which coincided with the small bit of pale light she thought she saw spilling over the lip of the pit's walls. It was 6:15 a.m., which meant she'd slept at least six hours, though she really had no idea what time she'd finally drifted off from exhaustion, fear, and the knowledge that the smartest option was to try conserving her energy as much as possible.

She probably could have slept even longer if it wasn't for the damn cold.

Kody turned on her phone's flashlight app, then pulled out her single water bottle and poured just a little of it so she could drink no more than a capful. Who knew how long she'd be down here.

Even worse than having been knocked unconscious, kidnapped, and thrown into a dark pit was being knocked unconscious, kidnapped, and thrown into a dark pit with no water whatsoever.

After that, she opened one of the protein bars, broke off an equally small piece at the corner, and chewed it slowly over and over until it was practically liquefied.

For now, that would have to be enough.

Conserving her energy also meant conserving her resources, which weren't all that great to begin with.

Before she turned off her flashlight app, she took one more quick scan of the pit around her, which only confirmed her previous suspicions.

This wasn't a natural hole in the ground, though the walls still crumbled and were uneven in some places. It was too perfect of a circle to have been naturally made. Someone had dug this into the cave floor, which meant this pit had a purpose, and now she was in it.

A surge of terror raced through her at that thought of what the purpose of this pit might actually turn out to be.

But then Kody closed her eyes and took deep, calming breaths. Panicking would only expend more of her resources, energy being one of them. The ability to calm down and think clearly and rationally about anything was another.

She didn't know how long she sat in complete darkness, breathing in through her nose and out through her mouth, trying to calm her rapid heartbeat and still her racing thoughts. For the most part, it worked.

Until she heard the same shuffling whisper of moving footsteps across the floor of the cave somewhere up above.

Someone was there.

Kody held her breath, listening more intently. Then the shuffling footsteps paused.

"Hello?" she called. "Is someone there? I'm down here! Please help me! Hello?"

Her voice echoed over and over within the pit and the rest of the cave above, but there was no reply.

She realized she shouldn't have expected one. Maybe she hadn't even heard footsteps. It could have been something else. A creature, the rustle of leaves blown through the cave entrance.

It could have been just her imagination and nothing else.

If no one was there, now might be as good a time as any to try climbing up the pit's walls again.

Even more determined this time to find a way, Kody

experimented first with several different areas of the pit's wall, feeling blindly in the dark for what felt like the best handholds. She did find several hard stones jutting from the dirt and, after testing several of them, decided this would be the best place to start.

After the first handhold, though, she couldn't get any higher. She had no light, no way to see where she was reaching, and no way to know exactly where she was putting her feet until they came down either on hard rock or soft, crumbling mud. Over and over again, she tried to climb the walls, each time finding several effective and promising handholds, and each time unable to get past them before either the walls broke away beneath her feet or she reached for a new hold and mistook a particularly solid clump of mud for another stone.

She had no idea how many attempts she'd made or how long she'd been at it, but when it finally got to be too much and she'd slid chest first down the wall again to land in a heap of crumbling dirt, her urgency, frustration, and fear got the better of her.

With a shrieking cry, Kody leapt to her feet and kicked at the dirt piles in front of her. Pebbles flew in all directions, bouncing off the walls and thumping back down into the dirt. Some skittered away across the pit's stone floor behind her.

That was all she had here. Dirt and pebbles and more dirt.

"Damn it," she hissed.

Then her thoughts stopped. Because what she *did* have was dirt and pebbles.

Who knew? Maybe they'd come in useful. Maybe she could build something, because at least she knew they were hard and wouldn't crumble away beneath any amount of pressure. It wasn't like she had anything else to do.

Heaving a sigh, Kody gingerly lowered herself to the pit floor and groped about, sifting her fingers through large mounds of dirt and damp earth and rooting out the small to medium-sized pebbles. Some had likely already been down there with her already, but most had come from within the pit walls where they'd broken away beneath her.

Eventually, when she thought she'd gone through it all, she had a decent-sized stash of tiny, hard stones at her disposal, all gathered together in a pile off to the side.

One more time, her dad's voice rang through her mind:

"Prepare for everything. And if you can't prepare, take an inventory. It's amazing how much around you can actually be used to help you when you've run out of other options."

So that was what she did.

Kody made her inventory quickly and efficiently.

A mountain of pebbles. A few sticks and twigs that had probably blown into the cave from outside. Her phone, now at sixty-one percent battery. One almost full bottle of water. Two protein bars, one missing a small corner. Her jacket. Her shoes.

And that was it.

Sighing deeply through her mouth, Kody finished her inventory and leaned back against the pit wall.

What she wouldn't give for some rope right now, which she'd had in her pack, but that had been taken from her.

Was there anything else she hadn't considered?

Before she could more thoroughly inspect herself, the sound of footsteps echoed again across the cave above.

Kody waited for the sound to either change or cut off entirely. At this point, she still wasn't sure if she'd pinpointed the source of those sounds, if they really were footsteps, if someone really was here in the cave with her. No use screaming herself hoarse again if no one was there.

There might not even be any use screaming down here if someone *could* hear it, should that someone be the men who'd thrown her down here in the first place.

The shuffling sounds echoed closer, then changed into smaller, gentler clicks and rumbles and whispering thumps. Then she heard metal clanging against either stone or more metal, and that had to be from a person.

"Hello?" she called. "I can hear you up there. I know there's someone here. Can you at least talk to me? Tell me you can hear me?"

There was no response.

"Listen, you really don't have to do this. Just let me go and I'll head right back home. I doubt I could even get back here again in the first place. I stumbled on this cave completely by accident. I wasn't supposed to be here. We can help each other. I hope you know that. If you just let me out of here, I'll disappear, and you won't ever see me again. You won't have to worry about that."

For a long moment, the cave was deafeningly silent. Then the clinking of metal started up again.

Kody closed her eyes and felt like giving up.

I can't give up. That's not what I do. That's not what I am. What would Dad say about this right now, huh? Think!

Unfortunately, her conversations with her father hadn't yet touched upon the small but obviously very real possibility of being kidnapped in the middle of the Northern California wilderness and thrown into a pit.

Technically though, this probably counted as a hostage situation.

I've heard plenty of stories about those. So I just need to get him talking if I can. Humanize myself, right?

"Listen," she said, her voice echoing more gently

through the cave because she wasn't trying to yell loud enough for anyone and everyone to hear her. Now she was just talking. "I can't believe this is actually what you want. I don't believe it. It's not what *I* want, trust me. We can get out of this. You can help me out of this, and nothing else has to happen after that. What's your name?"

The metallic clinking stopped for a moment, then picked back up again with no verbal response.

"My name's Kody," she continued. "Kody Anderson. I'm twenty-five. Grew up in Ohio. I'm just visiting, you know? Came out here a couple weeks ago. Staying not too far away from here. I didn't think I'd be heading all the way out to California for work, but you know, things happen. Life changes. Sometimes it throws you lemons."

Kody grimaced at that, talking about negative things.

"I'm still in school, actually. I'm this close to wrapping up my Master's in Environmental Research. Something I've always loved, you know? Looking at not just the environment as it is, but how people work with the environment as it is. How it can be used, how it can be changed. I mean, I guess at this point you can't really have an environment without people in the first place. We're all in it together.

"There's so much about this part of the country that I had no idea about before I came out here. I'm studying the land up here in these mountains. Some of the most beautiful I've ever seen.

"My dad taught me almost everything I know about backwoods hiking."

And she just kept talking.

At this point, Kody didn't pick and choose her words with any level of discernment as long as she focused on the positive. She opened up down there at the bottom of the pit, sharing with her anonymous captors stories of her travels across the country for school, reasons for choosing this part of Northern California in which to conduct her final bit of research for her thesis that would lead to receiving her Master's and probably being finished with school for a while.

She talked about her dad, their relationship, what she wanted to do after her schooling was over, where she thought she'd settle down. She talked about her mom, her dog, her friends back home, and the last time she'd spent quality time with them.

Through all of it, Kody didn't get a single response from the stranger above. The pounding clink of metal continued, though she noticed it paused every once in a while when she might have said something poignant, which only gave her further hope that maybe she was getting through to the guy.

"I've got a whole lot to look forward to waiting for me at home," she said. "My parents. They're gonna be so worried. They might even already be worried about me. I have no way to get a hold of them. Please, *please*, if you've been listening to me this whole time, if you can hear me, please help me get out of here. Even just tossing a rope down over the edge or, I don't know, dropping me a pickaxe or something. We can leave each other alone after that. I just want to go home, and I promise you I'll never come back. There's nothing for me here, anyway."

Now the metallic clinking had stopped. There were no more echoes within the cave, only the quickening in-and-out rush of her own breath as she waited for something, anything.

Still nothing.

After a few more minutes, she finally had to give up.

Whoever had been here with her, listening to her

stories, was now most likely gone again. Clearly, he'd decided not to lift a finger to help her.

Which meant she needed to help herself.

Gritting her teeth against the stiffness and her sore muscles everywhere, Kody pushed herself to her feet again, dusted off her hands despite knowing she was already covered head to toe in damp muck, and got back to investigating the pit walls with her hands.

Time after time, she thought she'd found a decent set of hand and footholds within the wall. Her hope surged every time she got her full weight off the ground. But each and every time, no matter how solid she felt scaling the wall, she never made it higher than three feet up.

She couldn't give up.

Her final attempt saw her nearly halfway, but when she paused to feel around for the next solid handhold, Kody slid back down again, her legs crumpling beneath her as the largest chunk of earthen wall yet broke away and spread out along the pit floor.

She wanted to scream at the walls now, but then a new sound from above made her stop.

Kody craned her neck, staring at the space where just a small bit of light poured over the edge of the pit's walls. A volley of pebbles toppled over the edge and dropped straight down into the pit with her.

She would have scrambled forward to collect them and add them to her stash, but now Kody couldn't take her eyes off the top of the wall.

Because she'd seen more movement up there too.

A shadow without any sound.

Two seconds later, a man's face slowly peeked out over the edge of the pit to stare straight down at her.

His face — a perfectly expressionless mask of apathy, Kody thought — didn't even look entirely human.

FOURTEEN

Sam
_____

THE FIRST FEW MINUTES OF RIDING IN SAM'S JEEP AFTER leaving the B&B passed in complete and highly awkward silence.

Sam wanted to tell Brad to never again introduce her as his wife or Kody's mother, under any circumstances, but the rational part of her that wasn't nearly as quick to anger and irritation reminded her this wasn't about Sam Salazar at all.

This was about Kody and her father, who had come all the way out here to Rush to find her. Nothing more.

"So here's what I'm thinking," Brad said, finally interrupting the silence. "Either someone took her, or they figured out that she was gone and wasn't coming back. They also figured out where she was staying, showed up at the B&B, and checked out for her after packing up all her stuff."

Sam choked back a laugh. "Or she came back early in the night and took all her own stuff."

"No." He shook his head. "There's no way."

"I mean, from an outside perspective, it's definitely

possible. Likely, even." She wanted to look at him, but she had to focus on driving. "Maybe something else is going on here."

"Yeah, if this were anyone else, I'd agree with you. But this is my *daughter*, Sam. I know her. She wouldn't just pack up and split like that without telling someone. Without telling *me*. I told you, we talk every day."

With a shrug, she had to concede to him on that one. "You do know her better than I do. What about her car, then? That was gone too. Susan didn't have anything to say about it, either. Any sign of her car in the last week and a half?"

"Not that I know of. I've talked to the County Sheriff's Department too. They haven't seen anything out on the highways, but they put out an APB. So if they do, I'll know about it."

"And the Rush PD have a description of her vehicle too?" Sam asked.

Scoffing, Brad rolled his eyes toward her and replied in a complete monotone, "This isn't my first rodeo, Salazar."

"Yeah, I know." She stared straight ahead. "This isn't the first time someone's asked me for help without putting all the facts down on the table first, either."

"Yes, the Rush Police have a description of her car."

"Good." Sam nodded curtly, though she wasn't remotely convinced that that actually was a good thing.

As far as she was concerned, the Rush PD had been devastatingly lax in their duties, especially during the last few years of Sam calling this town her home. Even more so in the last six to eight months.

Or maybe that was just how long she'd actually been paying attention.

Chief Colton could have all the facts at his disposal with a filed Missing Person's report and an APB out on both Kody and her car, and Sam still wouldn't necessarily trust him to wrap this up and find Brad's daughter, even with a million bucks on the line.

She wasn't gonna tell Brad that, though.

"So what now?" he asked.

She could feel him staring at the side of her face, but she didn't take her eyes off the road. "Well, normally, I'd suggest hitting up the Redwood. The bar where I work."

"You work at a bar?" Brad's self-satisfied smirk flickered in and out, which Sam did not fail to notice from the corner of her eye.

"That's what I said."

"How does *that* work exactly?"

She shot him a quick sidelong glance. "It works like work, Anderson. That's the only reason I show up there, and nothing's gonna change that."

It wasn't like she was trying to keep whatever she had going on with Chris a secret. And Brad had clearly discovered Sam's current dedication to sobriety and her attendance at NA meetings.

Mostly, it just wasn't any of Brad's goddamn business.

"All right," he relented. "That's fine. I'll back off. Then why would you normally suggest going to this bar, just not today?"

"The Redwood Rings is as close to the town gossip line as it gets," she said. "A handful of actual facts pass through all of it, if you know how to sift through the bullshit. Unfortunately for us, the Redwood's closed for the next couple days, probably. Hopefully no more than that. It's just not an option right now."

"So you're out of a job, then?"

Sam snorted. "No. I still have my job. This is just a mandatory vacation. Without pay. Or tips."

"That sucks."

"Careful. You're the one benefiting from it the most right now."

Brad chuckled, and Sam almost smiled with him but managed to keep a straight face.

They'd gotten along just fine in the past, years ago. Then again, getting along had turned into something else, and that wasn't anywhere close to what she wanted right now with Brad Anderson. She was willing to help the guy because of their history together in the same MP unit way back when, and that was as far as Sam could let it go.

"So what's your suggested alternative?" he asked.

"Who said I had one?"

"Come on, Sam. You wouldn't have started talking if you didn't already have a Plan B."

Clearly, the guy hadn't forgotten much about the way they'd worked together. Sam could've done with a little less familiarity, but the time for picking and choosing had definitely already passed.

"I want you to send me that picture of her," she said. "The one you showed me on your phone. I'll ask around town where I can. It'll take a lot more footwork than just popping into the bar, but it's a start."

"Sure." Brad pulled his phone from his back pocket, typed around a bit, then paused and stared at Sam's profile again for what felt like an hour.

"What?" she muttered.

"I mean... You want me to send it to you, I'm gonna need your number."

There was that stupid smirk again.

With a noncommittal hum of hesitation, Sam tilted her head and grimaced. "My number."

"Well I don't have a photo printout or anything. So yeah. That's how I'm gonna get it to you, right?"

No, she did not want Brad to have her number. But it

wasn't like she was trying to keep him away from her at this point. He'd found her without it anyway.

So she bit the bullet and rattled off a string of numbers, purposefully saying them faster than most people generally shared contact information.

Brad didn't miss a single one.

Then he typed around some more before finally shoving his phone back into his pocket. "There. Image sent."

"Great. So now we move on to other possibilities. Anyone Kody might have had trouble with?"

"In *this* town?" He was genuinely surprised. "She's only been here a few weeks."

"Come on, man. You and I both know trouble isn't necessarily contained by geographical location."

He snorted, then shook his head. "No. Nothing like that. Kody doesn't drink. Fortunately something she didn't pick up from me. She doesn't do drugs—"

"You sure about that?"

"Yeah, I'm sure. You know what, Sam? I kinda feel like you haven't been listening to me. I talk to my daughter every day. She tells me about everything she's doing, and *not* so I can keep my thumb over her but because she genuinely wants me to know. She's completely devoted to her schoolwork and her research and inching up on her Master's. She didn't have time for anything else."

"Or maybe she's had more time than you think," Sam suggested.

He opened his mouth and sucked in a sharp breath to respond, but no words came out. Brad's mouth clicked shut again, and he turned his head to stare out the front passenger-side window.

The silence returned, this time thickened by the tension of Sam having suggested very real possibilities the man clearly didn't want to consider, so she moved on. "How exactly did she find this interest of hers in environmental studies and research?"

"I don't know."

He'd answered way too quickly. With Brad in particular, Sam knew it meant he didn't want to talk about it.

So of course she kept pushing.

"Come on, Anderson. You talk to her every day. You two are like this, right?" Sam crossed her fingers and gave them a little shake in his direction. "I don't believe you, but hey. If you don't want my help looking under every single rock…"

"Christ, Sam." Brad puffed out a sigh and stared at her again, this time without any hint of his usual smugness. "You really get in there, don't you?"

"You came to me for a reason. Can't convince me now that it was just a happy accident."

"No, it wasn't."

When he still didn't start talking, Sam fought back another laugh. "And…"

"And…I think maybe I might've had something to do with her interest in things. From a distance, at least."

"I have no idea what that means," she said.

He looked startlingly uncomfortable now, shifting in the passenger seat, rubbing his palms along the legs of his jeans, tipping his head from side to side with the occasional grunt of indecision.

Must've been something pretty awful.

"Brad?"

"As far as I know, she first got interested in looking at the effects of civil unrest and international warfare on the environment, first at the local level, then all the way up to global. Or whatever."

"Oh." Sam raised her eyebrows, mulled over that fun

little thought for a minute, and decided to drop it right there.

Which was for the best.

Indirectly influenced by her dad's profession. No shit.

Neither one of them was about to start waltzing down memory lane to pull up their shared experiences from their time in active service, both before and after their assignments to the same unit.

Apparently, Sam would have to get used to hitting one wall after the other with this guy before moving on to the next step.

The pros and cons of asking an old Army buddy to help you find your missing kid.

The pros and cons of saying yes.

When the silence filling her Jeep was finally too much, Sam pulled out another avenue of consideration. "What about any friends of Kody's?"

"I mean, she *has* them."

She would have rolled her eyes if she wasn't still driving. "I mean if she's still in contact with friends, either from grad school or undergrad, high school, the neighborhood where she grew up, best friends, anyone she would've called to talk to if she found herself in trouble and needing a little help."

"Yeah, Sam," he griped. "Me."

"All right, let's pretend you and your daughter *didn't* talk every day. Next best thing."

"I'm sure she's got someone like that, yeah," he said, dipping his head to stare into his lap. "I mean, of course she did. She's a great kid. Everyone loves her. She has friends. I just...I don't know who they are."

"She doesn't talk about her friends?"

"Of course she does. Jesus, I feel like I'm under interrogation here."

Sam shot him a quick sidelong look. "Do you *need* to be?"

Brad clicked his tongue and didn't bother to answer.

She was pretty sure she'd asked it rhetorically, anyway.

"What I mean is I don't have their contact information," he said. "And I don't know their last names. There's no way to find them beyond that, and I just don't have those kinds of details."

"Fair enough. Maybe just start with that next time."

Brad puffed out a sigh but didn't say anything else.

"Any chance you have access to her phone records and her bill?" Sam asked.

"I'm not paying for it, if that's what you wanna know."

"If that was what I wanted to know, I would've asked. Hey, man, you came to me for help. This is me helping. If my line of questioning is annoying you, maybe this wasn't the best arrangement."

"Shit…" With a sigh, Brad shifted in his seat again and looked up at her. "I'm sorry, okay? I'm just tense. Worried. This whole thing…"

"I know. You don't have to explain it. I just need a little give-and-take here from you, right?"

Brad nodded, chewing on the inside of his cheek. "I'll see what I can do to get into her billing account. That's something I can work on in my own time."

"Sure."

"In the meantime, though, I need to find a place to stay. Don't get me wrong, living out of a big-ass SUV like mine has its perks every now and then, but it doesn't take long to realize I'm not as happy with sleeping wherever the fuck I can at forty-five as I was in my thirties."

"Forty-five?" Sam shot him another quick glance with a raised eyebrow and couldn't hold back a bark of a laugh this time.

"How's that funny?"

"I just … shit. You're not nearly as old as I thought."

"There's still a certain level of maturity that comes with it."

"Maturity my ass, Anderson."

Brad grinned. "So. On the topic of finding somewhere that isn't my car…"

He trailed off without finishing that sentence, and it took her a moment to notice he was staring at her again with that stupid smirk.

"What?"

He shrugged. "You've got a place, right?"

"Not for you to sleep, man."

"Oh, come on. Don't be like that."

"I'm not being like anything," she said. "I also don't think it's a good idea for me to offer or for you to accept."

A chuckle escaped him as he dropped a forearm on the center console between them and leaned slightly toward her. "I get what this is. You're saying no because you're worried you won't be able to resist me."

"Trust me, Anderson." Completely deadpan, Sam kept staring straight ahead to watch the road. "You're the last thing I can't resist."

He laughed. "All right, then what is it? Why not?"

"I mentioned my reputation in this town, right?"

"Uh huh. Not sure how that connects to where you live…"

"Look, you're here to find Kody and make sure she's all right. You found me to help you, and that's the extent of this arrangement, yeah? If it gets out that someone's staying with me in my trailer, who's also been riding around town with me and asking questions, even if it's about his daughter, it'll end up painting you with the same reputational brush I've been coloring myself with for the last two years."

"*Salazar...*" he said, a mocking lilt in his voice, "you really *do* care about me."

"Yeah, just keep telling yourself that."

SAM RETURNED him to the hotel, pulling up in the parking lot right beside his SUV.

"Thanks for the ride," he said, opening his door. "I'm gonna try to get into Kody's phone dashboard online. Does this place have decent internet?"

"I think so. Might have to ask at the front desk for a password."

"Cool. Let's go."

"Actually, I've gotta split for a couple hours," Sam said. "Got some errands to run, but once I've got those out of the way, I'll meet you back here. Maybe then you'll have pulled up something useful we can work with."

Brad chuckled. "No maybe about it. Yeah, that's fine. I'll wait for you inside."

"That café in two hours."

With a nod, he shut the Jeep's driver's-side door, and Sam was off.

Not only was she grateful to have a little personal space away from him again, but she did actually have errands. Fortunately, she'd have something to show for it too.

FIFTEEN

Sam

SAM WAS SO PREOCCUPIED WITH THIS WHOLE BUSINESS with Brad and his missing daughter, she almost didn't register the fact that the mom-and-pop pharmacy she consistently visited once a month for Ruthie Garrick's diabetes medication had raised those prescription prices by ten percent from last month.

She'd almost handed over her credit card without questioning it, but then she asked the pharmacist to double-check. She'd never paid that much for it before.

Sure enough, prices had risen.

"Man, talk about inflation, huh?" Sam said, trying to write the whole thing off as a joke.

The pharmacist took her comment very seriously. "Tell me about it. Even in a town like this, that's not gonna go over well for very long, if ever. Maybe it'll force some of the transient moochers out of Rush for good."

Sam fixed him with a wide-eyed look, blinked, then grabbed the bag of meds from him and took her leave.

This time when she knocked on Ruthie's front door,

with the paper pharmacy bag in hand, the elderly woman answered almost immediately.

Ruthie opened the door by all of three inches, scowled through the crack at Sam, and looked her up and down before her normally narrowed eyes widened in recognition. "Sam! What are you doing here?"

Sam almost laughed in the woman's face but managed to contain it to a splitting grin instead as she lifted the pharmacy bag in front of her. "Stopping by with your meds again, Ruthie. It's that time of month again."

She wanted to mention the fact that Ruthie had actually recognized her instead of asking who the hell she was and why the hell she was standing on an old woman's front porch, but Sam decided against it. Most likely, bringing it to the woman's attention would only shatter this brief moment of lucidity, and Sam kind of wanted to revel in it as long as possible.

"Well, isn't that just so dang kind of you?" Ruthie opened the door all the way and gestured for Sam to step inside. "Come on back and drop that off and tell me all about it. Oh, plus I owe you the cost of that insulin too."

Looks like Ruthie's having a good day.

Sam shut the front door behind them as Ruthie shuffled across her single-story bungalow house in one giant flower-patterned muumuu that could have been cut from the same fabric as her living-room curtains.

"How've you been, Ruthie?" Sam asked as they headed into the kitchen.

"Oh, fine, fine. Thanks for asking. You know, it's just little old me rattling around in this house all by myself."

"And your sleep? No more nightmares about Beth, I hope."

Ruthie stopped short and turned to look at Sam over her shoulder. "Who?"

Shit.

Sam wasn't sure she should be the one to touch that, but then Ruthie saved her the trouble.

"Oh, you said Beth." The woman laughed. "No, no, she's fine too. And no more nightmares for me. Or for Beth. Thanks for checking in."

Maybe the woman wasn't having such a good day for living in reality, after all. But at least she wasn't scrutinizing Sam with some of the thickest suspicion she'd ever been on the receiving end of, especially from someone who Sam ran regular errands for and stopped by to drop off life-saving medication once a month.

At this point, Sam would take what she could get.

She joined Ruthie in the woman's kitchen, which made her feel a little better when she saw all the dishes were washed and put away, and there wasn't another mess sprawling across the countertops. She set the pharmacy bag down on the kitchen island and smiled.

"Now *what* was I doing in here?" Ruthie asked, turning left and right and searching the floor as if her answers were there. "Oh yes. No. I remember. The cookies aren't quite ready yet. But I owe you money for my insulin."

"That's appreciated, thank you," Sam said, choosing to ignore the fact that there was no sign of any cookies in the oven, especially because the oven hadn't even been set.

Ruthie rummaged around in various kitchen drawers, then pulled out a bundled wad of cash and shook it in Sam's direction with a chuckle. "Now, don't you go rooting around through my cash drawer, understand? I trust you, which is the only reason I'm letting you see where I keep this."

"I'm flattered."

"You should be." The woman thumbed through quite a thick stack of bills before separating what she owed Sam for the meds. Then she practically shoved the cash into Sam's hands. "There you go. It's all there. Please and thank you. And would you like to stay for a cookie when they come out?"

Without waiting for an answer, Ruthie stopped on the other side of the kitchen island and ducked to open some cabinet drawers down there, which she peered into with a raised eyebrow before popping back up again and slamming the cabinet door shut. "Looks like they're almost ready."

Sam pressed her lips together, pocketed the cash, and chose not to mention the fact that Ruthie had fallen short on the total price of her meds by five bucks. Even without the ten percent increase, that was a small bit of change she was willing to eat on Ruthie's behalf, just because she didn't want to risk completely ruining the woman's day.

Not mentioning the nonexistent cookies baking in the kitchen cabinets was a given.

"I'd love to stay for cookies, Ruthie," she said. "Unfortunately, I can't. I have a lot of other things to get back to."

"Oh, of course you do. You're a busy, busy woman, aren't you?"

"Some days more than others," Sam muttered. "And just out of curiosity, Ruthie, do you know Susan? That woman who runs a bed and breakfast out of her home on the other side of town?"

"Who?"

"It's on — uh..." Sam snapped her fingers, trying to remember. "On Forest Street."

"Oh! Then there must be *two* Susans in this town, and I know both of them. Let's see, the one who runs, uh — Oh! No, that *is* the same Susan. Hooper is her last name. Steven's wife! Yes."

"That's the one." Sam nodded, only knowing they were

on the right track because she had, in fact, met Steven earlier today.

"Sure, I know her. Vaguely. Now, I wouldn't say we're close or anything, but... Well, did you know Steven used to be my dentist before his son took over? Look. Just look, Sam. What a beautiful job the man did!" Ruthie shuffled toward her, popped her mouth wide open, and started poking around in there with a finger, tapping teeth and still talking. "Of course, I didn't need nearly as much work as others..."

"Wow, look at that." Sam forced back both a laugh and the urge to reel away from Ruthie's gaping mouth, which might not have seen any other dental work since Steven Turner, D.D.O., had gone into retirement. "Sure did a great job there."

Ruthie's mouth clicked violently shut, which the woman didn't seem to feel. Then she leaned away from Sam and fixed her with a skeptically raised eyebrow. "Why are you asking about Susan, huh?"

"Like I said, I'm just curious."

"And not because you're sticking your nose into more business that has nothing to do with you?"

"I'm just asking around, Ruthie," Sam replied slowly, not letting herself take the woman's quirks to heart. If she had, she would have stopped coming by Ruthie's house months ago. "There was a woman staying at Susan Hooper's place. That woman recently went missing, and I'm helping to find her. So I went by the house to speak to Susan today, and I just wanted to ask you whether or not she's trustworthy. She seems to be the last person to see this young woman alive and well, and I'm wondering whether or not I can trust her."

"Well, I'm sure you can," Ruthie said. "I wouldn't necessarily call Susan a chronic liar, per se..."

When the old woman didn't immediately offer more information, Sam took the bait with a small measure of amusement. Of course Ruthie was starving for another opportunity to spread around town gossip, especially with someone who didn't already know what was happening everywhere else.

And since the Redwood Rings was temporarily closed, pending plumbing repairs, the living room of Ruthie's home was the next best thing for finding information about residents of Rush and their histories.

"But you *would* call her something else?" Sam asked, allowing herself to fall into the glaringly obvious trap. For Ruthie, apparently, Sam's conscious decision to play her game wasn't nearly as obvious.

"Oh well, I don't know if I'd call her anything, exactly." A small, knowing smile flickered at the corners of Ruthie's mouth as she shuffled sideways toward Sam, as if they were out in public and risked being seen together. "But Susan wasn't always the most satisfied woman with her life in this town."

Sam lowered her voice to the same level. "Like how?"

"For as long as I've known her, Susan Hooper has been a rather jealous woman. And to tell you the truth, I think she's secretly elated about the fact that poor Steven finally has dementia."

"Finally?" Sam frowned.

"This is just what I've heard and seen, mind you," Ruthie continued, sounding more lucid now than ever. Despite the oddities of what she was saying, she said it all as if she truly believed every word of it. "But Susan was always particularly jealous of her husband's freedom. His independence. Owning the dental practice. All the attention he got in town because of it. Now the poor man can't even wipe his own ass, but he has his dear wife to do everything for him. He relies on her for every single thing. Can't even leave the house without her. Can you imagine? She's much happier with that arrangement — actually, no. I've changed my mind. I'm sure she's *thrilled* by it."

"Wow. That *is* an interesting nugget of information to chew on," Sam said. "Thanks."

"Anytime." Ruthie dismissed the thank you with a wave of her hand. "I'm always happy to help you, seeing as you've been working so hard to help me the last few months since Beth, well… You know."

Sam nodded, studying Ruthie's wide, glinting eyes as the women held each other's gazes.

She's all there right now. Don't know how long that's gonna last, but it's nice to know it can still happen.

SAM STAYED another ten minutes to help tidy up around Ruthie's home, pretending the whole time that she was just trying to find something to do with her hands instead of cleaning up the old woman's house in fear that Ruthie would end up tripping over a pile of tossed-aside night-gowns in the middle of the hallway, or a pair of three-inch stilettos resting on the wooden floor in front of the couch. No way in hell could Ruthie manage wearing those now, and Sam had to stop herself from asking if the woman had secretly borrowed someone else's heels at some point in the last thirty years.

When she left, she felt surprisingly better about Ruthie continuing to live all on her own. Most of the time when Sam stopped by these days — which was twice a month for groceries and medication drop-offs — Ruthie had seemed just on this side of complete insanity. Maybe the woman had more good days like this, and it was just Sam's luck that she got to see all the not-so-great ones, however few and far between.

As she got back into her Jeep and pulled out of Ruthie's driveway, her phone buzzed in the center console with an incoming text. Sam wouldn't have known who'd sent it if it hadn't been for the shared picture of Kody above the text.

This was Brad's number.

No more sleeping in the back of an SUV. I'm in Room 8. Internet works fine here too. Come on by.

Sam stared blankly at the text, then dropped her phone back into the center console's cup holder and continued on her way down the road.

If that had been a face-to-face conversation, she would have reiterated her preference to meet up with him in the twenty-four-hour café attached to the hotel's lobby.

But saying so in a text would only further encourage him.

SIXTEEN

Sam

No, DRIVING FARTHER INTO THE CENTER OF TOWN TO STOP by the Redwood Rings wasn't technically considered an errand, though Sam had also wanted to ask Chris, if he wasn't too busy, whether he knew anything about a woman named Kody.

Since Christian, Levi, and Eddie clearly weren't going anywhere else anytime soon either, the Redwood seemed like the next best stop to hit multiple info-birds with one stone.

More than that, though, Sam had told Brad she needed a few hours. Her visit with Ruthie hadn't taken nearly as long as she'd thought it would, and she'd be damned if she was going to go straight to that hotel on the edge of town right after Brad's last text with his room number and all but an openly expressed invitation to enter it with him.

There still weren't any cars in the bar's front parking lot, but Sam was even more surprised to find Chris grinning at her like he'd just won the lottery.

She froze as the glass door swung silently shut behind her. "What happened?"

He chuckled. "Well I was thinking it was all good things today, but the look on your face is telling me otherwise."

Sam darted her gaze all around the bar's front dining room. It was just as empty as she'd expected, with Christian, Levi, and Eddie sitting together in a far corner table. Yet the eerie silence of the Redwood Rings in the early afternoon definitely made her feel like something was off.

Pair that with Chris' insane grin, and Sam was ready to expect anything. Namely, the worst.

"Well, I'm not immediately seeing anything off here," she said, "except for *you*. That's one hell of a creepy-ass smile, Chris."

Levi turned around in his chair and pointed at Chris by the bar. "Told you."

Chris spread his arms and glared at the guys in the corner. "What's wrong with my smile?"

"Makes you look terrified," Eddie said.

"Makes you look constipated," Christian added.

All three of them snickered and chuckled, shaking their heads before diving right back into their frothing pint glasses.

Chris scowled at them, then slowly headed across the bar to Sam.

"How's this, then?" he asked, his smile now returned to its usual crooked flicker.

"Much better. That doesn't make me think the world's coming to an end."

"Oh, for fuck's sake."

Sam laughed, and she definitely noticed the broadening of his smile in response but decided to give him a break for now.

"Whatever the reason," he said, "I'm glad to see you, Sam."

"Oh yeah? What's the occasion?"

He did a double take at her with a playful frown. "I need a reason to be happy to see you?"

"Most people do."

"Come on, Sam. You should know by now I'm not most people."

She pressed her lips together and decided not to walk right into that one, either.

"Actually, now that you mention it, something else *did* happen," Chris continued as he walked into the center of the Redwood's front dining room. Then he stopped, turned in a slow circle, and spread his arms. "What do you think?"

Sam raised an eyebrow and didn't know how she was going to answer that until Eddie said from the corner table, "Same old shit, different day."

The guys cracked up laughing again.

Chris shot her a look that said she ought to know exactly what he was talking about. When she didn't, she could only respond with a sheepish shrug.

"*Oh...*" she said a little too enthusiastically. "You mean everything's back to *normal*. Hey, congratulations, Chris. I'm really happy for you."

"Shut the hell up," he muttered, though his crooked smile remained. "And before you ask, no, we haven't opened up again. There's still a little more cleaning to do, so no, you don't have a shift tonight. Which now just leads me to my next question. Why are *you* here?"

"Come on, Chris," she said, adopting the same playful cluelessness he'd just given her. "I need a reason to stop by?"

"Considering that even when you do have a good reason to be here, on time, you're not... Yeah. I'd say you need a good reason. So what is it? Seriously, it's gotta be a good one."

"Careful now, son," Levi called from the table, raising his beer toward Chris. "Keep talking like that, you'll never see her walk back through those doors again."

Above the guys' barely restrained chuckling, Sam folded her arms and jerked her chin up at Chris. "Smart man. You should listen to him."

"Huh. Never thought I'd hear that from someone who actually means it."

Letting herself smile a little more, Sam approached him and pulled her phone from her back pocket before bringing up the image she wanted. "I do actually have some questions. Specifically, I'm wondering if you've seen this woman in here at all in the last couple weeks. She probably would've been up here in the front, you know, since I've been working the Back Bar."

Chris spent a good five seconds studying the photo of Kody on her phone, then flicked his gaze up toward her. "I don't recognize her. But I *do* recognize when Sam Salazar is up to something. What is it this time?"

"Trying to find someone."

"Uh-huh," he said with a deadpan stare. "And that's only half the answer, isn't it?"

Sam held his gaze a moment longer, half in playfulness and half in stepping up to the challenge. She knew he was trying to be friendly, to play it off like he wasn't that curious or concerned about what she'd been doing with her free time lately. She also knew that if she told Chris everything, he would, of course, just fall back into automatically worrying about her again anyway, which had become something of a pattern for both of them lately.

So she shrugged and decided to give him most of the answer, if not all of it.

Sam nodded at the picture. "This is actually the daughter of an old friend. She went missing, and I'm helping look for her."

"Oh." Chris took another look at the picture, seeming way more interested now. Or maybe just guilty for having brushed it off the first time. "Nope. Sorry. I really don't recognize her. She supposed to be a regular?"

"Not that I'm aware," Sam replied with a shrug. "I was told this young woman doesn't drink or frequent bars, but what kids don't tell their parents is usually volumes more than what they *do* tell their parents. Figured I'd take a stab at it. See if anyone here recognizes her."

"How long has she been missing?" Chris asked.

"About ten days. As far as we know."

"Wow, okay." Chris pressed his lips together and frowned at her phone one more time, even though she'd already turned off the screen. "Well, feel free to bring your friend by anytime, once the bar's back up and running again. Should only be a few days from now. Tell her she's got a drink on the house waiting for her if she wants it. Doesn't have to be the alcoholic kind. And feel free to pass along to her that I'll keep an eye out and ears open for anything about anyone who looks like her daughter."

Of course Chris would automatically assume an old friend of Sam's who asked Sam for help in finding a missing daughter would be a woman.

Brad Anderson definitely was not, but Sam didn't bother correcting the misconception. It didn't really matter, anyway. The whole point of stopping by the Redwood today was to ask after Kody, not to discuss the girl's parents.

Even if one of those parents happened to be an old Army buddy of Sam's from back in the day, who just also happened to be another number added to Sam's body count before she'd come to Rush.

And it really wasn't any of Chris' business.

"Thanks for that." Then Sam headed across the front dining room toward the corner table where Christian, Levi, and Eddie were currently holed up. "What about you guys?"

She turned her phone's screen back on to show the guys the same picture.

Each of them in turn took a good long look, leaning forward over their beers in consideration before shaking their heads.

"Nope, doesn't look familiar."

"Don't remember seeing anyone like that at all."

"Pretty sure if a face like that walked into this bar, I would've remembered."

Sam scoffed. "Yeah, I'm sure you would have."

"Whoa, wait. Hold on just a second, there," Christian added, stopping Sam from leaving the table as he reached toward her phone without really meaning to touch it. "Let me see that again."

Raising an eyebrow, Sam held her phone out under his nose again.

Christian squinted, tilted his head, then nodded. "You know what? Yeah. I think I *have* seen her before."

"Here at the bar?"

"Nah. Pretty sure we would've remembered someone like that in here."

"As long as someone like that was here *before* we reached our drink limit for the night," Levi added.

Eddie snorted. "You have a drink limit?"

"Pretty sure I did see her in town, though," Christian continued. "Don't know what she was doing. I didn't recognize who was with her. No one we run with, that's for sure. But I do remember seeing them have a conversation out on the street."

"What kind of conversation?" Sam asked.

"The talking kind." Christian looked at her like she was an idiot for asking that kind of question. "Didn't seem to be much of anything going on. Just a conversation. But I do remember I didn't recognize the fella. Young woman looked a little hot 'n bothered too. Not in the good way, mind you. Didn't think anything of it. Women do that from time to time."

"Right." Levi shook his head as he lifted his pint glass to his lips. "Because *you're* the expert on women these days."

"More'n *you* are."

"Thanks, guys." Sam nodded at them, leaving their table and the conversation before it could devolve into something completely unsalvageable.

Then she caught Chris' gaze again as she headed toward the Redwood's front doors. "Same goes for you. Thanks for the help and for keeping an eye out. And if anything else pops up in your head—"

"You'll be the first to know about it."

"The second," Eddie corrected from his table.

Chris scowled at him. "What?"

"She'll be the *second* person to know about it. Because if it comes to *your* mind, that done makes you the *first* person, don't it?"

Everyone else inside the front bar — which at this point was only Christian, Levi, Chris, and Sam — stared at him in silence. Then Sam cleared her throat and made it the rest of the way to the door.

"Catch ya later, fellas." Then she slipped out of the Redwood Rings.

. . .

Now that she'd exhausted her very limited options at the Redwood, Sam made her way toward the run-down hotel on the edge of downtown Rush to meet up with Brad again.

It felt strange to be back here after all the time she'd spent in this same hotel with Angela Copely when the woman had stayed here for weeks in search of what had happened to her daughter Dina.

The woman had brought a whole host of her own problems with her to Rush. She and Sam had gone over a large number of them in the twenty-four-hour café attached to this exact hotel. Sam hadn't been back since Angela and her daughter Laila had left Rush for good to go back home to Seattle.

The sad sight of the dilapidated but still functional building in the empty parking lot, even in the middle of the day, reminded her why.

When she arrived, she first stopped by the café just to poke her head in through the perpetually open doorway in case Brad had decided to wait for her at their originally agreed-upon location.

A quick glance around the empty diner-style establishment told her he hadn't.

So she made her way to Room 8, and only once she found said room on the hotel's first floor did she realize this was the exact same room in which Angela Copely had stayed.

Apparently, whoever assigned rooms to out-of-towners for short stays preferred to give them all the same lodgings.

Sam was fine with it, honestly. It just made it easier for her to find her way around the hotel.

Only now, when she approached the room, the hallway

filled with the sound of a man's voice rising in slightly louder-than-normal-conversation volumes.

It had to be Brad.

She only heard one voice, and it definitely sounded like his. Either the guy had totally lost it since they'd last spoken and was talking to himself when he thought no one else could hear, or he was having this heated conversation over the phone.

When she stopped just outside the door, Sam realized her hopes of such a heated conversation coming to an end with perfect timing had been unfounded.

The one-sided argument carrying on inside the room merely continued.

A minute later, Brad started shouting, the words rising clearly and succinctly through the hotel-room walls and door to spill into the hallway. "Because if I'd told you sooner, you would've wanted to come!"

Sam grimaced and thought about walking away again. By the sound of it, this conversation might end up taking longer than she cared to wait.

Then the room fell into complete silence, followed a few seconds later by a frustrated growl and a heavy thump behind the door.

If she had to guess, Sam would've said it was Brad punching or kicking the furniture around. Maybe even his own suitcase, if he'd packed one and bothered to bring it into the hotel with him.

But he wasn't yelling anymore. He wasn't arguing with whoever was on the phone. He didn't make any more noise after that.

Now seemed like a safer time to knock.

He opened the door almost instantly and paused when he realized it was Sam on the other side. With wide eyes, he just stared at her, then peered around her to quickly search the hallway. "Hey. You made it."

"Sure did."

Whether he'd already had his suspicions or something in her expression gave it away, when Brad met her gaze again, he grimaced. "Did you hear any of that before you knocked?"

Sam shrugged. "Just the yelling parts."

"So quite a bit of it, then." With a self-conscious chuckle, Brad stepped aside and motioned for her to join him in the room.

Sam entered and took a look around. The room was exactly the way she remembered from when Angela had stayed here, though that made sense. It was a hotel room. The exact same hotel room, even if the person currently occupying it couldn't have been more different than Angela Copely.

"Sorry you had to hear any of that, honestly," Brad said, turning away from her.

Sam stood there inside the open door, which she didn't feel comfortable closing herself because she didn't want to suddenly give the guy the wrong idea.

Seeing as it was just the two of them inside a hotel room together, shutting the door was more than likely to unintentionally imply a lot more than she wanted.

"Right." Brad paced across the middle of the room, running a hand over the top of his short-cropped hair. "That wasn't supposed to be a public thing, by the way. It wasn't really supposed to happen at all. Sorry."

"No need to apologize," she said.

"Yeah, well..." Another self-conscious chuckle escaped him. "Jesus. That was Denise."

"Okay." There wasn't much more Sam could say to that. She didn't know the woman personally — minus the one time the woman had walked in on her and Brad together, but that hadn't included any traditional introductions. Still, she knew enough about Brad's wife to understand exactly why he was acting so scattered now after a conversation with her. Made sense when this was an issue of their daughter missing.

"I'm gonna take a wild guess here," she said, "and say that you only told her about Kody just five minutes ago, yeah?"

Brad stopped pacing and looked at her head-on before letting out a heavy sigh. "That obvious, huh?"

"Doesn't take a rocket scientist, man."

"Can't argue with that. You know, it's been years since the divorce. And even sharing a kid, we still don't get along. Now that I think about it, we didn't even really get along that well when we were married. So I shouldn't be surprised, right? But you'd think things would've changed after all this time. I mean, all that bullshit about time healing wounds? Fuck that. She's *still* pissed at me."

Sam folded her arms and leaned back against the wall beside the still-open door. "Did it heal all *your* wounds?"

It was definitely meant as a rhetorical question, which they both knew full well.

True to form, Brad flashed her that winning grin of his she used to find somewhat exciting and maybe a little endearing, then glanced down at his bare forearm, which did in fact boast a long slashing scar he'd received in the line of duty before they'd ever met. "Only the ones you can see."

Sam wasn't going to encourage that kind of thing. She had no interest in sitting around and reminiscing about the good old days with a guy who still couldn't hold back from yelling at people over the phone, even if the most recent recipient of it was his ex-wife who probably still hated his guts now as much as she had back when Sam's involvement had given them a reason to end their marriage.

Brad stared at her with that stupid grin, probably waiting for her to laugh at his poorly timed joke. When she didn't, he puffed out a sigh and shook his head. The grin disappeared. "Yeah, I'm still working on all that."

"Speaking of working on it, what did you get out of Kody's cell phone account?"

"Right. I did get something." Brad passed her, leaving a surprisingly small amount of space between them when he leaned forward to grab the edge of the open door and swing it shut with a flick of his wrist.

Sam didn't move from where she'd set herself up leaning back against the wall beside the door. Again, she didn't want to give him any ideas. Standing perfectly still and barely reacting to anything seemed the best way to accomplish that.

"I managed to dig deep enough to pull out the most frequently dialed numbers on her records." Brad moved quickly toward the tiny desk built into the wall on the far side of the room, where his large tablet in a laughably bulky case rested on a frame. "Obviously there's my number. We can check that off the list. Then I had another buddy of mine look up the owners of these other numbers. Turns out these are definitely Kody's friends."

"And how do you know that?" Sam asked.

"I did tell you I'd heard their first names. She tells me about the people in her life. I just didn't have a way of contacting them on my own, but take a look at this. There's Annie Holden, Bethany Melrose, and Cassandra Hannity. Definitely recognize the first names, and these are all Cincinnati area codes. This is definitely them."

"All right, then." Finally pushing herself away from

the wall, Sam headed toward the desk to get a better look at the names and numbers pulled up on Brad's tablet. "Let's make some calls."

DIALING each of the numbers for Kody's friends in turn got them closer and closer to information they could actually use, one conversation at a time.

The first young woman sounded thrilled to be talking to Kody's dad, but all she knew was that Kody had taken off for Rush to finish up some work her Master's, and there was no more than that.

The second young woman had very much the same information, though it came with the added description of how incredibly excited Kody had been to head out to California for this research project and that it was all she could talk about for weeks on end before she finally made the trip out.

The only truly helpful information they received finally came from the last number on Brad's list. The young woman named Cassandra sounded far more self-aware and a lot more concerned about Kody's well-being and her whereabouts. She was the only one of Kody's friends who asked if she was okay, and Sam instantly marked this third young woman in her mind as the one who had to be the best friend, even if Kody wasn't aware of it.

There was a lot more of a connection between them simply based off the way Cassandra answered Sam and Brad's questions, not to mention the way she asked questions of her own, hoping to piece together whatever she could to help in the search.

They'd asked all three friends the same questions, but only Cassandra had anything to say when they asked if she knew of anyone who might have wanted to hurt Kody or who was upset with her for anything.

"I wouldn't say she was in trouble, really," the young woman said. "But she was pretty excited to get out of town. To just get away, period, you know? Halfway across the country. She hadn't had an excuse before then, but this finally gave her one. She needed some serious breathing room after Lucas. So this opportunity for going to Rush popped up, and she leapt on it."

"Who's Lucas?" Brad asked.

"Kody's ex."

Brad's mouth popped open. He blinked furiously at his phone put on speaker for these calls before he cleared his throat. "Right. Yeah, of course. When did they break up?"

Sam watched him intently but didn't say a word.

"Maybe two months ago," Cassandra replied. "Maybe a little longer. But he was really starting to get on her nerves, I know that. He was basically harassing her, and Kody couldn't wait to get out of town just so she wouldn't have to keep dealing with him."

"That's good to know," Brad said. "Do you happen to have this Lucas guy's number?"

"Unfortunately, I do, yeah. I've had to text him and even call him a few times to get him off her back. The guy doesn't really seem to take a hint all that well. I have no problem giving you his number. Is Kody okay?"

"That's what I'm trying to find out," Brad replied with a stiff nod. "She will be."

Then he got that phone number for the harassing ex-boyfriend, ended the call, and slumped back into the hard, uncomfortable, hotel-provided desk chair with a sigh.

"Didn't know about the boyfriend, huh?" Sam asked.

He slowly shook his head and stared blankly at the phone number for Lucas he'd written down on the pad of blank paper, also provided by the hotel. "That's something she would've told me about, right?"

"Not if she didn't think it was important. Obviously it wasn't, if they broke up a couple months ago."

"I swear to Christ," Brad muttered, "if this asshole did something to her…"

"Then we'll make sure he takes the right steps to correct some seriously shitty decisions," she finished for him. "*If* we can prove he actually did anything. Until then, Anderson, you gotta hold it together. We clear?"

"Yep." Clenching his eyes tightly shut, Brad rubbed his forehead for a moment, then dropped his hand back into his lap and grabbed his phone for another call. "Yeah, crystal clear, Sam. I'm good. No problem."

"I'm gonna hold you to that."

Sam kept a close eye on him as he dialed up the provided number, but she really didn't want to insert herself more than she already had. It wasn't her job to keep him in check. They didn't work together anymore. This wasn't an active case, as far as any of her job qualifications and current profession were concerned.

But if he showed any signs of losing it, Sam might have to back out of this before she could get much farther. Just to play it safe.

This Lucas guy made them wait through a full five rings on the other end of the line before he finally picked up, sounding like he'd just woken from a deep sleep.

Thirty seconds into the conversation, Sam realized that was just the way the guy sounded. It had to be.

For as worried and off his game as he was with his grown daughter incommunicado, Brad was impressively calm and lucid for this conversation with the young man who'd been dating her. Lucas showed the same level of restraint and maturity when he realized it was Kody's father calling, and they talked a little about where she was, what they'd been doing, and that she was missing, so Brad needed all the help he could get. That included hearing the truth straight from Lucas.

To his credit, the young man sounded genuinely surprised to hear that Kody was missing and just as genuinely eager and willing to do whatever he could to help find her and ensure her safety.

He didn't have much more information than her three girlfriends, though, so then Brad pulled out the big guns and told the kid he'd already spoken with his daughter's close friends.

"I heard you and Kody were on the outs for the last couple months, yeah?"

"If you mean, 'Did we break up?' I mean, yeah, man. A couple months ago."

"I also heard you were harassing her."

Sam shot him a quick look and wanted to remind him not to push things too far, but Brad ignored her.

"Harassing?" Lucas almost shrieked. "Are you kidding? Come on, man. I think Kody's amazing. You probably know she's pretty hard to harass anyway if she doesn't wanna be. I wasn't harassing her. We were talking a lot, yeah, about maybe getting back together. That's how things were looking."

"Then why did her friends think you'd just been causing her nothing but problems?" Brad asked.

"Honestly? Because she probably hadn't told them yet. Listen, I haven't really talked to anyone else either, because it's nobody else's business what Kody and I decide to do, together or separately. That's our private stuff. The only reason I'm telling you about it now is 'cause you said she's missing. Making sure she's okay is more important."

Brad paused, contemplating the young man's words, then cocked his head. "All right, Lucas. I believe you. What else can you tell me?"

Kody's ex sighed heavily. "Last time I talked to her, she seemed pretty spooked."

"You're gonna have to elaborate on that one, son," Brad said.

"I mean … *spooked*. You know. Like freaked out. Like something was bothering her. She wouldn't tell me too many specifics, but I think maybe she'd gotten into it with someone in town. Some kinda conflict. No, not physical. She called me, we talked about it. I think I helped her calm down afterwards. I don't know…"

Brad looked quickly up at Sam standing just behind him and to the side. She shrugged before twirling her finger in a get-more-information gesture. "Did she mention the person she got into with?"

"Sure did. Not easy to forget, either. Guy had the weirdest name ever. Some dude named Rip."

SEVENTEEN

Kody

EIGHT DAYS AGO...

KODY CERTAINLY HADN'T EXPECTED to find herself staring up into anyone's face, let alone that of a man who might or might not have been her captor and might or might not have actually wanted to help her.

This man's face, however, was obscured by shadow and the glare from the flashlight he aimed down at her in the bottom of the pit.

She could barely make out his features, though if she had to guess, she would've said this was the first guy in a hoodie and jeans she'd seen outside the cave when she was still hiking out on her own. He looked sort of young, but then sort of not. She had no idea why she thought it was both, but she couldn't narrow down his age.

She did know, however, that this wasn't the man with stringy hair who looked weirdly like Rip and had clocked her over the head with his walking stick.

That was a good start.

"Hi," she said, unable to look away from his face. "I'm Kody."

The man didn't respond. He merely kept staring down at her without moving, his expression too hidden in the half-light for her to tell what, if anything, he was thinking. She couldn't even be sure he was looking at her.

But now that she had his attention, getting him to talk was her next priority.

"What … what's your name?" she asked.

He inhaled deeply through his nose, then let it all back out again in a heavy sigh.

He doesn't wanna talk about himself. Makes sense. So just try another way…

"That's fine," Kody tried again. "You don't need to tell me your name. I get why you might not want to. But you don't need to tell me your name to help me out of here, right? Please. If you help me out of here, I'll just go. It won't take long. Just throw me a rope or something, and you won't even have to—"

"Can't do that." It was the first thing he'd said to her — the only thing — since she'd woken up in this pit.

Kody was so surprised by the curtness of his response and the audible pain behind those words, she couldn't hold back her own immediate reaction. With a snort, she spread her arms and shouted, "Why *not*?"

The man shook his head, then looked slowly over his shoulder before lowering his voice. "He wouldn't like it. My old man. He's … I just can't."

"Your dad?" Kody blinked, hoping the surprise wasn't ridiculously obvious in her expression now. "Listen, I know what that's like too. I'd do almost anything not to disappoint *my* dad. Probably already have by now, though. He's gotta be worried sick about me."

She'd thought drawing comparisons between them —

two grown adults worrying way too much about what their fathers thought — might draw a more empathetic connection between them. The guy hadn't told her *he* wouldn't like to help her out. Or that *he* couldn't afford to. If his dad hadn't been involved, maybe the guy would've instantly let her go.

Instead, the younger man whose face she couldn't quite see cleared his throat and started to turn away.

Kody was running out of options. And time with this one.

"Wait, wait, wait!"

He stopped turning away from her but still said nothing.

"At the very least, can I have my pack? Please? I packed it for a couple days. There's food in it, and more water, which I need 'cause I'm almost out of what I had on me. I'm hungry. I need both of those just to keep going. If there's nothing else you can do for me, can you at least get me my pack? Please?"

It was a total shot in the dark. Kody had absolutely no reason to believe that one of the men who'd tossed her down here — who didn't want to speak to her and who wouldn't let her go because he was terrified of his own father — would be gracious enough to hand over any of her things meant to continue her survival.

Hopefully, though, talking to him as much as she had already would humanize her a little more. Make this guy think about what he was actually doing here beyond trying not to piss off his dad. If he *did* bring her the pack, she had a few more days' worth of supplies, assuming no one let her out of here in the next few days. Maybe she could also get this younger-looking guy, clearly the more conscientious of the two, to open up to her a little.

Then she might have a chance.

It didn't surprise her that the guy offered no response to her request. After another moment of staring at her from the other end of his flashlight beam, he disappeared beyond the edge of the pit.

Kody practically held her breath so she could listen to the noises across the cave and form some logical rendition of what was happening up there. It just sounded like a bunch of footsteps, which could have meant anything.

And it was taking forever.

Trying to stay calm, Kody realized she had to move if she didn't want to lose it entirely.

She paced across the short diameter of the pit, circling round and round before crossing back and forth again. No matter how she looked at it, her options were incredibly few, and the chances of getting out of here in one piece were slim to none. She knew that.

This was one hell of a sticky situation.

It felt like she paced the bottom of the pit for an incredibly long time since the man had disappeared again. Though she thought the sound of him moving around up in the cave had stopped, she definitely didn't expect to see the guy's head poking out over the edge of the pit one more time before the weak beam of his flashlight filled the darkness around her again.

Kody blinked against the glare, then realized there was something in man's hands.

Something large and dark and ominous.

She couldn't for the life of her guess what it might have been.

She didn't have to.

A second later, the object plummeted from his hand down toward her.

Kody wondered for a split second if this was the thing with which he intended to kill her now.

A weighty but still relatively light thump pummeled into her chest with the swish of nylon. Kody's automatic reaction was to lift both arms and catch the bundle against her chest.

She recognized it instantly.

Holy shit, she was holding her pack!

"Thank you..." Her voice sounded raw and hoarse, though she'd expected it to tremble as a surge of hot, burning tears welled in her eyes. It was relief, yes, and gratitude, and something like rage because if the guy was willing to give her this one small thing she'd asked for, he had to be willing to help her more eventually, right?

Why wouldn't he just let her out now?

"Really, this means a lot," she added. "Thank you so much."

He didn't say anything as he stood there watching her. Then the beam of his flashlight flickered in a different direction, and Kody whipped her head up at the same time as another figure appeared over the edge of the pit.

It was little more than a dark, looming shadow in the shape of a man, and it moved too quickly for her to make out more details before the second figure lurched toward the man who'd thrown down her pack.

There was a smack and a solid thump, followed by a heavy grunt, and the younger man's form dropped out of view, as if he'd suddenly disappeared. His flashlight clattered out of his hand, rolling away and jerking the soft light up and down across the shadows and bumpy stone walls.

It felt like her brain took way too long to catch up with what her eyes had witnessed from below.

When the second man moved away from the pit's edge until she could only see the top of his head, Kody realized he'd just hit his partner in crime with one hell of a knockout punch and must now have been looming over the younger man's body.

That was when the yelling started.

Kody knew this was the long-haired Rip-lookalike with his deep, growling bark of commands and admonishments as he added what sounded like muffled kicks to another body.

If these two really were father and son, it was a seriously fucked-up relationship.

"What the hell do you think you're doing?" the older man roared, delivering more kicks. His son groaned. It sounded like tried to get up, but the beatdown only continued. "I told you not to say a goddamn thing. That was perfectly clear!"

As Kody watched, the older man's upright form dropped again, disappearing into what she imagined was some kind of straddling crouch over his own son. More sounds of unrestrained blows and grunts echoed around the cave.

"And you're over here doing exactly what I said not to fucking do!"

"Stop!" Kody shouted before she realized what was happening or that she'd been gritting her teeth and wincing against the sounds as she clutched her pack to her chest. "Please stop. You don't have to do this!"

She didn't expect the noises of such a beating to stop abruptly, but they did, followed by heavy, purposeful footsteps before the older man's shadowy silhouette appeared at the edge of the pit again. He didn't take the time to look down and study her like the younger guy.

The next second, his arm lurched out in front of him, and Kody had half a second to recognize the outline of a pistol at the end of it.

The gun went off the exact same second Kody stumbled backward and dropped to the floor of the pit.

The ensuing crack was deafening as it bounced off so much stone and condensed earth and enclosed space. A shower of dirt clods and pebbles sprayed into the air behind her, peppering her back and head.

She hunched forward, wrapped around her pack as she tucked her head toward her arms for protection.

Holding her breath, she waited for the pain to hit her. She waited for the certainty that, unlikely as it seemed, she'd just been shot.

When no other sounds echoed from above, Kody finally risked moving so she could check herself for injuries.

There was nothing. No bullet hole. No graze wound. Not so much as a scratch.

She had no idea if the older man with a gun was just a terrible shot or if he'd missed her on purpose, firing the round more to scare her into silence and submission than anything else.

Either way, the game had entirely changed now a firearm was involved.

Still breathing heavily and fighting not to freak out, she clutched her pack to her chest and listened in the near complete darkness.

A low, grunting moan. Lots of shuffling and scuffling around. Then the mixed echo of footsteps from two pairs of boots moving quickly away from the pit.

Kody stood perfectly still until all sound had disappeared. Then she waited a little longer.

Only when she finally decided the men were gone and she was on her own again did she realize she'd been trembling the whole time from head to toe.

That couldn't be helped.

The one positive she could pull from the situation was that she had her pack again, which was better than not having it. This pack was her lifeline, her emergency kit — everything she had deliberately packed to help her through sticky situations like this.

No, not *quite* like this.

Kody hadn't prepared for the unforeseen eventuality of being knocked unconscious with a stick, kidnapped, dragged into a cave, and tossed over the side of a freshly dug pit with one captor who seemed to have a conscience and didn't really want to hurt her and another who was angry enough and scary enough to beat his son and fire live rounds at the young woman crouching at the bottom of a hole.

She was working with what she had.

Not wanting to use any more of her phone's battery life, Kody felt around the outside of her pack in the pit's complete darkness. She'd used her gear more than enough times by now that she could clearly envision every part she touched with her fingers. In seconds, she found the front zipper to which she had attached the ridiculously silly Hello Kitty whistle.

But it wasn't there.

Her fingers started to shake again as she fumbled with the outside zipper again, tracing the line of the metal teeth and thinking maybe she'd attached that whistle to the second zipper. But no, the whistle was gone.

"Damn it," she whispered.

It wasn't really a surprise. If her captors had taken her gear off her, they no doubt had gone through it to make sure nothing would be a threat to them. Especially if they were going to give her her things before releasing her.

Which hopefully they did.

After that, she opened her pack and rummaged through

each item there, careful to set everything in the hollow between her crossed legs so she wouldn't lose it in the dark.

Time for another inventory.

She had another full water bottle, which was twice the size of the small one she'd kept in her jacket pocket, plus four more protein bars, an unopened bag of beef jerky, trail mix. Then came her survival blanket, which made Kody sigh in relief when she pulled it out, unfolded it, and wrapped the crinkling thermal material around her shoulders for the added warmth she'd been missing for days now.

But other things were missing from her supplies, not just the Hello Kitty whistle.

The coiled length of rope was gone too, just like the bear spray and utility knife.

What she did have, though, left her better off now than she'd been ten minutes ago.

At least she wouldn't starve down here for several more days.

Once everything was tucked securely back in her pack, the survival blanket finally started to insulate a little more heat back into her limbs. Then she decided to check her phone again.

The backlight was alarmingly intense, but she squinted against the glare and quickly scanned the only things she was really concerned with right now — he battery life, which was now down to fifty percent, and the complete lack of signal bars.

Neither of those things surprised her, but the lack of a signal was a little disappointing.

Even still, Kody was nowhere close to giving up yet. She quickly typed up another short text for help, mentioning she was in a cave and had been abducted with little cell service. Then she sent it off to her dad, hoping by some miracle it would make it out of this cave.

It took a long time for the next notification to pop up, describing the lack of service and that her most recent message was unable to send.

Debating the pros and cons of leaving her phone on and letting the power drain on the incredibly small chance that her messages might somehow get out into the world, Kody gritted her teeth and forced herself to shut off the phone.

Who knew when it might come in especially useful? And if she was going to be on her own down here for a while, with enough food and water to keep her alive as long as she was smart about it, she might make it long enough to have one good opportunity to call for help.

No way was she going to risk preemptively ruining it.

EIGHTEEN

Sam

"WHAT THE HELL KIND OF A NAME IS RIP ANYWAY? LIKE the abbreviation? R-I-P? Or what?" Brad spun around in the desk chair in his hotel room and scowled up at Sam. "Sounds like an asshole."

"He's a decent guy," Sam said. "Weird name notwithstanding. There are a lot of those in this town, though."

"Weird names or assholes?"

Sam snorted. "Both."

"Sam, please tell me you know this Rip guy."

She nodded and stared blankly across the hotel room, thinking. "Yeah, I've met him several times. Wouldn't necessarily say we're BFFs or anything, but he's a decent guy. Fair. Treats his employees pretty well, from what I hear. He's one of the bigger farmers up here."

"Farmers?" Brad asked. "Of what, exactly?"

She sent him a deadpan stare.

His eyebrows shot straight up, then he nodded once. "Right. *That* kinda farm. Jesus, and Kody was hanging out with a guy like that?"

161

"He's not bad people, Anderson. It's legal."

"That doesn't always mean a damn thing, does it? You have his number?"

"No. But I know his daughter. You do too now, actually."

"Come on, Salazar." Slumping back in the chair, Brad leaned all the way back against it, dropped his head backward, and ran both hands over his close-cropped hair with a massive sigh. "I'm not in the mood for fucked-up guessing games, all right? This is my kid we're talking about."

"It's not a guessing game. Meredith. She works at the Community Center. Runs the Twelve-Step meetings. You met her the other day when you were stalking me."

He sat bolt upright, dropping his hands into his lap, and blinked wide eyes at her before letting out a small, tired chuckle. "Oh. Yeah, I guess I do know her. Wasn't really all that helpful when I was asking about you, though. Didn't really give that whole *community vibe*, know what I'm sayin'?"

"Only to someone who shows up out of the blue asking creepy questions without explaining why he's here or how he knows me." Sam rolled her eyes and paced slowly across the tiny hotel room. "We should go talk to Meredith."

"We should go talk to Rip. If this is the asshole Lucas saw Kody running around with in town, he's first. I bet you anything he knows something. So where do I find him?"

Sam slowly looked over her shoulder at the man and tried to gauge what kind of mindset he was in.

Brad could handle his shit. She'd known that for years. But when it came to an emotionally charged situation, like his missing daughter or any of the other various personal

162

situations he'd brought to work with him in the past, the guy could get a little overheated.

Hell, a *lot* overheated. Dangerously so.

"I do know where his operation is," she said, then lifted a hand to stop Brad before he blurted out whatever new eager plan he'd suddenly cooked up in the last second. "But I'm going with you. No exceptions. I won't give you directions. I won't tell you where it is. We go together, and you let me do the talking. All of it."

With another flickering smile, Brad stood from the chair and lifted both hands in concession. "I can handle that. As long as we go right now."

She glanced at her watch more out of habit than anything else. "Yeah, I've probably got time."

Of course she had time. She was still temporarily out of work with literally nothing else to do. But it would take a whole lot more than this to get Sam to admit that out loud.

"UP HERE," Sam said, pointing out the front passenger window. "Turn right up here."

Brad practically slammed on the brakes to slow for the turn, ignoring the scathing glare she sent him. Then he slowed down even more and stopped several feet away from the enormous wrought-iron gates marking and blocking off the entrance to Rip's property.

"Damn," he said. "This guy's got decent security up here."

Sam took in the security cameras mounted on the gate posts on either side, plus the small booth that had been added on the other side of the gate. A line of four of Rip's security guys stood just on the other side of the gates, armed to the teeth and not afraid to show it.

She was pretty sure that was the outline of combat-grade body armor over their long-sleeve UV-proof shirts, but they were too far away to be certain.

"Yeah, he's definitely been cautious," she mused. "Maybe even a little *more* cautious lately."

"Why?" Brad whipped his head toward her. "Wasn't like this before?"

"No, he already had the gate and security guards. But the tower's new. The intercom's been updated too. And that team inside looks like they've beefed up their own precautions quite a bit. I wonder why."

"It's a fucking pot farm, Salazar. *That's* why."

"Maybe."

Sam didn't think that had anything to do with it. Rip's was a mostly legal business. She couldn't say one way or the other if the man engaged in less-legal enterprises in addition to the growing and wholesale distribution of his product. But it wouldn't have surprised her if that were the case.

Something else was going on here.

"Roll on up," she said, nodding toward the newly installed intercom system posted on a brand-new pole on this side of the gates. "We gotta call in."

"I've still got firepower in the back," he said, inching the SUV slowly forward across the crunching gravel drive. "Just saying."

"For what? Are you gonna blow up the speaker if you don't get what you want?"

Sam was grateful for the fact that he'd left both weapons in the back seat. At least the ones she knew about. It wouldn't surprise her if Brad had more concealed weapons on his person right now. She should have thought to ask.

The SUV rocked to a stop beside the intercom. Brad rolled down his window and punched the call button.

A low buzz flared from the speaker, followed by the same tinny voice that had greeted Sam every time she'd been allowed through these gates.

"Name."

Brad leaned slightly through his open window. "Yeah, listen—"

"It's Sam Salazar," she interrupted, leaning out of the passenger seat to make herself heard through Brad's open window. He scowled at her, but she ignored him. "Came up here to talk to Rip about a few things. Just hoping he's available."

A crackling bit of static came through the speaker.

"Did you make an appointment?"

"Uh, no."

"You gotta make an appointment."

"Since when?" Sam quipped.

More static, and when the guy answering calls at the gate spoke again, he sounded like he didn't want to be having this conversation at all. *"Listen, we've had some trouble with trespassers lately. Had to ramp up security. Rip's just not available, especially for house calls, without any forward notice. So if you want to talk to him, you gotta make an appointment. No exceptions."*

"What kind of trespassers?" Sam asked, squinting at the intercom box. "You guys got some competition up here, or somebody trying to steal your inventory?"

There was no answer from the intercom, so she decided to move on.

"All right, well, let me talk to Jordan, then. At least tell him I'm here. He can come meet us at the gate, if you want. Then you can let us in—"

"We won't. Not without an appointment. And Jordan's gone."

Sam sighed. "Gone how?"

"I don't know. Left town. He's done working here. The kid went back to, I don't know, Wisconsin or some shit. Listen, as much as we all like a good chat, I've got work to do. So make an appointment and then I'll see what I can do for you."

"And we do that how, exactly?" Sam asked.

"Look, lady, I'm not a secretary, all right? Call Rip. Set it up. Until then, I suggest flipping a one-eighty with that giant fucking cage you're in and getting on your way. There's nothing else I can do for you."

"All right. Understood. Thanks."

The security guard speaking to her let a derisive snort through the intercom before the low buzz returned, and that was the end of the conversation.

Sam slumped back into the passenger seat and shrugged. "You heard the guy. Back out."

With his lips pressed together in a grim line of frustration and disapproval, Brad jerked on the gear shift and hauled ass in reverse down the gravel-studded dirt drive back toward the slightly wider dirt frontage road.

He backed out to the left so they were facing in the direction they'd come, but instead of heading back toward town, he parked right there on the frontage road's narrow left-hand shoulder and shut off the engine.

"What are you doing?" Sam asked.

"I wanna show these assholes how goddamn serious I really am." Brad ripped off his seatbelt and jerked open the driver's-side door.

"Hold on, wait a second. You can't just roll up on them like that."

"Like hell I can't." The door slammed shut. Then he was marching toward the rear of the SUV.

Gritting her teeth, Sam spun around, quickly grabbed both the rifle and the pistol from the back seat, and returned them to her lap just as Brad opened the back door.

To find the back seat empty.

With a growl, he searched the floor and the rear of the vehicle, ran his hand along the back seat, then finally looked up into the front and found his weapons not where he'd left them. "Damn it, Salazar. What the fuck do you think you're doing?"

"I could ask you the same question," she said. "Because the way I see it, only one of us is out of line right now."

"Bullshit. Come on. Hand 'em over." He waved the firearms toward himself.

Sam didn't move.

Instead, she stared blankly at him and waited.

This could go one of two ways. Either he had enough working brain cells under all that rage and parental panic to realize he was going way too hard and fast right out the gate, or he had already long since passed that point and would just keep doing dumb shit until Sam finally helped him realize it.

They'd been through this kind of pattern before.

Glaring spitefully at her and definitely noticing his weapons in her lap, Brad pounded the heel of his fist against the back of the driver's seat. "Goddamnit! You're supposed to help me. Give me my fucking weapons, or—"

"Or what? Huh? You got a detailed plan for that? Because from where I'm sitting, it doesn't look like you've thought through anything at all."

"I swear to Christ, Salazar..." he growled through clenched teeth.

Still, she said nothing.

With a shout of frustration, Brad slammed the rear door shut, then stormed around the front of the vehicle, presumably heading toward the front passenger seat.

Looking at it from his perspective, Sam imagined the man planned to attempt getting his weapons from her by force. He was stupid, hot-headed, fueled entirely by his rattled emotions as a parent who couldn't find what happened to his kid. She understood that.

But she wasn't going to let him do it.

With one hand, she moved the rifle to the other side of the center console, and with her other hand, she lifted the pistol.

Brad jerked the front passenger door open so violently, the hinges squealed and creaked even in a new SUV. Then he stood there looming over her, his teeth bared in a grimace of rage as he prepared to blindly attack his only real friend in this situation.

By the time the door opened, Sam already had the pistol leveled at his chest.

No, she wasn't going to shoot the guy, but she'd switched off the safety just so he knew she wasn't screwing around.

"I don't give a fuck what you—" Brad stopped the second he saw the barrel trained on him, held in Sam's casual yet professional grip. His hands dropped away from the door, and at least he didn't lunge for the weapons.

He definitely didn't look happy, either. "What the hell?"

"I'll say it one more time," Sam said. "You need to take it down a notch."

"Quit fucking around, man. That Rip asshole knows Kody. He spoke to my daughter. Hell, he's probably the motherfucker who took her. And I'm gonna make him talk."

"Not if I'm the one with your arsenal." Sam nodded toward the pistol in her grip but kept her gaze on Brad.

"What are you gonna do about it, huh?" he seethed. "You gonna shoot me point blank, Sam? Just because I love my daughter?"

"Don't use her as an excuse for the way you're acting right now. I get it. You're scared. You're worried. You want results, and you think you're the only person who knows how to get them." She tilted her head, still training the pistol on him with an ever-steady grip honed by years of training and field experience. "I'm telling you right now, Anderson, you're not. I'm helping you because I know you. I'm holding this pistol right now because I know you. I'm telling you, get back behind the wheel and take us into town. We can't get onto Rip's property, and we're not doing this your way."

He glared at her, studying her expression and her posture and her hand training his own firearm on him.

They both knew Sam wouldn't actually fire a weapon at him, just like they both knew he wouldn't actually attack her just to get his hands on it.

She just needed him to know that what his amped-up emotions were telling him to do right now was at the bottom of their list of good choices.

Sam noticed it the second realization sank in and Brad's expression softened the slightest bit.

Good. He got in the picture.

He let out another sneering growl, then pushed himself away from the open passenger-side door. "You know what? Fuck you."

"You want me to drive too?" she asked. "Let you cool off a little more?"

Scoffing again, Brad slammed the door shut in her face, then stormed around the SUV back toward the driver's side.

With a heavy sigh, Sam re-engaged the pistol's safety, then laid both it and the rifle on the floor behind her seat.

Just like riding a fucking bike. You can go years without it, but once you get back on, it feels exactly the same as if you never stopped.

She's supposed that was one of the perks of having around old Army buddies from back in the day.

Right now, it was both a pro and a con. Sam just hoped Brad had gotten his shit together enough to keep from getting entirely out of control. It had been a long time since they'd worked together, and the last thing Sam wanted was to have to make the kind of hard choices one had to make to stop someone else from getting somebody killed.

BRAD DROVE like a lunatic back down the frontage road, toward the highway, and in the direction of downtown Rush.

Sam didn't say anything. She'd gotten him to back down at the gates of Rip's farm, and that was enough. She could handle white-knuckling the oh-shit handle beside the passenger-side window while Brad took the twists and turns of the highway at ridiculous speeds. But if bad came to worse, a vehicle as souped up as this could handle whatever his shitty driving threw at them.

Not that she wanted to test out its capabilities.

Despite his previous visit to the Community Center, Sam still had to offer a few detailed directions to get them there a second time. Brad was still riled up and had completely ignored her pre-emptive instructions until she shouted at him to take the next turn.

They came to a lurching, squealing halt in the parking lot, and Brad practically leapt out from behind the wheel to go take out his frustration and poorly masked panic on the completely innocent employees of and visitors to Rush's Community Center.

"Damn it," Sam muttered before she was right on his heels.

She jumped out of the SUV, darted around it to catch up with him, and leapt in front of him to cut him off. "Stop."

"You said we're talking to Meredith," he growled. "She's that Rip guy's daughter, yeah? So we'll talk to her. That's all I'm gonna do."

He tried to step around her, but Sam jumped in front of him again. "Not gonna happen. You're still riding on fumes, man. You need a timeout."

"Fuck off." He finally managed to slip around her again before marching toward the front of the building.

It wasn't like Sam could stand in front of him and physically stop him from barreling her over if he really wanted to, and it definitely looked like he wanted to.

But she wasn't going to let him storm in on Meredith and potentially turn to violence without exhausting the other alternatives first.

Clearly, he was still too elevated to handle any of this.

"I'm only gonna tell you one more time," she called after him. "You can actually listen to me and stop right now, or you can do this the hard way."

She knew he'd heard her. It would have been impossible not to.

He just wanted to ignore her.

With a heavy sigh, Sam rolled her eyes and took off

after him. She came up behind Brad and reached out to grab his shoulder. "Come on, Brad. This isn't—"

"Don't fucking touch me!" he growled, half-shrugging out from beneath her hand and half-shoving her away from him at the same time.

Sam stumbled backward, then hurried after him again, gritting her teeth. "You're not *listening* to me! This isn't the way to get shit done. Wake up!"

She grabbed his wrist this time, and a second later, Brad spun around toward her, roaring and raging with his fist cocked back.

He took his shot and swung.

Sam had seen it coming from a mile away, but that didn't mean it was any less disappointing.

She ducked his blow, skirted to the side under his arm, then popped up behind him and spun around to clock him a good one.

Right in the left kidney.

It wasn't hard enough to do any serious internal damage, but it definitely knocked him off balance.

And she knew it would hurt like a bitch.

With a cry, Brad staggered forward, his left knee buckled under the pain, and when he righted himself fully and turned back toward Sam, seething and ready to make heads roll, she pointed stiffly at his SUV and barked, "Stand down and get your ass back inside the vehicle, Anderson! Right the fuck now! That's a goddamn order!"

Her voice echoed across the parking lot, which she was grateful to see only contained a few cars, all of them empty.

The strength of her voice and the way she used it like this, the way she hadn't used it in years, surprised her. Part of it felt really good. Part of it made her want to turn around and run, but she held her ground.

Brad glared at her, sucking in hissing breaths through his teeth and favoring his left side where she'd hit him. "Seriously? You're gonna pull rank on me for something like this?"

"Fucking-A I will. If it means you get your ass back into that truck and let me do this the right way before you fuck up any other chances we have of finding your daughter. Have I made that clear enough for you?"

For a minute, it looked like Brad was about to start raging against her again. He still looked angry as hell, but the fight visibly seeped out of him enough for him to sigh, suck angrily on his teeth, then offer her a curt nod. "Yes, ma'am."

Sam stayed where she was and watched him half-stomp, half-hobble back to his SUV. Only when he slipped behind the wheel again and slammed the door shut behind him was she finally content enough to leave him and go talk to Meredith on her own.

Jesus Christ, can't we just leave the past where it fucking belongs? she thought as she climbed the front steps to the Community Center building. When she reached the front doors, she looked down at the knuckles of her right hand, which were now an angry red after one punch.

She didn't like pulling rank on anyone. She hadn't enjoyed it in the Army, and she sure as shit didn't enjoy it now. Fortunately, though, that was what it had taken to get Brad to listen to her.

Knowing that, Sam couldn't hold back a tiny smirk of satisfaction before she stepped into the Community Center.

NINETEEN

Charles
_____

SIX YEARS AGO...

"I JUST DON'T UNDERSTAND, Chief. My wife's been missing for forty-eight hours, and your people still haven't been able to find her."

Charles Putnam sat at his dining room table, trying not to let his anger and his fear overpower his conversation with Rush's Chief of Police. That was getting more difficult by the second.

"Like I've been telling you," Colton said calmly, "we're doing the best we can with the information we have."

"Well, it's not good enough!" Charles slammed a fist down on the table, making their coffee cups and the tray of spoons and coffee condiments rattle under the assault. "You've found no sign of my wife. You've made zero progress on the investigation. You assured me it was your top priority, but I'm starting to think I've done more work for the police to find my wife than the damn police have!"

When Charles finished his outburst, he quickly regained enough presence of mind to notice the disapproving but still remarkably calm look Colton sent his way. Only a man who'd been under fire from emotionally elevated people for quite some time could come up with an expression like that, but at least he didn't add fuel to Charles' fire.

Then Charles slowly sank back down into his seat at the table and cleared his throat. "Sorry."

"Understandable," Colton responded blandly. "No harm done. You're going through a rough time. I get it. The more you can hold those emotions in check, though, Charles, the faster we can get through this investigation and the search and bring your wife back home. Assuming, of course, she *wants* to come back home."

Charles shot the chief a quick scathing glance and folded his arms. "What the hell is *that* supposed to mean?"

Colton flipped through a small spiral-bound notebook on the table in front of him, then started speaking before he'd finished closing the notebook and returning it to the right breast pocket of his uniform shirt. "The way I've heard it told, you and Rose were navigating some bumpy marital terrain."

"We were not," Charles argued.

"That's not what I heard," Colton continued with a shrug. "Your wife had an affair, Charles. That kind of thing happens. It stands to reason that she might've made a habit out of it, and maybe she started up with the same kinda thing."

"That's not true," Charles said, forcing himself to remain calm.

"So she *didn't* cheat on you?" Colton asked.

"Well yeah, she did. But that was seven years ago.

Practically a lifetime. Way before Frankie ever came along."

"But there *have* been issues in your marriage," Colton continued.

"There were, but we got past it. Rose and I have been incredibly happy together. We worked through our differences. We both made necessary changes. We're completely committed to each other and to our son. It's not even a possibility now that she'd be running out on me. I don't want to hear you bring it up again."

Colton lifted both hands in concession and sat back against the chair. "Just doing my job. Which includes covering all the bases. Sometimes, the past has a nasty habit of catching up with us. Even when that past is distant and we thought it was over and done with."

"No. It's just not possible. Something *happened* to her." Charles fervently shook his head. "I can feel it, Chief. Something happened, and I need you to find her."

"All right. Okay." Colton nodded, though he didn't look particularly convinced. Still, he was clearly trying to be helpful despite the Rush PD's glaring lack of productive headway on Rose's case. "Well then, let's talk about—"

A burst of static rose from the police radio clipped to the shoulder of his uniform shirt before a tinny male voice filled Charles' kitchen.

"Chief, we've got a positive ID on a vehicle out here. Plates and VIN number match those on record for Rose Putnam. It's parked at the downtown bus station."

Charles' eyes widened as he stared at the radio on the chief's shoulder.

Colton watched the man intently and finally reached up to thumb his radio for a response. "Copy that, Nelson. Secure the scene and hang tight. I'm on my way."

"Rose's car," Charles murmured. "They found Rose's car."

"That's what it looks like," Colton said as he stood from the table. "But it's now part of our active investigation, so—"

"Finally!" Charles practically leapt from his chair and raced out of the kitchen toward the front of the house.

Colton drained the last of the coffee that had been offered to him in the Putnam residence, then gathered his jacket off the back of the chair. When he entered the living room, he found Charles standing by the front door with shoes on and jacket already pulled over his shoulders. "What are you doing?"

"I'm coming with you," Charles said, with no hesitation or reservation in his voice as he silently dared Colton to argue with him about this.

Finally, they'd found some sign of Rose, and Charles would be damned if he left it all up to the Rush PD now.

Whatever they found with Rose's car, Charles would be there with them, and whatever needed to happen after that, he would make sure it happened.

"I'm not so sure that's the best idea," Colton replied before shooting a poignant glance across the living room toward little Frankie, already half-asleep on the couch with the ear of one of his stuffed animals shoved into his mouth while cartoons played on the TV. "Your son needs you here."

"My *wife* needs me," Charles argued. "And that's why Evelyn's here."

He gestured toward his sister sitting on the couch beside his son.

At the sound of her name, Evelyn looked up at Charles and Colton and offered the men a tired smile. "Go ahead. I've got everything covered here. Frankie's on his way out.

You go do what you have to do. We'll be right here, waiting for you and Rose."

"Thank you," Charles murmured, then returned his full attention to Colton. "I'm coming, whether you like it or not, Chief. So we can go into this together, or you can deal with me following you to the scene and being a part of it anyway. I think we both know which would be easiest for everyone."

Colton pressed his lips together, took another quick sweep of the living room, then turned toward the front door. "Fine. But you keep your hands off the evidence, and don't get in my officers' way, understand? Or I will have you physically removed so we can get back to doing our jobs."

"Understood, Chief." Charles spun around and practically threw open the front door. "I know how this works. I've been writing stories about the cases in this town for years."

Then he marched out of the house and headed toward Colton's squad car.

"Uh-huh." The chief nodded at Evelyn, then silently left the house and pulled the door shut behind him.

THERE WERE two other police cruisers in the parking lot of the bus station when Colton and Charles arrived on the scene. The chief didn't bother telling Charles to wait in the car; the man had already made it perfectly clear he would be heavily involved in his wife's case, and he promised not to touch anything, so that had to be good enough for now.

It was definitely Rose's car. At least Charles was there to positively identify the vehicle and reconfirm what the Rush PD had already discovered.

But the vehicle was locked up tight, and no, Charles

did not have a second set of keys for the single car he and his wife had shared for years.

Just like his officers who'd arrived on the scene first had already done, Colton approached the locked vehicle and aimed his flashlight through the windows to see what he could see.

"What's that there?" he asked. "In the passenger seat?"

Charles shouldered his way past the other officers to stand beside the chief and get a good look for himself. "Candy."

"I'm sorry?" Colton asked blandly, briefly turning toward the man with his eyebrows raised.

"From The Toffee Shoppe. Rose stops by there almost every day before we have lunch together. That's what it says right there on the side of the bag, see? The Toffee Shoppe. Whatever's left in there, she was bringing home for Frankie."

Colton continued searching the inside of the vehicle with his flashlight, then finally gave the command for his other officers on scene to get the car open however they could without a spare set of keys. And if they couldn't, they'd have the thing impounded so they could break it open in a more controlled environment. Then he stormed across the parking lot.

"Where are you going?" Charles asked as he took off after the chief.

"We found her car in the parking lot of a bus station, Charles. I know you don't want to believe it, but all signs point to your wife having gone off on a solo trip of her own without telling you a damn thing about it. Or how it might not even be so solo."

"She wouldn't," Charles argued. "I already told you that."

"Well, let's go see what the folks who work here have to say about it."

Somehow, Charles kept his mouth shut and let the chief do the talking and the questioning when they walked inside the bus station.

The employee behind the ticket counter was a youngish-looking man in his mid- to late twenties who also looked incredibly bored by his job and maybe even his entire life, including the fact that Rush's Chief of Police now strode through the front doors of the station and headed right toward his window.

Colton asked the young man all the normal questions about vehicles left outside, whether or not they had security cameras on site. They did, but the recordings were erased at the end of every week on Friday nights to save room on the system's memory.

The chief extended a recent picture of Rose. "Do you remember seeing this woman here? Either Friday or yesterday?"

The clerk squinted at the photograph and wrinkled his nose. "No. I don't remember seeing anyone like this. Then again, yesterday was busy as hell. I doubt I'd remember one way or the other, you know?"

"Any idea why someone would leave their car parked indefinitely in the station's parking lot?"

The clerk shrugged. "I mean, folks do it all the time, like I said. Sometimes just because they can't find parking anywhere else. But plenty of folks also hitchhike out of Rush after leaving their cars here."

"She wouldn't have done that," Charles murmured, shaking his head. "Rose wouldn't hitchhike anywhere. She wouldn't just leave her car parked here either and disappear. Not with candy for Frankie in the front seat. Not when that's the only car we have."

"Charles." Colton turned toward him with a raised eyebrow. "I'm going to have to ask you to step back and let me handle this."

"She wouldn't *do* that!" Charles shouted, then thrust a finger at the clerk behind the ticket window. "You would have recognized her if you saw her come in here. Did you sell her a ticket? Look it up."

"It doesn't work like that, man." The clerk shrugged again. "We don't ask passengers for their personal details. Just come in and buy a ticket. Use it or don't. It's not like at the airport."

"Just look!" Charles shouted.

"All right, that's enough." Colton grabbed Charles by the shoulder and led him away from the ticket counter for a slightly more private conversation.

"What are you doing?" Charles asked. "Ask him. Tell him he has to look. You'll find that she wasn't here at all. Something happened to her. We need to go over the security footage and we need to—"

"What *you* need, Charles," Colton interjected, though he loosened his grip on the man's shoulder to hopefully show he didn't bear any ill will toward the guy going through one hell of a time right now, "is to go home. Be with your son. Let me and my department do our jobs. We'll find Rose if something happened to her, okay? We'll figure out what's going on here. That's what we do. But it's pretty damn difficult when you're looking over my shoulder and yelling at potential witnesses because you're getting a little overheated."

"I talk to witnesses all the time," Charles said through clenched teeth.

"Uh-huh. As a journalist, sure. But not about your missing wife, yeah? You're too close to this. Go home. Get some sleep. Focus on what you've got right now, which is a son who still needs you and a job you've still got to do when you get back to work tomorrow morning. I'll give you a call if anything else comes up."

With a frustrated sigh, Charles shrugged out from beneath Colton's hand, spun away from the chief and the ticket counter, and stormed back out of the station.

He didn't have a car to drive, so he headed out on foot instead. That was his only option.

But Charles Putnam did not go home.

He couldn't go home. Not now. Not when Rose was still out there, potentially in danger, waiting for her husband to find her and save her.

No, he didn't have the full force of the Rush Police Department at his every beck and call, but he sure as hell wasn't completely powerless in this situation.

So instead of walking home, Charles booked it on foot all the way across town toward *The Daily Rush*'s main office. He was a reporter, after all. This was his job, what he was good at. And he had to do something.

Sitting around at home with Frankie, no matter how much he loved his son, just wasn't an option.

There was no one in the building at this time of night, but that only made Charles all the more confident about what he needed to do. He headed straight for his office in the back, sat down, turned on his computer, and got to work.

He wrote out absolutely everything he could remember from two days ago when Rose had disappeared, what she was wearing, what they'd talked about, any and every detail from before and after their lunch date, which was the last time he'd seen or heard from her.

When he finished, Charles let out a heavy sigh, sank back against the back of his desk chair, and reread through all his notes and all the details that were still particularly fresh in his mind.

A knock on the inside of his open office door disrupted his focus, and he jumped in his chair before spinning it toward the sound.

"Sorry to interrupt," Patty said with a sheepishly apologetic smile.

"That's all right," he said with a tight chuckle before glancing behind her into the rest of the building's open office space. "I thought I was alone."

"I just stopped by to catch up on some extra work before we start up again tomorrow, Mondays being what they are. Then I heard you typing away in here. Is there anything I can help with, Charles?"

He frowned for a moment, then snapped his fingers and pointed at her. "Actually, yeah. Pull that file on all the different missing persons cases in Rush. The unsolved ones. You know, the women who've gone missing."

"Got it," she said with a nod. "Anything else?"

"No, Patty. For now, that's it. Thank you."

She left him alone to go pull those files. Charles drummed his fingers on the surface of his desk.

Chewing on the inside of his cheek, he pulled out his cell phone and played through Rose's final voicemail for what must have been the hundredth time.

TWENTY

Sam

SAM DIDN'T KNOW HOW LONG SHE'D BEEN PACING BACK
and forth in the hallway outside Meredith's office, but it
felt like damn near forever when the door finally opened
and a frail, skinny older man with a perpetual hunch and
gaping holes in the sides of his loafers shuffled out. She
puffed out a sigh of relief and murmured, "Finally."

The man shot her disapproving frown as she barreled
past him into Meredith's office.

Sure, maybe it wasn't the most respectful-to-the-
elderly thing to move so impatiently before he'd
completely stepped into the hall, but there wasn't a whole
lot of time to waste. She had one insanely riled-up Army
vet slash concerned father waiting in the parking lot right
outside, and she really didn't want to tempt fate by taking
any longer than she absolutely had to here.

This was about getting Rip's number, and that was it.

She stormed into the office and didn't bother shutting
the door behind her. "Meredith."

Meredith Graham looked quickly up from her desk and

batted her lashes before a small, tired-looking smile spread across her lips. "Sam. It's good to see you."

"Yeah, you too," Sam blurted as a force of habit she'd fallen out of a while ago but somehow found necessary to say in response right now. "How are things? Or whatever."

"Oh, well, you know... Honestly, I've been having a bit of a hard time, lately. Pretty much since Beth, if I'm being honest." The woman fiddled with a stack of loose papers on her desk, absently shuffling them together and tapping them upright on the desk's hard surface before setting them aside again. "It's been a struggle, which I know you already know. Listen, Sam, I do really appreciate that you came in to check on me, though. It's nice to see a familiar face in person outside of meetings."

Sam pressed her lips together, forcing herself away from the biting witticisms that had first popped up in her head about Meredith having a hard time without Beth because she couldn't find some other nutjob to focus on in her quest to martyr herself.

But that would have been too out of hand, Sam knew.

Plus, it wasn't like Sam hadn't been spending a lot of her own extra time getting involved in other people's business when those other people needed her help, too.

Now was not the time to be a hypocrite.

Still, she fidgeted awkwardly in the center of Meredith's office, swiping a few loose strands of hair away from her face before gazing briefly down at the tops of her sneakers. "Yeah, umm, sorry to hear that. Actually, I came by to ask you about Rip."

Meredith's tired smile morphed into a frown of confusion. "What about my dad?"

"I was hoping to get his number. I've never needed it before now, but apparently, anyone who wants to talk to the man now has to call him personally and schedule an appointment."

"Oh. That." Meredith sighed heavily and sank back in her chair. "There've been some issues up on his property recently. Trespassers. Folks thinking they can walk up onto someone else's farm whenever they want and do their own thing there."

"That's what all the beefed-up security at the gates had to say too." Sam folded her arms. "You know what's going on up there?"

"I'm not involved in my dad's business, Sam. You know that."

"Right. Of course. Which then just further goes to show that the best thing is to talk to him about it in person, so if I could just get that number…"

Meredith eyed her with the same type of scrutiny with which she eyed newcomers to meetings or people like Beth who seemed at one point or another to need more help than mere Twelve-Step programs could reasonably provide. This wasn't the first time she'd fixed Sam with that look, either. Fortunately, though, Sam's personal life and her personal decisions were not the current topic of conversation.

Lucky her.

With a heavy sigh, Meredith finally relented and tore her gaze away from Sam's face. "Yeah, okay. Just a second."

She opened her desk drawer for a pad of paper and a pen, then pulled out her cell so she could jot down Rip's number.

When she finished, she ripped off the top sheet of paper and extended it over her desk toward Sam. "That's his cell. But if you're wanting to talk to Rip sooner rather than later, you'll still have to wait. He's out of town right now."

Sam took the paper and folded it neatly before stuffing it into her pocket. "Any idea when he'll be back?"

"It's supposed to be tomorrow." Meredith shrugged. "Late tomorrow night, as far as I know."

"Well, at least I can call him and get something set up. Thanks for this."

Sam almost headed out of the office then but figured she might as well use the opportunity to ask a few more questions while she had Meredith's attention.

So she turned back toward the other woman. "Actually, now that I think about it, have you happened to hear anything about a Kody Anderson?"

"Is that the college girl who came up to do her research on environmental studies up at Rip's farm?" Meredith asked.

"Yep." Sam's eyebrows shot straight up in surprise. "That's her."

"Yeah, Rip mentioned her a few times over the last couple weeks. That he had meetings with her or that this student was spending some time up at the farm. I never met her personally, though."

"Did your dad ever mention anything to you about an argument he and Kody had?"

Meredith's expression went completely blank, though Sam had known the woman long enough to recognize it as Meredith's pissed-off-and-offended look. "Are you accusing my dad of something you can't prove, Sam?"

Sam shook her head. "No, not at all. It's nothing like that. I was just asking."

"Right." Meredith looked her up and down, then glanced at her watch. "Listen, Sam, I've got today's meeting to lead and prep for here in the next ten minutes.

You should stick around. Join the meeting. Be good to see you back in there."

"Yeah, another day," Sam said. "I've got a few things I need to get to."

"You know the program only works if you work it, right?" Meredith said.

Sam fought not to roll her eyes at the overly simplistic saying repeated ad nauseam in Twelve-Step groups and meetings. "Yeah. I know. I'll hit up another meeting sometime later this week, though. Thanks for the phone number, Meredith."

Then Sam hurried out of the Community Center as quickly as possible.

On her way through the halls, she pulled out the paper Meredith had given her and dialed up Rip's personal cell number.

The line didn't even ring but went straight to voicemail.

Normally, Sam didn't bother leaving voicemails, but this felt like one of those times where it was better to put her intentions out there even in a recorded message than wait for everything to fall into place all on its own.

So she let Rip's greeting play out and started talking after the beep.

"Rip. It's Sam Salazar. Listen, there's no reason for me to bullshit with you around this. I'm looking for Kody Anderson. She's gone missing. Last heard from almost two weeks ago now, and I heard the two of you had been working together on some stuff. Or at least that she was conducting some of her research out on your property. I figured you might have some more information that could help me find her.

"Your security team up at the farm is doing their jobs perfectly. They told me I need to make an appointment

189

with you now, so that's what I'm calling about. To make an appointment. This is my cell number, so when you get this, call me back. I heard you're out of town until tomorrow night, so I'll wait to hear from you. Thanks."

Then she hung up, stuffed her phone into the back pocket of her jeans again, and left the Community Center.

Sam had every intention of getting back into Brad's SUV with him and explaining that she'd gotten Rip's number and had already left the guy a message, with the caveat that they had to wait for the man to return from his out-of-town trip tomorrow night.

But when she reached the parking lot, Brad's giant, souped-up vehicle was nowhere to be found.

"Son of a bitch," she murmured.

Grimacing in frustration, Sam quickly dialed Brad's number, which she now had thanks to him texting her pictures of Kody.

She hadn't actually expected him to answer, so it came as no surprise when he didn't.

But it did make things slightly more complicated.

"For fuck's sake, Anderson. I told you to wait."

She had a feeling she knew exactly where the man had gone, assuming he made his decisions the same way now as when they'd served together.

And she might need a little help if she was right.

She skimmed through the other contacts saved in her phone, thinking about whom to call that would cause the least amount of conflict and offer the greatest potential for help. Who was the best person for that job, Syc or Chris?

"Aw, fuck it..."

Sam told herself she picked the number at random before making the call, but it didn't really matter. She just hoped she wasn't too late.

TWENTY-ONE

Sam

THE TWENTY MINUTES SHE WAITED FELT LIKE FOUR HOURS before Chris' truck finally pulled into the Community Center's parking lot. Before he'd even come to a complete stop, Sam had jogged toward his vehicle and opened the passenger-side door. The truck's wheels came to a rolling halt as Sam was already leaping up into the front passenger seat.

"Thanks for this, Chris," she said, quickly strapping on her seatbelt. "I really appreciate it."

"No problem," he replied with a casual shrug. "Nelson Taxi Service is always open for business."

She shot him a deadpan look and snorted. "I just need you to take me back to the hotel right on the edge of town. That's where my car is. And then, you know, I'll let you get back to your day."

"Sure thing." Chris pulled out of the parking lot and guided them back onto the road before saying anything else. Apparently, he couldn't keep his curiosity locked up for long.

Sam absolutely understood the feeling.

"So just riddle me this, though, huh?" Chris began. "How exactly did you leave your Jeep at the hotel but get stranded out here at the Community Center?"

"It really doesn't matter," she said, shaking her head.

"You sure about that?" Chris shot her a double take but inevitably had to refocus on the road. "Kinda seems like something that *does* matter, Sam."

"All right, fine. It does matter, okay? You're right. I just don't wanna talk about it."

He nodded. "Now *that* answer actually makes sense."

There wasn't any other conversation on the rest of the drive toward the hotel, and Sam couldn't get out of Chris' truck any faster.

"Hey, are you doing anything tonight?" he called after her before she could close the passenger-side door.

Sam froze. "Why?"

He let out a strained chuckle and shrugged. "All right, cutting the bullshit. I know you're not doing anything tonight, because we still haven't officially opened the Redwood back up again. So, since you seem to not have picked up on it, this is me inviting you over tonight. You know, company."

Sam studied his face, finally realized what he meant, and forced herself not to laugh. "Right. I appreciate that, Chris, but I'm gonna have to take a rain check. Sorry."

"Hey, no big deal. It's not like I don't expect that answer from time to time. Is this because of that friend you're helping?"

"Yeah, kind of."

"All right. Be careful, whatever you two end up getting into. If you need anything, you know you can always call me, right? I mean, I'm always here to help. I just can't guarantee I won't give you shit for it."

"Oh, that I *know* I can count on," she countered.

They both laughed, then Sam raised her hand in a final short wave before shutting the passenger-side door and hurrying across the hotel parking lot toward her Jeep.

That was great of Chris to have been so available and that he'd come to pick her up and take her back to her car without asking too many questions — or at least not more than any normal, sane person would ask of someone like her. She just really didn't want to get into the nitty-gritty details of what was going on with Brad and his daughter, not to mention the fact that Sam still hadn't corrected Chris' misconception of her old friend being another woman.

That was a fun bit of awkward conversation she was eager to put off as long as possible.

After hurrying to her Jeep and hopping inside, Sam pulled out her cigarettes and a lighter, lit up in the front seat with the windows down, and got in one glorious puff of nicotine before her phone rang.

She didn't recognize the number, and it hadn't been saved in her phone, but that had been happening a lot more frequently lately.

Sam's curiosity made it impossible not to answer.

"Hello?"

"Hello?" a woman replied. "Is this Sam?"

"It is."

"Oh, wonderful. Sam, this is Susan Hooper."

Sam almost choked on her next inhalation of bitter gray smoke and burning nicotine. She blew it out quickly and managed to get control of both her voice and her surprise. "Susan, hi. Thanks for calling. Did you find something?"

"As a matter of fact, I did. And I had to call you right away. You remember when I told you Kody had checked out with nothing but a note left in her room?"

"Sure," Sam said, ashing her cigarette out the window.

"Well, as it turns out, I did not actually throw that note away like I thought. Silly old me. I ended up turning the thing over and using the back of it to write down my shopping list for this week. I only found the thing because I stuck it to the fridge and thought I saw something through the paper from the other side. And what do you know? Here's her checkout note, right here in front of me, if you're still interested in taking a look."

"I am definitely still interested, Susan. Thank you so much. This could be incredibly helpful."

"Oh, I'm so glad to hear that. Come on by whenever you like. Steven and I are just here doing our thing. Unless, of course, you're busy…"

"No, no. I'll be right there. Thanks."

SAM MADE it to the bed-and-breakfast on the other side of town in record speed, where Susan met her at the open front door with a smile and a glass of iced tea in hand.

"You sure made it over here fast," she said.

"I was in the neighborhood," Sam replied.

"Come in, come in. Please. It's good to see you again."

Sam didn't particularly feel all that excited about walking back into the Turner-Hooper residence, though she *had* come to get that note from Kody, which had the potential to lead her right to possibly helpful next steps.

Susan, on the other hand, seemed more focused on having another guest in her home, which definitely wasn't what Sam was trying to be right now.

"Can I get you some iced tea?" the woman asked. "Or a glass of water? Cup of coffee?"

"No, thank you," Sam said.

"I just finished making a whole plate of finger sandwiches. Steven doesn't eat very many and there's no telling how many I can eat when there's no one else around to help me clear the plate. Would you like to join us for lunch?"

Sam got a grip on her manners and her patience and held on tight. "I wish I could stay, Susan. But I can't today. I've got a few other appointments. You called at just the right time in between them. Just that checkout note from Kody would be great."

The other woman seemed alarmingly disappointed by this rejection, almost like Sam should have felt obligated to entertain her host.

The awkwardness between them made Sam blurt out as a second thought, "Maybe some other time, though."

Susan's face lit up instantly. "Oh, that would be lovely. I very much enjoyed that last conversation with you and your husband the other day. Bring him by again, too, if you like. If he's not too busy."

Though it probably wasn't very effective, Sam at least tried to stop herself from grimacing at that bit of mistaken identity she hadn't bothered to correct, and now the woman was calling Brad her husband.

"Yeah, we'll see," she said.

"Fantastic." Grinning from ear to ear, Susan bustled off toward the kitchen, where doors and cabinets rumbled open and banged shut. She practically jogged back toward the enormous old house's entryway before delivering the checkout note allegedly left by Kody Anderson.

The woman handed Sam the note with the grocery list side turned up, so Sam flipped it back and forth a few times before she realized which side was which.

Then she found herself staring at the side that was decidedly Kody's checkout note.

. . .

Leaving early. Thanks for the accommodation.

   —Kody

SAM QUIRKED her lips in disappointment.

How the hell am I supposed to get the leads I need from a note typed out and printed like this?

"Thank you so much," she told Susan flatly. "This is what I needed."

The older woman tried desperately to get Sam to stay a little longer, either for refreshments or finger sandwiches or something else, but Sam had to quickly extricate herself from the B&B. First, because she didn't really have the time or the patience to stay and hang out with Susan Hooper chatting away about absolutely nothing. And second because she didn't know how much longer she could hold back her growing frustration at discovering that what she'd thought would be a helpful bit of evidence for her and Brad was actually now just one more complication.

Anyone could have typed this message on a piece of paper and left it in Kody's room, but they knew who she was and where she'd been staying and that she wasn't supposed to have checked out this early, all to hide their tracks. So no one would think anything unusual had happened, like a young woman disappearing or still being in danger.

All this told Sam it was incredibly unlikely that Kody had checked herself out or written this note or gathered up all her things before vacating the premises.

She now had a whole new can of worms open right in front of her.

Specifically, who had typed this note, when they'd broken into the bed and breakfast to retrieve Kody's things, how they knew so much about her in the first place, and what the hell they'd done with her.

Sam didn't know where to go next after Susan's house, so she went straight home. Though she didn't really have anything to do back inside the Deville, for some inexplicable reason, she was overcome by the urgent need to clean her trailer top to bottom and end to end.

Somewhere during the process, Dog had found himself inside the Deville with her, though Sam didn't remember letting him in after she'd gotten home. Now, while she cleaned and grumbled to herself about Brad's anger issues and Susan Hooper's loneliness and desperation for company, Dog lay sprawled out in the center of the trailer, watching her.

After a while, Sam couldn't help but notice the way he didn't take his eyes off her, his bushy canine eyebrows twitching back and forth to follow her footsteps. Every now and then, he let out a low whine and a rather disgruntled-sounding chuff.

The next time he did this, Sam finally had to stop with a damp rag in hand and a spray bottle of watered-down cleaning solution in the other, then stuck the backs of both hands on her hips. "Yeah, I know. This isn't my usual M.O. Trust me, Dog, this is as weird for me as it is for you, but I need something to do."

Dog snorted and lazily flopped over onto his side.

"I'm cleaning up for *me*, okay?" she told him. "And it doesn't help anyone to just let their own messes keep piling up around them. So this is me taking pride in my surroundings. That's because I like the feeling of a clean space, *not* because I'm expecting any kind of company now or in the near future or ever."

Dog stared blankly at her, then pushed himself up onto his haunches and dipped a head between his hind legs.

Sam snickered. "Yeah, okay. No need to ask you how you feel about it. Read you loud and clear."

She wasn't ready to admit to herself that she still halfway expected Brad to push her boundaries more than he already had. Specifically when it came to coming over to her place.

Sam didn't really have guests over, and when she did, it was pretty much just Chris.

Now, though, she subconsciously wanted to make sure this fellow ex-MP and longtime friend of hers didn't see what daily life in a cheap-ass trailer park in the middle of nowhere in Northern California looked like.

Since when did she start giving a shit?

Her phone buzzed on the tiny sliver of the Deville's kitchen counter, each time moving slightly closer to the edge of the cracked, scratched-up, chipped Formica surface.

Sam stretched her neck out over the kitchen counter and saw it was Brad calling.

"Nope. Not dealing with that today. If he wants to be a douchebag and bail on me and leave me stranded without a ride anywhere, he can go fuck himself."

She kept cleaning, which didn't take very long at all because the Deville was tiny and there wasn't much to do.

Sam didn't get along very well with others when there wasn't much to do.

She didn't get along very well with *herself* when there was nothing to do.

Reminded now that she was still a better version of herself when not left entirely to her own devices, she swept her phone off the counter, snatched an ice-cold can of Coke out of the mini-fridge, and headed outside.

The second the Deville's front door squealed open, Dog leapt to his feet with another snort and raced past her, shoving the door aside with his snout and bounding down all two front steps before booking it toward the firepit.

Syc was out there in his chair, doing his daily thing. He had the fire crackling away in the pit with a half-smoked joint hanging loosely from his lips and his eyes closed.

At first, she thought he was asleep, though that didn't stop her from making her way to the lawn chair unofficially marked as hers around the firepit and plopping down into it.

Syc didn't move when she cracked open her Coke can, or when she glugged almost half of it down in one breath, or when her phone buzzed loudly in the lawn chair's cup holder.

Brad again.

She wasn't going to answer this time, either.

A minute later, her phone buzzed again. Sam ignored it again.

She almost jumped out of her skin when Syc took a long, slightly whistling drag on his joint and blew the white cloud out around the joint still resting between his lips before he finally took it out. "Sounds like you got some calls."

Sam glared at him. "I thought you were asleep."

"What if I was? You gonna go run away and hide now that I'm awake?"

She snorted and drank more Coke. "How's everything been looking lately after the whole zoning debacle?"

"Debacle." Clicking his tongue, Syc slowly shook his head. "Ain't heard a thing about it. Far as I know, everything got signed off on down at City Hall real quick, no more questions asked. Just the way I like it."

"That's good to hear."

"Uh-huh."

"What about that thumb drive I gave you?" she asked. "You have to use that at all?"

"Nope." Syc lazily swung his arm out over the side of the lawn chair to ash his joint over the grass beside him. "Thing's still locked up as tight as Little Pete's mouth about the whole thing."

"Good." Sam nodded. "What'd you end up doing with it?"

"It's safe, Sam. Don't you worry about that."

If anyone else had said it to her like that, it would've instantly made Sam worry about it.

But from Syc, a quick and casual reassurance like that went a lot farther. He'd done her several solids in her two years and change of living in Rush. He was on her list of top three people she didn't think were completely full of shit in this town.

They sat around the firepit in silence again. Dog eventually padded his way back toward them, sniffing the ground or throwing his head up to catch something interesting on the air. Then he finally gave in and flopped onto his side in the grass in his normal spot between the lawn chairs.

In that moment, everything felt right, oddly enough.

Sam could be temporarily without a job or even a hardset date for when she could get back to the one she had — plus an unexpected and probably unwelcome blast from the past having rattled her chains in the last several days and another missing young woman to find, hopefully in time to keep the worst-case scenario from coming to pass — and still be pretty damn okay.

She also had this — sitting around the fire with Syc and Dog, a cold drink in her hand and a cigarette between her lips and not a goddamn word spoken because it just wasn't necessary to fill the silence.

So few people actually got that these days.

Though Syc was the one to break the silence again, she didn't begrudge him that. At least he didn't spew a load of bullshit every time he opened his mouth.

"Did that guy ever find you?" he asked.

"What guy?"

"Who showed up here asking about you?"

"He did, actually. Turns out I did in fact recognize the back of that head."

Syc snorted. "You're welcome. Who is he?"

"Just an old Army buddy," she said, shaking her head.

"He causing you trouble already?"

"Nothing I can't handle."

"Doesn't mean you have to, though. Just saying."

"Ever the fountain of irrefutable wisdom," she said through a chuckle.

"Careful, Sam," he said. "Keep using big fancy words like that, and Dog's gonna start thinking you've turned on him."

Dog didn't move a muscle even at the sound of his name.

The plastic cup holder in Sam's canvas lawn chair buzzed loudly again with the next phone call, which she ignored.

Before it stopped ringing, Syc grunted, pulled out a beer bottle from wherever the hell he'd been hiding it until now, cracked it open with a hollow clunk and hiss, then shook his head as he lifted the bottle to his lips. "You gotta do something about *that*, though."

"Not a conversation I'm ready to have right now."

"Not a noise I'm ready to keep listening to right now, either," Syc replied gruffly. "It's annoying as hell. Answer the damn phone or turn it off."

Pressing her lips together to fight back a smile, Sam stared into the crackling firepit and took a mental note.

Sycamore Fox wasn't one for modern technology, no, but she hadn't figured him for the type who couldn't stand the sound of said technology in someone else's hands.

One more moment of silence, then her phone buzzed again.

This time, she felt Syc's sidelong glare settling on her face and didn't even have to look at him.

She snatched her phone out of the cup holder, saw it was not Brad this time but a call from the Rush PD, and immediately wrote it off as yet another call she didn't want to answer take.

But it was the *police*.

With her luck, it was probably Chief Colton, and with her luck, if she didn't answer, that would just end up bringing a whole bucket full of messy chunks pouring down on her head when she least expected it.

With a groan, Sam relented and took the call.

"Yeah," she said.

"Miss Salazar?" a man asked on the other end of the line.

"Sam," she corrected. "That's me."

"Sorry to bother you, ma'am," he continued, instantly marking himself as either a brand-new rookie to Rush's police force or a poor, clueless bastard who still had no idea who she was. "I'm calling on behalf of one Bradley Anderson."

Shit.

"Uh-huh…" That was all she could say short of cussing out the booking officer or whoever was calling her.

"Do you know him?" the man asked.

"Unfortunately, yes."

"All right, well, we have Mr. Anderson in custody

down at the station. He was picked up and processed for multiple compounded assault charges earlier today. Normally, I wouldn't be making calls on anyone's behalf like this, but the guy just won't shut up about calling you specifically to bail him out."

Sam choked on her Coke.

She fought to catch her breath, cleared her throat several times, then said wryly into the phone, "Is that so?"

TWENTY-TWO

Kody

SEVERAL DAYS AGO...

KODY HAD no idea how long she'd been in the pit. All she knew was that she was still down here, and she hadn't come up with any new ideas for how to get herself out.

Now that her phone's battery had dwindled to thirty-eight percent, she'd shut it off and promised herself she wouldn't turn it back on again for anything, even a light to see by, until she was certain any message or phone call would actually make it through to its intended receiver.

Of course, that could only happen if she were ever let out of this damn pit in the first place.

There was no telling what her two captors had planned for her, but as long as she was still alive, there was still a chance.

That was the single bit of glowing optimism to which she still clung as time slipped away from her in the near-constant darkness and near-constant silence within the cave.

With no light to see by, no tools to help her make other tools to make an escape from the pit a viable option, and nothing else to occupy her thoughts, Kody turned instead to taking meticulously detailed mental notes of everything she heard in the cave.

Hopefully, if this went on longer than another day or two, she could come up with a pattern of when her captors entered the cave, what it sounded like they were doing, how long it felt like they were there, and what various degrees of minimal light poured into the cave entrance from outside during each of the men's visits.

She catalogued everything, finding it a lot easier than she'd expected to remember those details because she didn't have anything else occupying her mind.

More than that, Kody knew if she didn't find something to focus on, she'd end up going down an even deeper, darker hole inside herself, fearing the worst before it happened and losing all hope before there was ever really a reason to.

The way she looked at it, there was never a good reason.

For the most part, she found a pattern of the men's noises easy to put together. The younger man, she was pretty sure, was the one with the lighter, more hesitant footsteps. Kody heard the shuffling sounds of his movements around the cave a lot more frequently than she heard the other man's.

After a while, she started to wonder if the son in this father-son kidnapping duo just stayed in this cave all the time and hardly ever left. After all, he'd been the one she'd seen standing outside the cave in the first place when she'd walked into that small valley she was never supposed to have found.

The younger man's footsteps moved even during the

night as well, or as close to nighttime as Kody could guess. Moments when almost no light at all came through the cave, when everything was the most silent, and even when she'd managed to wrap herself tightly in the survival blanket and doze off for a few minutes at a time, she would be startled awake by the soft whispering footsteps of the younger man shuffling around the stone floor above her.

He never came to talk to her again, even at night when they were alone. Or so Kody assumed.

The older man, the one who'd clubbed her in the head and who had apparently beaten his own son for speaking to her, seemed only to show up during the daylight hours.

Kody recognized this by her ability to barely make out the silhouette of her own hand in front of her face. The upper layer of the cave probably held a lot more light during the day, but very little of it spilled into the pit.

Only when there was even that small amount of light did the older man's loud, furious, stomping echo around the cave mix in with his grunts of frustration and disapproval.

After what Kody guessed was two more days, or at least two more periods of sleeping through what felt like the darkest hours at the bottom of the pit, the cave filled with altogether different sounds.

Clattering and clinking. The tight, sharp crackle of hinges tightening, almost like glass withstanding as much pressure as possible right before it shattered. There were metallic clangs and heavy bangs, something that sounded like an enormous trunk being dragged across the cave's stone floor, and a lot of small, lightly tinkling echoes, like one of them was tinkering with a toolset or some kind of complex contraption.

Kody was more confused and curious about the source of these new sounds than anything else up to this point.

She couldn't for the life of her figure out what they were doing. Of course, neither man was going to answer her when she asked, so she stopped asking.

The first thought that made sense as an explanation was that they'd started up some kind of drug operation in the middle of nowhere, and she just happened to stumble upon it at the exact wrong time.

She'd heard of meth labs, ranging from disastrously amateur to impressively expert, set up in all kinds of strange places around the country. That kind of thing seemed like it was constantly making the news.

None of that made complete sense, though. If she was sitting in a pit inside a hidden mountain-cave meth lab, she would have been able to smell it.

The only thing she could smell was the dankness of the cave, the dampness of the earth and the pit's walls all around her, and the sharp stink of her own body after however many days she'd spent down here trying to hold her growing terror at bay.

Eventually, it didn't matter how many days or nights it had been, or what kind of patterns she'd noticed. Kody had finally reached the end of her patience for sitting quietly like a good victim and waiting for the worst to happen, as it inevitably would.

She'd been listening intently to the sounds in the cave for what felt like the last fifteen minutes or so. Then again, fifteen minutes here could feel either like five seconds or ten hours. But she felt confident it was just the younger man here, the more compassionate one, the son, alone and by himself. She hadn't heard anything of the older man's presence, and she had to do something.

"I know you've got a lot on your shoulders right now," she called out. Her voice was hoarse and raspy from misuse and the necessary dehydration she'd forced herself into so she could preserve her water supply. "I know you know what the right thing to do is. You wouldn't have given me my pack otherwise. And I'm grateful for that. Can we talk again, just you and me?"

The noise in the cave had stopped abruptly the second she'd started talking, but that was to be expected.

When the younger man still refused to be baited back to the edge of the pit again, Kody just had to keep going.

It was all she could do.

"I get that you can't just let me go. That would be more trouble for you. I understand that now. Message received. I just…" She sighed heavily and swallowed.

Her voice had started to tremble while she spoke, and that definitely was not the kind of image she wanted to portray now. Not when she was trying to ask her younger captor for his help again.

"Please," she continued. "I just need to get word to my dad to let him know I'm alive, at the very least. Or if you can somehow get a message to him, then maybe he can find me and no one will ever have to know it came from you.

"My dad's name is Brad Anderson. He knows I'm in Rush. I normally talk to him every day, but I haven't since I've been down here, obviously. Can you get word to him for me? Call him, maybe? Brad Anderson. His number is…"

Kody rattled off her dad's cell number, slowly and deliberately articulating each digit, grateful for the fact that she'd memorized his number in the first place.

Over and over, she repeated her father's name and phone number. She didn't have any way to see down here, even if she could write a note. But maybe her captors had pen and paper or their own phones to jot down important information like this.

Name and number. Name and number. Again and again until Kody felt she was chanting it like a mantra.

Like a life-saving meditation.

Maybe if the younger man in the cave heard it enough times over and over like this, it would stick in his head too.

Maybe it would get through to him enough that he might at least attempt to contact her dad.

Before she knew it, footsteps shuffled across the cave floor, echoing closer and closer to the pit's edge.

Kody's voice only grew louder, her spirits lifted by the idea that the younger man might actually deliver a message to her dad.

Shuffling footsteps sounded just like the way she'd catalogued the younger man's movements. But in a short-lived moment of horror, Kody realized she had drastically miscalculated everything.

It was the older man's head of stringy, shoulder-length gray hair popping out over the edge of the pit with a sharp, gruff bark of, "Cut the shit, you stupid fucking bitch!"

Maybe he should have shot her when he'd had the chance, because Kody wasn't about to let this opportunity slip through her fingers.

She leapt to her feet anyway, more scared of the older man but unwilling to just sit there and keep cowering. "Please! Please just let me out of here! I promise I won't—"

"We'll let you go when we're damn good and ready," he snapped. "That ain't now. So until we get to that point, you're gonna sit down. You're gonna shut up. And you're gonna wait 'til the right time."

She took a few steps backward and swallowed thickly, her neck craning painfully so she could stare up at the silhouette of the older man bending forward, his stringy hair wavering like a curtain of thin ropes along either side of his face. "How long is that gonna be? I can't last down here forever. I need food and water. I'm running low already. And it's so cold down here. If I don't get something warmer, I'm gonna end up freezing."

"I told you to sit down and shut the hell up! You don't need shit. You can move. You've got enough down there with you to last. You'll live. And you'll choose to keep living if you know what's good for you. Which means I don't wanna hear a goddamn thing out of this pit unless it's after I asked you the fucking question!"

The man spat into the pit, then spun around and clomped back across the cave.

Kody's chest heaved with quickening breath as her anger and rage and fear heightened all together in equal parts. Her fists clenched so tight at her sides that her forearms ached from it, and the sound of her teeth grinding in her head drowned out the last of her captor's footsteps.

But then everything fell perfectly still and silent.

Chances were both men had left the cave again. But she really didn't care anymore.

She had to do something with all this energy boiling up inside her.

The only option she had was to let it out in one long, hoarse, seemingly endless scream that filled the cave with its echoing rage and filled her own head with a vibrating pain.

It still wasn't enough of a release.

So she gasped for air and screamed again. Loud and long and without holding back.

She didn't give a fuck if her captors heard her now. Most likely, they were just going to kill her anyway. So what was the point of playing their game by their rules when they'd rigged it completely against her anyway?

TWENTY-THREE

Sam

SAM BURST THROUGH THE DOORS OF THE RUSH POLICE Station and headed straight for the receptionist at the front desk.

The woman's greeting smile faded when she saw who was heading her way, but she quickly tried to correct her expression. "Can I help you with something?"

"I got a call earlier today about Brad Anderson. You guys have him in holding right now. Booked for assault charges." Sam gritted her teeth and had to force out the rest of it. "I'm here to ... post bail."

"Oh." The receptionist's eyebrows went straight up, and her gaze bounced fervently around the surface of her desk before she finally found what she wanted. "I can help you with that. I just need you to fill out this form and sign each of these affidavits beneath. Then I'll collect the bail money, of course."

"Of course," Sam muttered, reaching for the pen and clipboard the receptionist slid across the desk toward her.

"And on that top page there," the other woman said, "if there are any other stipulations of his bond you would like to add in writing, those will be made clear to Mr. Anderson when he—"

"I know how this works," Sam interrupted tersely, already halfway through signing the paperwork. "Thanks."

The woman kept her mouth shut after that, her lips pressed together in a grim line as she first watched Sam fill out all the paperwork, then counted the bail money Sam had to pull out of the slow-as-hell ATM on her way here. Three different times, the woman counted it by hand before she put all the cash through one of those electronic money-counters more often seen in banks than in police stations before she finally checked off that the appropriate amount had been paid. Then she signed her name as the station's administrative witness to the entire process.

"Do you acknowledge that if Mr. Anderson misses his court hearing, for any reason, the money you've put up for his bond will become forfeit and a warrant will be issued for his immediate arrest and incarceration?"

"Yep," Sam replied blandly.

The receptionist stared back at her for a moment, then shuffled the paperwork, snapped the rubber band around the stack of cash, deposited everything into the front drawer of her desk, and picked up her phone to dial an internal number.

"Go ahead and take a seat," she told Sam. "This won't be long."

That was bullshit.

Sam waited in the precinct lobby for forty minutes for Brad's bail to be posted, for the information to be entered into the system, for his arresting officers to be notified, and then for someone else to walk to the other side of the building and unlock the holding cell before escorting Brad back through the building.

He was cuffed again by the time they led him out into

freedom once more, but the officer dropping him off in front quickly released him. He didn't say a word as he nodded for Brad to get the hell out of there.

Sam stood as Brad headed her way. When he saw her, he attempted a smile, though it was made difficult by his split and swollen bottom lip.

She didn't smile at all.

As he reached her in the lobby, she also noticed the raw, bright red of his scraped knuckles and the rip in his button-down shirt.

"You look like shit," she said.

Brad scoffed. "You should see the other guy."

"You should've called someone else to bail your ass out. This is the last time I'm doing it. For real."

His smile disappeared. "Yeah, but thanks for—"

"Shut up," she hissed, then spun away from him and marched back through the station doors.

She didn't particularly care whether or not Brad followed her, which of course he did. She made it to her Jeep, and he jogged to catch up with her and meet her there, grimacing as he briefly pressed a hand to his ribcage.

"Sam, I'm sorry," he said. "I know it wasn't the best—"

"No. It wasn't. Actually, this shit is *exactly* what I told you not to do."

"I know," he said.

"And you had to fucking go and do it, anyway."

"I screwed up, okay? I know that."

"You're damn right you screwed up! And I just had to cough up more cash than I make in a month to keep your ass from rotting behind bars for who knows how long. The police in this town don't exactly operate through the quickest legal channels when it comes to outsiders. You're one lucky dumbass, you know that?"

"Yeah, I know," he replied with a shrug. "Especially since it turns out that Rip guy wasn't even on his farm in the first place."

"Shit, Anderson," Sam growled. "*I* could've told you that. He's out of town until tomorrow night. Which I found out, by the way, by *not being a fucking idiot.*"

With a grimace, Brad shoved both hands into the pockets of his jeans.

"I got his number, and I left a message to hopefully make that appointment with him, but now who knows if that's ever gonna happen." Sam tossed her hands in the air. "I seriously doubt Rip'll wanna talk to either of us after you beat two of his security guys to hell and back."

"Four, actually," Brad muttered.

Sam puffed out an exasperated sigh. "Jesus Christ, man. Listen, you came up here to find me, because you wanted my help finding your daughter, yeah?"

Brad's gaze flickered around the parking lot before finally settling on her face, and he offered a quick, self-conscious nod.

"And I'm willing to help you," she continued. "Honestly, I am. But for that to happen, I need you to let go of the fucking wheel and let me drive this thing, yeah? You're too worked up to know up from down, obviously, and I'm not pulling your ass out of the fire if you're too bone-headed to walk right back into it again.

"We have to do this as much by the books as possible, whatever book that is, but it's the one that doesn't involve threatening and assaulting armed guards at one of the biggest commercial marijuana farms in the state, all right? Or anywhere. You keep your hands to yourself, you keep your mouth shut, and just stay where I can see you. That's what I'm here for."

"Yep." Gazing at his boots, Brad bounced on his toes

with his hands still in his pockets. and nodded. "I got it, Salazar."

"You damn well better," she snapped. "Or you and I will have serious issues."

She felt mostly confident in his understanding of their agreement when Brad didn't open his mouth again. So Sam decided to move on. "While you were out there being a moron, I found something else too."

"Really?"

"Susan Hooper called to say she found that checkout note Kody left in her room at the B&B. So I stopped by to pick it up." Sam reached into her pocket and pulled out the folded note with Susan's handwritten grocery list on one side and the typed-up checkout note printed on the other.

Brad practically snatched it out of her hands and skimmed it desperately before his face contorted into a bitter scowl. "Damnit."

"Yeah, that's about the same thought I had too," she said.

He shook his head. "My daughter didn't write this."

"Obviously."

"No, I mean, this didn't come from her. She didn't write it, she didn't type it, this is someone else pretending to be Kody. Look. The spelling mistake? She never would've let that fly, even just for a simple note like this. And after spending two weeks at the B&B, she would've left something a little more personal for the owner. Like an actual letter from a real person. This is just somebody trying to cover their tracks."

"I considered that a possibility too," she said. "Any idea who might have had knowledge of where she was staying, or access to her things, to get inside the shed in the backyard?"

"The motherfucker who took her, that's who," he growled.

Before Sam could say anything else, Brad tore up the printed note into dozens of tiny pieces, ripping it up as if he had claws at the end of his fingers and bunching it all up into a messy fist before chucking it at the parking lot pavement.

Well there goes our evidence.

"I can't fucking believe this!" Brad's voice cracked, and he turned his back to Sam, presumably so she wouldn't see him starting to break down now. "What happened to her? I know my kid. I know she would've taken every precaution possible. I know she wouldn't have walked into anything unprepared. Someone else did this. I know it. Someone took her, and whatever they did to her, I have to—"

"Hey." Sam set a hand on his shoulder. Brad instantly stiffened beneath her touch, but she didn't let him go. She let him stand there, his is back to her, for as long as he needed. "We're gonna find her, Brad. We'll get to the bottom of it, I promise. The two of us, working on this together, putting our heads together like we used to to get something done. Come on, you know what it takes to see this through to the end. We'll find your daughter. If she's even half as smart as you've made her out to be, I'm sure she's hanging in there. She'll make it through. Don't lose sight of that, all right?"

Brad's shoulder slumped forward. He let out a massive, hollow sigh, dipped his head in a not-so-reassured nod, and looked over his shoulder at her. "Was everyone this positive when your daughter was gone?"

Sam stared at him, momentarily at a loss for what to say to that low fucking blow until she realized she didn't actually have to provide an answer.

She couldn't.

Instead, she dropped her hand away from Brad's shoulder, swallowed, and nodded toward Rush's Main Street just off the station's parking lot. "Go back to the hotel. Take a shower. Maybe get something to eat. And don't leave your damn room until I tell you I've got something else, okay? When I do, you'll be the first person to hear about it."

Brad scanned the street in the direction of the hotel, which happened to be on the other side of town, then raised his eyebrows. "How am I supposed to get back there? They impounded my truck."

"Last time I checked, both your legs still work."

With that, Sam climbed behind the wheel of her Jeep, shut the door, and drove off.

The only thing that made her feel any level of confidence in Brad's ability to not start more shit was the fact that he *didn't* have his car right now.

Kind of hard to stomp his way up the mountain to Rip's farm again, or anywhere else in or around Rush, without his wheels. Trekking around on foot would give him the time he needed to cool off and pull himself together.

Hopefully, Sam would have more information for him later today.

WITH A WHOLE SWELL of new and disturbingly unfamiliar emotions boiling through her, Sam figured the next best place to go at this very moment was to pay Hector a visit. She was headed in that direction already when her phone rang again.

Sam wasn't in the mood for conversation of any kind,

and she almost ignored the call until she saw it was Rip calling her back.

So she pulled over onto the shoulder, cut the Jeep's engine, and answered.

"Hey, Rip. Thanks for calling me back."

"What the fuck, Sam? I leave town for thirty hours, and everything goes to shit. Then I hear some douchebag picked a fight with my guys, and *you're* the one who bailed him out."

"I'm sorry about that. The guy's a hothead, Rip. He got out of control and seriously screwed up."

"You can say that again."

"It won't happen again," she said. "You have my word on that."

The man growled out a sigh from the other end of the line. "Listen, I don't know you all that well, Sam, but based on the few interactions we've had, you're all right. I like you well enough. That won't last if your pals can't pull on their big-boy pants and handle their shit like adults. If it happens again, it's on you."

"Fair enough. Actually, the reason my friend was at your farm in the first place is the same reason I called you earlier. His daughter's missing, and the guy's getting pretty desperate for any kind of information on what happened to her and where she might be right now. So if I need an appointment to talk to you, when you get back into town obviously, I'm happy to make one."

"No appointment," he grumbled. "That's just a waste of both our time. Go ahead and ask your questions now. If I can help you over the phone, we can get this off both our plates that much faster without forcing anybody into close physical quarters, because that clearly doesn't solve anything."

She swallowed her biting retort to that.

It wasn't Sam's anger issues that had laid Rip's security guys out, or that had put Brad in cuffs, but here she was, speaking on his behalf.

Probably better that they had this conversation over the phone, yeah. The sooner the better too.

"Brad's daughter," she started. "Kody Anderson. I heard you know her."

"Grad student. Yeah. Came out here for field research or whatever. She came by my farm a couple times a few weeks ago, asking if she could shadow some of my employees and get a feel for how things worked, how we ran things. She seemed more interested in the effects of farming on the land versus the political bullshit or whatever that normally comes with young people trying to get a look at the place. I opened my doors to her. She's a smart girl."

"I also heard you were seen having an argument with her in town," Sam added. "Kody's ex-boyfriend mentioned you by name. I guess Kody said the two of you got into some kinda disagreement."

"Uh-huh."

She waited for him to go into further detail, then rolled her eyes when he didn't and added, "Can you tell me what that argument was about, Rip?"

"She had more questions about … I don't know, two weeks ago. Normally, we got along just fine, which was easy enough. She stuck to her own business, to do her own research. That was all well and good with me. But then she just kept riding me for a time to sit down and talk about whatever she wanted to talk about with her paper or whatever. I just didn't have the time for it."

"All of a sudden?"

"Pretty much." Rip sighed. "We're having some water issues on the farm. The day we argued in town was the day those issues started, and yeah, I got a little heated, because a threat to my crops at that point is pretty self-explanatory."

"How did that argument end?"

"I told her to get off my ass about it, and when I fixed the issues I was dealing with, I'd reach out to her so we could talk. I guess she did a little digging on her own after that, because two days later, this girl was back up at my farm asking for me, saying she knew we were having problems with our irrigation and water sources and said she wanted to help."

"That makes sense," Sam said. "She was already familiar with your property at that point."

"And then some," Rip said. "I wasn't gonna take her up on the offer, but she laid out a damn convincing plan and said she wanted to look into it. So I unofficially hired her to find the problem. Day after that, she found me again, wanting to know where we got our water for the crops. I told her where it was. We've been channeling irrigation from the same place for damn near thirty years."

"You gave her detailed instructions?" Sam asked.

"Yeah."

"And those were…"

Rip cleared his throat. "Simple and easy. Past the farm on the frontage road, past the new cemetery, take a left, follow the road for ten miles to the pull-out parking lot right there on the shoulder. Then it's about a twenty-mile trek from that pull-out into the valley and the lake right there. Easy as that."

"Thanks, Rip. Did you hear from her after that?"

"No, actually. She didn't call. She didn't show up at the farm again, either. Like she just vanished off the face of the earth at that point, and I figured she felt like she got in too deep over her head with this kinda thing. I don't know, got scared. Packed up and went home."

"Well, that's not what happened."

"Damn." He cleared his throat again. "Tell you what. I'm coming back to town early tomorrow morning. I'll reach out when I've settled back in here, and if you like, I can meet you at that turnoff first thing. We'll head to the lake together, and I'll show you the place myself."

"That would be the most help I've gotten from anyone so far, Rip. Thanks. I'll wait to hear from you."

TWENTY-FOUR

Charles

Present Day

Despite everything we've been through, we still somehow managed to make things work.

When taken in the context of *The Daily Rush* newspaper being managed and operated efficiently for the last several years, even in today's sociopolitical climate, Charles Putnam could absolutely acknowledge how fortunate they'd been.

Especially now as he looked over the compiled numbers for the paper's ad revenue this month.

Small towns like Rush had a hard enough time keeping smaller businesses afloat long-term. For local newspapers, it could be even harder. But they were still here, still taking up space, still moving along.

Charles looked up at the framed photo he kept on his desk, this one of him and Frankie, just the two of them.

His son had grown up so much in the last several years. He was a good kid, a smart kid. So whenever Charles looked at this picture, or at any picture of them taken in the last six years since Rose's disappearance, he could tell immediately that the smiles on both his and his son's face weren't entirely genuine.

They looked happy, sure, but neither of them truly were.

Not completely. Not the way they would have been if the love of Charles' life and Frankie's mother had been around to live through the last six years with them.

A knock on the open door of his office made Charles glance up across the room, then another smile graced his features in real time. It was genuine, though nothing like the smiles he used to give back when life had seemed so much simpler.

"Hey." Patty remained by the open door with her knuckles poised against the wood for a moment longer. "Are you busy?"

"Not too busy for you," he told her. "Come on in."

She crossed his office quickly, stopped to bend down toward him for a quick kiss, then frowned and placed her hands on her hips.

She'd done a lot more of that lately, especially after they'd started dating almost two years ago. Charles imagined it was because now Patty was privy to how much time he *didn't* spend with work.

It was a lot less time now than it had been when Rose was still around.

Sitting back in his desk chair, Charles looked up at her and feigned an even broader smile. "What is it?"

"I'm just stopping by to see how you're doing."

"But you look like there's already something wrong." Charles spread his arms. "So come on. You might as well say it while we're here."

Patty tucked her shoulder-length brunette hair behind

her ear and pressed her lips together before finally speaking her mind. "I'm getting a little worried about you, Chuck."

"Oh really?"

"It's just that... You've been working yourself really hard lately. Maybe a little too hard. Honestly, I think you might need a break."

Charles scoffed and turned back toward his desk. "I don't need a break."

"Honestly, though. When was the last time you even had one? When was the last time you took a day off? Hell, even the afternoon?"

"The news doesn't operate on a nine-to-five schedule, Patty. You know that."

"I also know that a human being can't survive on twenty-hour workdays and old packets of Pop-Tarts you pulled from the back of the cabinets in the staff kitchen. Don't get me wrong, you're setting a new record for it, but it won't last forever."

"All right. Message received." When he looked back up at her, the concern on Patty's face hadn't changed one bit. "And something tells me you didn't step into my office just to comment on my eating habits."

"Well, *someone* has to. But you're right. There *is* something else."

When she didn't immediately say what it was, Charles put his work down again and turned to face her directly. "So what's up?"

By now, they'd been dating long enough that he could practically read each and every one of her expressions. The one he was getting from her now, though, didn't stoke much confidence.

"Patty?"

She shook her head, sighed, then grimaced before a

halting, hesitant reply finally burst from her lips. "It's important. I know it's important and, well, no one else is going to bring it up to you, so I'm the one who has to do it. I just … I don't wanna be the one to…"

"To what?"

"To open up old wounds, Chuck."

That was all she had to say. Charles needed no further explanation, nor did he wonder at the cause of the sinking, gnawing pit curdling in his gut.

That was all she had to say, and he knew.

"You found something about Rose, didn't you?" he asked.

Patty frowned at him, then stepped away from the desk only to grab the single, incredibly uncomfortable chair against the wall beside his office door. She dragged it with her back toward his desk and sat so they could have this conversation without her looming over him. "I just got off the phone with my contact at the station. Another woman's been reported missing, Chuck."

She pulled out her phone to show him the picture of the young woman in question, but Charles didn't need to see it.

Just like he didn't need to specifically hear that this new information was connected to the disappearance of his wife six years ago. He already knew what the young woman looked like.

Dark hair. Dark eyes. Wide, beaming smile.

He wouldn't look directly at Patty or at her phone when he spoke next. "There's a striking resemblance to Rose, just like the others?"

Patty slowly lowered her phone into her lap and nodded.

The next second, Charles grabbed the bottom righthand drawer of his desk and jerked it open with a loud bang. His hands and fingers had gone into that drawer so many times to pull out the exact same file so many times that he no longer had to look at what he was doing.

The folder he'd wanted slapped down onto the surface of his desk, and he stared at its closed cover for a moment.

It was happening again.

Charles loudly cleared his throat, then stood abruptly from his chair and swiped the file off his desk to take with him. "I'll be back later."

"Do you want some company for this, Chuck?" she asked. "Because I can absolutely come with you."

"No." Charles grabbed his messenger bag and his jacket, then paused and turned back toward her to lay a gently reassuring hand on her upper arm. "No, I have to do this alone. And I need you to be there for Frankie if I'm not back in the office by five. Can you go to the house and wait for me there? I don't want him to be alone, but I really have no idea how long this'll—"

"Of course I will." Patty grabbed his hand off her arm, held it in both of hers, and quickly kissed the back of it. "And it'll take as much time as it needs to take. Frankie and I will be waiting for you at home when it's finished."

IT WAS ONLY a few blocks from the newspaper's headquarters to the Rush Police Station on a relatively calm and quiet afternoon.

Charles' heart pounded in his chest, his pulse rushing in his ears and drowning out every other sound as he strode down the sidewalk along Main Street.

Despite how long it had been since feeling like this, on the verge of something important, maybe the most important thing he'd ever done, all the old sensations, hopes, and doubts came rushing back to him as if they'd never left.

Then he was at the station, pulling open the swinging glass doors, and walking inside.

With his shoulders squarely rolled back and his chin held high, Charles headed straight for the receptionist desk at the front of the building and tried to smile at the woman sitting on the other side of it as he approached.

"Well, look who's here," she said, folding her hands on top of the desk. "Charles."

"Madelaine. I need to speak with Colton."

The woman sighed and cast a long glance at the far end of the precinct lobby. "He's really busy right now, Charles."

"I get that. Chief of Police is a hard job. I still need to speak with him."

"Would you like to make an appointment?"

"Sure, I'll make an appointment for right now. Just let him know I'm here." Charles gestured toward the phone on her desk and nodded, hoping it looked more encouraging than threatening.

In no way did he want to start a scene, especially not at the police station itself, but he'd been turned away by Chief Colton, by the junior and even senior officers tasked with upholding law and order in Rush, and by almost every single town employee in the process over the last six years.

He'd learned since that if he wanted anything to get done, or for anyone to take him seriously, he couldn't take no for an answer.

Madelaine seemed to understand that as she studied his expression, and she reached for the phone in its cradle on her desk with a nod. "All right. I'll tell him you're here. Why don't you go ahead and take a seat over there, and when the chief's available, we'll let you know."

"Thank you." Charles drummed his fingers on the

surface of her desk, then spun curtly around and marched toward the ridiculously uncomfortable chairs lining the lobby wall.

He had never been arrested in his life, but he imagined the experience felt quite a bit like sitting in those chairs.

Still, it had to be done, and he had to talk to Colton about this new missing woman.

The time ticked by with a kind of anticipatory slowness that made him want to pull out what little remained of his hair these days. Charles flipped through his own personal file on the missing women's cases while he waited. Then he stuffed that back in his messenger bag and drummed his fingers on his thighs. Then he surfed through his phone, which he hated to do out in public, but he wanted to make sure the time hadn't gotten away from him, that Patty or Frankie hadn't called him since he'd left the paper.

There was nothing.

Just like there was nothing from either Madelaine or the Chief of Police.

Charles leaned forward over his lap, propping himself up with forearms on his thighs, and watched the goings-on in the lobby.

He would stay as long as it took to get just five minutes of the chief's time. Surely, the man could spare five minutes.

He waited so long that the pressure and anticipation and, admittedly, perseverant muddle of nerves made him stand from the chair and take off for the lobby's public-use restroom.

A nervous bladder had plagued him since he was in high school. Although, these days, the affliction only really came back to torture him like this when he was particularly excited about something and far more emotionally invested in potential outcomes than he otherwise would have been with anything else.

It was a quick trip, sixty seconds if that, including washing his hands. What would sixty seconds be after he'd sat in that god-awful chair for who knew how long, waiting for someone to tell him he could speak to Chief Colton?

The second he opened the restroom door and headed back to the chair, he caught sight of the back of the chief's uniform just as Colton slipped through the station's front doors and headed down the stairs toward a squad car in the parking lot.

"Wait a minute!" He jogged across the lobby, whipping a strap of his messenger bag over his head and shoulder, and glared back at Madelaine, pointing at her. "Did you tell him I was here?"

"I did," she said, spreading her arms. "I told you he was busy."

"Damnit." Charles ran the rest of the way toward the front doors, burst out of the station, and almost leapt over the entire set of stairs, waving an arm wildly overhead to catch Colton's attention. "Chief! Chief Colton! Hold on. I just need a moment of—"

The harsh, echoing slam of car doors shutting cut him off. Several squad-car engines were already running, and then those squad cars were pulling out of the parking lot faster than seemed appropriate to take off away from the station and head out to handle important police business.

Which, according to the Rush PD, Charles Putnam clearly was not.

Seething with indignation, Charles stomped a foot into the asphalt and spun around in a tight circle. "Fuck!"

Every single time.

This was exactly the way Colton had treated him in the

twelve months following Rose's disappearance six years ago. He was nothing more than a nuisance, a grieving husband, a man too hung up on hope to realize that what he hoped for was impossible and a waste of everyone's time.

This wasn't.

Through all those years, raising his son on his own, running *The Daily Rush* as its senior editor, keeping the threads of journalism and truth and public awareness tied together, using whatever he could at any given time, he'd thought Chief Ralph Colton would at least afford him the courtesy of five goddamn minutes.

Now boiling with the rage of being ignored and dismissed like that — and to be honest with himself, he genuinely believed Madelaine had told Colton to get out of the station the second Charles had headed for the restroom — it felt like Charles had gone back in time to the early days after his wife had disappeared. The beginning of yet another unsolved mystery involving women who'd gone missing in and around the town of Rush, California.

Fine, then. If Colton and the entire Rush PD weren't going to help him help someone else this time, that was on them.

Charles would just have to take things into his own hands again. He would come back with real results, with proof. He could feel it in his bones this time.

When he stopped spinning in circles and cursing Colton under his breath, Charles stopped on the station's front sidewalk, facing the front of the building. His gaze landed on the wide sign against the building's outer wall — a public police bulletin board of sorts, where pictures of all the people who'd gone missing in Rush and had never been found were posted.

Their smiling faces contrasted drastically with the

terror and despair that came hand in hand with having to create missing persons posters in the first place.

Taking a deep breath, Charles walked up the steps again and approached the bulletin board. His gaze was automatically drawn toward the old picture of Rose that had been up there since the day he'd reported her missing six years ago.

She was so beautiful, his wife.

His *deceased* wife, he had to remind himself. She was declared dead six months after she disappeared, though her body had never been found, and that particular case remained unsolved, just like so many others.

Charles had tried to move on. He and Frankie both had.

Easier said than done, and it didn't stop the thick lump from forming in his throat as he gazed at Rose's dazzling smile aimed straight at him from the bulletin board.

After a few more seconds, Charles diverted his attention to the other images on posters of the other missing women. They came in all shapes and sizes, all ages, all walks of life, these women.

He was looking for one in particular.

The newest one.

He found the printed Missing poster of her intact just to the right of center.

Kody Anderson.

Reported missing twelve days ago.

And, of course, she bore a definitive resemblance to Rose.

Long dark hair. Dark eyes. Wide, brilliant smile. Healthy-looking. Happy.

He wasn't going to just stand by and hope the professionals actually did their jobs this time.

No. This time, Charles would do whatever he had to do to find the evil son of a bitch responsible for these kidnappings and disappearances. And then, if he had to, he'd ensure justice was served.

Within the confines of the law or beyond them.

He snatched the missing poster of Kody Anderson off the bulletin board, then crisply folded it in half and tucked it neatly into his messenger bag hanging against his hip before he started his walk home.

TWENTY-FIVE

Sam

SAM CONTEMPLATED TURNING HER JEEP AROUND ON THE frontage road to head back to the hotel so she could tell Brad in person about Rip's phone call and the new information he'd given her.

But the whole reason she'd wanted to talk to Hector in the first place still flipped and turned and swirled in her mind.

To avoid the complacency that tended to lead to worst-case scenarios, in her personal experience, she decided it was better to continue with her original plan first. If she felt like she needed to talk to Hector, that was most likely the best thing for her to do right now. And after that, she'd have to see.

Plus, she didn't quite feel like she'd gotten enough space from Brad after having bailed him out of jail to immediately go see him at the hotel again with her patience intact and her anger under control and buckled down.

It just wasn't the kind of anger she'd expected to feel now, especially after their last conversation.

So she pulled off the shoulder and kept heading across town toward Hector's auto shop.

Honestly, it looked more like a junkyard.

Maybe once it had been an auto body shop, but Sam hadn't seen anyone out here, either in the garage or out in the yard out back, doing much of anything other than tinkering with a bunch of old junk and listening to obnoxiously loud music.

Sam parked up front, got out of her Jeep, and strolled around the property, looking for its owner. No one was inside the tiny trailer used as an office building. There wasn't anyone wandering about the garage or yard, either.

As it turned out, Sam stumbled upon even more tinkering while looking for her sponsor.

This particular kind just so happened to be with a woman in the back seat of a rusted-out 1957 Chevy Station Wagon.

Which Sam knew immediately because that same car was the only thing moving in the yard behind Hector's shop. Squeaking, rocking from side to side. And there was the top of Hector's hat, just barely visible through the rear window before a woman's hand slapped up against the glass pane, followed by a piercing shriek.

Sam stopped a few yards from the vehicle and cocked her head.

I guess that might *mean she's enjoying herself.*

Not exactly the kind of private moment she wanted to walk in on, whether it was Hector's or anyone else's, but it couldn't be *that* private. He was practically out in the open about it.

She started to turn around to head toward the trailer and wait for him there, but the situation was made that much more awkward when Hector's head popped up above the line of the windows and he looked right at Sam.

Great.

A low bark of a laugh she'd only heard from him maybe twice rose from the inside of the old car, muffled through the windows. The murmur of two voices followed, with a whole lot of scuffling around and attempts to subtly pull most items of clothing back on into a half-assed state of dress.

Trying to pretend she hadn't seen or heard anything and also wishing that were the case, Sam headed back toward the office anyway.

Behind her, the car door squealed open, the carriage squeaked as it bounced around on the tires, and Hector cleared his throat. "Sam."

"My bad," she called back, raising a hand in the air without turning around. "I can wait."

He laughed again, which was odd to hear so many times in such a short span. "Don't act like it's something you've never seen before. We're all adults here."

Before she could figure out how to respond to that in a way that didn't make her look like even more of an asshole, crunching footsteps approached her from behind across the gravel and dry grass and bits of broken metal pieces. Then Hector was walking beside her.

He'd buckled his jeans and clearly hadn't taken his hat off while entertaining said unknown company in the back of the car, but his oil-stained fingers worked quickly to finish fastening his button-down shirt while they walked side-by-side.

Sam couldn't bring herself to look at him.

"I'm sorry," she said. "That was not part of the plan, you know. I didn't mean to interrupt."

"I'm not upset about it, if that's what you're thinking."

"You know, I was actually trying *not* to think about it in too much detail."

He snorted. "I get it. Just, you know, maybe call next time before you show up."

"Noted."

They walked the side of the yard to round the front of the property, where Sam's Jeep came back into view.

"So, what's up?" he asked.

"Well, I wanted to talk to you," she said, still hesitant. "But I guess maybe now's not the best time."

"Self-pity doesn't suit you at all, Sam," he said. "Even less than it suits most other folks. I'm walking next to you now. Made myself available. We can forget the ten minutes before this ever happened and just move on."

She shot him a sidelong glance and smirked. "Only ten minutes, huh?"

"Unless you wanna hear about everything before that..."

"Shut up." Huffing out a laugh, she shook her head and thrust both hands into the pockets of her light jacket.

"All right, then. Pleasantries are over, Sam. So, what's up? You obviously came by to talk about something. You feeling okay?"

"I'm good," she said. "Just feeling a little confused, I guess."

"How come?"

"Well, right before I dropped by, I had a conversation with someone. This person mentioned Sophie in a way that seemed kinda shitty at the time. Really, just any mention of her at all feels shitty when it's coming from someone else."

All traces of light-hearted joking had disappeared from Hector's face now, and he slowly nodded in understanding. "And you came right here after."

"Yeah."

"'Cause this person mentioning Sophie made you wanna use again?"

They reached the front of the garage, where various vehicles were parked or raised on lifts in varied states of disrepair.

Sam stopped walking, leaned back against the frame of the garage's open door, and folded her arms. "No, actually. I *don't* wanna use."

Hector took off his hat, ran a hand through his closely cropped hair that had gone almost entirely gray, then placed his hat on his again. "Yeah, that *is* some real heavy shit."

"That's the thing," Sam replied, overlooking his sarcasm. "I normally get so worked up about this kinda thing, but today, I'm just … I mean, it makes me sad, yeah. But I don't feel like I need to tear shit apart or go off the deep end or anything."

"So you feel like you gotta make an emergency out of it?"

"I'm not trying to. Am I sad? Yeah, of course I am. I miss her. Talking about her always breaks my heart, but I'm … weirdly okay." Sam's heart pounded in her chest, louder than her own thoughts, and she had to shake her hands out to move some of the energy. "It's actually starting to freak me out now, honestly."

"All right, I can see that. Just stay here with me. Just right here. I need your help with something, huh?"

Sam let out a bitter laugh. "Didn't seem like you needed a whole lot of help before I showed up."

"Circumstances have changed a little, and now something requires assistance."

"What is it?" she asked.

"I need you to take a breath."

Sam glared at him.

"Come on, now." Hector twirled a hand, motioning for her to hurry up and get to it already. "Take a breath. If you're gonna help me out, I need you to help me out."

Rolling her eyes, Sam did what he instructed and took one long, deep inhale before puffing it all back out again.

Hector shrugged. "It's a decent start. How about one more time, just for good measure?"

She took another deep breath and fought the urge to flip him off because of it.

"Now, this part is real important, Sam," Hector said, turning to face her squarely and dipping his head toward her to fix her with a serious frown.

"Okay."

"I know it doesn't feel like it," he said, "especially when you're putting yourself through the wringer because of it, but this is a *good* thing."

Sam blinked dumbly at him, then puffed out a wry laugh. "You gotta be shitting me."

"Nope. Listen to what I'm about to tell you. Don't just toss it out with everything else. It came to me for a reason, and it might just be what you need to hear from someone you know ain't gonna bullshit you."

Sam glanced around the empty, quiet garage, then shrugged. "Okay, I'm listening."

"You're moving through this, yeah?" he said. "It's all part of the process. Someone brought up Sophie today, and you didn't react the way you're used to reacting. Means you're healing."

"Sure, that's easy enough to say. But what if I'm just—"

"I wasn't finished," he interrupted, holding up a hand for her to stop.

If anyone else had done that, Sam would've slapped the hand away and really let the person have it for talking to her like that. But this was Hector, so she let him continue.

"Just because you didn't go straight to wanting to use or get piss-drunk somewhere and try to kill yourself doesn't mean you love her any less. Doesn't mean you don't miss her. Doesn't mean you're broken or that you dropped your soul somewhere in the parking lot. All it means is you're exactly where you're supposed to be, and that's gonna get easier and easier with a little more time. You hear me?"

Sam stared at him, not quite sure what to say until she finally let out a massive sigh and sagged against the garage door's frame. All the tension that had been growing inside her the second she realized Brad's mention of Sophie hadn't sent her into a complete tailspin lightened, fizzling out into more of a background awareness of the changes she was experiencing right now.

What kind of changes, no one could have prepared her for, because they were the kind no one ever actually understood until it was happening right there in the moment.

"Yeah," she said with another sigh. "I hear you."

"Good." Hector nodded. "You notice how you're not freaking out right now?"

Sam rolled her eyes again but couldn't help a small chuckle this time. "Message received."

"I'm just making sure. Don't really wanna keep hearing about someone freaking out about not freaking out, you know? That ain't useful information for anybody. But now you got a little taste of what it's like. You just keep moving through it, one day at a time, one hour at a time, hell, one minute. That's what you need. You're doing the work, Sam. That's what matters."

"Thanks," she said, swallowing thickly. She finally dared to look up at the man who had inadvertently become her sponsor in a moment of fairly poor judgment on her part a few months ago, not to mention the mistakes Sam had also made before choosing to talk to Hector about them instead of downing an entire bottle of whiskey on her own.

Hector's kind smile eased her further into the kind of comfort that only existed between people who had gone through this same thing and understood the effects of it on the same level.

"Feel any better now?" Hector asked.

"Yeah," she said. "A little."

"Well then, you're welcome."

He looked like he was about to say something else, but then incoming footsteps joined them in the garage.

Sam and Hector both turned at the same time to see a woman entering the garage. They obviously noticed her before she noticed them, because she walked almost halfway across the garage before looking up to see Hector and Sam beside the open door. "Oh. Sorry. I wasn't trying to interrupt. If you need to finish your meeting—"

"I think we just finished wrapping everything up," Sam said, shooting Hector a sidelong glance. "Don't worry about it. You didn't interrupt anything."

Hector smirked at her, then nodded at the woman. "We're all fine over here, Liz."

"I'll go ahead and let you two get back to … work." Sam nodded at the woman, then shot Hector a quick wink that made him snort before she pushed herself away from the garage's doorframe to head back to her Jeep. "Thanks for your time, Hector."

"Uh-huh. You still have my number, right? In case you need to get a hold of me again."

"Don't worry, I've still got it. And I will definitely call first next time. See you around."

Then she was on her way back to her Jeep, with the sound of Hector's low, quiet laughter following her. She couldn't help cracking a smile of her own, especially when she heard the woman trying to speak subtly as she walked away.

"Next time, I'll just put up an 'Out for Lunch' sign."

"Naw." Hector laughed. "It'll just turn away the wrong kinda folks, anyway."

Shaking her head in disbelief tinged with amusement now that the worst of her internal crisis was over, Sam climbed back up into her Jeep and started the engine.

Yes, cell phones had been invented for a reason, and it was on her to remember that even an older man like Hector, who had somehow agreed to become her sponsor through the Twelve-Step program, had a life of his own, whether or not Sam knew anything else about it.

Now that Hector had talked her down from not really needing to be talked down anymore, which was a new and ridiculously confusing state to be in, though he seemed to think she'd get used to it fairly quickly, Sam had the mental and emotional bandwidth again to think about where she wanted to go and who she wanted to speak to next.

She was still waiting for the next call from Rip once he got back into town and was ready to meet with her for a little hike out to the lake serving as his property's water supply. There was still no word from Chris about when business would be up and running again at the bar. There was no reason to return to the Redwood Rings.

So now Sam found herself without any excuse not to get back to Brad so they could compare notes again and she could tell him about the new information she'd gotten so far in regard to the kind of relationship Kody and Rip had had, specifically a sort of temporary employer-employee relationship focusing on her ability to solve one major problem for Rip's farm and his entire business as a whole.

She pulled up Brad's number and made the call.

He answered on the first ring.

"Sam, you gotta get back to the hotel," he said. "Right. Fucking. Now."

"Yeah, that was the plan. I just had a few things to take care of first, but I got some good information I think you should hear."

"You know what? So did I," he said. "A fucking breakthrough, that's what this is. Get your ass over here so we can go over everything and figure out next steps, yeah?"

"Give me about fifteen minutes."

SAM HAD GOTTEN SO USED to driving up to the dingy hotel on the edge of town that she wasn't expecting anything important or even of any real interest to happen along the way. Especially not when she pulled her Jeep into the parking lot and hopped out to head for the hotel's entrance.

So she was completely unprepared to see Big Pete Wilder and his wife Elaine walking arm in arm together toward the very same hotel.

The sight of Rush's biggest, wealthiest, self-proclaimed hotshot and the man who did in fact own the majority of the town was the last thing Sam would have expected to see in a place like this. More often than not, Sam found him as a begrudging customer in the Back Bar of the Redwood Rings.

Most certainly *not* walking into a cheap hotel at the edge of town more fitting of transient workers and tourists and folks down on their luck enough that they needed a last-minute place to stay but couldn't afford something better.

But then she remembered the Redwood Rings was still closed for now, which meant the Back Bar was also closed. So the regular locals had to go somewhere instead until Chris opened the place back up again, right?

But why the hell would Big Pete come here? And, even stranger, why would he bring his wife?

Pete and Elaine had just entered the hotel's poor excuse for a lobby when Sam finally finished crossing the parking lot. By the time she made it into the building, the Wilders were headed straight for the front doors of the twenty-four-hour café attached to the hotel.

Before they stepped inside, Big Pete looked back over his shoulder as if he thought he could feel something strange there behind him. Then Sam was certain he'd seen her, because there was no way to miss each other at this point.

The man looked almost terrified, like Sam's presence here meant he'd been caught doing something he shouldn't have.

If anyone deserved to feel that kind of pressure for no reason, it was Big Pete Wilder.

Sam ignored him completely and just kept walking. She had an old Army buddy to meet in a hotel room anyway. She hadn't come here for awkward conversations in a twenty-four-hour hotel café with the real man behind the curtain of running a town like Rush. Despite the fact that his son, Little Pete, was Rush's official mayor, Pete Senior was the one calling all the shots.

Sam found herself surprisingly amused and satisfied by the instant look of bafflement on Big Pete's face when he'd seen her, followed by a hint of embarrassment and instant frustration when he realized he didn't have anything close to the same effect on Sam as she seemed to have on him.

Namely that he still couldn't stand to be in the same room with her despite how often circumstances put the two of them in the same room together.

It was interesting to see him here, especially with his wife, yeah. But Sam had more interesting things to focus on right now, and for the first time in a long time, she truly didn't believe that Big Pete Wilder had anything to do with the current case she was unofficially trying to solve on her own.

TWENTY-SIX

Kody

SEVERAL DAYS AGO...

KODY FELT like she was swimming through a thick soup of time, like the minutes and hours she used to pay such close attention to no longer existed.

Maybe they never had in the first place.

She had no idea how long she'd been down here in this pit. She'd lost complete track of the days and the time. She'd even stopped listening for sounds of her abductors entering the cave with any real measure of consistency.

Either that, or Kody had simply lost her ability to tell the difference.

This whole time, she'd been trying so hard not to give in, turning her phone on to check the time and the date, to check the phone's battery percentage, to try over and over again — most likely with the same non-existent results — to get some kind of service signal. Enough at the very least for a text to her dad to get out and reach him.

So she had no idea how long she'd been trying not to turn to relying on her phone, either.

But then the darkness, the solitude, the cold, hunger, thirst, and loneliness all got to her, and she just couldn't hold it together anymore.

Kody pulled her phone out of the pocket of her light windbreaker and held down the side button to power on the device.

It seemed to take forever to get the thing started. When she finally did, a glaringly bright light filled the intensely thick darkness at the bottom of the pit, momentarily blinding her.

Kody waited for her vision to adjust, then finally looked at the date and time digitally stamped across her phone's screen. Her eyes recognized the shape of numbers, but her brain was too slow in processing them before her cell phone practically erupted with buzzing vibrations and obnoxious notification banners blooming into existence on her screen, one after the other, over and over again.

Her phone made so much noise, she hoped her kidnappers couldn't hear it.

But then she stopped thinking when she realized she'd just received a plethora of texts from both her parents.

That little detail was the most surprising of all in the moment. Since when did both her parents ever do anything together?

Kody quickly searched through the texts, all of which carried on in similar fashion. Her parents were asking where she was, wondering what had happened to her, asking if she was safe, if she needed help, reminding her that it had been days since either of them had heard from her, and now they were both getting incredibly worried.

Her eyes filling with tears, Kody quickly typed up a message to send to them both, something quick and simple to let them know that she was still alive, that she was okay, that she didn't have a lot of food, water, cell battery, and that she needed them to hurry up and find her or she was afraid the worst would actually end up happening and nothing could prepare any of them for that.

She finally finished typing up the text, pressed the send button, and...

Nothing.

"Oh, come on," she growled. "You gotta be kidding me."

She shook her phone in the air, then thumped it against her other hand a few times, as if that would kickstart access to a signal. They probably weren't anywhere close to this cave, and she went back through her texts and saw, to even more heightened frustration, that while Kody had received so many incoming texts from her parents, her smartphone still marked her sent texts asking her dad for help as undelivered.

"How does that even happen?"

Her parents' texts got all the way out here to her, but her own messages never left this very pit and this depressingly dark and silent cave.

That didn't make sense.

Maybe she just had to be in the exact right spot to get the exact right type of cell service, so she could be sure her SOS texts were getting out there to her dad. Then he'd be able to come find her. It was still possible to get out of this.

Kody might still survive.

That new flare of hope burned through her so forcefully, she couldn't think about anything else.

Kody walked along the bottom of the pit, holding her phone up as high as her arm would reach to try and catch the cell signal. She'd had it. She knew she had, otherwise those messages wouldn't have come through on her end. She just had to find the perfect spot.

A brief flicker of one signal bar made her stop and suck in a sharp breath of anticipation with a renewed flare of hope. She hadn't dared to let herself hope this much until now, but the proof was right there in front of her. Something had gotten through. She could still do this.

But no matter what she did or how much she waved her phone around, she couldn't get that single signal bar to come back.

I just need to get higher.

She slipped her phone into the back pocket of her jeans and prepared to get busy with an escape plan again, this time with an actual possibility of escape and rescue spurring her forward.

This could work.

She slammed the toe of her hiking boot into the side of the pit wall and, to her surprise, relief, and a small level of wry amusement, her boot punched through the thick dirt wall and settled into it to form a viable foothold.

"Yes," she whispered.

Holding herself steady, Kody got a little more leverage between her outstretched arms in the curving walls of the pit, figuring out in record time how to press outwards with both hands to shimmy up the wall as if she were trying to climb a chimney.

She'd heard that phrase used once in reference to rock climbing anyway. This couldn't be that different.

She moved her feet up again, kicking a foothold into the wall. Kody couldn't see where her hand and footholds would be, but now for some reason, she had developed the ability to feel the best places for them anyway. She was actually pulling herself up.

She was actually climbing the walls of the pit.

Foot, hand, foot hand…

She was halfway up now, getting some real traction.

Higher now, and the top of the pit looked so close above her. Just a little bit farther.

As she stretched up one arm to find another handhold, she felt the packed earth beneath her left foot slide away and give, then her right foot.

"No, no, no, no!"

In a last desperate attempt, Kody kicked upward, lunging for another handhold above her.

Her fingertips caught on a strong bit of rock poking over the edge, and for a split second that felt like an eternity, she dangled there from the fingers of her right hand. All she had to do was just get her feet steady beneath her.

Then a massive chunk of the wall gave way beneath her weight. It was like someone had peeled away a layer of dirt just to watch it slide back to the floor of the pit.

Just to watch Kody fail.

She scrambled to find another hold as she started to slide down, but everything gave way. Nothing stuck. Nothing could hold her weight.

The next thing she knew, there was nothing beneath her.

Arms flailing, she dropped in a shower of muddy earth and clods of dirt, small pebbles, and a rumbling whisper of earth breaking away beneath her.

She landed hard on her backside and instantly felt something crack.

For a brief, stunned, horrified moment, she thought she might have broken her tailbone or a leg or something vital.

But that would have been excruciating, right?

When she recovered from the shock of falling three-quarters of the way down into the pit again, she leaned sideways and reached down toward her hips, then beneath her to the base of her tailbone.

Her fingers brushed something hard and square in the back pocket of her jeans, and she froze.

"Oh shit..."

With trembling fingers, her hand dove into her back pocket and closed around the offending object. The thing she'd felt snap.

She pulled out her cell phone and almost broke down.

She could no longer see. It was still dark at the bottom of the pit, and now zero light whatsoever came from her phone even though she'd left it on to try and catch the signal.

As soon as she pulled her phone out of her pocket, part of the screen crumbled away in her fingers. A corner of the device broke free and toppled to the floor of the pit with all of the dirt and pebbles.

Running her fingers over the surface of the screen only confirmed the worst.

She'd cracked it. She'd completely destroyed her one method of contact with the outside world, and now what was she supposed to do?

This was it. This was the end for her.

Kody was quickly running out of food. She only had one and a half protein bars left and only a few sips of water. She was freezing most of the time, even with her survival blanket. Every bit of inventory and gear she'd had at her disposal in the beginning of this nightmare was now gone, used up for nothing more than her own efforts to stay alive at the bottom of this pit in a cave, kept here by two complete strangers who clearly didn't give a shit whether she lived or died.

A strangled croak of a sob escaped her as Kody realized this was the end, that she had gone as far as she could go, that with her phone crushed and no way to get any messages out to her parents, the rest of her hope had shattered right along with the screen.

Her legs gave out beneath her, and she sank like a dead weight through molasses to the floor of the pit.

It was hopeless. She had nothing left. She might as well just give up now.

Those thoughts tugged at her until Kody started tugging back, because she didn't have anything else to do.

She clawed at the wall of the pit as she sagged in despair against it, another sob bursting from her lips. Then the thick dirt wall in front of her gave way beneath her hands. She pulled out a giant clump of wet earth that stayed together in her hand until she squeezed tighter and it crushed apart to sift through her fingers.

Then a new idea hit her.

What if trying to climb up out of the pit wasn't the best method at all and never had been?

The dirt was clearly too damp and too fragile to take the entirety of her weight on its edge. But what if she tunneled *through* it? What if she tried to climb sideways through the earth instead of straight up?

Sucking in a sharp breath, Kody scrambled on hands and knees back toward the wall and started to dig.

Not that she had that much experience digging tunnels by hand or any other method, but it couldn't be that hard, could it?

Her unprotected fingers clawed into the damp earth over and over, breaking out huge scoops of mud and the occasional pebble.

It came out a lot faster than she'd expected this way, and she doubled down in her efforts to move faster and faster.

Hope flared through her again, giving her the impossible strength to keep going, to keep prying into the pit's wall, to keep digging.

The more she dug, the more hopeful Kody became that this was her way out. She could actually do this.

She lost all sense of time again, but now, she was focused on one objective only and time didn't matter. As long as she kept going, as long as she made headway on this tunnel, everything would be all right.

She still had a chance.

Finally, she'd scraped away something large enough to fit her head and most of her shoulders into, which she had to do now in order to reach farther back and keep tunneling into the pit's wall.

She might actually make this work.

She might actually get out of here.

With her body halfway in the tunnel, Kody forced herself to keep moving, to not think about what else might happen.

Or what was waiting for her. Or what her captors might do to her if they found her here and saw her trying to dig her way out.

She scratched at the pit walls even faster.

Whether it was because of her haste or because the damp earth of the pit walls just couldn't take it, she knew she'd completely screwed herself when the first large clump of mud dropped away from her hands before she even had a chance to dig it away.

Then the ceiling of her newly formed tunnel dropped, falling down on her in one massive sheet of thick, heavy, cold mud.

The second she realized what was happening, the rest of the tunnel was caving in on her, dampness and heavy earth filling in the space she'd just created, falling on top of her, drowning her.

Too thick, too heavy, covering her completely.

She couldn't breathe.

Struggling wildly, Kody kicked out at anything and everything behind her. She pushed herself backward through the mud, her heart pounding in her chest and her lungs burning already from lack of air.

In a final desperate shove, she launched herself backward out of the tunnel, the rest of which collapsed right there in front of her as she tumbled backward onto the floor of the pit.

A raw, searing gasp tore through her throat, and she finally sucked air back into her burning lungs.

By the time she stopped gasping, her entire body was trembling. She was cold, exhausted, sore everywhere. Her fingertips had gone numb, and now she was covered in muck and had neither the strength nor the will to try again or even to pick herself back up and keep going.

For the first time since she'd found herself down here, in this pit in the back of a cave in the mountains, Kody completely lost all sense of composure.

She broke down sobbing, her body sagging against the wall of earth beside her. Mud and dampness clinging to her skin and her hair and the backs of her hands, and she didn't even care anymore. She was exhausted, hungry, dehydrated, terrified.

And no one was coming to help her.

The terror and the helplessness finally overwhelmed her. Then a new emotion popped up seemingly out of nowhere to join the others.

Pure, unadulterated rage unlike anything she'd ever felt before.

Kody was hardly capable of coherent thought at this point, her body and her mind running on empty, which meant running on survival and nothing else.

Rage fueled her, but only enough to nurture a raw, curdling, animalistic scream of fury and hopelessness.

The sound seared her throat on its way out, coursing through her entire body, sending flushes of heat up her spine and across her limbs and instantly leaving her breathless and exhausted.

But of course no one answered her screams. Just like no one had answered her pleas for help.

No one could hear her all the way out here in the middle of nowhere.

Or, if anyone *could* hear her, they just didn't care.

TWENTY-SEVEN

Sam

BY THE TIME SAM MADE IT TO ROOM 8 AND STOPPED TO knock on the door, she still wasn't sure she was fully prepared to look Brad in the eye again without succumbing to the urge to make snide comments or blatantly remind him of what an ass he'd been. Today, especially.

So when she heard his footsteps crossing the room toward the door, then saw the handle turning from the other side, she decided it was best just to barrel in head first like she did with pretty much everything else and get right down to the reason she was here.

And that reason did not include bringing Brad with her to follow up on any other possible leads until she had something real and much more concrete that he couldn't screw up all on his own.

When the door opened, Sam blew straight through the doorway, muscling a surprised Brad aside as she stopped toward the center of the small hotel room without waiting for a hello.

"Okay, listen," she said. "I'm going to tell you something, and it's—"

259

She stopped at the sight of a man she didn't know now standing from the chair behind the tiny desk built into the wall. Then Sam looked over her shoulder at Brad and cleared her throat. "Didn't know you already had company."

"Well, don't let *that* stop you," he said. "You were on a roll."

She shot him a deadpan glare, to which Brad responded with a rumbling chuckle before he gestured toward the man now on his feet beside the desk chair. "Sam, meet Charles Putnam. My new development."

Instantly, Sam returned to taking a more detailed inventory of the man in Brad's hotel room. She nodded at him in casual greeting before asking, "You know where Kody is?"

Charles' surprised expression, which hadn't quite gotten the chance to morph into a smile or any other kind of greeting, fell even further at her question. "Unfortunately, no."

Brad snapped his fingers and pointed at the man. "But he knows where to start."

"Interesting development, for sure." Sam folded her arms and leaned back against the wall before nodding at Charles. "So let's hear what you've got. *After* somebody tells me how the two of you know each other."

"We don't, really," Brad said. "I mean, not until, like, an hour ago."

Charles cleared his throat and focused his attention on Sam to bring her up to speed as well. "I'm Senior Editor at *The Daily Rush*. The paper got a tip about another woman in Rush reported missing nine days ago now. As soon as I heard, I figured her family would be here by now too. First logical first place to start was at the hotels. This one was only number two on my list, but as it turns out, knocking door-to-door does occasionally produce the desired result."

He gestured toward Brad, who spread his arms and raised his eyebrows at Sam. "Small world, right?"

She ignored his attempts to make light of this, which Brad wouldn't have done if it were just the two of them. Right now, she was more interested in learning about Charles, because a reporter getting involved in an unofficial investigation Sam herself had taken on for an old Army buddy made things infinitely more complicated.

"And you wanted to ... what?" she asked. "Talk to the family? Put out a story about what they're going through and publicize the difficulties of losing a child?"

She hadn't meant to go that far, but she hadn't been able to help the searing vitriol from her voice, which now made it perfectly clear she did not approve of Charles' involvement or the idea of him writing anything about this situation.

Brad sucked in a sharp breath through his teeth and grimaced.

Charles looked back and forth between them, eyes wide, and pressed a fist to his mouth in a poorly veiled attempt to clear his throat and start over. "I'm sorry. We clearly started off on the wrong foot and under completely different assumptions about why I'm here. To make this clear, Sam, I'm not trying to write a story. Not now. And I'm definitely not trying to dig in deep and hurt anyone just to sell a few more papers."

He paused to study her reaction, which remained well hidden on purpose, before continuing. "I'm actually here to help you find Kody and, hopefully, solve the whole mess of other cases involving missing women in and around Rush. Because I think whoever abducted Kody is the same person responsible for at least half a dozen missing persons cases in the area. I want to settle this for good."

"Oh." Sam pressed her lips together, then nodded at *The Daily Rush*'s senior editor before gesturing for him to continue. "What makes you think this is a serial situation?"

Charles glanced at Brad as if asking for the man's permission to retell his story now with Sam present.

Part of her admired that in him. At least the men knew he was answering to the missing girl's father when it came to sharing sensitive information like he was about to.

"She's been helping me from the beginning," Brad told him. "Whatever you have to say from here on out, you can say in front of Sam."

That seemed good enough for Charles.

"I believe Kody's disappearance is just the latest in a pattern of women who've gone missing in Rush over the last thirty years." The man turned back to the tiny wall desk, picked up a stack of papers there, and handed them straight to Sam. "Take a look."

Sam quickly realized they were all Missing posters going back thirty years, just like he'd said. The page on top was Kody's poster, with the young woman's smiling face taking up the majority of the leaflet. Then, while Sam flipped through one poster after another, Charles continued his story.

"Six women in total now, as far as I've been able to put together. There may be more, but right now I'm going with six. Each of them with similar features. Dark hair. Dark eyes. Smiling. Friendly. Clean cut. Like clockwork, a new woman fitting this description has gone missing every five years since it started. Until Kody. For some reason, there's a six-year gap between her disappearance and the last. Doesn't fit the pattern *exactly*, which I haven't been able to explain yet. Everything else about her disappearance, though, adds up."

Sam flipped to the last poster in the stack of women's smiling faces arranged from oldest to most recent after Kody's. Though this final poster was dated for six years ago, it was also the most well-worn within Charles' collection and clearly had been handled quite often for quite some time.

The second she looked up at Charles with a curious frown, he picked up on her unspoken question.

"The last disappearance before Kody," he told her, "was six years ago. My wife Rose."

"What happened to her?" Sam asked.

Charles slowly shook his head. "She just never came home. The police had no leads. Probably couldn't have come up with one if their lives depended on it. At first, they tried to convince me she'd left town. That she'd grown tired of me or had fallen for someone else. But that just wasn't Rose. She wouldn't have done that. She certainly wouldn't have left our four-year-old son without a word."

Sam flipped through the Missing posters again. "What about these other women? Besides their physical characteristics, any other commonalities?"

"Between the first four? Yes. They were all out-of-towners. Either visiting or part of the transient workforce. None of them had any roots here before they arrived. Or, if they'd stopped to settle down for a bit, it was on a temporary basis, from what I can gather."

"Which would also fit with Kody's disappearance," Brad added.

"A student staying at a B&B for six weeks while conducting field research up in the mountains?" Sam nodded. "That tracks. What else?"

"The first three women were migrant workers," Charles continued. "Seasonal. Trimmers up on the mountain back when things weren't quite as aboveboard with the marijuana industry as they are now. The fourth woman who disappeared five years before my Rose was a sex worker. But with all four of them, everyone just assumed these women left town without speaking to anyone, without giving notice, without any conceivable reason. They just ... disappeared. Apparently, the cases were marked unsolved, and the Rush PD dropped their cold-case files into the archives to be buried under even more paperwork over the years."

"Including Rose's case?" Sam asked.

The muscles of Charles' jaw clenched and unclenched rapidly. "Yeah. Everyone tried to tell me that was the case with Rose too. But I knew better. I've always known better. I know there's a serial killer involved, either right here in town or somewhere close by in the mountains. The five-year pattern was consistent until Kody, but I'm certain she's the latest victim."

"Were any of these women's bodies ever found?" Sam asked handed the stack of posters back to him.

"No, actually. None of them." Charles paused, then quickly looked up at Brad again. "But I know you still have time to find your daughter. We have to act fast, but there's still a good chance to bring her home safely. Alive."

"It's an interesting theory," Sam mused.

"But it's worth a shot," Brad interjected.

"It might be," she said. "But I'm not convinced that's what's happening here."

Charles' shoulders slumped forward as he gaped at her. "You too?"

"Don't lump me in with whoever else you're trying to

lump me in with," she corrected. "I'm just saying I have more information too since the last time Brad and I talked."

She didn't think it was the appropriate time to mention his run-in with four of Rip's security guards earlier today and the necessity of her bailing him out of jail hours later. From the way Brad stared back at her, though, she knew he was thinking something along similar lines.

"I got in touch with Rip Graham this afternoon," Sam explained. "Turns out Kody was working with him on his property and in the general area around it for her research. She was helping him with some irrigation issues. Finding the cause of problems he's been having with the farm's water supply. He seems to think she might've gotten lost out on the mountain, looking for the lake that feeds into his property."

Sam nodded at Brad. "He agreed to take us up there tomorrow. Show us exactly where the detailed directions he gave Kody led. Then we'll canvas the area, look for evidence of her having been there. So far, that sounds like her last known whereabouts. She could still be there, for all we know."

"Mountains on the west side of the highway?" Charles asked.

"I think so."

"There's a lot of open land up there," he added. "A lake, definitely. More than one, if I remember correctly. Multiple series of caves all within about ten miles of each other. I'd like to come with you, if you don't mind."

Brad looked stunned by the unexpected turn of the conversation but said nothing.

Sam shook her head. "It's probably best if you stay in town and let us handle the search on the mountain.

"I've studied more maps of the area than I care to

admit in the last six years," he argued. "And I've had my suspicions for a long time that the killer we're looking for is up there in that general area. Either in a cabin or hiding on a bit of private property or holing up in one of those caves, maybe. I could help."

"What makes you think this alleged serial killer is in the mountains?" Sam asked.

"It's the Northern California wilderness," Charles replied quickly. "Way more places to hide a body where no one could find them. Who knows how many wild animals could have picked up the scent and disposed of the evidence without the killer ever having to lift a finger—"

"We're not talking about bodies," Brad interjected, then swallowed thickly as he stared at a stain on the hotel room's worn carpet floor. "Not now. Not until we know for sure. But we still need to go up there and look. If Kody's up there, if she got lost somehow or taken, we might still be able to get to her in time."

Sam studied both men staring back at her, each of them battling his own pain at the loss of someone he loved and apparently waiting for *her* to make important decisions around here.

With a shrug, she said, "Then I guess our next step is to meet Rip up at the turnoff past the cemetery tomorrow. And yeah, Charles, I think you should come with us."

TWENTY-EIGHT

Sam

AFTER THEY ALL AGREED TO MEET BACK AT THE HOTEL AT 7:30 the next morning, Charles admitted he should probably head home. He also offered to leave the Missing posters behind in case they wanted to look over the details, but Sam assured him that wasn't necessary. So he packed up the rest of his things and slipped out of the room.

Once he was gone, Sam realized she should probably be on her way home too, seeing as now it was just her and Brad alone in his hotel room, with all the important information already discussed between them.

No point in hanging around and sending mixed messages.

Brad, however, wasn't quite ready to end the conversation for the evening.

"I get why we're going up there tomorrow with this Rip guy," he said. "I understand where you're coming from, Sam, but I think it's just gonna end up being a waste of time."

"Because it was my idea?"

"Come on. I wouldn't have asked for your help if I

thought your ideas were worthless. No, I'm saying this because Chief Colton actually searched the mountain days ago. Took a search party with him and everything."

"Chief Colton?" Sam clicked her tongue. "Well, I'm sure he thought he was doing his job. But honestly, I don't trust him to thoroughly investigate much of anything, not to mention find your daughter."

"Oh, but you trust the owner of a pot farm and who knows what other kinds of less-than-legit businesses to give us a better lead than the professionals?"

Sam spread her arms. "As far as I know, everything Rip's involved in nowadays is above board. Totally legit. And if it's not, he's too smart to do something that would implicate himself in any type of crime. Especially a kidnapping or a serial murder spree. He was openly working with Kody. He told me he'd hired her to help him solve the issues with his water supply. Doesn't make sense that he'd be this forthcoming if he was responsible."

"Still." Brad shrugged, then ran a hand over his short-cropped hair. "That seems like a long shot."

"So does Charles' serial-killer theory. I mean, it *sounds* convincing, sure. Sounds like an easy answer, all wrapped up in a neat little bow. But the guy's drawing way too many conclusions from not nearly enough evidence."

"All those missing women in the last thirty years?" he asked. "That's not enough evidence?"

"Not beneath the surface, Anderson. Look, all six of these women, including Kody, were completely different ages when they went missing. Different professions. From different parts of the country. Sure, they have a similar physical appearance, if we're taking that in the loosest terms possible. Dark hair. Dark eyes. Nice big smile. Seriously, though, if we're categorizing a serial killer's victims by those characteristics alone, *I* might as well be next on the list."

He snorted and sat on the edge of the bed.

"The resemblance is too slight," Sam continued. "It's a very thin theory with too many holes. Did you look at the dates each woman was reported missing?"

Brad wrinkled his nose and muttered, "No, but I'm sure *you* did."

"They didn't even disappear around the same time of year within those five-year periods. One was in the fall, one in summer, two others in the spring. It just doesn't add up. I'd call it a flimsy guess at best. Not even a real theory, all things considered."

"What about his wife?" Brad asked. "Don't you think the man would have his details down pretty damn straight if he's trying to figure out what happened to his wife?"

"Not really." Sam puffed out a sigh. "Honestly, I'd just call it wishful thinking. He's too close. The man lost his wife. She disappeared on him, sure, but that doesn't mean she was kidnapped and murdered. It doesn't mean *any* of these women were.

"Looking at it objectively, it's just as likely that every single one of these women left town of their own volition and just decided not to say anything to anyone about it. And here's Charles, just trying to make sense of his wife leaving him. Easier to believe she was kidnapped and murdered than to accept the fact that maybe their marriage just wasn't gonna last."

"You think he's making it up," Brad said.

"I think the guy's grasping at straws. That he's creating a pattern where there really is none and looking for all the ways new details fit the pattern while ignoring a hell of a lot more evidence that refutes the pattern's existence in the first place."

"So why didn't you just say that to him?"

"That's not my job."

Brad's upper lip twitched in the beginning of a sneer that didn't quite make it to the rest of his features. "And you think I'm just as delusional, don't you?"

Sam fully faced him from the other side of the room and tilted her head. "I think you're just as scared. And for good reason. I also don't know nearly enough about your relationship with your daughter to come to a conclusion about it either way. Sure, it's a lot less likely that even a grown child disappears on purpose without telling anyone, including their family, but it's not unheard of. I'm not saying that's what I think Kody did. I'm saying this is a lot more complicated than we've been giving it credit for so far, and it just keeps getting more complicated the farther we go."

"We can't just give up, Sam. I'm not giving up on her."

"That's not what I said." She walked slowly across the room, feeling like an ass now for having shot down so many possibilities for finding his daughter. "And I wouldn't suggest giving up in the first place. Never. We'll find her. I know we will. We just have to be smart about which leads to follow and which ones to put aside when they're less likely to get us anywhere useful. Honestly, a serial killer in Rush is one of the least likely scenarios, in my opinion."

Closing his eyes, Brad sighed again and seemed to hunch farther into himself. "You know this place better than I do. I'll give you that."

"And you know your daughter. We'll get her back. Heading up the mountain with Rip tomorrow is a good start, I can feel it. And regardless of his business industry, I trust him. He doesn't have any reason to give us the runaround on something like this, especially when he's dealing with his own problems beyond a missing student who kinda worked for him for a while."

"All right." Brad's tense posture softened a little before he nodded. "All right, fine. We'll go up there in the morning, and I'll give this Rip guy a chance to prove me wrong. Even if he does have a stupid-ass name."

"Our best bet, by the way," Sam added, trying not to let him see her smile, "is to look into everything we can and narrow it down from there. We can get back to doing that first thing in the morning."

"Yeah." Brad slid his hands down his thighs where he sat, leaned over his lap, and propped himself up with his head hanging between his shoulders.

Sam waited a moment longer for him to say anything else. Clearly, he wasn't in the best of moods, but it wasn't her job to fix his moods, either. She'd handled his last bout of idiocy and hot-headedness that had landed him behind bars because she was the only one around capable of doing it. Plus, Sam wasn't just going to leave a friend in jail.

What he was going through now, though?

She couldn't let other people's problems become her personal responsibility.

There was helping people in need and using her skills and her training and her field experience to do so, and then there was getting way too personally involved.

For Sam, the line between them was clearer now than it ever had been.

It was time for her to go.

"I'll see you back here in the morning, then," she said, taking off for the door. "We'll meet up with Charles, then head up the mountain first thing."

Brad didn't immediately say anything, so she took that as her moment to disappear and give him a little privacy, if nothing else.

She'd just grabbed the door handle and started to pull it down when Brad stood from the bed.

"Sam, wait."

She paused, fingers still wrapped around the metal lever, and looked over her shoulder at him.

He was already crossing the hotel room toward her, his expression halfway between eager self-confidence and the kind of burrowing doubt that usually went hand in hand with a person not wanting to be alone.

Sam recognized those conflicting emotions a second before he reached her, and then he proved she was just as skilled with evaluating his frame of mind as she'd been over a decade ago.

"Thank you," he said gently. "For all your help with this. I know I've made it a little harder for you then I probably should have."

She snorted. "Just a little."

"That's not what I'm trying to do. And I want you to know that I'm grateful you're even willing to put your neck out for me like this."

"We had each other's backs in the day," she said with a shrug. "I don't see a good reason why that should be any different now. Assuming we ignore your quick stint in county jail."

Brad chuckled. "I was hoping we could."

"And as long as you don't pull that shit again, we can forget about it."

"Sounds good."

Before she had a chance to say anything else or continue opening the door, Brad took another step toward her, reached out, and gently grabbed her free hand before lifting it in front of him. "I was also hoping you might wanna stick around a little longer."

"Did you find something else you wanted to talk about?" she asked.

"No, Sam. I meant staying here with me. You know, two people who already know each other pretty damn well. Who already know they enjoy each other's company. It's hard to be alone through something like this, anyway and... Well, you've always been good at helping me forget."

The whole time, Sam was acutely aware of her hand in both of his, of how close he stood, of the look in his eyes as he spoke to her.

There was no confusion about what the guy wanted right now.

This definitely was not the kind of situation in which she'd wanted to involve herself. Not with Brad. Not with anyone, really. Emotions riding high with missing children and cold cases and potential serial killers wasn't really her thing.

For some reason, though, she didn't pull her hand away. She didn't quite stop him, either.

Not yet.

Brad leaned closer. "I would really like it if you stayed."

The next thing she knew, her back was pressed up against the hotel room door, Brad's hands were cupping her cheeks, and he was kissing her the way she remembered him kissing her way back when — before either of them had realized how stupid they were being, before either of them had figured out what it meant to have something worth losing and then ended up losing it anyway.

For the briefest moment, Sam actually considered giving in and staying.

What was the harm in it, after all? One night wouldn't change much of anything.

Then again, she'd thought the exact same thing years ago, and she'd been wrong.

Things were just too complicated. They were complicated before Brad had shown up in a Rush, and they would still be complicated after he left when this was all over.

The fact that all this went through Sam's head *as* he was kissing her probably wasn't a good sign, anyway.

When Brad pulled away and looked down at her with hooded eyes silently pleading for her to say yes, Sam made up her mind.

She gently pushed against his chest until he stepped back, then shook her head. "It's probably not a good idea."

He studied her expression a moment longer, then shrugged and backed away. "Yeah. You're probably right. Figured it was worth a shot anyway."

"Well, *one* of us has to think about how things play out all the way to the end. I guess that's why you came looking for me."

Brad chuckled and ran a hand through his hair again. "Must be."

"I'll see you in the morning." Sam finally opened the door. "Goodnight, Anderson."

Then she stepped quickly out of his hotel room, pulled the door shut behind her, and leaned her back against it for a moment to collect herself.

That was a close one.

Sam just couldn't afford close ones anymore. At this point in her life, it was as simple as that.

When she exited the hotel and made her way toward her Jeep in the parking lot, the last thing she expected was to be met with another familiar face here.

Especially one that had always looked so pissed off to see her anywhere nearby.

Which meant that when she caught sight of Big Pete

Wilder standing outside the hotel's entrance with his hands thrust into the pockets of his dress slacks, Sam ignored him completely and kept walking. She didn't stop or even slow down on her way to the Jeep.

"Salazar?"

"Don't worry, Pete," she called, tossing a hand in the air without turning around. "I'm on my way out. You can pretend you never saw me."

"That's not what I had in mind," he said.

She just kept walking.

After all the different sides of the man she'd seen in the last year alone, plus the alarmingly high instances of him storming into the Back Bar on a rampage and repeatedly accusing her of meddling in either his personal or business affairs, the last thing she wanted was another altercation with the man who considered himself above not only the scrutiny of others in Rush but the majority of its laws and regulations as well.

"Salazar," he called again, and now his footsteps were following her too. "Will you just stop a goddamn—"

"Listen," she said tersely, "I've had an insanely long day. Not that I'm about to get into it right now, even with you, Pete, but whatever's going on, whatever you think I did, I've been way too busy to even pretend I had anything to do with it. So if you don't mind, I'd really just like to go home and sleep it off. You can hunt me down and accuse me of some shit I also didn't do some other time."

His footsteps quickened across the asphalt behind her. "That's not why I'm here."

"Well I won't tell anyone I saw you here, either, if that's what you're worried about. Goodnight."

"Sam, *please*..."

Oddly enough, that was the one thing Big Pete Wilder could have possibly said to get her to stop and reconsider.

To be honest, Sam hadn't even been sure the word 'please' was a part of the man's vocabulary until just now. The fact that he'd said it to *her* set several alarm bells clanging away in Sam's mind all at once.

She stopped halfway to her Jeep and turned slowly to face him, surprise and curiosity and suspicion all mixing together at the sight of the enormous man looking like a terrified little schoolboy as he finished approaching her in the parking lot.

"Because you said please," she told him, "I'm going to ask you what you're trying to get out of this right now. But I really don't have the time or the patience to play guessing games."

Pete scowled at her, his lips pressed tightly together, but that normal expression of his now looked pinched and highly uncomfortable as he glanced quickly around the parking lot.

The sun had gone down about half an hour ago, so a little natural light still filled the sky. The rest of the light in the parking lot came from the weak streetlamps dotting the hotel's property, though it was more than enough light to see by if there had been anyone else out there with them.

There wasn't.

Even still, Big Pete looked highly uncomfortable and quickly rubbed his forehead before murmuring, "I'm actually doing this because I want your ... help."

Sam almost lost it.

A bubbling snort escaped her, followed by a choked-off laugh, which she held back only because she knew laughing right in Big Pete Wilder's face was not the smartest decision for anyone. Especially her. But she couldn't hold her wry amusement in check any more than that. "Say that again."

"You heard me," he grumbled, still looking around as

if they were in a crowded lobby instead. "I need to talk to you. Can we do this in private?"

He gestured toward his car — the only shiny black Mercedes making an appearance on this side of town, something infrequent enough for it to stand out like a sore thumb.

"Private. Sure." Sam turned away from him and headed back toward her Jeep. "If you wanna talk so badly *in private*, why don't you hop up into my mobile office, Pete? Otherwise, I'll see you later."

She'd meant it as a jab to his pride and how ridiculous his request was, nothing else.

To her complete astonishment, once Sam climbed up behind the wheel of her Jeep, she got a perfect view through the front passenger-side window of Big Pete also approaching her Jeep. Without pausing or looking around again or even stopping to wait for a more direct invitation, he jerked open the passenger-side door, hauled himself up into the front seat beside her, and pulled the door shut again with a muffled slam.

The Jeep rocked slightly at the sudden and astoundingly rare addition of the weight of a man Big Pete's size.

All Sam could do at first was stare blankly ahead through the windshield, unseeing, wondering what the hell could've possibly happened to this epic asshole sitting at the top of Rush's socio-economic food chain to make him climb up into *her* vehicle for a private chat.

What could a man like him possibly need her help with?

Pete sat in her front passenger seat as if he'd been threatened into it instead. With his brow deeply furrowed and his lips pursed in aggravation, he glared at the top of the dashboard, grunted, and said nothing.

"This is as private as it's gonna get, you know," she

finally said. "You might as well just say what you need to—"

"It's Elaine." Pete sighed, and his frown deepened even farther. "She's in this … I don't know. This *phase*. Got in touch with a group of folks on the east side of town. Not the best type. Not the kind she'd even speak to, normally. They've got this fucking commune out there, up in the woods, and she's been spending more and more time there lately."

For the life of her, Sam couldn't imagine a more awkward conversation.

"So your wife has some new friends." Sam shrugged. "Congratulations."

"That's not it, and you fucking know it," he hissed. "I don't give a shit about her having friends. She should. I can't be everything to *her*. I'm already everything to everyone else."

Sam fought not to roll her eyes.

"Thing is, she's been spending way more time with these hippie freaks out there than is good for her or anyone else. She leaves early, comes home late, won't tell me shit about what they're doing out there, and she hasn't been to the club since… Hell, since all that ghost bullshit a few months back. And every time she comes home after being with these people, she starts spouting a whole load of shit I don't understand. I'm not even sure she understands it, either, and I'm at the end of my rope with this."

"Uh-huh." Sam leaned sideways against the armrest of the driver's side door but couldn't quite bring herself to look straight at the man. "You know, I bet you guys could find a pretty decent marriage counselor around here."

"Cut the shit, Salazar. This is serious. I don't like it any more than you do, but I need someone to look into exactly what these people are doing with my wife day in and day out and why she's got so suddenly caught up in their ... whatever the hell they're doing out there. And I want *you* to look into it."

"I bet you do," she said flatly.

"This isn't a command or some type of threat or anything like that," he added. "I wanna hire you to go dig up everything you can about these commune freaks and help me get my wife back."

"No shit." Sam forced a cough to stop herself from laughing in his face again, "I'm sure whatever it is, Elaine can handle herself. She's a smart woman. I think the best thing for you to do is just to let her have her space for this."

"By hiring you, I mean I'll *pay* you. In cash."

"I already have a job, Pete. I sling drinks at the Redwood Rings and the Back Bar. In case you haven't noticed, there's no PI office with my name on it in town."

"Ten grand to start," he muttered. "Another ten at the end when you've dug as deep as you can go."

Holy shit.

If this had been anyone but Big Pete Wilder, of *course* Sam would have said yes.

Instead, she said, "This isn't something I do, Pete."

"Another twenty grand on top of it if you can convince her to come home and never go back to these shitheads," Pete added with a grimace as he stared straight ahead through the windshield. "That's more than worth your time."

"Okay, you're clearly not hearing me." Sam shifted quickly in the driver's seat to face him as much as possible and sternly added, "The answer's no."

Big Pete finally looked at her, blinked, then shouted, "Why the fuck not?"

"Because I've got enough on my plate right now as it

is. Because you hate my guts. Because I can't stand you, either. Because no amount of money in the world would get me to help *you*. And because I can't figure out why the hell you'd wanna hire *me* for anything."

"Trust me, Salazar, I'm not in love with the idea any more than you are. As much as it pisses me off, you seem to be the only person in this whole goddamn town who actually knows how to find answers to relevant questions, even when other folks are trying to keep those answers private."

"And you want me to … what? Just roll right up to this commune and start asking questions?"

Big Pete shrugged. "If that's what you think is the best way to handle it."

A bitter laugh escaped her.

The man probably thought everything around here was easier for Sam Salazar, all because she was an outsider. She hadn't grown up in Rush. She didn't have any familial ties. As far as anyone else was concerned, she was as much of a transient worker and drifter as any of the trimmers who came by to work on the farms, blowing in with the breeze one minute and whipping right back out again the next.

If she were Big Pete Wilder, she would probably expect someone like herself more than capable of infiltrating a hippie a hippie commune like this, and having it a whole hell of a lot easier than someone with deeper ties running through the pulse of this town.

None of that mattered anyway.

"Sorry, Pete," she said flatly. "I can't."

"Fine. Twenty thousand up front, another twenty when you're done, and that's it. I won't go higher."

"This isn't a negotiation. It's still a no."

"Are you fucking kidding me?"

For a moment, her Jeep fell eerily silent, especially considering such a large, loud, energetically enormous man sitting right next to her. A silent, speechless Big Pete was even more unpredictable than a loud and bellowing Big Pete, which he only reconfirmed for her when he exploded two seconds later.

"What the fuck do you mean, you can't do it?" he roared.

"Exactly what I said." Somehow, even with her ears ringing after his outburst in her fully closed vehicle, Sam managed to keep her voice even, level, and under far more control than this man had ever exhibited in her presence. "I *can't* do it. Sorry, Pete. You're gonna have to find someone else to research your wife's hobbies in secret."

"You little—" He started to lean toward her, then stopped himself, seemed to grab hold of his emotions and whatever his boiling anger had almost prompted him to do, then thrust a finger toward her anyway. "You're making a mistake, Salazar. All you had to do was say yes, and I could've cleared away so many problems for you. That's over now. The offer's expired."

Sam clicked her tongue and replied in a bored-sounding monotone, "That's really too bad."

"I swear to Christ, if you say anything about this to anyone—"

"Nobody listens to me in this town anyway, Pete," she interrupted. "Remember? They all believe whatever *you* say, and you've made it perfectly clear I can't be trusted."

He leered at her, eyed her up and down with something like pure hatred, then threw open the passenger-side door. Once he hopped out, he nearly took the door off its hinges when he slammed it shut behind him.

Sam didn't bother watching him cross the parking lot. She didn't want anything to do with him after that, including seeing him, or thinking about him, or wondering why the hell he'd really come to her about any of this, because she didn't trust a word he'd said.

Instead, she pulled quickly out of the hotel's parking lot and booked it as fast as her Jeep would take her back to Birdsong Park and the Deville and her lawn chair beside the firepit.

Her only immediate plans were to eat a piping-hot microwave dinner in all of two minutes before flopping down onto her tiny bed in the tiny trailer and spending the next several hours completely unconscious.

TWENTY-NINE

Sam

THE NEXT MORNING, SAM GOT UP BRIGHT AND EARLY. THIS was surprisingly easier than she normally would have expected, simply because she'd managed to get into bed at a decent hour the night before.

She supposed she had the Redwood Rings' plumbing issues and last-minute closure to thank for that.

After showering in the park's communal facilities and eating a quick breakfast, she was out the door and headed to her Jeep, stopping to give Dog a quick scratch behind the ears on her way.

Syc was already outside in his usual seat by the fire, his daily wake-and-bake joint already lit in his hand as he called after her, "Got everything you need?"

"Pretty sure, yeah. Why? You gonna worry about me while I'm gone?"

"Didn't say that. This is about me trying to avoid as much trouble as possible. Normally, that wouldn't include me making this kind of offer, but if it keeps you and your friend from getting into even more trouble on your own... Want me to come along with?"

"You don't think we can handle it on our own, huh?" Sam chuckled. "If I didn't know better, Syc, I'd say you actually care what happens to us out there."

"Yeah, but you know better." He puffed on his joint. "Still, the offer stands."

"Nah, we're good. Rip's gonna meet us up there right off the highway. I'm pretty sure that's where one of the trailheads starts, and then he's coming with us as a sort of guide, I guess. But thanks."

"Huh." When he spoke again through an exhale, his voice came out thickly muffled by all the smoke. "Well, if anyone knows the area well enough, it'd be him."

"That's what we're thinking too. Pretty much in his backyard, so it looks like we've got it covered."

Syc waved a hand in farewell without looking at her, choosing instead to stare into the smoldering embers of the firepit like he usually did. "Just don't expect me to wait up for you."

Sam laughed again as she made it to her Jeep. "Of course not. That's what Dog's here for."

SINCE THEY'D AGREED to all meet at the hotel at 7:30 a.m., Sam tried her best to be slightly early. She succeeded by a whole five minutes, which was saying a lot.

She fully expected to find either Charles or Brad — or both of them — waiting for her outside Room 8, but she didn't get that far after entering the hotel's pitiful lobby.

Instead, she had a clear view of both men sitting at a booth together in the attached twenty-four-hour café.

That hadn't been part of their previously discussed plans, but at least they were comfortable enough with each other to start a conversation without Sam present.

And to have breakfast together, apparently.

They were just finishing up their meals when she joined them. Instead of choosing either of them to snuggle up close to in the booth, Sam pulled up a free-standing chair from a nearby table, though she assured them she'd already eaten and wasn't hungry.

"We still ordered you a coffee," Brad said before sliding the full mug toward her.

"That's something everyone needs," Charles added with a nod, the picture of seriousness. "Whether or not you've already had some, am I right?"

"Trust me," Sam said, reaching for the steaming mug, "I'm the last person to turn down a free cup of coffee."

Once the guys settled their check, they all left the hotel together. Brad didn't argue with her when she reminded him of their deal — they'd go up together to meet Rip in her Jeep. Sam was tempted to also remind him that he'd lost his driving privileges, but that would've just been more salt on an open wound.

The guy's SUV was still in police impound, so the issue was settled for them, anyway.

Charles, however, insisted on driving his own car, just in case he needed to get somewhere else or they ran into any sort of conceivable trouble along the way.

Sam didn't see a reason to argue with him on that one.

More than that, she was grateful he'd offered to drive himself. Any more than one passenger in her Jeep at a time was enough to give her a headache and distract her from driving. One passenger was best.

Zero passengers was preferred, but Brad made it clear he'd rather ride with her than with Charles.

They piled into the vehicles and took off past the hotel, down the main strip of road toward the highway, then north up the highway toward the frontage road leading directly to Rip's property and not much else.

Sam drove right past the enormous wrought-iron gates marking the front entrance to Rip's farm. It didn't escape her notice that while they passed those gates with all the extra beefed-up security — including four guards that might or might not have been the four graced by an intimate meeting with Brad's fists the day before — Brad stared dutifully straight ahead through the front windshield. He didn't even twitch in the direction of Rip's property, nor did he say a thing.

Rip's instructions to the pull-off area where they planned to meet were fairly simple and easy to follow. They passed the old cemetery first on the left and took the left turn just past the new cemetery, also on the left, this one slightly easier to spot from the frontage road. After that, it was just another ten miles or so before they came upon the turnoff, and that was it.

The turnoff could be considered a small parking lot with enough room for five mid-sized vehicles. It also provided access to a decent overlook view across this part of the mountain, and there was plenty of space for both Sam's Jeep and Charles' sedan as he arrived closely behind her.

Even once they'd turned off the frontage road and pulled both vehicles to a stop in the lot, though, there was still no sign of Rip's truck.

"He said he'd meet us here around this time, right?" Charles asked as he got out of his car and cracked open a new plastic bottle of water.

"That's exactly what he said." Sam dusted off her hands and walked slowly across the dirt pull-out. "He's probably just running late. We can wait a few minutes. I'm sure he'll show up soon."

When soon turned into fifteen minutes later and there was still no sign of anyone else this up here — no sound of truck engines coming up the mountainside to join them — Sam started to wonder if maybe Rip had found new information or maybe new trouble with his farm that had quickly erased their meet-up from his mind.

As far as she knew, he wasn't someone who easily forgot his appointments. A man like Rip Graham didn't get to where he was in his line of work by being dependably forgetful or unreliable.

"Sam." Brad stopped pacing at the far end of the turnoff and impatiently spread his arms. "We've been waiting up here for…what? Almost half an hour now?"

Charles glanced at his watch. "Almost forty-five minutes."

"Yeah, great." Brad shot the man a skeptical look, which went entirely unnoticed. "Even better."

"Kody came here to look at Rip's water source," Sam reminded them. "It's just as important to him as everything else, and he's got an investment in finding her too. He'll be here."

But then it became clear that Sam was starting to promise things on behalf of a man who clearly wasn't going to hold up his end of their agreement this morning.

She was also smart enough to realize that both Brad and Charles had become increasingly more eager to get started down the trailhead toward the lake — and increasingly less patient.

The first time Sam dialed Rip's number to check on him, the line rang once, then cut off without offering an option to leave a voicemail. Then she tried twice more but quickly realized that the issue all along had been the lack of service here.

Still, she didn't want to leave Rip completely in the lurch. There was no way Brad or Charles would agree to just turn around and reschedule this for another day. Not now that they were already here.

So Sam went with the next best option.

After fiddling around in her glovebox, she found a pen that still worked among three others that had already run out of ink, plus a piece of paper that had probably once been some kind of important documentation for the Jeep but had now faded through time and heat exposure and some sort of oily substance spilled somewhere in the glovebox's vicinity sometime in the last decade. That piece of paper did, however, have one almost completely blank side, which Sam used to quickly scribble out a note.

At the very least, it was important he knew they'd gone ahead on purpose. If he showed up like they'd planned, he'd find the note with his name written across the top in incredibly large letters.

'RIP. We headed up the mountain already. Meet us at the lake. Sam.'

THEN SHE ADDED THE TIME — 8:42 a.m. — and left the note on her dashboard for him to find.

"Let's go."

∼

IT WAS A BEAUTIFUL DAY, crisp and cool but not freezing, with plenty of sunshine and enough morning birdsong to fill what might have otherwise been a slightly awkward silence among the trio.

No doubt about it, the first part of the hike was fairly difficult. A number of fallen trees blocked much of their path in the beginning. Once they got past those, the terrain rose in a sharp incline, forcing them to climb over rocky outcroppings and up a wall of slick, loose shale at one point just to get back to the trail reappearing on the other side.

All this left them with little energy or focus for conversation anyway, for which Sam was grateful.

During an outing like this, searching for a missing person where tensions ran almost as high as hope, there was no telling what kinds of things might pop out of anyone's mouth when they paid more attention to traversing the mountainside than to what was said out loud.

If she hadn't had to focus so hard on the hike — or hadn't been so drastically aware of both men in front of and behind her, moving stiffly with sharp winded breath — she would have called this one of the more beautiful hikes she'd been on in some time.

Sam found herself feeling a little guilty for appreciating the view now and then, knowing that Kody was out there somewhere, hopefully still alive and waiting for someone to pick up her trail and come find her.

After almost two hours, they'd only found one thing up there in the hills that wasn't a natural part of the area around them.

An old, dilapidated log cabin peeked out from between thinning trees in an area that didn't technically count as a clearing. The place was well hidden, though poorly maintained. The wooden front door had almost completely rotted away from any recognizable shape and hung precariously from its top hinges. Two of the front windows had been busted in, which meant that when they finally got the door open and stepped into the cabin, the main room was littered with layers of old leaves, dried pine needles, dust, and a scattering of old insect husks.

Beyond the single ripped-open and warped condom wrapper on the far side of the cabin's main room, there was nothing else to indicate that anyone had been up here in quite some time. All three sets of their footsteps left significant prints in the thick layer of dust coating the warped wooden floors, which had stretched and buckled enough beneath the weather patterns over the years to form dangerously large gaps between each slat.

Sam shook her head and headed back toward the cabin's front door. "Totally abandoned. I wouldn't put stock in anyone having been up here recently. Definitely not Kody."

"I was thinking the same," Brad said.

Charles investigated a little further. He was the only one to poke his head into the back hallway and the one other small room built at the rear of the cabin, but when he emerged again to join Sam and Brad outside, he had nothing new to report.

They had to keep looking.

No sign of Rip's recent presence here crossed their path even on the last leg of the trek toward the lake. Sam hadn't expected to find the guy catching up to them and crossing their path at the abandoned cabin, but she did think he might have passed them by while they were investigating and potentially beat them to their destination.

When they first spotted the lake from the top of a valley ridge they'd spent half an hour diligently climbing, the breathtaking view was almost enough to make Sam forget why they were here.

But she didn't.

They were here to find Kody, and that was exactly what she intended to do.

Another precarious descent over slippery shale and ground covered in layers of pine needles that slid and tumbled beneath their feet down the steep incline finally got them to the valley floor and right up to the edge of the lake. Only when they'd approached it this closely was it clear that the water feeding into and out of the lake had been efficiently dammed.

The lake was incredibly full. If this had happened during the rainy season, the surrounding valley would definitely have flooded. This time of year, though, the water remained in the lake basin, though just barely. Its pristine surface glistened under the light breeze while the dark shapes of small fish flitted about beneath, avoiding the reflected shadows of larger birds occasionally passing ahead.

There was no sign of anyone out here, either. No clues left behind. No clothes or the remnants of a campsite or discarded food. Nothing to suggest anyone had left the comfort of civilization in town to spend their time up here in the valley's wilderness.

Except for the fact that the lake itself had been dammed.

"That's not a natural occurrence." Sam headed toward the site of blocked water.

"No it's not," Charles replied as he followed closely behind her. "I think there's something in the original town ordinances about damming certain bodies of water out here. For the most part, it's illegal. Has been for the last several decades. Natural bodies of water can be diverted as long as it doesn't affect the overall ecology of the surrounding area, which looks like what Rip's been doing. The reasoning behind what can and can't be used and in which way is more complex than I can pretend to fully understand, honestly."

"But not too complex for an Environmental Studies grad student to grasp," Sam added. "Right?"

The man frowned at her. "I suppose not."

"Kody definitely would've known," Brad said. "She picked this part of California specifically, and she knew what she was getting into out here as far as environmental effects were concerned. Trust me, I heard all about the research she did on local industries and their effects in this part of the state on certain ecological changes."

Sam paused on her slow walk around the lake to look at him over her shoulder. "Are you saying she would've known about the laws prohibiting dams like this one?"

With a snort, he shot her a wry smile in response, though just made him look that much more worried. "It wasn't obvious?"

"That's a yes," Sam murmured as she continued walking again.

"So this dam is here on purpose," Charles added. "Just not above board. That's what this means."

"This has to be the lake Rip mentioned," Sam said. "The one that feeds into his water supply. And there's the source of his current water issues right here. Someone blocked it off, and it wasn't him. He wouldn't sabotage his own business like that."

"You sure about that?" Brad asked.

She met his gaze before nodding. "I'm sure. Someone else might try something like this, if they got themselves into a tight spot financially and were trying to go for insurance payouts or something, but not Rip."

"I agree with Sam," Charles said. "That man works and lives on an enormous farm. Has more wholesale distribution contracts with California dispensaries than one man alone should ever be allowed to have at one time. You wouldn't think it by looking at him, but financial pickles are the least of Rip Graham's worries. At least, not the kind that would make him desperate enough to dam up his own water supply. No, he wouldn't do this himself."

"Then someone else decided to do it for him instead," Sam added. "Or *against* him..."

Charles pointed at her. "That seems a lot more likely."

"That someone would purposefully sabotage his water supply?" she asked. "And reasons for that would be..."

"One of his competitors," Charles offered with a shrug.

"Someone's sabotaging his grow business," Brad added.

Sam folded her arms and studied the closest dammed area of the lake. "Someone who wants Rip to fail in his business to make sure whatever he tries won't work out. Or somebody wants to divert his attention and his resources away from his actual plants. Waste his time in having to come up here and fix this issue."

"Does he have a whole lot of competitors in this area?" Brad asks. "You know, specifically other people growing and selling weed."

Sam and Charles looked at each other, then she shrugged. "My guess is at least three others. But I don't claim to know the inner workings of this place nearly as much as someone who's been here a hell of a lot longer than I have."

"As far as the rest of Rush is concerned," Charles continued, "I'm an outsider too. But yeah, I'd say that's fairly accurate. There are a few other farms out here. Much smaller operations than Rip's with a little more of a mom-and-pop feel to them, so to speak. But they do all right for themselves. As far as I know, Rip's always been a businessman who welcomes competition and innovation, even in his own industry."

"I heard he offered the best wages for trimmers too during the season," Sam said.

"Yeah, that sounds accurate to me."

"Any idea who might've wanted to start trouble with him by blocking up his water source?"

The Daily Rush's senior editor scratched his head. "Your guess is as good as mine, here. Wish I could give you more."

Despite the frustrating lack of answers, Sam was still determined to get to the bottom of this. In order to do that, they had to go down every possible rabbit hole and leave no stone unturned, not only to find Kody but now to pinpoint who might have wanted to damage Rip's business or his reputation in the area or both.

Honestly, she had no idea where to even start looking for people who made that list. This was, for all intents and purposes, a completely foreign world to her.

Maybe I should've taken Syc up on his offer to join us. The man smokes enough weed to know exactly where it all comes from and who's involved.

With no immediate solutions at hand, the trio continued around the lake, studying the terrain around the illegal dam and looking for any other evidence that might have indicated someone else's presence here.

For the most part, the valley remained particularly undisturbed. The only real evidence was the dam itself, and beyond that, it seemed they'd reached another dead-end.

Sam was about to call it and say they should head back to the vehicles. At the very least, it was probably best to wait to hear from Rip again before they decided on their next course of action. Specifically whether they should continue with a broader search along the mountain or simply turn their sights elsewhere.

But before she could get that far, a thick set of clouds swooped lazily in front of the sun. The sky darkened, removing the sunlight's glare from the lake's surface and making it much easier to see quite a bit farther in the distance.

Sam still shaded her eyes with a hand over her forehead, but now she could actually see what was in front of them on the far western side of the lake.

"Did you guys see that?"

Both Brad and Charles looked up in the direction she was staring, but their blank expressions and lack of response told her they had no idea what she was talking about.

"Up there." She pointed. "There's a cave over that way. See it? That first dark spot right on this side of the ridge. Looks like there are at least two more past it. Could be a whole series of caves up here. Maybe interconnected, maybe not."

"But not very likely to be empty," Charles added. "Especially if there's someone up here trying to hide something they don't want to be found."

Sam turned toward Brad and fixed him with a questioning gaze. "Maybe we should go check it out."

THIRTY

Kody

SEVERAL DAYS AGO...

SHE'D PROMISED herself she would never let it get to this point.

But after who knew how many days and no change in her circumstances — other than the fact that she'd consumed the last of her food what felt like two days ago and the last drops of water sometime this morning — Kody was finally starting to lose hope.

Her entire body was one massive ache. She couldn't focus on anything, including pinpointing the pain and discomfort because it was everywhere now, joined by the permeating chill that seeped into her survival blanket, which now failed to protect her. The cold had eaten through her skin and into her bones, just like her hunger and dehydration, and Kody had run out of options for improving her current circumstances in any way.

She knew it was important not to give up. Her conscious mind — which felt like it had been fading in and out lately — reminded her that oftentimes, the line between life and death, between survival and just not making it, came down to the presence of hope.

Simply put, those who believed they would make it through any life-altering horror — or at least those willing to convince themselves survival was still possible — had significantly higher survival rates than those who let the pain, hunger, despair, and overwhelming helplessness run the show.

Sometimes, though, giving up and giving in and letting death take over started to look preferable to survival.

Kody had already found herself entertaining thoughts in this vein. That realization had terrified her more than any lack of food or water or the endless possibilities of what her kidnappers might have in store for her.

She didn't want to die.

Of course she didn't, but sometimes, the idea of letting go — of curling up on the bottom of this pit, wrapped in the crinkling survival blanket, with nothing else around her but dampness and darkness and the damned chill that had now become a part of her — seemed like such a relief.

The thought crept up on her when she wasn't paying attention. How liberating it would be to stop fighting, to stop thinking about when the men would come back to the cave or when they would finally decide that leaving her here no longer served their purposes.

How easy it would be to stop worrying about when she'd get more water at the very least or food as an added miracle.

Sometimes, the sudden weakness of her body terrified her even more than the thought of death itself.

Then, when she noticed these were the actual thoughts floating through her mind, that they came from her and no one else, that she was actually entertaining throwing in the towel, she instantly redoubled her efforts to distract herself.

The thoughts were always there, but she hadn't given in to them. She hadn't given up.

Not yet.

There was still time for fate to pull a one-eighty on her.

Though her phone was completely useless now, and all her rations had run out, and she had never been so cold or sore or weak in her life, Kody wouldn't let herself give up.

She didn't have the energy anymore to try another physical escape. The walls of the pit had crumbled significantly around her. The tunnel she'd dug that had collapsed on her had filled the bottom of the pit with a lot more mud than she'd expected, while the steady drip of water somewhere above in the cave echoed constantly around her, taunting her now with the promise of water that was obviously so close yet impossible to reach.

Kody pushed herself away from the wall of the pit and crawled slowly, achingly forward on hands and knees as she felt around in the dark for puddles or the wettest, sloppiest bit of mud she could find.

Closer to her collapsed tunnel, she found one such puddle when her partially numb fingers slid across the squelchy grime.

Trying to keep her hands from shaking, she gathered up as much mud as she could into two hands, packed it into a loose ball, then lifted the whole thing above her head and threw her head back with her mouth open. She waited in the dark for the disastrously few drops of water squeezed from this ball of mud to drip into her mouth.

They were cold, silty, and tasted like drinking rocks, but it was something.

It was all she had.

It still wasn't enough.

That simple task alone wore her out completely. With a massive sigh, she sat back and slumped against the wall again. She couldn't keep this up for much longer, either. If she didn't get more water soon, she wasn't going to make it.

Kody could have sworn she felt parts of her body already starting to shut down. Although she no longer had any viable form of recording the passage of time, she had a sneaking suspicion that what had at first felt like small, short bursts of random catnaps were actually moments of unconsciousness brought on by malnutrition, dehydration, and exhaustion.

It wouldn't have surprised her if she'd slept for twelve hours straight without being able to tell the difference. Even the amount of sleep that she'd had had done nothing to revive the tiniest spark of her energy.

Feeling like she might be about to drift off into that unnecessary unconsciousness again, Kody forced herself to think about something good, something she loved, something that made her feel some measure of hope still.

Her mind instantly turned to her parents.

She knew they were both incredibly worried about her. She knew they had both noticed she was missing and had tried to get in touch with her. She did her best not to think about her mom and dad in the worst of their worried state right now but instead as her favorite versions of them.

Her mom making her hot chocolate and the best damn four-cheese grilled cheese in Ohio. Her dad laughing at one of her jokes, the unmistakable pride and admiration reflected back to her in his eyes as she described her latest accomplishments and shared the best parts of her dreams for the future with him.

Those memories made her smile, until it occurred to

her again, brutally and without warning, that these memories might very well be the last she ever saw of her parents.

The last experience she might ever have of the people who had created her, raised her, and loved her.

Memories were all she had now, because the odds were unequivocally stacked against her.

Most likely, she was going to die in this pit.

The last thing she wanted was to break down crying. Her body couldn't afford to lose any more water.

More than that, though, she refused to spend what were probably her last hours sobbing on the floor of a pit in a dank, musty cave.

Kody Anderson wouldn't go out like that.

No way in hell.

She couldn't, even if there was no one else around to witness her final moments.

If nothing else, she still had *some* of her pride intact.

The stinging in her eyes brought by oncoming tears she refused to shed finally settled again, and Kody puffed out a soft, weak sigh. At the very least, she could still get a grip on herself, and that was something when she had literally nothing else.

A loud click and clatter echoed across the hard stone floor of the cave somewhere up above.

Kody froze, momentarily holding her breath so she could listen better.

What was that?

At first, when no other sound followed, she wrote it off as a chip of loose rock having fallen from the cave wall or ceiling on its own.

But then the footsteps started, and she couldn't deny those really were footsteps.

Her captors stepping back into the cave.

That had been one of the hardest things for her to come

to terms with while she'd been left down here. Kody couldn't decide whether it was better to have the occasional company of other people while she was trapped down here — even if they ignored her completely and clearly didn't give a shit about what happened to her — or if she preferred being entirely alone.

In the beginning, she might have been more motivated toward escape attempts when she knew the men were gone, forced to rely solely on herself because no one was there with her. Maybe, if the men had never entered the cave, she might have tried harder.

Maybe the mere knowledge of her captors' presence had dulled her senses and made her dependent on begging them for help.

It seemed odd that, even with the men moving in and out of the cave on a timeline she could no longer follow, she still felt so miserably lonely.

It *seemed* odd, but at her core, she knew it wasn't.

"Hello?" A male voice echoed softly through the cave, not quite a whisper but definitely not shouted at top volume, either.

Kody almost laughed at the sound.

Great. The hallucinations are finally kicking in.

But then she heard soft, hesitant footsteps moving across the cave floor above her. Metal clinked against metal, more small pebbles and stones cluttered across the floor, and the man's voice rang out again. "I know someone's been in here. If you thought you cleaned up after yourself, you need to work harder on covering your tracks."

Kody's mind felt so sluggish and slow.

Was she really hearing this right now? Did the man who owned that voice actually exist, or was she losing it?

The footsteps echoed closer, followed by a quick

flashing beam of low light streaking across the top of the pit.

Then she realized, far later than she should have, that the voice definitely didn't belong to either of her captors. This was someone completely new.

Someone had found her!

"Help…"

The word croaked out of her throat in a strangled cry. Or maybe she didn't make any sound at all. She couldn't really tell either way, but she had to keep trying.

"Help," she called again. "I'm down here. Help me. Please…"

Her voice was so weak; just that small bit of shouting left her entirely winded, and she sagged against the wall of the pit again, fighting to catch her breath.

"Hello?" the man called again.

"I'm down here," Kody panted. "I'm … I'm trapped. Please don't leave me!"

After that, the cave fell silent again.

She held her breath, hoping to hear something else. Then her mind ran away on her again, and in seconds, she'd almost convinced herself that she *had* been hallucinating.

Tears sprang to her eyes again as she dropped her head back against the muddy wall of the pit.

"No, no, no," she moaned. "Please don't leave me down here by myself. Please don't leave me here. I can't … I can't…"

This was it. She knew it.

This was the moment where the last hope to which she'd clung for so long finally abandoned her.

This was the deepest, darkest bottom of hopelessness, and this was as far as Kody was going to get.

She might as well just give up now. She might as well just—

A bright flash illuminated through her closed eyelids, and she blinked rapidly before finally opening her impossibly heavy eyes.

The bright light disappeared. She tried to focus her vision in the dark, but the next second, the blinding whiteness enveloped everything, aimed straight at her.

Kody pressed herself back against the pit wall, scrambling to get away from the light, blinking and grimacing and barely able to lift her hands in front of her face.

"Holy shit. Kody?"

"Oh my god," Kody whispered, struggling to rise.

It was Rip.

"Oh my god, you found me! You're here! *Please* tell me this is real…"

"Finding you in the bottom of a giant hole like this? Yeah, kid, it's real. Are you all right? You hurt?"

"Nothing sunlight and a giant meal can't fix," she said with a weak laugh. "I mean, I took a hit to the head a while ago, but other than that…"

"We gotta get you out of here. Can you walk?"

"Yeah, I think so." It felt like it took forever for Kody to push herself up to her feet, but she managed it somehow. On wobbly legs, she staggered toward the far wall of the pit over which Rip now loomed. "How did you find me?"

"We can get to that part later. Right now, we gotta get you out of here." Rip propped his flashlight on the cave floor beside him, the bright beam streaking across the open top of the pit as he lowered himself to the ground and stretched out on his belly.

"Come on, kid," he said, extending a hand down over the edge. "Come on. Grab my hand, and I'll help you out."

Kody's heart fluttered in her chest as she finished hobbling toward the wall and reached up with a weak, trembling hand.

All the hope and renewed energy she'd received from finally being found down here almost disappeared completely when her upstretched fingertips still fell short of Rip's offered hand by a good six inches.

"I can't reach. I'm too far down."

"All right, well, you got anything down there you can climb on top of?"

"If I did, I already would've gotten myself out."

"What about the walls? Any handholds or footholds? Can you climb even just a little way? Two, three feet—"

"No," she said. "I already tried climbing the walls. It's all mud. Just keeps breaking apart. I can't."

"Shit. Okay." Rip pushed himself first to his knees, then stood. "Hang tight. I'm gonna go find something to help pull you out of here."

"There might be a rope up there somewhere. It was in my pack, but it's gone now."

"I'll find something." Rip's voice echoed from farther away now.

Kody started to let herself relax in the knowledge that she was finally being saved. Someone had found her.

Then the details of her circumstances came rushing back. Instantly horrified, she slapped both hands against the wall of the pit and shouted, "You need to hurry! Before they come back. If they find you in here, they'll—"

A loud clang of something metal hitting either the cave wall or its floor cut her off.

"Rip?"

The only reply she got were the muffled echoes of a quick, heavy scuffle from up above. Something heavy and thick thudded down on something else, followed immediately by a grunting groan and another thump.

Then the cave filled with the sound of hobbling footsteps and long, slow, whispering drags across stone and dirt. Heavy breathing. The sounds of hard labor drawing closer with every second.

"Rip?" Kody softly called again.

The beam of his flashlight wobbled across the top of the pit, then a dark shape loomed in front of the light, growing larger by the second as it rolled into view at the pit's edge.

The next thing she knew, Kody was staring wide-eyed at an enormous, hulking object tumbling over the edge and dropping down into the pit until it crashed right on top of her, and she went down with it.

THIRTY-ONE

Sam

AFTER SUCH A FRUITLESS SEARCH BOTH ALONG THE mountain and inside the series of caves by the lake, Sam, Brad, and Charles quickly agreed the best next step would be to head back across the mountain toward their cars before deciding anything else.

When they returned to the turnoff — covered in sweat, a light dusting of red-brown dirt, and a few scratches from sturdier bushes and brambles — there was still no sign of anyone else having come up here.

No indication that Rip had even made it to the turnoff lot the first place for their agreed-upon rendezvous.

With a sigh, Charles shook his head. "I really thought we were gonna find something up there today. I was sure of it."

"We only searched one part of the mountain," Sam said. "And we're definitely not done. There's still a lot more."

Brad folded his arms. "Would've been a lot more helpful with that Rip guy, though."

Sam nodded. "And I'm gonna find out what happened with that this morning so we don't run into this kind of issue again."

"I'm gonna head home," Charles said as he unlocked his sedan and opened the driver's-side door. "Take another look at my files. See if anything else stands out that I might've missed before. I'll be in touch if I find anything."

Sam nodded. "Same here."

With nothing else to do, Sam and Brad piled into her Jeep, then they took off down the frontage road, just a few minutes behind Charles.

Sam drove quickly, going over and over their morning in her mind, trying to find what she'd missed. Rip was supposed to have been out here with them, but something hadn't quite added up.

Had she misheard him? Maybe he wasn't back in town yet.

Thinking about Rip, though, reminded her they were all the way up here now and would pass his property on the way into town anyway.

She didn't say a thing about it to Brad but simply slowed at the turnoff to Rip's property entrance and parked the Jeep at the very end, making sure to leave plenty of room for other vehicles to pass through if necessary.

"What're we doing *now*?" Brad asked.

Sam jerked the gearshift into park, cut the Jeep's engine, and turned to him with the most serious scowl she could muster. "*We* aren't doing anything. I'm gonna go talk to those guys standing by the gate, see what's going on with Rip, and *you* are gonna keep your ass in this seat."

He chuckled softly. "Very funny."

Sam had already started to open the driver's-side door, but she abandoned that for the moment and resumed glaring at him. "It wasn't a joke. No way in hell am I letting you waltz right up to those front gates again. I don't give a shit if you feel like you have yourself back under control now. You've been out of jail for less than twenty-four hours. You stay here."

"Come on, Sam. That's totally unnecessary."

"So was beating on Rip's security guys just because you didn't get the answer you wanted," she snapped back. Then she leapt out of the Jeep, snapped her fingers, pointed at him, and added, "Stay."

She practically slammed the door shut before trudging up the dirt road leading right to the front gates of Rip's farm.

She'd already made up her mind about it. If Brad refused to listen to her now, she was done with him. She'd still keep looking for Kody, but it wouldn't be as part of a ride-along, and she wouldn't be feeding him any more information until she had a concrete answer.

Fortunately, Brad actually listened to her this time, which made this a whole hell of a lot easier. With him safely tucked away in the Jeep, she could actually have a conversation.

Part of her expected the guards to bristle at the sight of her Jeep in the drive, but then Sam remembered they'd been in Brad's SUV the first time they'd come up here together. Of course, these guys knew by now that Brad and Sam at least knew each other, if not that they were old friends from back in their Army days.

Fortunately, though, that didn't seem to matter to the security guys. They watched Sam approach, and one of them stepped closer to the gate, lifting his automatic rifle enough to make it clear he knew what he was doing with it but not actually making any threatening moves just yet.

"Hey, there," she called to them, raising a hand in greeting.

One of the guards nodded in response, but that was it.

Only when Sam finally reached the giant wrought-iron gates did she notice these were in fact the same four security guards Brad had tried to strong-arm yesterday. She didn't know them personally, but each man boasted some form of evidence from their tussle with her Army buddy.

The one standing closest to her had a black eye and a split lip, which might or might not have been the reason he didn't offer so much as an attempted smile in her direction.

"Not opening the gates today, lady," he told her, shaking his head. "Not after your rabid dog got loose."

His gaze shifted past her toward the Jeep.

Damn. So they *could* see Brad in there.

Sam spread her arms, acting casual but also wanting to show she was currently unarmed. "I had nothing to do with that, and I'm sorry it happened. I put his collar back on, though. He knows to stay in the Jeep."

"Good for you," the guard replied with a grunt. "Still not opening the gates today."

"What if I promised to leave him out here and just step inside on my own? I need to talk to Rip."

"Rip's not here," the guy said. "Even if he was, the answer would still be no. You'll have to wait 'til he comes back. He went up the mountain this morning for an appointment."

"Oh, I know." Sam reached the iron gates and stopped. "That appointment was with me. But he never showed."

The guard's eyes widened, then he glanced at a second security guy who'd come to join him at the gates before lowering his rifle on its strap and pulling out his cell phone instead. "Hold on a second."

He dialed a number, then pressed the phone to his ear.

Confused frowns and disturbed scowls darkened all around as the first guard stared blankly at nothing while listening to the phone. Then he abruptly jerked it away from his ear and shoved it back into his pocket. "He's not answering calls, either."

"Could've told you that," Sam said. "I was thinking maybe something came up on his schedule this morning and he had to take off for it instead of meeting with me."

The guard scrunched up his face. "Nah, he wouldn't've gone somewhere else without letting somebody know first. He's a real stickler about shit like that. Being punctual. Always being in contact. Letting everyone know what he's up to so we're all on the same page and nothing falls through the cracks."

"Good habits to get into." Sam nodded past the gates. "Especially in this line of work."

None of the guards reacted.

The first guy, however, pressed a fist to his mouth, thumped his knuckles against his lips a few times, then pulled his phone back out. "I'm gonna make a few more calls."

"Sure." Sam stuck her hands in the pockets of her light jacket, content to wait it out.

She couldn't make out what the guards were saying to each other in murmured voices. She couldn't even make out this side of the conversations the closest guard had over the phone. But in only a few minutes, the commotion in front of her picked up, and several people on Rip's property moved about all at once, including another man driving up to the gates in a beaten old pickup.

"You know where Rip was supposed to meet you this morning on the mountain?" the first guard asked.

Sam spun back toward him and nodded. "Oh yeah. Just came from there."

"Go on up with Richie and Allen," he said, nodding at the pickup. "Show 'em exactly where you were, and we'll figure out what happened."

"No problem." Sam walked casually back to the Jeep as the mechanized wrought-iron gate let out a low, warning buzz. Then both sides slid apart at the middle, rolling away from each other on enormous wheels.

The old pickup's engine rumbled loudly behind her until she hopped back up into her Jeep and shut the door.

She sat there for a moment, feeling unnaturally stiff in the driver's seat before she finally cranked the Jeep's engine back on.

"What's up with all that?" Brad asked.

After pulling a tight U-turn in the drive, Sam waited at the end of it, looking up into the rearview mirror until Richie and Allen pulled all the way through the front gates. "Turns out nobody here knows where Rip is either. Honestly, I wasn't worried about him until *they* were worried about him."

"They know what happened?"

"Just that he's missing and no one's heard from him."

"More than enough cause for concern."

She shot Brad a quick sidelong glance with a flicker of a frown before slowly letting the Jeep roll forward so she could turn onto the front edge road again. She wanted Rip's guys in the truck behind her to have plenty of time to easily follow her up the mountain. "Understatement of the year, man."

THE TURNOFF beside the frontage road still showed no signs of Rip's truck or anyone else having arrived after Sam, Brad, and Charles left the first time.

Sam explained to the occupants of the two trucks of

Rip's men who'd followed her that this was where Rip had told her to meet for their appointment. She also explained why — that he meant to lead her up the mountain for a tour of the farm's water source, where Kody was supposed to have been in the first place.

"And he just never showed," she finished. "We did find the lake, though. It's dammed up. Looks like it has been for a while. Figured you guys might've wanted to know about that too. Might be the reason for your water problem, yeah?"

Richie — a man in his early forties, his skin already tanned and leathered from working outside for decades — rubbed a hand through his hair before covering it all with his cowboy hat. "Goddamn. Thanks for saying something. We should've had someone come up here a while ago, but we've been dealing with some break-ins too. Trespassing issues on the farm. Just never had the time."

"Totally understandable," she said.

"We'll take care of the dam," he said. "Few sticks of dynamite'll do the job just fine. Then we're back in business."

Ritchie barked instructions to the other men, who opened and closed truck doors, rummaging around in supplies before three of them took off along the trailhead toward the lake.

"Thanks for your help with that," Richie added.

"No problem. If you hear from Rip, just let him know I'm waiting for a call. Still haven't had that appointment."

"Yes, ma'am." With a dip of his head, he turned to get to work with the rest of his men, presumably to fix said water issue at Rip's farm in a single explosive trip. Literally.

Sam hopped back into the Jeep and couldn't get the thing turned around fast enough to head back into town.

"I'm guessing that didn't go so well," Brad said after a few minutes of tense silence.

"For the farm? Actually, things are looking up. But now I've got two people missing up here on this mountain, and I don't like the way it smells."

THIRTY-TWO

Sam

SAM'S ONLY OPTION NOW WAS TO DROP BRAD OFF AT THE hotel, which would give each of them space to brainstorm separately before they made any other moves.

She was too baffled and admittedly concerned by Rip's alleged disappearance to focus entirely on piecing together evidence from Kody's disappearance too. Not now, anyway.

What she needed was a good long think, some fresh air, solitude, quiet, maybe even a fire to stare into…

Suddenly, going right back home to Birdsong Park for a few hours sounded like the best idea she'd had all day. Maybe she'd even make herself a sandwich.

She pulled into the hotel's parking lot, operating on autopilot with her mind so preoccupied by new developments.

She and Brad both got out of the Jeep and headed silently side-by-side toward the building.

About halfway there, Sam realized what she was doing and stopped. "Wait."

Brad stopped a few feet in front of her, then turned around with a wide-eyed look of surprise. "You good?"

"Yeah. But I'm thinking it might be best if I—"

She didn't have the chance to finish. What happened next seemed occurred in such quick succession that she could hardly discern the order of events.

A deafening bang rose from across the parking lot somewhere behind her.

Brad's gaze flickered over her shoulder, and his eyes widened in instant terror — the kind of unexpected shock that makes all coherent thought flee.

The sharp, staccato clack of either ridiculously strong heels or crutches of reinforced steel hurried closer, followed by a woman's low, furious shout. "What the *fuck* do you think you're doing?"

Sam couldn't help but turn around. She didn't necessarily assume the woman was shouting at her, but who *wouldn't* have wanted to see the source of a sound like that? Maybe catch a few seconds of decent drama playing out right in front of her?

She certainly didn't expect to immediately become a part of that drama herself.

The second Sam registered the furious-looking woman stomping toward them, the strangest feeling of déjà vu washed through her, like she was supposed to know who this was.

"Denise?" Brad practically shouted beside her.

Then it hit her all at once.

Denise Anderson.

Or, at least, that *used* to be her name back when she and Brad were still married.

Shit.

"W-what are you doing here?" Brad stammered.

"Oh sure," the other woman snapped as she finally

caught up with them. The deadly-sounding clack of her heels stopped on the pavement. "Say it like *that's* the most important question here and you have no idea what's happening. Well *here's* a question for you. What the hell is *she* doing here?"

Sam lifted a finger, as if that would get anyone's attention, and murmured, "Just dropping him off at the hotel and getting out of here."

"Oh no." Denise actually stepped in front of Sam, blocking her escape as the woman folded her arms and glowered. "You've made yourself a part of this all over again, so now you're gonna stick with it till the end and see it through this time. No easy getaways."

Denise's angrily narrowed gaze ripped right back up to settle on Brad again. "The least you could've done was tell me the two of you are seeing each other again."

A nervous-sounding chuckle that made her instantly want to jump into a ditch erupted from Sam's throat. "No. We're definitely *not* seeing each other again. We never were, really—"

"Deny it all you want," Denise snapped, turning her nose up to look down it at Sam. "I'm not a fucking idiot, okay? The two of you getting out of that Jeep together in a hotel parking lot, hurrying inside like you can't wait to be alone? I might not have picked up on the signs the first time, Sam, but believe it or not, I've learned a thing or two in the last decade and change, thanks."

Sam puffed out a sigh, which was her only immediate alternative to bursting out laughing at both the high levels of discomfort and the fact that nothing she said right now would be well received by Brad's ex-wife either way.

Fortunately, Brad had learned a few things in the last decade as well.

Namely, the importance of stepping in and correcting

Denise's misconceptions. Which, given his complete lack of it the last time Denise had found them together, seemed remarkably ironic.

The only time the guy had the guts to tell her the truth was when she'd assumed *incorrectly*.

"Hold on, Denise," he said, lifting both hands in an attempt to placate her. "We just—"

"I don't need to know the details of your personal relationships at this point, Bradley," Denise hissed. "But at the very least, I *do* deserve a little bit of respect. I'm not an idiot, I have eyes, we've all moved on. Just give me the common courtesy of telling me."

"We're not together," he finally blurted, then shot Sam a quick look.

All she could do was shrug and shake her head and hope Denise didn't freak out as much as she had the first and only time she'd found Brad and Sam together, and that had been well before the divorce.

Probably the cause of it, even, which Sam was fully ready to admit and accept.

That had been a long time ago. She hoped she'd changed as a person since then, in positive ways, but she wouldn't be getting any reassurance about that right now.

"Funny." Denise looked back and forth between them. "I don't believe a goddamn word out of your mouth, Brad. I wonder why that is."

"Not that you have any reason to believe me over him," Sam added quickly, "but it's the truth. This is strictly platonic."

"Oh, is it?"

Brad looked quickly around the parking lot, and despite it being entirely empty with no one to witness this fun little quarrel of a misunderstanding, he gestured back toward the hotel's entrance. "Can we finish this inside? In private."

"No, you can't just sweep all this under the rug," Denis scoffed. "And I thought you actually gave a shit about what's happening right now."

"Of course I do," he countered. "That's why I'm here. I heard Sam was in Rush, so I found her to ask for her help. She's one of the best, and I know for a fact I can trust her."

"Was that before or after you started fucking her again?"

"Okay..." Sam lifted both hands in concession and tried one more time to sneak back across the parking lot toward her Jeep. "You two obviously need to have this conversation alone."

"You don't need to go just because she doesn't wanna listen, Sam," Brad said. "Don't leave."

She clicked her tongue. "I really should, though."

"Is that true?" Denise asked. The explosive vitriol in her voice had faded just enough to imply she might actually listen this time.

The woman clearly still hated Sam's guts, and Sam absolutely couldn't blame her for it.

It still didn't feel safe to answer the question, even when Denise had aimed it directly at Sam.

When she glanced at Brad and he merely shrugged, the deep plea for help behind his eyes was at complete odds with the casual way he offered non-answers.

I wouldn't be able to make good decisions at a time like this, either, if it was my kid still missing out there. Fuck it.

Sam turned back toward Denise and slowly nodded. "It's true. Brad found me a few days ago. Creeped me out at first, though. I thought he was stalking me."

Denise snorted. "No surprise there."

"Hey, hold on…" Brad interjected.

Both women ignored him.

"But then I figured out it was him," Sam continued, "and he told me about Kody. Asked if I could help him find her because the police hadn't done much of anything. And honestly, I don't trust them to do what needs to be done with something like this, either."

"So you *did* call the police, huh?" Denise asked, glaring at Brad again. "Did you give them the whole sob story, or just the parts that made you seem like a good dad?"

"Ouch," Brad murmured as he dipped his head. "Actually, I told them everything I know."

"What about her?" Denise nodded toward Sam, meeting her gaze with a pert, know-it-all cock of her head. "Did he tell you about his relationship with my daughter?"

"A little," Sam confessed. "But I don't know the whole story."

"No, of course you don't know the whole story. Brad doesn't tell anyone the truth, even when he's begging for their help. So I'm only gonna say this once, Sam, on the small chance that you just ended up being another victim of this man's complete idiocy, and then I'm moving on. Just so there's no confusion, I don't care if he asked for your help. My daughter won't be going anywhere near you. You're the one who destroyed our marriage. You're the one who left her without a father for years. So whatever he's promised you in exchange, you're not getting it, and you can go back to your own life when we're done here."

Sam's mouth popped open in surprise. "Actually, he didn't offer anything."

"Let me guess," Denise continued. "He told you this fantastic story about how close he and Kody are, right?

320

Their father-daughter bond? He's just *so worried* about her and needs to find her now, or he won't know what to do with himself?"

Sam had only enough time to shoot Brad another quick glance and see the man shaking his head with a heavy sigh before Denise continued.

"What a fantastic story that would've made. If it wasn't complete bullshit. I bet he left out the part where he and Kody were estranged, right?"

Sam paused.

Of all the things she might have expected to come barreling from Denise's mouth, that wasn't on the list.

Frowning, she looked at Brad again, but now he wouldn't look either woman in the eye.

"Actually, no," Sam replied. "He didn't tell me that part. I got the impression he and Kody were really close."

"Of course you did," Denise said. "Because the man who told you that is a chronic liar and a piece of shit, as evidenced by the fact that when I finally kicked his ass out, not long after you came into the picture, Sam, Kody was eleven. And he didn't lift a fucking finger, all that time, to see her or speak to her or do anything for her. For almost fifteen years, okay? No contact since she was *eleven*."

"No, I definitely didn't hear that part," Sam said.

"Well, now you know." Denise tossed a hand in Brad's general direction, as if they were discussing a hunk of meat at the butcher's instead of a living man who could hear everything she said about him. "The only reason he knows anything at all about Kody going missing is because I called him about a week ago. Hadn't heard from my daughter in three days, couldn't get a hold of her, and despite my better judgment, I thought that maybe, for some bizarre reason, Kody had found her father, gotten in touch with him, and... Well, if she wasn't *with* him, then I don't know, she might have told him where she was going."

Sam blinked, nodded slowly, then turned toward Brad again. "Funny. That doesn't sound anything like what you told me. Is it true?"

Brad grimaced like a man stuck between a rock and a hard place who'd just realized he wouldn't be able to wriggle himself out of it this time. With another heavy sigh, he ran a hand over his close-cropped hair again and cleared his throat. "Yeah, it's true."

"See?" Denise leaned toward Sam and thrust her hand even farther toward Brad. "Lying piece of shit."

"All right, will you let me finish?" Brad shouted at her, though he was clearly trying not to lose his cool.

Sam felt for the guy insomuch as Denise made it particularly difficult not to become frustrated with her. But he'd been lying to her this whole time.

"Whatever you think you have to say," Denise told him, "it's already been said. This woman doesn't need any more of your lies."

"Well you don't even have all the facts, Denise, so maybe you should shut your mouth and listen for once!"

The audible snap of the woman's jaws clamping shut might have echoed across the empty parking lot.

Even if it didn't really, Sam's mind played the sound over and over again. She now expected Denise to fully lose control of herself and start a different kind of scene that most likely could not be contained to the privacy of this empty parking lot.

The last thing Sam wanted was to get caught up in this. Not here. Not in Rush. Not while she'd done so well to keep her head down and her nose relatively clean the last few months. For the most part.

"Fine, then," Denise said with another flippant toss of

her hand toward him. "Fill me in on the new details, Bradley. I'm sure they'll change everything."

The man sighed, regained an admirable measure of his composure, then turned toward Sam. "What Denise just said ... about Kody being eleven when I left and us losing contact after that—"

"You mean you *abandoning* your daughter?" Denise interjected.

He ignored her, though the muscles of his jaw clenched even more furiously now. "That part's true. I hadn't spoken to Kody for a long time, and I really wasn't a part of her life at all."

Denise scoffed again. "How is that any different than—"

"Until about two years ago," Brad finished. "She found me somehow, for whatever reason, and wanted to talk. At least, that's how it started out. I think she just wanted to know who her father was, or maybe to get a better understanding for the man who walked out on her and her mom. Honestly, when she first reached out, I told her no. What's the point of exposing your own kid to the truth of exactly what kind of piece of shit you are? They've got good enough imaginations. But..."

He scratched the side of his head and cleared his throat again. "But she kept at it. Kept calling me, wanting to meet, until eventually I said okay. Then, well, things just kept going from there, I guess. We started talking regularly. Couple times a month, then it turned into a couple times a week, and for the last six months or so, I've been hearing from her every single day. Even if it's just a text. We've definitely been in contact, and that part wasn't a lie."

Sam pressed her lips together, not knowing what to say or even what to think with these two warring versions of the truth, each composing the full extent of the story as each of Kody's parents saw it. She wasn't sure who to immediately believe, but what Sam *could* tell was that they both fully believed their own sides of the story, so maybe both were true.

"Are you serious right now?" Denise asked, gaping at her ex-husband.

"I've got no reason to lie about this, Denise," he said. "Not when our child's missing."

"Why didn't you *tell* me?"

A bitter laugh escaped him as he gestured toward her. "Really? You think the first thing on my mind was how excited I was to tell you I'd reconnected with our kid? If I had to guess, that's probably why Kody didn't tell you, either."

"And what the hell is *that* supposed to mean?" Denise shouted.

"All right, hold on a second." Sam almost stepped between them, instantly thought better of it, but kept talking anyway because this was the kind of situation that needed to be immediately addressed. For Kody's sake, first and foremost, if not for anyone else's. "Here's what we know, okay? We know Kody's missing. She's not where she was supposed to be, specifically staying at the B&B on the other side of town. She's not answering her phone.

"We haven't found her vehicle, and she's lucky enough to have two parents who care about and who came all the way out here to this middle-of-nowhere town to help each other find her. I get that things are tense and there's a lot going on, but at the very least, we should be able to focus on helping Kody before anything else. Then, after that ... I mean, what happens, happens. We can all agree on that, at least, can't we?"

For the first time, Denise looked embarrassed instead

of filled with nothing but pure rage. She blinked quickly, lowered her gaze away from Sam, and nodded without a word.

Brad, on the other hand, stared at Sam as if she'd just galloped into the parking lot in full on white horse and in full fucking battle armor to rescue him before carrying him off into the sunset.

She gave him a once over and snorted. "Why are you looking at me like that?"

"What?" He blinked quickly before shaking his head. "I'm not…"

"Forget it." Sam turned back to his ex-wife. "Look, Denise, I'm sorry for the misunderstanding here. I had no idea about any of this, really. All I'm doing is helping Brad look for your daughter and make sure she's okay. He's not paying me. I didn't ask for anything in return. I don't *want* anything. I'm good at what I do, and no one should have to fight tooth and nail just to convince someone else that their kid's worth protecting. If you don't believe anything else I say, you can absolutely believe that."

All the frustration and anger and exasperation so deeply etched across Denise's features softened as she stared at Sam. Then the woman surprised them all when she nodded and replied, "I do, Sam. And for that, I'm more grateful than I can say."

Anything else after that would have sounded ridiculously awkward, so instead, Sam cleared her throat and tried one more time to make her way toward her Jeep. "You two need to catch up. Brad, you should tell her everything we've found out so far. We can meet up and talk about next steps later, but right now, I gotta get going."

"Please stay, Sam." Brad took off after her, reaching for her, but she skirted around his grasp and thankfully avoided being physically held back now too. "We can work this out. It's better if you're here."

"It's not," she blurted. "Not now. Take care of this with Denise. It's more important. We can move forward later."

"But you're part of this now," he pleaded, "and I need your help."

"And *I* need to get my ass to a fucking meeting!" she hissed. "Because if I don't, in about three hours from now, I won't be in a state to help anybody with fucking anything, including myself. I gotta go."

Whether it was the words themselves or how vehemently she delivered them, Brad stopped chasing her down and just stood there in the parking lot instead, gaping after her.

Sam could feel his gaze on her as she marched back to her Jeep. She'd managed to avert major crisis mode with both Brad and Denise in close proximity, with Sam herself right there in the middle of it — a position she'd promised herself years ago she would never find herself in again, but here they were.

She didn't blame anyone for that. This time, there was no one *to* blame. Except maybe Brad for not having thought to give Sam the full scope of his relationship with his daughter or the fact that it had only really existed for the last two years instead of Kody's entire life.

She understood why he might not have wanted to reveal all that, but it didn't mean she wasn't still pissed at him for lying to her. By omission, sure, but it was still a lie, and it had still left her high and dry when Denise arrived to spit out the rest of the information Sam absolutely should have had from the very beginning.

It shouldn't have surprised her that Brad Anderson still hadn't outgrown his juvenile habit of lying to women or friends or anyone in his life when he wanted something out of them.

The only good thing, she realized as she booked it in her Jeep toward the Community Center, was that she now knew exactly how she felt about the situation.

Yes, she was pissed at Brad and absolutely validated in feeling that way. Fortunately, how she felt about him didn't change the way she felt about finding his daughter, nor did it affect her determination or her ability to do so.

Everything else aside, finding Kody before something truly awful happened to her was the best-case scenario and number-one priority, and Sam would do whatever she had to do to make that happen.

Even if the other bullshit in between rattled her so hard that she used a meeting as a last-second excuse to get out of someone else's sticky situation.

THIRTY-THREE

Sam

SAM STORMED THROUGH THE FRONT DOORS OF THE RUSH Community Center as if what she'd find inside could solve all her problems all at once.

She definitely would've gone straight to the meeting room if there had been a meeting at this time of day. She knew she was way too early, but saying it out loud had been the only thing she could think of to get Brad off her back while she tried to leave him and his ex-wife to their own devices.

Still, that didn't mean she couldn't use a little support all the same. Even when there wasn't any meeting in session, there were always people at the Community Center during regular business hours. Meredith was one of them.

Sam didn't look for the woman in the meeting room but went straight to the administrative wing and down the hall toward Meredith's office. Before she even reached it, she heard Meredith's muffled voice echoing slightly against the blank white walls and linoleum floors. Her office door was open, but Sam stopped outside it when she realized Meredith's current conversation was on the phone instead of face-to-face with someone else.

A quick peek inside told her Meredith was as visibly upset as she sounded. The woman's eyes were red-rimmed again. She definitely looked like either she'd been crying or she was about to, her voice subdued and almost lifeless when she wrapped up the conversation.

"Well please just keep me informed. I want to know everything you do, all right? Thanks."

She ended her call, set her phone down on the desk, and heaved a massive sigh that sounded more like hopelessness than relief. She still hadn't noticed Sam standing there on the other side of her open office door, so Sam knocked gently and cleared her throat.

"Was that your dad?"

Meredith whipped her head up her bowed head and frowned. "No. No one's seen or heard from him since he left to go help *you* up on the mountain. Apparently, you're the last person who saw him."

Sam shook her head and slowly entered the office. "I didn't. He planned to meet us at the turnoff, but he never showed."

"Uh-huh." Meredith's frown deepened into a critical scowl. "But he was still coming to help you, Sam. What exactly did you get my father involved in all of a sudden?"

"I asked him some questions about the grad student who's gone missing. She was working with Rip, and he offered to help me up the mountain."

Meredith scoffed, a bitter smile creasing her lips as she stared at the paperwork on her desk. "I can't believe you would drag him into one of these bullshit missions of yours, Sam. You have to know by now that they do more harm than good. For everyone."

Sam stopped halfway across the office and folded her

arms, blinking in surprise. "What exactly is *that* supposed to mean?"

"You getting involved in everyone else's business, and that's not even what you do," Meredith snapped. "It happens every time you get involved. You don't actually help, do you? No, you just end up making things worse. Remember how sideways everything went with Beth after you had to insert yourself into *her* life and—"

"Okay, wait just a minute," Sam interrupted. "Let's get this part straight first. Beth was on her own mission, okay? I didn't insert myself into anything. She *asked* for help, and I was the only person in this whole damn town willing to sit down and actually *listen* to a thing she said. Because you and everyone else thought she was completely insane. Beth wanted what she wanted, she wasn't going to stop, and I couldn't have stopped her. But I had nothing to do with the choices she made. You have to know that."

"All I know," Meredith said, slamming her hands down onto the surface of her desk before pushing herself to her feet, "is that Beth was getting better before *you* started screwing around with her life. And now she's gone. And I still don't know what to do with that."

"Oh, come on, Meredith." Scoffing, Sam spread her arms. "We all felt Beth's death. All of us. We all know the tragedy that could've been avoided. None of us wanted to see that happen. It's been months, and you're still trying to blame me for the fact that Beth chose to kill herself? You know what? I'm starting to think you've got something seriously personal against me, because I'm not the one making all these problems. Either that, or ... I don't know. The way you're being such an asshole about it, you'd think you were in love with her or something."

Meredith froze behind her desk, eyes wide. She blinked once before her eyes took on a sudden glint of malice and she sneered at Sam with a whispered, "Fuck you."

More surprised than anything else, Sam stepped forward. "Meredith."

"Don't." Meredith snatched her purse off the end of her desk, slipped the strap over her shoulder, and added, "I'm done making myself available to you, Sam. I'm just ... *done*."

The woman stormed around her desk, across the office, and past Sam without a word before she disappeared in the hallway.

"Shit," Sam whispered.

She hurried after the woman, feeling like an ass now because she'd let her annoyance and irritation start running her mouth for her. That never turned out well for anyone.

"Meredith," she called before the other woman disappeared around the final corner.

This definitely wasn't some kind of bluff designed to end the argument.

This was real.

Even still, Sam followed Meredith all the way out of the Community Center, calling after her one more time once they were outside.

Meredith made a beeline across the parking lot toward for her vehicle, got into it, and slammed the door hard enough and loudly enough that consequent damage to the frame wouldn't have come as a surprise. Then she peeled out of the lot and barreled out of view toward town thirty seconds later.

Then it was just Sam, standing there like an asshole without anything to show for efforts.

On top of that, now she just felt like shit.

That was not how this conversation with Meredith was supposed to have gone at all.

Yes, Sam had grown tired of Meredith blaming her for Beth's death and warning her away from helping anyone for months now. That didn't mean she'd grown tired of Meredith herself. She hadn't come here for a fight, but clearly, that message hadn't been properly delivered. Or received.

For a moment longer, Sam stood at the top of the Community Center's front steps, staring at the last place she'd seen Meredith's vehicle.

She'd have some amends to make for this one. Now, she realized, on top of regretting having upset Meredith so much, Sam also recognized the tightening of guilt in her stomach.

What if what Meredith had said about Rip were true?

What if, simply because Sam had involved the man by asking him questions about Kody, she really had endangered him?

What if she was responsible for Rip going missing and, by default, something had happened to him while he was out there?

With her cheeks burning, her stomach clenched in knots, and her teeth gritted in frustration, Sam returned to her Jeep and left the Community Center to head for downtown Rush. There was only one other place she could think of right now that might be of any help to her whatsoever.

THE REDWOOD RINGS' parking lot was empty, the entrance to the front bar unlocked. Sam entered with one easy tug on the glass front doors. She immediately found Chris standing behind the bar with his weekly checklist on a clipboard in hand while he went over inventory.

He paused when she stepped inside, briefly looked up

from his clipboard, and went right back to work. "We *are* still closed."

"And I didn't even have to ask," Sam said as she headed toward the bar.

"You didn't have to. The fact that you're here means you have questions and I'm the only one who can answer them. Can't think of anything else you'd need from me."

At first, seeing Chris had brought her a much-needed level of relief and comfort.

The minute he'd opened his mouth, though, those feelings disappeared.

Something was wrong.

There was no playfulness in his voice, no smile when he looked up at her. For Chris, everything he'd just said had been standoffish and brusque, nothing like his regular self around her. Plus, he wouldn't look up at her but instead seemed particularly engrossed in his checklist.

Great. What happened here?

Instead of joining him behind the bar, Sam sat at one of the empty barstools and drummed her fingers on the bar, watching him.

Chris didn't say anything. He didn't stop working either.

"So what's going on?" she finally asked. "More problems with the bar that need fixing before we're back in business?"

"Just doing my due diligence. Gotta make sure everything's squared away before I open the doors again. Can't really afford to close down a second time after this. So, I'm making sure I do it all right the first time."

He moved away from her down the bar to inspect the mini fridge and its contents.

"Something else happen?" Sam asked, trying not to sound desperate. He was really acting odd.

"Nothing going on here, Sam. What about you?"

"Oh, you know…" Her fingers tapped across the bar's surface in front of her. "Just trying to stay busy."

"Sounds like you have been."

"What?"

As if he'd been hoping to get to this exact point through their entire conversation, Chris finally set down the clipboard and looked up at her for longer than half a second. "I heard you've been running around town with some guy the last few days."

"Christ…" Sam smothered a groan and briefly dipped her head to rub her temples. "Let me guess. Big Pete thought he'd come check on how the repairs are going and just happened to mention it."

"Something like that, yeah."

"First of all, I'm not *running around town* with anyone," Sam clarified. "And second, Big Pete's just pissed at me again."

"Anything I should know about? For the sake of self-preservation, of course."

"Not as far as I can tell."

They stared at each other for a moment. Sam couldn't help but think Chris looked like he was waiting for her to say something else — to divulge more information or maybe ask the right kind of question. She had no idea what either of those might be, but something was going on here.

Then she realized she really had stopped by the bar looking for Chris, wanting to speak to him, hoping he'd have a little free time to spend with her.

She'd actually come here looking for comfort, and not the kind she was going to get while sitting on one side of the bar while he did inventory on the other.

Clearly.

"So the bar's still closed for now?" she asked.

"And you'll hear all about it when we're back open," he replied gruffly.

"You're not expecting anyone to come by today? No service providers or contractors or anything?"

Chris looked up at her again, this time with a flicker of a curious smile at the corner of his mouth. "Why the sudden interest in my tremendously boring duties as a bar owner, Sam?"

"I don't actually give a shit about all that." She slipped off the stool and headed around the end of the bar, holding his gaze. "Like I said, though, I'm just trying to stay busy. Looking for ways to pass the time now that I'm temporarily out of a job."

He set the clipboard down again. "You came *here* for that?"

Sam glanced toward the swinging doors that led into the kitchen and then farther back through the building. "Honestly, I was thinking more of finding it upstairs…"

Pursing his lips, Chris studied the newly tidied bar, then scanned the empty front room and cleared his throat. "Yeah, I guess inventory can wait."

By the time he hurried away from the bar to head after her, Sam had already slipped through the swinging kitchen doors to make her way toward the back staircase, grinning.

THEY LAY in bed together afterward in Chris' apartment above Redwood.

Sam silently patted herself on the back for having pinpointed exactly what she'd needed as a positive outlet for her growing frustration this morning.

Now she lay on her back with the thin sheet pulled up over her chest and her hands folded behind her head, studying what she could of Chris' bedroom without moving. "This is new."

"What is?" With a light chuckle, he rolled onto his side to face her, propping his head up in one hand.

"I'm just realizing this is the first time I've seen your place under natural lighting," she said. "You know, like during the day."

"If you're gonna try to tell me that has an effect on performance too, we might have a problem. 'Cause I'm just not buying it."

"I didn't say anything about performance," she said with a laugh. "You got nothing to worry about."

"Just the natural lighting, apparently."

She smirked and closed her eyes, letting herself sink into the comfort of being here, just the two of them, where they didn't have to pretend to be anything else than whatever they wanted in this exact moment.

For the first time, Sam could actually acknowledge that comfort in the safety she felt around Chris without feeling depressingly guilty about it or terrified of what it might mean in the future.

For the first time in a long time, she didn't worry nearly so much about letting herself get close, and that was okay.

"Listen," Chris said. "About Big Pete coming in to tell me what you've been up to lately..."

Sam huffed out a sigh. "He's just trying to start shit. You know that."

"Sure, I do. But I still have to ask. Was it true?"

"That I've been running around town with some other guy?" she asked with a chuckle. The laugh died the second she looked at him beside her, his eyes wide with genuine curiosity and a small amount of concern behind them. "Kind of an odd topic to bring up right after sex in the middle of the day, but okay. If we're defining *running around town* as giving rides and helping him look for his missing daughter, then yeah. It's true."

"Who is he?"

Sam almost laughed when she noted the closest thing to jealousy she'd heard in Chris Nelson's voice since they'd met. "He's an old Army buddy, Chris. We served together, and that's it."

"All right. If you say that's what he is. I'm just hoping I'm not some … stand-in for this other guy."

"What?" She rolled her eyes. "No, of course not. There's nothing between him and me other than we used to work together. A long time ago. He figured out I was here in Rush when he realized his daughter was missing, and he asked me for help, Chris. That's it."

"Okay." He studied her face for a moment, then reached out to trail a finger across her bare shoulder. "I believe you. I just think you could've said something and corrected me when I assumed this friend was a woman."

"You're right. From here on out, I'll correct every single misconception that comes out of your mouth without fail. I promise."

Chris laughed, pushed himself up off his side, and leaned over her to kiss her again.

THIRTY-FOUR

Charles

PRESENT DAY

"DAD, are you done yet? I'm *starving*."

"Hold on, Frankie. I'm almost done. Just got a few more..."

Charles loomed over the printed papers, unclipped case files, sheets of scribbled notes, and photos he'd spread out all over the kitchen table, his focus centered entirely on studying the puzzle he'd been trying to put together for the last six years with zero results.

"Seriously?" Frankie stomped into the kitchen, stopped on the other side of the table, and picked up one of the pages. "It's late. We were supposed to eat, like, an hour ago."

"We will," Charles replied absently. "I just need a few more minutes."

"You said that an hour ago."

"Damnit, Frankie! Can't you see I'm busy? I'm still working. Will you just — Hey, put that down! What are you *doing*?" Charles skipped around the table and snatched the paper from his son's hands before slapping it back down in place again.

His son glared up at him and said nothing.

Charles sighed. "Look, I'm sorry I snapped at you. I just need to focus on this. I'm really onto something this time, and all I need is—"

"Forget it." Rolling his eyes, Frankie spun around and marched across the living room. His pounding footsteps echoed up the stairs and down the hall to his bedroom before he slammed the door shut behind him.

Charles hardly noticed any of it. He was far too involved in the details of these now six unsolved cases of missing women in and around Rush.

Missing women he knew in his bones had all been abducted and murdered by the same assailant over the last thirty years.

He was so close to solving these, to figuring out what happened to Rose, now that he had more current information with the most recent missing woman. Maybe if he was fast enough, he could put all the pieces together before Kody had to die too.

Nobody in his life seemed to understand that.

His intense concentration was interrupted again by a brief knock on the door, followed by the soft squeal and click of it opening and shutting again. Then Patty appeared in the entrance to the kitchen. "Chuck?"

"I'm busy," he snapped.

"I can see that," she calmly replied. "But there's a difference between busy and obsessed, babe. Okay, I think it's time for you to take a break."

"I don't *need* a break, Patty. What I need is to figure out what the hell I'm missing. I can see it. It's right here in front of me. I just have to find the last piece. I know I can find it. I have to…"

She gently touched his shoulder from behind and guided him away from the table to face her. "Charles. Take a break."

He frowned, skimmed all the papers covering the entire surface of the kitchen table, then blinked up at her again. "What are you even doing here?"

"Oh, nice of you to ask. I'm here because your son called me, Chuck. He's worried about you. And he's hungry." She nodded toward the kitchen island. "So I brought pizza."

"Oh, shit. Thanks for that."

"You're welcome." Patty pulled gently on his arm again. "Now why don't you put all this away for now? I'll set the table, and we can have dinner."

"I can't put it all away." He gestured toward the semi-organized mess. "I can't. I've got it all set out in the most efficient way."

"Fine, forget the table. We have the island and the bistro chairs. I'll set our places there instead tonight. Come on. Can you grab us all some waters, at least?"

"Yeah. Sure." Charles walked aimlessly across the kitchen, his mind constantly turning back to the facts of six surrounding six open-ended and unsolved missing persons cases he knew in his core were all connected.

Patty clinked around in the kitchen, pulling out plates and napkins and setting places for them at the island. Just when she was about to call upstairs for Frankie, the ten-year-old bounded down the stairs with an echoing crash like a stampede of rhinos in the house and skidded to a stop as he entered the kitchen.

"Frankie, come on," she called after him anyway. "No running in the house. You know that."

"Yeah, I do," he said. "I just thought it was 'stop paying attention to the rules' day or something."

That finally ripped Charles out of his thoughts, and he turned around to shoot his son a warning stare. "That's enough. Patty came over with pizza, so you need to say thank you and be polite. Hear me?"

Frankie marched toward the kitchen island and the open box of pizza, looking right up at Patty. "Thank you. Otherwise, I would've starved to death."

"Frankie..." Patty sighed and watched him closely, not sure exactly how to handle that, because she'd been worried about the same thing for days now. She didn't stop him either when the boy grabbed a plate, dropped three hulking slices of pizza onto it, and turned around to carry his meal back upstairs.

"Hey," Charles called after him. "We're having dinner together. Come sit down."

"Why?" the boy called over his shoulder without slowing. "You're just gonna sit there and think about work anyway. It's not like you can't wait to get back to *that*."

More clomping footsteps up the stairs, another slam of the door, and Charles let out a heavy sigh. "I just can't win with that kid."

Patty stared across the kitchen at the living room beyond, her gaze captured by the entire far wall of the living room almost completely covered in more scribbled notes and drawn lines and six Missing posters of six different women. "Can you blame him?"

"Seriously?" Charles stuffed almost half the first slice of pizza into his mouth, chewed it way too quickly, and swallowed before washing it down with a half-full glass of water. "You're taking his side now?"

"Honestly, it's hard not to when a ten-year-old boy has

342

to call someone *else* for dinner because his own father refuses to feed him."

"I'm not refusing, Patty. I'm just busy. You know what? My parents used to make me wait till eight or nine in the evening sometimes before I got my dinner, and if I ever asked for food or talked to them the way he just talked to me, I'd be in my bed right now. With an empty stomach. Nursing a stinging cheek instead."

"You are not your parents, Chuck," she said. "You're Frankie's parent, though. He needs his father, and right now, you're—"

"Right now, I'm trying to find the connections between these women," Charles said as he walked into the living room, cramming the second half of the pizza slice into his mouth. He stopped a few feet away from the wall, holding his plate in both hands, and studied the pictures.

Patty hopped down off the bistro chair pulled up to the kitchen island, leaving her partially eaten pizza behind on the plate because now what little had remained of her appetite was gone too. "Okay, this isn't easy for me. I've been keeping my mouth shut, hoping you'd come around. That you'd see what's going on here. But at this point, Chuck, I'm getting really concerned."

"Tell me about it," he muttered. "All these different pieces... They *almost* fit together, but not quite. And now this last young woman, this Anderson girl? Six years since the last one, and she was a lot more established here in town than—"

"I'm not talking about the damn cases, Charles!" Patty shouted as she stopped beside him and grabbed his arm. "I'm talking about *you*."

He turned toward her and searched her face. "What about me?"

"I'm worried about you. About you diving into these

343

cases again. You're getting yourself all worked up. I mean, you remember what happened right after Rose left, don't you?"

"She didn't leave," he snapped. "She was taken. I know she was taken, and I thought you believed me."

"I did. I *do*." Patty grabbed his empty plate, set it on the coffee table, then took both his hands and held them just as fervently as she held his gaze. "I do believe you. But this is starting to look a lot like it did back then. Frankie's a lot older now. He might not remember everything from six years ago, but he remembers enough. And he's scared, Chuck. He thinks he's losing his dad."

Charles rolled his eyes. "He's not losing me."

"He's not old enough to know the difference," she said. "And honestly, I'd argue that yes, this is bordering on obsession again, honey. And if it gets that bad again... Last time, you managed to pull it all together so you could keep Frankie with you. Your son. That's what's most important. But this time, if you let this happen again, Charles, it's gonna be a lot harder to win that custody battle a second time. Your sister's gonna end up with Frankie, and you'll be alone, and I know that's not what you want."

"I won't be alone," he said. "I have you."

Patty raised her eyebrows and fixed him with an otherwise deadpan expression. "Not if you keep going down this road in the same way."

He ripped his hands out of her grasp and turned away to face the wall of Missing posters again. "Thanks for the support."

"You know I support you, Chuck. What I *can't* support is you diving down this rabbit hole that has no conceivable end."

"I don't need reminding, Patty!" he shouted. "Jesus

Christ, I'm trying to solve these cases. I'm trying to fix this!"

She slowly shook her head. "That's not your job."

"No, you're right. It's the police's job. And they're failing at it. Might not be my profession, I'm not getting paid for it, but this *is* my business, Patty. This is my *wife*."

His final word hung in the air between them before she took a step back. "Your *late* wife."

Gritting his teeth, Charles scoffed and looked back up at the posters. "You know what I mean."

"Actually, I don't think I do anymore. I don't understand any of this. I have no idea why you can't be in the here and now, Charles. With us. With your son. And with me. Yes, your wife went missing, and it was a terrible tragedy. You and Frankie will never be the same. But if you can't move on, what's the point of any of this?"

He couldn't look at her, it was too much, and she just didn't understand. She couldn't.

Charles had to do this. There was no other option.

"I can't have this conversation right now," he said. "You're obviously worked up, and I have a lot of work to do."

"No, it's fine. Forget it. *I'm* the one being unreasonable now. I'm obviously standing in the way of the only thing you want right now, so I'll just remove myself and save you the trouble."

She stormed across the living room, through the kitchen, and jerked the front door open. A muffled sob filtered through the house before the door slammed shut.

Charles barely heard the rev of her car's engine outside before Patty drove off, leaving behind an almost full box of still-steaming pizza.

It was her own damn fault if she couldn't see where he was coming from.

These cases had to be solved. The serial killer clearly had to be stopped. The Rush police hadn't done shit about it six years ago, or every five years before that for the last three decades, and they clearly weren't going to do anything about it now. Even when another young woman had gone missing and there might still be time to find her and save her before she ended up like all the others.

Before she ended up like Rose.

With a trembling hand, Charles pulled his cell phone from his back pocket, scrolled through the few saved voicemails in his inbox, and pressed play on a very specific message left there six years ago.

Rose's voice played through his phone's speaker, her words oddly slurred but not incoherent as she told him something about an appointment and asked him to pick Frankie up from daycare at Juana Aguayo's house.

The last things she'd ever said to him, and even then, Charles had failed to be there for her. He'd failed Frankie. He'd failed everyone.

There was no coming back from that until he made this right.

His eyes burned, his vision blurred a little, and he sniffed just as a small shape appeared in on the far side of the living room.

"Where's Patty?" Frankie asked.

With another quick sniff, Charles swiped at his eyes with the back of a hand and stuffed his phone back into his pocket. "She left."

"Why?"

"Because she's emotional," Charles said, dismissing the whole thing with a brusque flip of his hand. "If she wants to storm out, that's on her. How's the pizza?"

When he finally turned away from the wall of Missing posters to look at his son, he found Frankie glaring at him again. Not just in annoyance this time — the kind that seemed far too mature to come from a ten-year-old — but now with a fierce anger that quickly brought tears to the boy's eyes. His bottom lip trembled.

"Why do you have to *do* this?"

"Frankie... It's just... You wouldn't understand."

"No, I *don't* understand. Because you never even try to explain it to me. You don't even *talk* to me, and then you just told Patty to go home? She just got here!"

"I didn't tell her to leave, son. She got frustrated and left all on her own."

"Yeah, because of *you*!" Frankie shouted. "That's what you do! You just ruin everything. You're wrecking my whole life, and now I'm stuck here with you, and you can't even make me dinner or eat pizza with me or pretend like you care about me at all!"

"Don't be ridiculous. Come on. Of course I care about you."

"Doesn't seem like it." The boy sniffed. "All you do is work. And then ... what? Some other lady goes missing, everyone's worried about her, and you think you're the one who has to find her? Who *cares* about all this stupid crap?"

"Watch your mouth," Charles snipped.

"It's the dumbest thing ever!" the boy shouted, his fists clenched tight and his face reddening more by the second. "Why can't you just get over it, huh? Mom wasn't kidnapped. Nobody took her. She just *left*!"

"You don't know what you're talking about," Charles growled.

"She left you, and she left me," the boy continued. "She just didn't love us anymore, and she went somewhere else, and you can't handle it, so you have to ruin everything else. *I* handled it, Dad, and I'm ten! Why can't you just let it go?"

A pain so startlingly acute and heavy pierced through Charles' chest. For a split second, he thought he might be having a heart attack and instantly regretted cramming that slice of pizza into his mouth one half at a time.

But then he saw the tears streaming down his son's furiously red cheeks and realized this was a different kind of heart pain altogether.

"Frankie." His voice broke on that one word as he stepped toward his son, then he cleared his throat. "Listen, buddy. It's not as simple as all that."

"Yes, it is!" Frankie screamed. "But you don't want anything to get better, so it never will!"

The kid spun on his heel and raced upstairs again, his muffled cries echoing back down behind him until, for the third time tonight, as far as Charles was aware, he slammed his bedroom door shut.

Only this time, Charles also clearly heard his son flopping down onto his squeaky mattress and screaming into his pillow.

At least it was a relatively healthy outlet for the boy's frustration.

Charles just didn't have it in him right now to try to comfort his son. No, once he'd put all the pieces together, once he'd solved these cases and found out what had really happened to Rose, *then* he could concentrate on the present.

Until then, he just didn't have enough of himself to give to every other facet of his life trying to pull him in what felt like a hundred different directions all at once.

So he returned to the kitchen table and studied the notes and case files and photographs of all six missing persons cases.

He didn't notice when the sound of Frankie crying in his bed upstairs finally stopped.

The only thing that broke his attention again was when his phone rang in his back pocket, and he hastily pulled it out. He didn't bother to look at who it was before accepting the call.

"Hello?"

"It's me." Patty sounded like she'd spent all day crying, though it had only been about half an hour.

Charles looked at his watch and mentally kicked himself. No, it had been more like two hours.

"Hey," he said. "Listen, Patty, I—"

"No, you don't have to say anything. I wanted to say a few things, and we don't have to make a big deal out of it. I just want you to hear it all from me, and then I'm going to bed."

"Okay." Charles pulled the chair up from under the table and sat in it for what might have been the first time all day. Only then did he realize his legs were killing him.

"First," she said, "I don't want there to be any confusion about these missing women and unsolved cases. You know how I feel about it. I don't like how much of an obsession this is becoming again for you. It's dangerous, and I don't want to see you or Frankie get even more hurt than you already have been.

"But I *do* understand. I know how important this is to you. I know why you can't just let it go. And I care about you, Chuck. So I'm behind you on this. If it's what you need to do, it's what you need to do, and I'll help however I can."

Hearing those words, all the fight deflated out of him in a single moment. All his defensiveness and his irritation with the rest of the world that just couldn't get it through their thick heads that this was something *he* had to do.

Now finally, someone was telling him what he'd been

waiting to hear for the last six years, and the worst part was that it had taken this long to hear it.

"Chuck?"

"Yeah, I'm—" He cleared his throat and had to try again. "I'm here. Thank you."

"You're welcome. And that leads to the other reason I called you. I just heard from my contact with the police, Chuck, and I … well, it feels important enough to tell you. It feels like something you should know. Two vehicles were just pulled out of a gorge up the mountain. They're still investigating, but it could mean something."

Charles' heart thumped in his chest, and he sat up straighter at the table. "It could definitely mean something."

THIRTY-FIVE

Sam

"IF YOU'RE STILL TRYING TO FIND WAYS TO PASS THE TIME, like you said... Wanna stay for dinner?"

Sam finished tugging her jeans on and buttoning them before she turned around to fix Chris with an apologetic smile. "Maybe another time. It's late. I should be getting home."

"It's nine o'clock, Sam," he said. "Since when did that start counting as late?"

"Since I actually haven't been home all day. And Dog's probably worried out of his mind by this point, you know? Seems like every time I leave Birdsong, he falls into an existential crisis."

Chris snorted. "Poor Dog."

"Tell me about it." Sam shrugged her light canvas jacket over her shoulders, then hurried toward him and surprised them both by standing on her tiptoes to place a quick kiss on Chris' cheek. Her eyes widened when she realized what she'd just done and how effortless it had been in the moment. Then she cleared her throat and tried to cover it all up again, even when Chris made no effort whatsoever to hide his blooming smile.

"So, I'll see you later, then," she said.

He turned a playful frown onto her. "I hope so."

"Don't look at me like that."

"Like what? I'm actually feeling happy about something. That bothers you?"

Sam rolled her eyes. "Forget it. Let me know when we're back open for business, yeah?"

"That was the plan all along," he called after her as she hurried across his apartment.

Chris leaned back against the living room wall with his arms folded and watched her cram her feet into her sneakers.

She could feel him watching her. She could practically feel that ridiculous smile she couldn't help but find annoyingly cute and had to break that weird silence with something. "Hey, I've got a question for you."

"Of course you do."

"Have you heard anything about this commune-type place just east of town?"

"Yeah, actually," he said. "Real off-the-grid kinda spot. Hillside Farms or something like that."

Sam finished tying her laces and stood fully upright. "Know anything else about it?"

Chris shrugged. "They grow a whole lot of produce, from what I've heard. Vegetables, mostly. All kinds of farm-to-table stuff. They've got a stand on the side of the highway, farther out by their property, and I think they might have actually started selling to that café on the corner in town."

"So just a bunch of farmers then?" Sam nodded, her bottom lip thrust out in an over-exaggeration of hard thinking. "What about any other rumors about the place? Heard anything from the guys or around the Redwood about the commune being some kinda front for, you know … something else?"

Chris raised an eyebrow. "Like what?"

She playfully rolled her eyes and turned away from him to face the door. "I don't know, Chris. That's why I'm asking."

"Nope," he said, following her toward the front of his apartment. "Unfortunately, I haven't heard any new conspiracy theories about vegetable-growing commune cults in Northern California. Sorry."

She couldn't help but laugh as he opened his apartment door for her. "Yeah, I can hear it in your voice just how sorry you are. Try not to let it ruin your night."

"Well if it starts to, I know exactly who to call to come out and make me feel better."

With a snort, Sam hurried down the stairs and let herself out of the Redwood Rings.

SHE'D ONLY BEEN DRIVING out of town for five minutes before her phone rang.

It was Brad.

Not knowing what this conversation had in store or how heated it might get even over the phone, Sam decided it was best to pull over along the wide shoulder through the center of town to answer it. Otherwise, she had a feeling Brad would just keep blowing up her phone all night.

"Look," she said when she answered, not even bothering with opening pleasantries, "I know this is important. I know you came up here to ask for my help. But you really need to be with Denise right now. She's in town, and you guys obviously have a few things to work out, and I don't want to be in the middle of—"

"Whoa, Sam, hold on. You don't have to go there, okay? I'm with Denise right now, actually. She's the one who said I should call you."

Sam pulled the phone away from her ear, frowned at the number on her screen just to make sure it really was Brad, then was suddenly grateful she'd decided to pull over for this one.

"Seriously?"

"Yeah. Listen, I normally wouldn't call you this late, but I just got off the phone with Charles. Apparently, the police found two vehicles up in a gorge somewhere. They're pulling them out right now, haven't identified them yet, but honestly, I don't know how to get up there. I wouldn't be able to give Denise accurate directions, anyway, so we were hoping you might—"

"I'm on my way," Sam blurted. "Give me, like, three minutes."

TRUE TO HER WORD, Sam pulled up in front of the hotel in under five minutes. Admittedly, she'd been driving a little over the speed limit, but she could live with that. The bulk of the Rush Police Department's attention and resources were being pulled up toward that gorge tonight, anyway.

More than anything else, though, Sam drove quickly because she was flat-out worried.

Though she wasn't the praying type, she silently hoped to whatever existed out there greater than her that neither of these newly discovered vehicles belonged to either Kody or Rip. That would make this whole thing even more of a giant disaster, and she already felt terrible about getting Rip involved in this and possibly being the reason he'd now gone missing in the first place.

When she pulled up at the hotel's front entrance, both Denise and Brad were already standing outside the front doors, waiting for her. They both hurried toward the Jeep and, with zero preamble, let themselves in.

Sam was only marginally surprised by the fact that Denise elected to sit in the front with Sam while leaving Brad to hop into the back.

She figured that was less because the other woman enjoyed her company and more because she didn't enjoy riding in the backseat of anything.

What surprised Sam even more was the complete change of Denise's demeanor, especially toward her.

"Thank you for doing this, Sam," Denise said, strapping on her seatbelt.

Blinking in surprise, Sam shot her sidelong glance and nodded. "Yeah. Of course."

With her next glance up into the rearview mirror, she caught a glimpse of Brad in the back seat. He met her gaze in the reflection and nodded.

Looks like we're all on the same page for this one. That's nice.

Then they were off.

Charles had given Brad fairly detailed directions for finding the gorge in question. While it would have been difficult for any out-of-towner to find based on those instructions alone, Sam found it with remarkable ease.

When she pulled her Jeep up to the scenic overlook off the highway by the gorge, the shoulder was packed with emergency vehicles — a firetruck, four police cruisers, a tow truck with some serious cable winch capacity, and all the accompanying emergency response professionals.

The gorge was just off an old logging road, which Sam

hadn't visited before, but she knew enough about the area to know they were relatively close to the sawmill up here.

She parked the Jeep at a respectful distance from the other emergency vehicles, then got out.

Denise was right behind her, Brad following shortly after.

The first person on the scene to notice their arrival was Charles. He ducked beneath the police tape stretching across the area and hurried toward Sam to meet her first before anyone else did.

"Hey," he said. "Glad you could make it."

"Thanks for calling Brad about it," she said. "Looks like we might actually have something here."

"Yeah, that could go either way, honestly." Charles grimaced. "I'm here covering the story. This is what I've got so far."

Charles looked over his shoulder at the team of various emergency professionals, all of whom were far more inter-ested in doing their job right now than in paying close attention to what the local reporter was doing with a trio of onlookers beyond the boundaries of what was now being treated like a crime scene.

"Normally," he continued, "this old logging road is closed off. There's a gate about a mile down. You drove through it. It's usually closed and chained off, but some hikers lost their way earlier this week, apparently, and they reported the gate had been vandalized. Or at least it looked that way. The chain was broken, and the gate was hanging crooked off its hinges. Logical conclusion is vandalism, I guess.

"Instead of opting for any kind of police investigation, though, it looks like the sawmill decided to take matters into their own hands. They sent a few men up here to take a look at the gate. Protect the private property. Repair what needed to be repaired. They fixed the gate, then double-checked to make sure no one else was trespassing on the property. Nobody camping out illegally on the road that's supposed to be closed or taking up space once the gate had been broken into. And that's when they found the vehicles down in the gorge."

"And we don't have any idea who these vehicles belong to?" Sam asked.

Charles' frown deepened as he slowly shook his head. "Not yet. But we're about to."

THIRTY-SIX

Sam

THE RUSH PD HAD ALREADY CLOSED OFF THIS PORTION OF the road, blocking it with police cruisers first and then cordoning it off with tape and temporary roadblocks.

None of that, however, was much of a deterrent for the various civilian citizens of Rush who, each of them in their own way, thought it was their own personal business to be here tonight.

Everyone wanted to get a first look at the vehicles currently being pulled up out of the gorge.

Charles led Sam, Brad, and Denise closer to the collection of emergency responders and easily slipped them all beneath the police tape under the guise of his being there as a local reporter and nothing more.

From the way he eagerly watched the goings-on, Sam had a distinct hunch that Charles Putnam had a lot more skin in the game than he was letting on.

She already knew about his wife and the fact that the man truly believed all these disappearances were connected via one thirty-year-old serial-killer streak. For

Charles, she could tell, none of those other disappearances were old. None of them were in the past.

From the terrified expression he tried so hard to hide, she had a feeling the man was reliving the same horrors of the night his wife disappeared all over again.

Surprisingly, though, Charles wasn't the one causing a scene right now and giving the police — namely Chief Colton — a harder time than they already had in pulling up the vehicles.

No, right now that was Meredith Graham.

The woman had clearly received a similar call about the vehicles' discovery, and she'd come up here to get immediate answers as to whether or not one of those vehicles belonged to her father.

As the woman pled with several other police officers to let her pass the tape to get a closer look, Sam noted the glaring change in Meredith's disposition now compared to the way they'd parted earlier today.

The woman was no longer angry. Now, she was purely concerned, her eyes wide and her voice growing in volume every time she assumed saying the same things over and over again, only louder each time, would make the officers understand her better than the time before.

Someone should at least acknowledge that she's here and why.

"That's Rip's daughter, right?" Brad murmured as he stepped up beside Sam, nodding in Meredith's direction. "The one who works the Community Center, yeah?"

"Meredith," Sam said with a nod.

"I just need to see if that's his truck!" Meredith shouted. "Ralph! Ralph, *please*!"

She kept trying to poke her head around the officer currently trying to get her to step back.

It would have been impossible for Chief Colton not to

hear her calling him by name. So he finally turned around and told the officer to go check something else on the scene while he went to speak to Rip's daughter.

"Meredith. This is an active investigation, all right? And a potential crime scene. It's marked off for a reason."

"I get how this works, Ralph," Meredith snapped back. "But you know me. You know my dad. I just need to see if it's his truck, okay? Just let me in to get a good look."

"I can't do that right now," he said, doing an admirable job of keeping his cool despite practically being harangued from the other side of the police tape. "Go home, Meredith. When we know something, we'll call you."

"You'll know something now, and I want to see!" she shouted.

Sam had been watching their conversation with curiosity, so she hadn't noticed Charles slipping away from her, Brad, and Denise before the paper's Senior Editor stood beside Meredith and inserted himself into their conversation.

"She's already here, Chief," Charles said. "She got a call. There's a chance one of those vehicles belongs to her father. Just let her take a look."

"*You're* not supposed to be here, either, Charles," Colton said, his frown deepening. "None of you are supposed to be here."

"I'm here as a reporter," Charles said. "Story for *The Daily Rush*."

"I don't give a shit. This isn't open to the media. However people found out about this, now is *not* the time to barge into an active investigation and start making demands. This has nothing to do with you—"

"This has *everything* to do with me, Chief, and you know it," Charles retorted. "And *I* know this new missing woman is related to Rose's disappearance."

"Come on, man." Colton rolled his eyes. "Not again. Not now."

"I have to know. And I'm staying here to get the full story from the very beginning."

"This is not the way I wanted tonight to turn out," Colton muttered as he forced himself to look away from the civilians causing him even more trouble. "Listen, I need both of you to go home so my men and I can do our jobs."

Then his gaze landed on Sam standing slightly back, with Brad and Denise beside her, and his scowl only deepened. "No. Ah, Jesus, no. What are *you* doing here, Salazar?"

"I'm with Kody's parents," Sam said, gesturing toward Denise and Brad. "It's important for them to see what's going on up here too, don't you think?"

"No. It's important that the law enforcement professionals have enough space to do their jobs," Colton growled. "I think it's pretty damn hard for any of us to do that when we've got civilians just standing around, rubbernecking the whole damn thing and impeding our work."

"We're not in anyone's way, Chief," Charles interrupted. "We're all standing right here. I just wanna see what comes up out of that gorge."

"That's not how this works!" Colton barked.

The loud, grating growl and chug of the cable winch pulling the first vehicle up over the lip of the gorge nearly drowned out everything else.

Then Meredith used the brief moment of distraction as her opportunity to duck under the police tape and head straight for the edge of the gorge.

"Shit. Meredith!" Colton barked. "Get back here. There are rules."

"Don't talk to me about rules, Ralph!" she shouted

over her shoulder, quickly dodging the outstretched hand of another officer attempting to stop her. "My father's missing, and I *need* to see this."

Other officers stepped up in an attempt to stop her too, but Colton gave in and lifted a hand to call them off. "Let her go."

Sam watched the strange interaction between Meredith and the Chief of Police with growing curiosity.

He sure changed his mind pretty damn fast.

Once Meredith was clear of the other officers, she jogged toward the tow truck pulling up the first vehicle just as the hood of that first vehicle emerged from below.

Men shouted. Hands reached out. The cable winch let out a grinding screech before chugging again and redoubling its efforts to lift the rest of its heavy load over the edge.

Meredith's raw gasp was easily heard over all the other noise as she darted forward. "Oh, no," she moaned, bringing both hands up to her mouth. "Oh, no, no, no…"

Colton was beside her in an instant, looking like he wanted to offer some kind of reassurance or comfort, but that clearly would have been a futile effort at this point.

The only thing Meredith could do, just like the other civilians who weren't supposed to be here, was watch in horror as Colton and his officers investigated what they could of the truck that had just been recovered.

It didn't take very long before Colton left the vehicle and approached Meredith again. She stared at him with wide, terrified eyes, but he had to tell her anyway. All it took was one slow, solemn nod and a softly murmured, "I'm sorry, Meredith."

"No!" The woman lurched forward toward the edge of the gorge.

This time, the officers closest to her were forced to

intervene when it looked like she was about to throw herself off the edge of the cliff.

"Oh, my God, no!" she screamed. "Did you find him? Is he down there? Is there a body? Oh, God…"

Colton shouldered his way past his men, pulled Meredith aside, and put his arm around her. "There's no one down there. The truck's empty. It's banged up, but that's his VIN number and his license plate. No sign of a wreck. He could still be out there, okay?"

"Of *course* he is," she said, sniffing and wiping her eyes. "Of course he's still out there. He has to be."

"We'll get forensics working on it as soon as possible," he told her. "In the meantime, Meredith, really, I need you to go home. You've seen everything there is to see here."

It looked like the woman was about to comply, but then the cable winch on the tow truck grumbled and squealed again as its next bit of cargo was steadily pulled up the side of the gorge.

No one moved while the second vehicle rose toward them. Not even Meredith.

But when the Subaru Outback appeared over the edge of the drop, Denise practically screamed.

The sound made Sam jump, yet not before Kody's mother had ducked under the police tape, avoided several officers' attempts to stop her, and run all the way up to the car. "That's her car! Oh, my God. It's Kody's car!"

Sam looked at Brad still standing beside her.

He'd gone completely white, his face a blank, expressionless mask.

It wouldn't have surprised her if his legs gave out beneath him at that moment, but he didn't seem to notice anyone else around him at this point. Not even Sam.

"Ma'am!" Chief Colton shouted this time, turning his

attention onto Denise. "Ma'am, you have to stay behind the tape!"

"That is my daughter's car!" Denise shouted again, pointing as the rest of the vehicle was pulled and pushed and towed up onto the turnoff beside the road. "My *daughter's* car! Do you understand? I'm not leaving until I know what happened to her!"

"It's gonna take us a bit of time to figure out, ma'am," Colton replied. "Please. This is an active investigation. Civilians aren't allowed to—"

"Oh, Jesus, no!" Both of Denise's hands clapped up over her mouth as one of the other officers approached Kody's car to unlock the trunk.

He paused when he looked inside, then glanced back over his shoulder. "Chief?"

"Kody!" Denise screamed before racing past Colton and practically throwing herself at the Subaru's open trunk.

With a shout of surprise and frustration, the officer who'd opened it reeled backward, fighting to keep his balance as this crazed, grieving mother leapt toward him.

Denise's hands thumped down onto the edge of the trunk as she stared inside, gasping for breath and searching every inch of the open space.

Not having moved beside Sam, Brad inhaled sharply and muttered, "Oh fuck…"

"Oh, my God." With a cry, Denise reinforced her grip on the edge of the trunk, now holding herself up from dropping to the ground when her legs wobbled and gave out beneath her. "Oh, my God. It's just her suitcase."

She turned partially around to find Brad still standing on the other side of the tape.

"Just her suitcase!" she shouted, her voice quivering with unshed tears now. "She's not here."

Brad let out one long, heavy sigh and said nothing.

After a quick initial search of Kody's car as well, the officers confirmed no sign of a body in either vehicle or at the bottom of the gorge, but they still had to run forensics on the inside of both vehicles. For now, none of them were any closer to finding either Kody or Rip.

"Mrs. Anderson?" Colton asked, stepping toward her.

"Hanson," she said, straightening away from the Subaru's trunk. "Denise Hanson, actually."

Colton shot a quick glanced at Brad behind the police tape and standing next to Sam. "Got it. Ms. Hanson. I'd like to have you come down to the station with me to answer a few questions. Standard procedure interview with family members who may know something. This could help us search for your daughter. If we could do this tonight, that would be best."

"Um ... sure." Denise blinked furiously, her gaze darting back and forth between Kody's car and the chief's face. "Interview. Yeah, I can ... I can do that. If it'll help, absolutely."

With a nod, Colton left her and strode quickly back down the road toward the police tape cordoning off this crime scene from the rest of the eager-eyed civilian onlookers, none of whom had taken 'go away' as an appropriate command to follow.

"The rest of you," he called out to everyone else at once, which was at this point Meredith, Sam, and Charles, "get your asses back down this mountain, call it a night, and let the Rush PD do our jobs. This is an active police investigation, and unless we call any one of you specifically for questioning or assistance in this, none of you are authorized to involve yourselves beyond this point.

"I swear, if I have to repeat myself about this to anyone I see here right now, I *will* be making arrests for interfering with an investigation, and there *will* be charges brought against you, and you *will* spend at least one night behind bars down at the station. Maybe two, depending on how much lip you give me in the process. Is that clear?"

No one said a word.

Colton seemed satisfied enough that he'd made his point and nodded at Brad. "Mr. Anderson, I'll be in touch with you in the morning. Ms. Hanson?" He turned toward Denise. "Now that I think about it, it might be better if you come down to the station for that interview tomorrow.

"Maybe both of you at the same time so you can go through your daughter's belongings together. Everything will be taken out of her vehicle and processed as evidence, and then we'd like you to help us catalog what's there. Note if there's anything potentially missing from her belongings that might also point us in the right direction as to where she might be now or what might have happened to her. First thing in the morning, I'll give you a call to remind you to come down."

Both Kody's parents nodded, looking similarly shell-shocked, and neither of them could offer any form of verbal consent.

Just as Colton was turning around to head back toward his officers, Sam cleared her throat and stepped toward the line of tape.

"Chief?" she called after him.

He stopped, turned to look at her over his shoulder, and — Sam could have sworn — actively fought not to roll his eyes. "It's over, Salazar."

"Oh, yeah, I know. Both vehicles recovered. You've all done a great job tonight. Can I have a word real fast?"

Scowling again, Colton muttered something to one of his nearby officers, hooked his thumbs through his belt loop, and approached her. "Make it quick."

"There's no coincidence about it, Chief," she told him. "Both of these specific vehicles were dumped here in the same gorge, found at the same time. Kody was working for Rip up at his farm. You knew that, right?"

"Of course I knew that. What's your point?"

"My point is, whoever took their cars and dumped them here... It's the same person. I mean, that's obvious enough after tonight. Whoever has Kody, wherever she is right now, I'm willing to bet damn near anything that Rip's there with her too."

Colton shot a quick look back at the two newly recovered vehicles, then nodded at Sam and for the first time ever didn't look like he wanted to arrest her on the spot just for existing. "I was coming to the same conclusion myself. Which means this has turned into something a lot bigger than any of us thought."

THIRTY-SEVEN

Kody

SEVERAL DAYS AGO...

KODY COULDN'T STOP STARING at the body.

After the pain of being practically crushed by at least two hundred and thirty pounds of man toppling down on top of her, she'd managed to wiggle her way out from under him, and now couldn't bring herself to move any closer.

She didn't know how long she'd been huddling there against the opposite wall of the pit. The only thing going through her mind now was that her captors had just killed someone and dumped his body into the pit as a sign of exactly what they intended to do to her — whenever the hell they decided it was time.

It wasn't just anybody, either.

It was Rip.

He'd found her. He'd come for her. He'd been trying to help her escape. He was the only person who had, and now

369

he was dead, lying there on the other side of the pit in a crumpled heap.

The loss of her one and only attempted rescuer was more painful and more terrifying than the moment she'd found herself trapped down here in the first place.

Her eyes stung with tears that wanted to well up and spill over, but she wouldn't let them.

It didn't matter how much her kidnappers wanted to scare her with this macabre gift or warning or both. She would never let herself break down the way she wanted to. Not while those men were still up there. Not where they could see.

She knew they were still there. Both men made such a ridiculous amount of noise doing god knew what. She just wished it would stop, but there was nothing she could do now.

She couldn't even stop staring at Rip's motionless body down here with her.

The one thing that did get her to stop was completely unexpected.

A sharp, reverberating bang way off in the distance — something that sounded like it could have been a gunshot but from much farther away.

As soon as Kody's conscious mind cataloged the noise as something massive and explosive, a violent rumble moved through the cave and down into the walls and the floor of the pit itself. Small stones, pebbles, and clumps of mud shivered away from the pit's walls around her. A decent portion of them landed on Rip's body. A much larger collection of loosely packed mud trembled in the wall behind her, and she heard the first bits of it sloughing off just in time to leap to her feet and avoid being buried by the pit's thick mud walls for a second time.

Then she stared at the place where she'd just been sitting and couldn't help but wonder what the hell was happening out there on the mountainside.

Was that an earthquake?

What else could have possibly had that same effect?

A low moan rose from the other side of the pit, making Kody jump in surprise before she spun around to stare at Rip's corpse.

The corpse that moved, stirring slightly as it groaned again.

"Holy shit, he's still alive!" she shouted.

Kody leapt across the pit toward him and crashed to her knees beside his mostly motionless form.

How could she have been so stupid, thinking he was dead?

She should have checked him over the instant she realized what had fallen down on top of her, felt for a pulse, and looked him over far before now.

But at least he was still alive. At least she could try to do something about it and help him in whatever way possible.

As carefully and gently as she could, Kody searched the man's unconscious form first to check him over for injuries, which clearly existed, otherwise he wouldn't have spent this whole time unconscious.

She found his phone first, which wasn't useful at all for contacting the outside world without service down here, but it did provide light for her to see by.

She instantly took advantage of the light, using it to get a better look at Rip's current state. He seemed perfectly fine. No clearly broken bones or limbs sticking out at horrifying angles.

Then she shined the light on his head.

A nasty gash stretched from his temple to almost the top of his head. When she gently touched it, her fingers came away sticky with his blood.

More than that, he was still bleeding. A lot.

Kody cursing herself for having been too terrified to use her brain.

This whole time, Rip had been lying there at the bottom of the pit, bleeding from his head, and she'd just thought he was dead and didn't bother to check. She couldn't afford any other stupid mistakes, or this man's death would be on her instead of on the men who'd tossed him down here.

With Rip's phone now lighting the pit for her, Kody hastily rummaged through her pack, looking for anything she could use to help staunch the heavy flow of blood from Rip's head wound. The only thing she could come up with now, the only thing she had on her, was an extra menstrual pad tucked away in one of the side pockets, left over from one of her previous adventures.

In a pinch, it would do the job just as well as anything else.

She ripped open the packaging, tossed aside all the extra plastic wracking, and pressed the thick cotton padding against the side of Rip's head to use as a compress.

Hopefully, with enough pressure that didn't hurt him even worse or freak him out, she could get the bleeding to stop. Then they could move on from the most depressing emergency to what came next.

The first time she checked beneath the pad, the bleeding still hadn't stopped, so she immediately reapplied it and acted on instinct.

"Somebody help us down here!" she screamed. "He's

bleeding! Badly! Please, we need to get him medical attention, or he's going to *die* down here!"

She'd called out on instinct, not thinking about how her captors would respond to her pleas on someone else's behalf — or that they would do anything differently than they'd done for her.

She definitely didn't expect such a quick response, which came in the form of the older man shuffling toward the edge of the pit to look down on them, his stringy gray hair hanging down around the sides of his face like a moth-eaten curtain.

"Please," Kody called as she cradled Rip's head in her lap and craned her neck to look up at the older man. "Please, you have to help him. He's not gonna make it."

The man's eyes flickered back and forth in the dim lighting, his expression impossible to read when it was covered in so much shadow.

The shadows, though, did not hide the older man's gruff clearing of his throat and grotesque hocking before he spat a thick glob down into the bottom of the pit with his prisoners.

Then he disappeared from the edge and from Kody's view, and she fought back another round of tears threatening to burst free.

"I know you're still up there," she called, this time intending for the younger man to hear her, hoping he might act despite his father's continued presence in the cave. "I know you don't agree with what he's doing to us. I know you want to do the right thing. I know you have a conscience and a heart. You brought me my pack, didn't you? That means something. You want everyone to make it out of this alive, and that can't happen if this man doesn't get medical attention *right now*. Please, you have to do something for him."

She didn't necessarily expect a response. She hadn't gotten one in so long, it had become a normal, natural thing for Kody to shout into the ether and hear absolutely nothing in reply.

Only this time, Kody was no longer on her own.

This time, she had someone to help, to protect. It wasn't all on her — or at least didn't have to be, as long as she could get the help he needed.

Rip had found her, after all. If one person had found her, that meant it was possible for others to do the same.

A new flare of hope surged within her, bringing with it more adrenaline-induced energy than she thought her body could provide in its current state.

But she wasn't going to sit here questioning it.

She was going to use it.

Her captors would never help. She already knew that. But now things had changed.

Now, Rip was down here now too, and he'd come with his own stash of resources, however few and meager.

Chances were they were different than her own, and it was time to take inventory again. Together, the two of them might just make it out of here alive, if they played their cards right. If they were smart.

If she could stop the bleeding and keep him from dying so he could help her out of this.

Turning the man over as quickly and gently as possible while trying to keep the padded compress pressed against his temple, Kody searched with her one free hand through Rip's pockets. She'd already found his phone, which now she realized was just about out of battery and wouldn't make it much longer.

Then came his wallet. No use to either of them down here.

A lighter emerged from his front pocket next, followed by a small, tightly wadded-up plastic baggie filled with...

What was that?

Kody lifted the plastic baggie to her nose and sniffed. The familiar scent almost made her burst out laughing despite their dire circumstances.

Leave it to Rip to consider this little baggie one of the most important aspects of being prepared for anything. He was a farmer, after all. It made sense that he had some of his own crop on hand for personal use.

She set the pungent baggie aside with all his other belongings, which didn't amount to much, and she focused instead on keeping the pressure on his head wound and keeping him slightly elevated with his head in her lap and hoping he pulled through.

At this point, hope was once more the only effective tool she had.

But it was better than nothing.

And it was better than where she'd been before her captors had thrown Rip down in here with her, because until she'd seen him looming over the edge of the pit, reaching his hand down toward her, Kody had already lost all hope.

Now, that had changed.

Her hope would only grow more powerful when Rip gained consciousness — *if* he gained consciousness, and she prayed he did. The sooner he recovered from his fall and head injury, which might or might not have given him a mild concussion like hers, the sooner they could both be on their feet, trying something new.

Kody considered herself fairly fit. Barely over a hundred and twenty pounds. Rip was up there in age, sure, but he was strong, worked the farm himself all day, every day, despite his dozens of employees. She could get him back on his feet. She could stand on his shoulders and hoist herself up over the lip of the pit, then she'd figure out a way to get him up, maybe even with her own rope he'd failed to find before their captors had found him.

In a split second, it seemed Kody Anderson had gone from complete hopelessness and terror to renewed by this second chance that had literally fallen right on top of her.

Now, taking care of Rip, getting him conscious again and on his feet, was her new mission, and she devoted everything she had to it.

He didn't make it easy, though.

She sat there for what felt like a ridiculously long time, battling with the urgency to get going and the adrenaline racing through her while also fully understanding the need for patience. The man had a fairly severe head injury. She couldn't just slap him back into consciousness, no matter how much she wanted to.

After a while of him lying in her lap, the bleeding had finally stopped, and Rip started to wake up.

Kody's heart leapt in her chest.

"Oh my God, Rip, you're okay," she babbled. "I was so worried. I thought they threw you down here with me because you — I didn't know you'd been hit so hard in the head. I got the bleeding to stop. Now we just need to put our heads together and think of a way out of this, you and me. I know we can do it. Rip?"

The man's eyelids fluttered, and he moaned again before his eyes rolled back in his head. A few seconds later, he was blinking, starting to take in what little of their surroundings existed. His lips moved in a muttered cadence, but Kody couldn't understand a word he was saying.

"Look at me. Hey." She gently pressed a hand against his cheek and turned his head so he looked right up at her.

"Hey. It's me. It's Kody. You're gonna be okay, all right? We're both gonna be okay. It's the two of us, and we can do this."

Rip's eyes widened, then a slow, almost lazy smile bloomed across his lips. He tried to reach for her face and proved his vision was also affected when he missed. Instead, his fingers closed gently around nothing but air beside her head. "It's you."

Kody huffed out a laugh that sounded both hurried and tremendously relieved. "It's me. You found me. I can't thank you enough for that, but now we both need to figure a way out of here."

"I never thought I'd see you like this." Rip's gaze flittered back and forth across her face, interspersed with his eyes rolling back in his head again before he focused somewhat on the young woman hovering over him. "But I'm glad it's you, Meredith."

"Tell me about it. I'm glad it's *you*. I can't believe—" Kody stopped herself when his last words fully sank in.

"Wait, who am I?" she asked, then gently patted him on the cheek again to get his attention. "Come on, Rip. Hey, look at me. Who am I?"

His smile flickered in and out, just like his weakening consciousness. "You're a pain in my ass," he murmured through a tired laugh, "but you're still my daughter."

"Oh shit." Kody swallowed, kept the pad pressed against Rip's temple just in case, and sat there at a complete loss for what to do.

Rip was alive, all right, but he was clearly delirious, couldn't tell the difference between the young woman who'd temporarily worked for him for all of a week and his own daughter, who was at least twice Kody's age, if not more. No way could she count on him to get up and walk out of this cave, even if there was no one there to stop them, let alone stand up long enough beneath the weight of her entire body to lift her up to the top of the pit.

They were screwed.

They needed a doctor.

Rip needed help, and if he didn't get it, she had no doubt now that he was going to die.

If Rip died, Kody was pretty sure all hope for her was completely lost as well.

THIRTY-EIGHT

Sam

SAM OFFERED TO DRIVE BRAD AND DENISE BACK TO THE hotel after leaving the top of the gorge with Chief Colton's reassurances that he'd contact them again first thing in the morning. She was more than willing to drive them both around, and neither of Kody's parents tried to argue against accepting this kind of help.

She pulled the Jeep up directly in front of the hotel's entrance so they wouldn't have to walk very far and waited for them to extricate themselves from the vehicle.

Before Brad shut the rear passenger-side door after climbing out, Sam looked back at him. "Hey, if you guys need anything, I'm just a phone call away, all right?"

He looked at her with glazed eyes and attempted one hell of a pitiful smile. "Thanks, Sam. For that. For all this."

"No problem. Get some rest, huh? We'll get more answers tomorrow."

"Goodnight." Then he shut the door and was on his way to the hotel entrance, coming up behind Denise.

Before she even reached the hotel's front doors, Kody's mom stopped in her tracks and burst into tears. She

379

buried her face in both hands and clearly tried to quiet her own sobs but didn't do a very good job of it.

Sam was more than sympathetic to the situation. No one could blame a mother for being brought to tears by her worry over the welfare of her child. It didn't matter how old that child was or how long they'd been on their own as an adult. It was just one of those truths of being a mother, something Sam would always understand.

What she didn't understand, though, was what Denise must have felt right now. Yes, the woman was upset. Yes, she feared for her daughter's safety and even Kody's life, but she also had someone there to comfort her through the loss.

Not even the loss, really, but simply the fear of it. The worry that she would get word from the police with no hope behind it, merely the sad, undeniable confirmation that her daughter was gone.

Sam knew what that felt like. Hell, she'd been reliving that feeling every day for years, putting herself through the proverbial meat grinder because she'd felt for so long that she deserved it, that she had to suffer if she'd ever loved her daughter at all.

But she didn't have any experience whatsoever with being comforted through those harrowing emotions. By anyone.

When she'd lost her Sophie, Sam had had no one. She'd been all on her own, without a shoulder to cry on or a loving arm to wrap around her the way Brad wrapped his arm around Denise now as he guided her through the hotel's front doors.

No, Sam had been completely alone. She had suffered alone and grieved alone and made so many wrong choices alone. With no one around to warn her away from those choices.

No one to hold the kind of space for her that allowed someone grieving like that to make better choices for themselves, either.

It would have been nice to have some kind of support around Sophie's death the way Denise and Brad had each other. Even if they weren't still together, they shared the same daughter. Unlike Sam and Ian, they didn't completely hate each other's guts.

That was what had come between Sam and her daughter's father in the end. Then again, neither of Kody's parents were responsible for the death of their only child, either.

With a heavy, sinking weight in the pit of her stomach, Sam watched the preemptively grieving parents until they disappeared through the hotel's front doors. Then she peeled out of the parking lot with no idea where she wanted to go or what she wanted to do.

Her first thought was that maybe she should talk to someone, to not be alone while thoughts of Sophie flooded through her mind while an unsolved missing person's case like this was so fresh and so new and taking up nearly all her free time. But the more she thought about it as she drove, the more she realized she wasn't actually as negatively affected by the similarities as she would have been even just a few months ago.

She'd been thinking about Sophie today, yes. Of course she had. She was helping an old friend look for his missing daughter, feeling his pain and his fear and his urgency right along with him as if it were her own from years ago. At the same time, she was so much more disconnected than she'd ever been before when something reminded her of her baby.

This felt exactly the same as the last time Brad had

mentioned Sophie in a barbed quip about trying to offer reassurances to the parent of a missing child.

When he'd said that the other day, it had definitely tugged on her heartstrings. She'd thought about her Sophie and felt the pain and longing and love that no longer had anywhere to go.

But it hadn't completely destroyed her.

Nor was it completely destroying her tonight, and that was still entirely new.

Maybe she was moving through this, after all.

Maybe Sam would end up being relatively okay, and that was a hell of a lot better than being a complete fucking mess.

Maybe she didn't need to talk to anyone about what she felt, about maybe wanting to use, maybe not, about whatever changes she was going through personally at the moment.

She probably would have called Hector again if she'd been feeling any of those things, but the onslaught of negative and exhausting emotions never came.

Then a new idea hit her, which ended up being a good reason for her to call her sponsor anyway.

She sent the call to his number, then figured it was probably better to pull over for this conversation. Better safe than sorry, especially now, right?

He answered almost immediately.

"Hey, Sam. Everything all right?"

"Yeah, everything's fine. No emergencies, no issues. It's kinda weird."

"Well enjoy it while it lasts," he said with a chuckle. "So then to what do I owe the pleasure of this evening phone call?"

"I need your help, actually."

"Where are you?"

Sam peered through the front windshield. "At the corner of Main Street and Nightingale."

"Wait right there," he told her, his voice as calm and even as ever. "I'll be there in five minutes or less, and we can talk face to face. It's always better that way, if you ask me."

"I'll be here."

True to his word, Hector pulled up at the cross streets in barely under five minutes and left his truck engine rumbling away behind her Jeep. He left his truck, marched towards Sam's vehicle, and opened the passenger-side door before climbing up into the seat beside her. Then he pulled the door shut, let out a contented sigh, and turned toward her with a gentle smile. "What's up?"

Sam shrugged. "Now that we're here, this definitely feels like something I could've just asked you over the phone."

"I told you I'd be here in person. I prefer not to talk over the phone anyway, if I can help it. Better for the soul to actually see the face of the one you're talking to. Feels real."

"Okay…" Sam let out a wry chuckle and ran a hand through her hair. "I'm wondering if your mom might be willing to talk to me tonight. I don't know if it's too late, but I have some questions for her, and they'd really help me out with this … unofficial case of mine, I guess. You know, what I've been working on. Helping a friend."

"This the Army buddy of yours?" he asked.

"His daughter went missing almost two weeks ago. She was working up here." Sam shook her head. "And I get that your mom hasn't met her and doesn't know anything about this young woman, but I think there might be some connections to someone she did used to know.

And I don't wanna just go storming up to her in her home, asking random questions about the past."

"Wouldn't be random," he said. "Or a problem. But I'm glad you asked all the same. Come on, you can follow me back to my place."

"Right now?"

"It's ... what, ten thirty?" Hector flashed her a crooked smile that lasted all of two seconds. "Trust me, Mamá Juana puts most of these college kids to shame with her late-night hours. It'll be fine, Sam. I promise."

Without waiting for her to agree to driving out to the Aguayo family property to speak to his mother, Hector leapt out of the Jeep, got back into his truck, and slowly pulled out to give her plenty of time to catch up and stay on his tail as they headed toward the other side of town.

THE AGUAYO FAMILY COMPOUND, as Sam had come to think of it, looked almost exactly the same as the one and only other time she'd been here. At least half a dozen vehicles were parked on the perfectly manicured lawn spanning the property, which also housed three different manufactured trailer homes, all with their own individual spaces but clearly all part of the same property. LED lights of various bright colors were strung up on all three of the front porches, some of them flashing in the darkness. While Sam could clearly hear several voices from one, two, or all three houses rising in friendly and easygoing laughter, the general vibe around the place didn't feel so much like a party this time.

Maybe it was the lack of *mariachi* music being played at deafening volumes.

When she got out of her Jeep, Hector was already

waiting for her with his hands in his pockets. He nodded toward the middle house, and Sam silently followed.

She didn't know what she expected from walking in on the Aguayo family compound — at least four generations of Aguayos all living together, mostly working together, and sharing their lives as one of the longest-standing immigrant families in Rush. She certainly hadn't expected to be greeted with so many beaming smiles, nods, family members standing to shake her hand and tell her their names with a happily added, "*Mucho gusto*," before she moved on to the next.

"*Quién es?*" a loud, matriarchal voice called from what Sam could only assume was the kitchen.

"Mamá," Hector replied as he ushered Sam along with him, "I'd like you to meet someone."

Then they were in the kitchen, and though she hadn't met the woman personally, Sam already knew there was no mistaking Juana Aguayo for anyone else.

Hector's mother was shorter and physically smaller overall than Sam had expected, but her petite frame bustling around the kitchen exuded authority softened by the big-heartedness and ever-watchful omniscience that seemed to go hand in hand with any large family's matriarch.

Sam couldn't pin it down exactly, but she also noticed a fieriness to the woman as Juana moved about, tossing handfuls of ingredients into pots bubbling away on the stove, filling the kitchen and the entire house with the unmistakable scent of cooking onions and freshly chopped cilantro with a hint of Mexican spices underneath it all.

Juana still faced the stove when Hector and Sam entered the kitchen, intermittently wiping her hands on the brightly colored apron covered in geometric patterns between stirring a ladle in a huge pot and adding more ingredients to something else.

"*Obviamente, mi hijo*," she said, "*pero no conozco a nadie que no todavía haya conocido*."

Hector stopped in the kitchen with that kind of smile only a grown man in his mid-fifties could fix on his own mother. "That's because you haven't met her yet. This is Sam."

Juana spun away from the stove, wiping both hands on her apron again. Her gaze landed instantly on Sam's face before she looked Sam up and down with a knowing smile. Then she winked at her son. "*Oye, mi vida. Es demaciado joven para ti, no?*"

Hector forced a cough to cover up his laughter. "Not necessarily."

"What did she say?" Sam muttered from the corner of her mouth as she tried to smile.

Hector leaned toward her and whispered, "She says you're too young for me."

Sam couldn't help but snort. "I see. Definitely just friends," she added a little louder this time so Juana would hear.

"*Momento, momento*." Juana finished bustling around the kitchen, then finally removed herself from all the delicious-smelling food to come meet Sam for real.

"*Mucho gusto*, Sam," she said, holding out her hand.

"Oh." Sam took the woman's hand, which came with its own surprisingly firm grip, then shot Hector another quick, uncomfortable look. "I don't actually speak Spanish. At all. Sorry."

"*De verdad?*" Juana's eyes widened, then she fixed her son with a playful frown before finally releasing Sam's hand. "Well, it's very nice to meet you. Any friend of

Hector's is always welcome here. I am surprised you don't know Spanish."

Sam wrinkled her nose. "I'm adopted. And I guess my parents didn't exactly feel it was important for me to know any other language, so..."

"*Entonces,* you can practice your Spanish with Hector, *sí*? He's a very good teacher, my son. Extremely patient."

Sam's smile widened with very little effort. "I definitely know *that*."

"It will be good for you both." Juana wagged a finger between Sam and Hector. "He gets to teach. You get to connect with your roots."

Sam felt like a complete idiot when all she could do was shrug, at a complete loss when Juana burst into Spanish and back into English again.

"Everybody wins," Hector translated with the faintest hint of a smile lingering on his features before he cleared his throat.

"Right," she said. "Maybe."

He shrugged. "If you ever wanna learn, I'd be happy to teach you."

"Because your mom suggested it?" she shot back before realizing that probably wasn't the best response.

Hector barked out a startlingly loud laugh and shook his head. "Contrary to popular belief around here, Sam, I don't do everything my mom tells me."

"*Cuídate, mi hijo.*" Juana wagged a finger at him again. "Your mother hears everything and sees everything. No matter how old you are. Or how grown up you think you are."

"Of course, Ma'am," he said with a deferent nod, still smirking. "I know that."

A burst of laughter rose from another room in the same house.

Juana's gaze darted in that direction, then she clicked her tongue and rolled her eyes. "Always something so funny to laugh about. Sam, will you be staying for dinner?"

Sam froze, not having expected a dinner invitation just after 10:00 p.m.

"If you can stay, please stay," Juana added. "Our home is always open to you. It will be good for you. Get some real Mexican food. Maybe your body will remember where you come from, eh?"

Sam couldn't think of anything to say. This entire conversation had taken a turn for the unbearably awkward — dinner invites and staying late in someone else's home with their entire family in attendance, not to mention an entire family that all lived either in the same house or at the very least the same property of three different homes. It was completely beyond her wheelhouse.

And Hector wasn't any help now, either.

The man stood against the wall of the kitchen with his arms folded, smirking at Sam and clearly waiting for her to step out of her comfort zone — which didn't even exist here — and ask Juana the questions she'd come to ask.

"Maybe another time?" Sam hesitantly replied, though it came out sounding like the most insecure question of her life. "But thanks anyway. For the invitation."

"Hmm." Juana looked her up and down one more time, then shrugged. "As you wish. Like I said, the invitation is always open. You come for dinner whenever you like. Hector will tell me the next time you are coming, and I will make sure to have my *pozole* on the stove."

"That sounds great." Sam had to fight to keep herself from grimacing.

Change the subject now. You sound like a fucking idiot.

"Actually…" She cleared her throat. "Mrs. Aguayo—"

Juana barked out a laugh and turned briefly away from the stove to fix Sam with a gleaming smile. "*Qué es esto*? Missus? *No, por favor*, Sam. Juana. Please."

"Juana." Sam wished the lump in her throat would just fucking go down already as she swallowed. "I was hoping I could talk to you about someone you might remember from a handful of years ago."

"I remember everyone, Sam." The woman tossed a hand over her shoulder as she went back to her boiling pots and items cooking away on the stove.

"Do you remember a Rose Putnam?" Sam asked.

"*Ah, sí, sí.* I remember the woman very well. Such a sad thing that happened, yes? Poor Frankie. Their son. I used to watch him during the day while his parents worked. Ran a daycare right here out of this very same house until *los peques* just became too much for me to handle all at once."

Hector chuckled. "You mean *your* family grew too big for you to handle anyone else's?"

Juana thrust a finger toward her son and rattled off something long and impossible to follow in Spanish, but Sam thought it sounded very much like something from the mouth of a woman no one would want to mess with if they knew what was good for them.

"I know there were stories all over town about it when Rose disappeared," Sam continued.

"Ah, yes." Juana nodded as she worked. "So many stories. People do love to talk about everyone else, don't they?"

"What do *you* think happened?"

The woman shrugged over the stove. "Who knows? I certainly do not. To be honest, I thought at first that her husband ... Charles, yes? I thought he killed her."

Sam choked on her next breath. "Really?"

"Oh, this happens so much. You would be surprised." Juana waved a hand behind her again, dismissing the whole thing. "But then I changed my mind."

Sam found herself leaning forward toward the woman, waiting for the rest of that explanation to be offered up. She heard Hector chuckle again and figured she might need to prompt his mother into saying more. "And what made you change your mind?"

"It was the way he *was* after Rose disappeared," Juana replied. "The man was so lost, yes? So very sad. As if he walked through a cloud every day and could not find the sun again. And I tell you this, a man who murders his wife does not carry on so long about her death afterwards. That kind of man wants to move on. He wants to let that wife die so he can live without her the way he wanted. Charles did not do this. He … how do you say it? He fell apart, yes? Almost lost his boy. We all thought his sister was going to come take Frankie away to keep him safe. Charles even tried…"

She paused, took one step away from the stove, and closed her eyes to cross herself with a muttered prayer before continuing. "He tried taking his own life, but even that did not work. After all this, I felt what he showed the world was much more than pretending, yes? Even after that, he still did not let her die. I think he is dating a woman from the paper who worked for him. But even with that woman, Charles still writes about Rose."

Sam frowned and tilted her head. "What do you mean? As in he writes about her in the paper?"

Hector nodded. "Every year on the anniversary of his wife's disappearance, *The Daily Rush* runs a feature on Rose and the other women who've gone missing in and around this town."

"*Qué triste.*" Juana clicked her tongue and shook her

head. "Charles is the man keeping Rose's memory alive in this town. The only one, I think. Many people would have forgotten her if he did not do this. So I asked myself, why would he spend all this time remembering her, reminding all of us about her, if he was the one who killed her? This makes no sense to me. Does it make sense to you?"

The woman leaned over one of the pots, dipped a smaller spoon into it, and quickly blew across its surface before tasting it. Then she spun around to look directly at Sam again and raised her eyebrows in question.

With her hands now deeply settled in the pockets of her light jacket, Sam met Juana Aguayo's gaze and shrugged. "I don't know. Why do any of us do the things we do?"

Beside her, Hector let out a low hum of agreement and nodded.

Juana broke into a beaming grin and shook a finger at Sam. "Héctor, I like this *amiga* of yours."

He snorted and shot Sam a sidelong look. "Yeah, she's all right."

THIRTY-NINE

Sam

THE NEXT MORNING, SAM WAS AWAKENED FAR EARLIER than she would have liked by her phone buzzing constantly on the tiny bedside table next to her head.

With a groan, she slapped her hand down several times before finally closing her fingers around the stupid phone. Then she blinked groggily at the bright glow behind the backlit name of the current caller.

Brad again.

Her immediate reaction was to ignore the call completely and try to get at least a few more hours of sleep. But then she remembered why he'd be calling her this early in the first place and didn't particularly want to be any more of an asshole today than she might have already been since he'd found her.

So she answered.

"Please tell me you don't get up this early every morning," she grumbled.

"Well, I don't know about Brad, but I've actually always been a morning person."

Sam sat bolt-upright in her bed, covers flying off her lap. "Denise! Sorry, I thought—"

"Don't worry about it. I *am* calling you from his phone." The woman sounded far friendlier than Sam had ever heard her, which instantly put Sam on a groggy, half-asleep defensive.

"Is everything okay?"

"Um, well… We're fine. Everything's … fine. But Chief Colton just called, and we have an appointment at the station to meet with him and go through Kody's things. You know, what they found in her car last night."

"Yeah," Sam said, trying to blink out the rest of her fatigue. "That's good. You guys should go down there. I hope they don't give you any problems."

"Would they normally?" Denise asked.

"What? Oh. I mean… No, they shouldn't. I was just… Sorry. I just woke up."

"Oh, I'm sorry," Denise said quickly. "I didn't mean to—"

"No, it's okay. Really. Better than an alarm clock."

"Listen, Sam. I was actually hoping… Well, *Brad* and I were hoping you'd be willing to go down to the station with us this morning. Maybe you can help us go through Kody's things. There might be something there Brad and I would miss that you wouldn't, you know? It doesn't hurt to have an extra pair of eyes. Someone who's a little more neutral in all this."

"Neutral." Sam dipped her head to pinch the bridge of her nose. "Yeah, um … you know what, Denise? I can absolutely be there. Just give me a bit. When's your appointment?"

"In half an hour."

"I'll meet you guys there as soon as I can."

. . .

FORTUNATELY, Brad and Denise hadn't been waiting much longer than ten minutes when Sam finally rolled into parking lot of the Rush police station. They each greeted her with tired, slightly haggard, but still hopeful smiles when she got out of the Jeep.

There wasn't a whole lot of conversation, but that wasn't surprising. This was one hell of an appointment to make with any form of law enforcement, and Sam just hoped she could provide more help to Kody's parents than not.

They entered the station together, checked in, and waited for the notified officers to come lead them into the back room where they were set to review evidence gathered from Kody's vehicle.

It was only fitting, Sam thought, when the officer who finally appeared greet Brad and Denise this morning turned out to be Chief Ralph Colton.

He strutted around the station's front desk, looking only at Brad and Denise with a semi-compassionate smile as he extended his hand. "Good morning. Thank you both for coming down first thing. I'll walk you through this, and it shouldn't take very long at all."

"Thank you," Brad said.

"The three of us, actually," Denise added, sticking a thumb over her shoulder.

At the same moment, Sam stood from the ridiculously uncomfortable chair in the station's lobby and instantly locked eyes with Colton. "Morning, Chief."

His smile disappeared, replaced by that perpetual scowl she knew so well. She could have sworn the man's face trembled with restrained rage as he forced himself not to yell at her in front of the out-of-town parents of Rush's most recent kidnapping victim.

"Salazar," he murmured. "I guess I should've expected this."

Sam spread her arms. "I'm just here at the family's request."

"Great." He spat out the word as if it were poison, then flashed another tight, disgusted-looking smile at Brad and Denise before gesturing for all three of them to follow him into one of the station's back rooms.

When they entered, they found Kody's collected belongings laid out on one large banquet table in the center of the room.

"This is everything we pulled from your daughter's vehicle last night," Colton said. "It's all been logged and entered into the system as processed evidence. Feel free to look through everything. You can touch it, of course, if you feel the need to go through things more thoroughly. Just know that we have a record of everything on this table, so I have to make it clear that nothing leaves this room until this case is closed and we release evidence to the family. Take your time, though. And if you need anything or have any questions, I'll be right outside."

Denise and Brad both thanked the man. Sam shot him a beaming grin she and Colton both knew didn't mean she was actually happy to see him.

The Chief of Police stepped out of the room and closed the door behind him to give them a little more privacy.

Then the searching began.

Kody's suitcase had been systematically opened and unpacked, her clothes laid out in neat piles across the table. With them were several spiralbound notebooks, multiple textbooks she'd brought with her from school, a few pamphlets and flyers for the town of Rush she could have picked up anywhere, and a business card for Home Sweet

Home Bed & Breakfast, with which Sam was already quite familiar.

"Just at a first glance," Sam asked, "do you guys see anything that looks out of place or something you expected to find here that's missing?"

"Her phone," Denise said.

Brad nodded. "Her backpack. The one she takes on hikes."

"That makes sense." Sam nodded. "She was supposed to be heading up the mountain to look around the lake. Obviously, she didn't quite make it."

They spent another ten minutes going through Kody's things but couldn't come up with anything else that was obviously missing or raised any more suspicion than it otherwise would have.

Then Sam opened the door to the room and invited Chief Colton to come back inside with them because they had a few questions.

She also explained what they'd discovered. The phone, the backpack, all things that made sense in this particular situation weren't out of place at all.

"Is there anything else you and your officers might've found that maybe we didn't notice?" Sam asked.

Colton slipped his thumbs through his beltloops again and shook his head as he eyed the table covered in evidence. "Nothing comes to mind. We did send out a search party when she was first reported missing. Combed the whole damn mountain over the course of almost twenty hours. Didn't find any sign that she'd been up there at all. Zero evidence, honestly. Finding her vehicle in the gorge last night was the first lead we've had."

Scrunching up her face in an obvious attempt not to break down crying, Denise picked up one of her daughter's textbooks and quickly flipped through it. Then she shook her head and set it back down on the table. "There's nothing else here."

"All right, then." Colton nodded. "Would you folks like some more time in here?"

"I think we've seen everything we can see," Brad replied.

"Sure. Right this way, then." Colton gestured into the hallway.

Brad and Denise slowly fell in line behind him.

Sam stayed behind just long enough to pick up the business card from the bed and breakfast on the other side of town. She flipped it over and widened her eyes when she found a phone number hastily written across the back.

Once the back room had cleared out, she pulled her phone from her pocket, snapped a quick photo of the back of that business card with the phone number, then returned the card and hurried out of the room before anyone else noticed she'd fallen behind.

FORTY

Kody

THE BOTTOM OF THIS DAMN PIT HAD BEEN COLD AND DAMP since the very beginning of Kody's imprisonment in it. She'd known that, yes, but now the levels of dampness had begun to change. Not for the better.

The only reason she'd noticed the change at all was because she shifted around in her current position on the floor, trying to help Rip sit up more comfortably. When she jammed her hiking boot down into the mucky floor beneath her, the instant squelch of much more watery mud beneath her weight was unmistakable

Just to be sure, she also pressed her hands down into the mud to feel it for herself.

Sure enough, it was cold, wet, and left her fingers dripping.

Not a good sign.

She was about to say something to Rip about it but stopped when the sound of two angry, arguing men's voices filled the cave.

"...won't last forever, and they obviously found it. We have to help them out of there before—"

"I didn't ask for your opinion. I told you to do your fucking job!"

"Yes, sir."

Footsteps echoed through the cave again, but Kody no longer cared about what those footsteps meant for her personally, no matter the direction in which they moved. The only thing she could think about now, the only thing that mattered, was getting Rip some medical attention because he was not doing well. That was perfectly clear, especially in this cold and damp in the cave, in the bottom of a pit that now seemed to be filling with more water every second.

"Hey!" she shouted, trying not to shake Rip too much while she supported him in her lap. "Hey, if you're still up there, we really need to get him some help down here. He's in bad shape. He's not gonna make it."

There was no response, as usual.

"I'm serious! If we don't get him help, he's gonna die down here!"

That wasn't what she wanted. It was difficult to say out loud, but they had to understand what was at stake and what they'd done. If killing their prisoners hadn't been their plan all along, they were going to end up with a lot more on their hands than just a curious grad student at the bottom of a pit and a semi-unconscious farmer.

They'd make themselves murderers after this.

A surge of guilt flowed through her, and she recognized what she'd just said and how she'd said it. The last thing she wanted was to scare Rip or make him panic, either before or after he fully regained his wits.

But there was no sugar-coating it now. He was in deep shit. He needed far more medical attention than what she could provide last-minute with random spare supplies on hand, and all Kody had to work with now was the hope that these men in the cave would take her seriously and realize the potential consequences facing them if they didn't *do* something.

Yet again, there was no answer, and the cave fell silent.

With a heavy sigh, Kody turned her attention back to Rip.

"Come on." She patted his cheeks and blew on his face — glistening with sweat but still looking remarkably pale even in the almost non-existent light down here — and did everything she could think of to wake him.

At first, she didn't think it would do much at all, but then Rip finally started to stir. The sight of it renewed what little hope she'd regained since realizing he wasn't dead after all.

The man groaned heavily.

Kody fought to stay calm.

"Hey, there. You're awake again, Rip. It's Kody. Can you tell me how you're feeling?"

Another groan escaped him, and he looked momentarily confused to find himself lying in a dark, cold, damp place with no light and nothing familiar around him and a strange young woman cradling his head in her lap.

"This is … a cave," he murmured.

"Yes," Kody said, fighting back a grin that felt like victory. "That's right. We're in a cave, Rip. Not exactly the best scenario, here, but it's good to know where you are."

"Fuck, my head." He reached slowly toward his temple, which fortunately had stopped bleeding. The worst of it was over, at least.

Kody gently deflected his hand. "No, don't touch it. You've got a pretty nasty gash there on your temple, Rip. I got the bleeding to stop, but we definitely shouldn't mess with it until we've had a doctor look, all right?"

He blinked wearily and tried to sit up a little. He

couldn't quite manage it by himself, but she did note the weight and pressure of his body leaning against hers lessened slightly.

"What doctor?" he asked.

Yeah, that was going to be a bit of a problem, wasn't it?

"Right now, there isn't one," she told him. "We're in a cave somewhere up on the mountain, Rip. I tried to find the lake, but I must've taken a wrong turn somewhere, and I ended up... Well, here. So did you."

"I know this cave." Rip's voice was slightly muffled, like he still wasn't fully awake again as he spoke, but he did seem perfectly aware of his surroundings now, if not much else. "Yeah, I *know* this cave. It's on my land. My land on the mountain. How did I ... get here?"

"I was asking myself the same thing," she said. "Honestly, I'm pretty sure you came out here looking for me."

Rip twisted his head around to try looking at her, blinked wide eyes to focus on her face, then cracked a tired, lopsided smile that didn't reassure her all that much. "Oh, yeah. I remember you. The water girl."

"That's right." Kody couldn't help but laugh. "I'm the water girl. Kody. I'm really glad you found me down here, but now we're *both* down here instead of one of us helping the other get out."

"Yeah, the water girl... You were supposed to find the lake."

"I know," she said. "And I'm not trying to alarm you or be the bearer of bad news more than I have to, but we've got another water issue right here in front of us."

Rip frowned, then dipped his head to look at the floor of the pit beneath them, which was difficult enough to see in the thick darkness. "It's wet down here."

"Right. And it wasn't this wet when those men first brought me here. Do you know who they are?"

The man scrunched up his face, as if the act of deep concentration physically hurt him, then shook his head. "I remember coming to look for you, but after that... I have no idea how I got here."

"That's okay," Kody reassured him. "It'll come to you eventually. Do you know anything about what's happening with the water right now? Seeing as this is a cave on your property."

He took longer than she would have liked to come up with an answer, but it wasn't like either of them were going anywhere anytime soon. Which was, yet again, all part of the problem.

"This pit," he said, gazing slowly around. "We need to get out of here."

"Yep. That's what I've been saying. All right, here we go."

She helped the man rise to his feet in a jumbled mess of groaning and grunting and slipping around in the mud. Then they were both finally on their feet, and Rip got a better look — or feel — around.

"This cave," he repeated. "It's usually flooded where we're standing right now. This is all supposed to all be underwater. It's part of my water system and the irrigation for the farm."

He spoke slowly, contemplatively, as if each word took several seconds on its own to form in his mind before he could remember how to form the sounds with his mouth.

At least he was making sense.

"So its natural state down here is totally submerged." Kody cleared her throat. "Good to know."

"How did it get like this?" Rip asked, turning in a slow, staggering circle.

She felt awful for the guy. He'd clearly been hit way too hard over the head, and maybe if he hadn't, he'd remember more about what was going on here.

That didn't change the fact that they still had to get out as soon as possible and a hell of a lot faster than Kody had previously needed, because now the threat coming at them from below was far more immediately dangerous than the threat of the men from above.

"I bet they're the ones who did this," she said, nodding up toward the edge of the pit. "I bet these men blocked off the water somehow so they could dry out this cave. Any idea why they'd want access to it?"

Rip slowly shook his head. "No clue. But it makes sense, if that's what happened."

A silence hung between them then, like an unspoken plea for some kind of miracle to help them out of this.

Kody stepped toward the wall and stopped with the much louder, much more watery splash and squelch of mud around her hiking boots. Then she looked down to see the water level at the bottom of the pit had risen drastically.

Now it was no longer what it felt like a densely packed floor or possibly even stone beneath her but muddy and dangerously wet, with now half an inch of water coating everything.

"You know," she said with a wry laugh, "if the water keeps rising, we might have our instant way out of here."

Rip turned to frown at her.

She shrugged. "If it floods, we can just rise with the tide and swim our way out."

It was a poor attempt to lighten the mood, but it was all she had.

Rip didn't seem to find it very funny, and she couldn't blame him.

They both knew, after having sat here at the bottom of this pit for so long, that the water rising to join them wouldn't actually float them out the way she'd joked. This pit was too full of mud and loose earth. The more water rose through the pit's floor and the walls around them, the more it would pull down those same walls with their own weight. Everything would become heavy, wet, freezing mud. It might as well have been quicksand at that point.

Kody had already experienced it herself when trying to dig sideways through the pit walls. She didn't want to think about how much more terrifying it would be to get buried alive beneath an entire pit full of that same heavy mud, which was all they would have once the pit flooded.

There was no swimming out, that was for sure.

"All right," he said. "We have to try getting ourselves out. Come on."

Rip stepped closer to the wall and bent at the knees with a grunt. "You need to stand up on my shoulders. I can push you out, and then you help pull me up."

"Rip, I don't know if that's such a good idea." Kody looked him over from head to toe. The man could hardly stand, let alone hold a hundred and twenty pounds on his shoulders, even for a little while.

"It's the only way out," he said. "I can handle it. Come on."

She didn't want to do this, but he was right. It was their only option.

So she tried to steady herself against the pit walls, but they kept crumbling away from her hands.

Every time she tried to get a little more height, maybe keep Rip from taking all her weight, more of the wall fell away beneath her touch like she was trying to climb a damn sandcastle.

Rip definitely hadn't recovered enough of his strength

to make this a viable option. When Kody got one foot up onto his shoulder at an awkward angle, he rose, trying to lift her up with him, and his knees buckled instantly. They toppled together onto the floor in a muddy heap.

Over and over and over again, they tried to get her up on his shoulders so he could hoist her out. Every time, either Rip couldn't hold her up long enough, or the quickly disintegrating walls of the pit just kept giving way beneath the slightest pressure.

The last time they tried it, an enormous chunk of sloppy mud sloughed off the pit walls to spill down all around and on top of them. It took them a few minutes to pull each other out of the mess before they were both back on their feet.

And now the water was up past their ankles.

"This isn't working," she said.

"Yeah, I picked up on that." Rip cleared his throat and nodded. "There's only one thing left to do now."

"And that is?"

He turned away from her, lifted his face toward the top of the pit, and took a deep breath.

"Help!" he bellowed, his voice exploding up into the cave above them. "Somebody help! We're down here!"

Kody watched him for a minute in dumbstruck silence.

If screaming for help was this man's last resort and he'd already resigned himself to using it, they were seriously fucked.

So she took a deep breath and added her screams to his.

FORTY-ONE

Sam
_____

IN THE FRONT PARKING LOT OF THE RUSH POLICE STATION, Sam told Denise and Brad she thought it was best if they went their separate ways for now.

"I'm gonna go home," she said. "Look through a couple things, but I'll meet you guys back at the hotel later. I'll give you a call."

"Thank you so much, Sam," Denise said.

Brad narrowed his eyes. "Go ahead and spill it now, Sam. Whatever you've got cooking."

"Might be nothing," she said with a shrug. "Might be something, but I don't know yet. So I'm gonna go check it out, all right? You two go back to the hotel. I'll be in touch."

She waited there in the parking lot until Brad finally relented, got into Denise's car with her, and they drove off. Then Sam pulled out her phone with the picture of that number scribbled on the back of the Bed & Breakfast business card and made the call.

Time to see who it belonged to.

The phone rang twice before a man answered.

"This is Zach."

Sam blinked. "Zach … Turner?"

"Yeah. Who's this?"

"Oh. Sorry. This is Sam. Sam Salazar."

"Oh!" A short laugh escaped him. "Hey, Sam. I wasn't expecting to hear from you. How are things? Your tooth's not still bothering you, is it? I was sure I'd taken care of everything last time you were in. Do you need to make another appointment?"

"No, my tooth's fine, thanks. I was actually wondering if I could come by and talk to you in person."

"Sure. Is everything okay?"

"Just wanna ask you a few questions."

"Well…" The hesitation in his voice was unmistakable. "You know what? If you can get over here to the office right now, I have a little bit of spare time before my next scheduled patient."

"Great. I'll see you then."

Sam hopped up into her Jeep and headed back to Rush's main strip out.

How convenient that the number led to Zach the dentist, who also just happened to be on the other side of downtown.

When Sam reached the old brick building where the Turner dental offices were held, after parking her car in the lot of the closed-down bus terminal, she couldn't help feeling that same overwhelming sense of foreboding bordering on terror again.

No, she wasn't going to the dentist for an appointment. She wouldn't have to sit in that chair. But somehow, just knowing there was a dentist inside on the second floor made her skin crawl.

Get over yourself. This is a social call. Your teeth aren't even involved.

It amazed her all over again how old the building truly was. She approached the door, made her way through the wide lobby on the ground floor, then moved up the stairs, following all the signs toward the Turner Dental offices.

The front door was once again propped open for her, as if that in and of itself would be more inviting and make incoming patients feel that much more at ease.

Not Sam.

She walked in and was greeted by the same receptionist's beaming smile.

"Hello. Do you have an appointment?"

"Not today," Sam said. "I just stopped by to speak with Zach for a minute. He knows I'm coming. Said he had a little bit of free time."

"Well, he will any minute, now," the receptionist replied. "He's still with a patient, but as soon as he's finished, I'll let him know you're here. Can I get your name, please?"

"Sam Salazar."

"Feel free to take a seat. He shouldn't be much longer at all."

After five minutes of waiting, Sam realized she probably should have asked the receptionist for her own personal definition of "not too much longer." Waiting only made her boredom soar through the roof until she finally had to break the silence just so there was more than the low hum of whatever motor pumped bubbles into the sad-looking fishtank on the other side of the room.

"You know, I still can't get over how old this building is."

"Oh, I know." The receptionist nodded sagely. "This place has been around since the very beginning of Rush, almost."

"Without a whole lot of structural renovations too," Sam said. "It must cost a fortune to heat in the winter."

"It's not so bad now, actually. The whole building used to be heated by an old boiler down in the basement, and that was definitely expensive. But the owners switched to electric heating about four years ago, and since then, it's been a lot more consistent, at the very least. And less expensive with shared utility costs, for sure."

"Huh. Sounds like a smart move for everyone." Sam turned in a slow circle and walked toward the front desk. "Were you the receptionist for Zach's father too?"

"Steven?" The woman's smile blossomed even wider. "Oh yes. I've been working behind this desk for over twenty years now."

"That's a lot of patients."

"It's a lot of years."

Sam pulled her phone from her back pocket and scrolled through her saved pictures while she spoke. "Would you by any chance happen to have seen this young woman around town in the last few weeks or so?"

She turned her phone around with the picture of Kody pulled up on display.

The receptionist took a nice long look at the image, then shook her head. "No, sorry. She doesn't look familiar. But if she'd had an appointment here on a Friday, I wouldn't have been here to see her anyway."

"Why's that?"

"I don't work on Fridays. It's always been that way. Not something I requested, just a rule Steven had in place when I started with him. I guess the habit just continued when Zach took over. I sure do miss Steven. Don't get me wrong, working with his son is wonderful too. Brings this place more into the present. Of course, there are always certain changes, even when a business stays in the family. There are pros and cons to both."

"Totally natural," Sam said. "If you aren't here on Fridays, who handles reception?"

"Oh, well, back when her husband ran things here, Susan would man the front desk and check patients in. She stopped doing that when Zach took over, though. So now the current Doctor Turner likes to tell patients to just let themselves in. They show up, sign in, and meet him in the back on their own time, I guess."

"Open-door policy, huh?"

"Something like that." The woman chuckled. "Don't ask me how or why, but it seems to be working well for him."

Interesting.

FORTY-TWO

Sam

FIVE MINUTES AFTER HIS PATIENT LEFT THE LOBBY WITH A smile at the receptionist and a thank you, Zach emerged from the back, drying his hands off on a paper towel before he tossed that in the trash behind the front desk.

When he saw Sam hunched over in front of the fish tank, scrutinizing the lives of the dental office's aquatic pets on display, he chuckled through a wide grin. "Enjoying the fish?"

Sam jerked upright and spun around before offering him a lopsided smile in response. "Maybe envying them a little. Unless you're about to tell me fish have teeth too."

"Not the kind I deal with on a regular basis. Listen, I've got about twenty minutes until my next scheduled patient, so that's what I can give you now. Do you wanna go grab some coffee before I have to be back?"

"I will never say no to coffee," Sam said.

THE DAY WAS clear enough and warm enough to make a mid-morning walk more than pleasant, so Zach led the

413

way to what he referred to as one of the best hole-in-the-wall cafés he'd ever seen.

"I didn't know that was a thing," Sam said. "I mean, tiny restaurants and bars, sure. But coffee houses?"

"It's definitely a thing. And it's definitely worth it."

With their twenty-minute time limit, she couldn't help but start with a few friendly and non-intrusive questions while they walked. "And you like being a dentist, Zach?"

He shot her a surprised look, then smiled with an easy shrug. "Yeah, I enjoy it now. It was hard at first, to be honest. I wasn't sure it was what I actually wanted when I went to dental school, but, well, I was too stubborn to try anything else. As it turned out, I'm a far better dentist than my dad."

"That's a self-confident assessment," she said with a laugh.

"He was definitely good at what he did," Zach continued. "And he took care of lots of mouths in this town. But when I took over the practice, I realized all the pieces of the bigger picture he'd been missing that I was able to provide, just because I'm younger and had slightly different training. Exposure to newer techniques. That kinda thing. And I proved to be a better businessman too. That might've been the biggest surprise of all, honestly."

"Your dad didn't do well running the practice?"

"It wasn't that necessarily. But my dad never really did much to grow his business. He was more content with what he had and to keep it at that. He'd take on new patients, yeah, but he didn't put much time or effort into growing his patient list or revenue from the practice."

Sam nodded. "Gotcha."

"My goal here, honestly, is to earn enough in profit over the next year, sooner if possible, to support putting my dad in a care facility full-time. My mom's been watching him since his dementia took a turn, and I get why she wouldn't want to send him away for full-time care. But she's getting up there in age too. She deserves a break. And when my dad has his bad days, they're pretty bad days."

"That's an admirable goal," she said.

Zach laughed. "Maybe you could tell *her* that. It's a point of contention between us. Has been for a while."

"Sorry to hear that."

They reached the coffee shop, which Sam never would have guessed was a coffee shop before stepping inside and seeing it with her own eyes. They went straight to the counter first to place their orders, and the coffees were ready almost immediately.

Sam suggested they take the empty corner table to sit down and finish their chat. Zach had no problem with it.

She gave herself a moment to truly appreciate her to-go cup of fresh, hot, black coffee, which was a hell of a lot better than she'd expected.

Zach laughed at her reaction. "I told you."

Then it was time to get down to brass tacks.

Sam pulled out her phone, opened up the picture of Kody, and showed it to him. "How well do you know Kody Anderson?"

Zach barely glanced at the picture and tried to cover up his ensuing expression with a long sip of coffee. "Not that well, honestly. I'd seen her around town once or twice."

"But you knew her well enough to give her your direct personal number, right?"

He froze and raised his eyebrows in clueless surprise.

Sam shrugged. "Your phone number was found in her things the police recovered from her vehicle. On the back of one of your mom's business cards."

He scratched the back of his head and nodded. "Oh. You caught me red-handed."

Sam folded her arms and sat back in her chair. "So you do know her."

"Yeah, I know Kody. Fairly well, actually. Not as well as I want to, but I thought it was heading in that direction. I met her at my folks' place while she was staying there as a guest."

Sam nodded.

"We started talking, pretty much hit it off right away. And yeah, I liked her. But I had to, uh … keep it on the down-low, more or less. Didn't want my mom to know I was interested in her in a long-term way, I guess."

"How come?" Sam asked.

He glanced quickly around the café, but the few other patrons didn't pay them any attention. Even still, he leaned slightly forward over the table and lowered his voice. "My mom can be a little intense when it comes to relationships."

"Sounds like you had a relationship with Kody," she said.

"I thought I did. I know she's incredibly intelligent and beautiful. Funny. All the things I like, and I definitely thought it was something with her that might go somewhere. We went on a handful of dates. Honestly, I would've said they went really well, but now…"

Slowly sipping her coffee, Sam held his gaze and leaned toward him over the table as well. "I want all the details, Zach. Don't leave anything out. Because you know she's gone missing, right?"

"Yeah. I had a feeling that was what you wanted to talk about."

"Well, we're on a time crunch." She lifted her to-go cup toward him in a silent toast. "So I'm expecting you to fit in as much information as possible in the ... what? Twelve minutes you've got left."

"Basically, we kept the dates and the fact that we were interested in each other secret from my mom. She's nosy. She's picky. But, you know, I'm a grown man. Kody's a grown woman. Didn't think it would be that much of an issue. I spent the night with her in that shed out back at my folks' place. I mean, it's been converted."

Sam nodded. "I've seen it. Keep going."

"Right. I headed out the next morning to go to work, and my mom saw me leaving through the back yard. Should've realized she'd be awake that early, probably, but again, adults. It's not like we're in high school."

"No, it's not." Sam slurped more coffee. "What happened?"

"She tore me a new one is what happened," Zach replied with a sigh. "Went on and on about how Kody wasn't good enough for me, that I deserved someone better. It's not like she could give any examples, and that was humiliating, to say the least."

"And it didn't worry you when Kody disappeared and was reported missing?"

The man grimaced and shook his head. "No. When she disappeared, I didn't know she was technically missing. I just assumed she'd packed up and left town on her own. After the way my mom reacted, I wouldn't have wanted anything to do with me or my family, either, if I were Kody. And on top of that..."

He grimaced again, dropping his gaze to the tabletop.

Sam nodded. "Keep going."

He took a deep breath. "I'm pretty sure it got a little intense. That *I* got intense. You know, I thought things between us were heading in one direction. I wasn't a hundred percent sure, but I had my suspicions. And part of me thinks I just read way more into what Kody and I had than what was actually there. I'm not sure she felt the same way."

"So you assumed she checked out of the B&B, just like your mom thinks too, yeah?"

"Exactly. But she didn't go back home, did she?"

"Doesn't look that way, no. Zach, you say your mom didn't think Kody was good enough for you. Would you have any reason to believe she might have hurt Kody in any way?"

He barked out a laugh. "What? Are you serious?"

"Stranger things have happened," she said with a shrug.

"No." Zach sat back in his chair, his smile flickering in and out as he drank more coffee. "Absolutely not. That could never happen. You know how old my mom is, right? She's barely hanging on just taking care of my dad. There's no way she has it in her to hurt someone after running their place on top of everything else."

"But she was angry enough to have done something, right?" Sam asked.

"With *me*. She was angry with me. She wouldn't have taken it out on Kody. She's not like that."

Sam shrugged and dipped her head towards the table. "Hey, I hear ya. Had to ask. This thing between you and Kody was something I didn't know about until I called you this morning and you answered."

"I get that," he said. "I realize now I probably should've said something about it once I heard from my mom that Kody's parents thought she was missing."

"Yeah, probably."

Zach practically jumped in his seat, then pulled a cell phone from his back pocket and frowned at it.

"Everything all right?" Sam asked.

"Yeah, just a call. From a number I don't know. I don't usually get a lot of those. Now I've had two in one day."

"Might wanna answer it."

He clearly tried to laugh it off but was too surprised or concerned or something else to pull it off.

Sam would have liked to see what number pulled up on his phone on the off chance that Zach still wasn't being entirely honest with her and did actually know who was calling him.

But he answered.

"This is Zach." The dentist's eyes widened. "Chief Colton. Yeah. No, I didn't expect to get a call from you. How did you ... All right. Sure. I'm at that coffee place just a few blocks down from my office building. It's on the — Yep, that's the one. Sure, I'll be here."

He set his phone down on the table and frowned at nothing.

"My guess is Chief Colton found that business card with your number on the back just a little later than I did," Sam mused.

"Right. I'll have to call Cindy. Tell her to cancel my next patient."

"You'll be fine," she told him and she stood. "Just tell him the same things you told me, and it won't hurt at all."

He looked blank and far away when he tilted his head to look up at her. "You think?"

"Sure." Sam took her coffee with her and stopped only to pat her dentist on the shoulder. "Hey, at least it's not like going to the dentist."

FORTY-THREE

Sam
_____

SAM DID NOT GO BACK TO ZACH'S DENTAL OFFICE AFTER she left the coffee shop. It wasn't necessary anymore, and she had other places she would rather be instead. Next steps to think about.

So she walked right back to the closed bus terminal to pick up her Jeep and instead continued toward the opposite side of town to pay Susan Hooper's B&B one more friendly visit.

"Sam!" Susan greeted her with a beaming smile and her arms thrown open almost as wide as the front door of her home. "I did not expect to see you again so soon. How are you?"

"I'm fine, thanks. Hope I'm not interrupting anything."

"Oh no, not at all. Come inside, please." The woman ushered Sam inside, quickly shut the door, and bustled away down the foyer toward the main sitting area of the house. "Can I get you anything to drink, Sam? Yes? Some tea? I've got lots of iced tea."

"No, thank you," Sam said. "I'm fine. I won't take up

too much of your time. I just have a few more questions for you."

"And I am happy to answer them." Susan nodded curtly, stopped in the center of the enormous living room, and plopped right down onto the longest couch beside her husband's armchair before folding her hands in her lap. "How can I help?"

Sam entered slowly, taking in all the same details of the bed and breakfast's sitting area, which once again included Steven Turner sitting in his usual armchair, looking vacant and a little bored and not moving.

"Hi, Steven," she said. "It's Sam again. We met a few times earlier this week. Good to see you."

The man didn't respond or offer any reaction to her presence, which she honestly didn't expect anyway.

Then Sam sat on the couch opposite Susan and scooted forward until she sat at the edge of the cushion.

"So what can I help you with, Sam?" Susan asked.

Sam folded her own hands, crossed her thighs, and leaned slightly forward. "This is probably going to be a little awkward, Susan, but I just had coffee with Zach."

"Oh, how nice."

"And the way he explained it, you didn't really seem to like Kody all that much. Apparently, you and your son had a pretty big fight over it."

Susan's smile instantly disappeared, and she smartly cocked her head, clicking her tongue. "Is that what Zach said?"

In the armchair beside her, Steven grumbled something unintelligible, his fingers twitching rapidly against the upholstered armrest until it looked far more like he was tapping them intentionally instead.

Sam shot a quick glance toward the man and lowered her voice. "Is he all right?"

"He's fine," Susan assured her. "Try to ignore him if you can. Really. This is all part of our normal every day."

With a heavy grunt, Steven turned. Flopping his other arm down on the armrest facing Sam, he propped himself up and turned even more toward her. His eyes narrowed to wrinkly slits of suspicion as he scowled at her, his lips pursing and relaxing like even his facial muscles didn't have the strength to maintain one expression for very long. A low growl rose from his throat before he blurted, "You got a mouth full of rot. It needs fixing!"

Sam huffed out a laugh as she lifted a hand to the side of her jaw where she'd had her cavity filled. "Yeah, I'm working on it."

"I'm sorry my son felt it appropriate to give you such a warped representation of what actually happened," Susan continued, ignoring both her husband and Sam. All the previous bubbly, hospitable energy she'd exuded every other time Sam had stopped by had disappeared now too. The woman looked deadly serious. "And I'm afraid it was actually the other way around."

"How's that?" Sam asked, slowly pulling her gaze away from Steven's twitching scowl.

"I wasn't upset because I thought my son was too good for Kody," Susan continued. "Kody is too good for *him*. It was *her* I'd warned off dating my son. I didn't want her to get hurt. You know, in the short time she'd stayed here with us, I felt like I'd gotten to know her more than enough to understand things would never have worked out well between them. That sweet young woman would've only ended up heartbroken and devastated in the end, with nothing to show for it. And yes, Zach and I fought over this, but... Well, now you know what it was really about."

Sam tilted her head, nodding at the woman's version of

events. "Is there a particular reason you thought Zach would just end up breaking her heart?"

"Too many to count." Susan sighed. "At this point, I've already forgotten most of their names. My son is something of a womanizer, truth be told. It's unfortunate, and I thought we'd raised him better than that, but there's just something in him that doesn't quite understand the value of a good woman or how to treat her. Not something either of us are proud of."

"I see," Sam said. "So you were just trying to avoid one more romantic casualty for your son, huh?"

"Exactly." Susan sat back on the couch, crossed one leg over the other, and folded her hands on her top knee before her hostess's smile returned. "I just didn't want Kody to get hurt."

Steven grunted again in his chair, even louder this time. "Kody! Kody's in the oven!"

"What was that?" Sam asked.

Heaving an exasperated sigh, Susan pushed herself to her feet and strode right out of the sitting area toward the kitchen. Both Sam and Steven could see into the kitchen from where they sat while Susan demonstrated for her husband by pulling open the oven door and waving a hand around inside.

"See, Steven? Oven's open, right here. No Kody in it. *No one* in it, as a matter of fact."

With a surge of energy Sam certainly hadn't expected the man to find, Steven pushed himself out of the armchair on wobbly legs and shuffled out of the room toward the back of the enormous house.

The oven door slammed shut. Then Susan bustled back in from the kitchen, shaking her head. "I'm sorry about him..."

"He just took off into the hallway back there," Sam

said, gesturing in that direction. "Do you need to go help him?"

"No, when he's ready to get up, he's ready to get up. Best to just let him have the run of the house when he's got the energy for it. He's not on his feet all the time or able to get back on them once he sits down, so this is about all the exercise he gets these days." Susan plopped back down onto the couch and swiped a few loose strands of gray hair away from her face.

Sam had the distinct impression that there was something else going on here between the elderly couple. Something she was missing. Something Susan might have been sugarcoating quite a bit about their current situation, but Sam still had no leg to stand on.

It wasn't her place to be concerned for Steven if his own wife, who lived with him and took care of him day in and day out, said he was fine. What else could she do?

"Does your husband ever get violent with his dementia?" she asked. "I know it doesn't always happen that way, but I've heard of people struggling with that sometimes."

"Oh, no." Susan dismissed the whole idea with a casual wave of her hand. "That man wouldn't hurt a fly. Not now, and not back before the dementia. We're lucky that much about him hasn't changed."

As if they'd planned its timing, a loud crash came from one of the back rooms, followed by the rumble of drawers opening and slamming shut again before several heavy thumps and lighter clatters filled the back half of the Victorian mansion.

Susan frowned in the direction of all the noise. "The *furniture*, on the other hand..."

"Would you like me to call Zach?" Sam asked. "See if he can stop by to lend a hand?"

"No, no." The woman leapt back to her feet with surprising spryness and gestured with fluttering hands for Sam to stay seated. "I can handle Steven just fine on my own. Not to worry."

Sam also stood. "Thanks for your help, Susan. That definitely cleared some things up."

"Anytime," Susan called over her shoulder as she power-walked across the sitting room. "I do mean that, Sam. You come back absolutely any time. The door is always open. That's a standing invitation. We would love to have you again. We'll talk soon." Then she disappeared into the hallway and Sam was perfectly content to let herself out.

The second she pulled the front door shut behind her, however, also happened to be the same second Chief Colton shut the front driver's-side door of his squad car parked up close and personal in Susan's driveway.

Sam grinned.

Colton's scowl darkened into the angriest, most twisted version she'd seen yet. "Goddamnit, Salazar," he growled as he stomped toward her. "I swear to Christ, I've had it up to *here* with your shit."

"That's your best hello yet, Chief," she told him with a quick nod as she walked down the front porch steps. "Good to see you too."

"No it's not. It's *not* good to see you. You know why? Because I've been seeing you everywhere. Every time I turn around, there you are, Salazar. Canvassing my crime scenes. Interrogating my witnesses. Interfering with my open investigations."

"I wasn't interrogating anyone," Sam said, spreading her arms. "I'm just asking a few questions around town on behalf of the family. Which, last time I checked, isn't illegal."

426

"Well I suggest you go back and recheck all the other laws you seem to have forgotten so easily. This won't end well for you. I can tell you that much."

"I know you're not threatening me, Chief," she said, pausing just in front of him.

When Colton thrust a finger in her face, it took everything she had not to laugh at how much like Big Pete Wilder the man looked in that moment.

Guess his boss is starting to rub off on him too, huh?

"It's not a threat," he said. "I'm promising you right now, Salazar, if I see you with one more witness on my case, if you even turn up in the same place, coincidence or not, I *will* arrest you for interference myself, and then I'll get you the fuck out of my way and *keep* you out of my way until I damn well feel like letting you go. You're not in the Army anymore. You have no jurisdiction here, and it's time for you to stay in your goddamn lane. Are we understood?"

"Perfectly." After flashing him a tight smile, Sam slipped past him on the narrow front walkway to head back to her Jeep.

FORTY-FOUR

Kody

IT WAS IMPOSSIBLE TO IGNORE THE RISING WATER LEVELS around them, and now that water had become a major problem.

It was now up past the middle of Kody's calves and steadily rising by the minute. Worse than that, it was freezing cold, like it had come straight from the glacier runoff in the mountains to seep up under them from below somehow.

With her lower legs submerged, her feet soaked all the way through, and her toes completely numb, Kody couldn't stop shivering. Even with her survival blanket wrapped around both her and Rip as they huddled together against the wall of the pit to try to maintain the necessary body heat between them, getting warm was impossible.

They might have had a better chance at escape — or at least more intensive and productive brainstorming sessions — if it hadn't been such a struggle in the first place just for Rip to remain on his feet. The man kept sinking where he stood, his back sliding against the pit wall behind him and bringing more giant chunks of mud down around their feet, as if this pit were a particularly hairy dog with severe allergies and a terrible shedding problem.

A very wet dog.

Kody had to keep pulling Rip upright again, supporting him with one of his arms wrapped around both her shoulders so he wouldn't collapse in the water. That would come with its own set of dangers and potentially deadly disasters, like hypothermia. Or drowning. The water was high enough now for that to be a real threat on multiple fronts. More so for Rip than for Kody, but for how much longer, she had no way of knowing.

No matter what, they both had to stay conscious for as long as possible.

So she said through chattering teeth, "Tell me about your morning."

It was a stupid question given the circumstances, but she wanted to keep him talking. At the very least, that would help him stay alert, and it would help her preserve her strength and energy if it meant she didn't have to support most of his body weight on her own.

"My morning?" Rip asked, panting between enormous shivers wracking his entire body.

"Assuming today was the morning you headed out here to come looking for me," she said. "Sorry if I'm off by a few hours. Or days. Kinda hard to tell time in here."

Rip huffed out a weak laugh. "Hell, I got up. Ate breakfast."

"Oh, *breakfast...*" Kody rolled her eyes, her mouth instantly watering at that one simple word. "I love breakfast. What was it?"

"Sausage links," he said, fixing her with a frown half-confusion, half amusement. "Fried 'em myself."

"Hot grease and everything, huh?" Kody nodded. "Then what?"

"Then I took a shower. And yeah, I know, you don't have to tell me. Shower would be really fucking great right now." They both let out weak chuckles. "Got dressed. Hopped in my truck and hit the road. Then I after that, I…"

For a terrifying second, Kody thought the man was about to lose consciousness again. She tightened her grip on his wrist with his arm still dangling around her shoulders and tried to catch his gaze. "Rip? You still here with me?"

"I'm still here." He cleared his throat, then shivered again. "Just can't remember what came after leaving home. I rolled through the farm's front gates and headed up the road, and the rest is just … gone."

Great. Can't keep him talking about something he doesn't remember.

"You called me Meredith earlier," she said instead, changing the subject because she had to keep him talking about *anything*. "When you first came to after they dropped you down here with me. Do you remember that?"

"Not really." He started to reach up toward his wounded temple but then thought better of it. "Now that you mention it, I can see how I would've done that. You kinda look like her." Rip squinted down at her and wrinkled his nose. "Through fuzzy vision and a bad concussion, sure."

Kody's smile felt a little warmer now, but only just. "Meredith's your daughter, right?"

"That's right."

"You two get along? I know she's grown, but… I don't know, I guess I always kinda figured the whole parent-child thing got easier as everybody got older."

Rip grunted and wobbled a little before quickly finding

his footing again in the muck beneath them. "A common misconception."

"So that's a no, then?"

He responded with a non-committal hum. "We get along just fine, sure. So long as we don't talk about anything personal or business related or political."

"Oh, good. That leaves a whole lot of conversation topics for a nice long dinner together."

A wheezing laugh burst from the man's lips before he coughed violently and wobbled again on his feet. One more groan, then he cleared his throat again. "Sounds like you've already got it figured out. You and your folks the same way?"

"Sometimes. My mom and I used to be close before I moved out on my own. There are definitely things I don't tell her. Just to keep it on the safe side."

"Wise choice," he said. "Perfectly normal. Everybody does it."

"But my dad … I feel close to him *now*. I mean, I don't tell him everything, either, but we talk every day, even if it's just a text or something. Or at least we used to. Before…"

"Uh-huh."

Kody puffed out a sigh, but it came out as a shuddering gasp through her full-body shivers and chattering teeth. "My parents split up when I was eleven. My dad left, and I didn't hear from him again for a long time. My mom didn't want to talk to him. She didn't want *me* to talk to him. And she didn't talk *about* him, so it was like he never existed in the first place."

"Sometimes, that's for the best."

"Yeah, that's what she told me." Kody thought she felt something dripping down her face and quickly wiped it away with the back of her hand, but she could no longer feel most of her hand or most of her face. "But then I went away to college. I graduated. Got into grad school."

"Uh-huh."

"And I realized *I* wanted to talk to *him*. So I found him. This was a couple years ago, and we reconnected. Sometimes it feels like I didn't grow up without him. But it's always still there in the back of my mind that there was so much time I could've spent with my actual dad. I didn't get to..."

Her voice broke at the end. She sucked in a quick breath, telling herself not to cry because what was the point of something stupid like that now?

Still, when she started talking again, she couldn't keep the tremor out of her voice. If it hadn't been so dark in the pit, she would have noticed her vision blurring anyway.

"Now, just when I thought I was doing so well with everything, I've let both my parents down. I just disappeared on them, you know? They obviously have no idea where to look for me. They haven't heard from me. They have no idea where I am or what happened or if I'm even alive right now. I think I've been down here for a few weeks, but I lost count. And they'll probably never know. That's the worst part."

"Come on now." Rip sniffed, then readjusted his arm around her shoulders so he could jostle her a little in something as close to a hug as his weakened body could manage. "Don't talk like that."

"It's not hopelessness," she corrected him. "Nothing like that. It's just... This doesn't make any fucking sense. That's all."

"Shit hardly ever does, kid."

"No, I mean, I honestly don't understand why I haven't been found yet. Why *we* haven't been found. I left a detailed map in my car showing the exact route I'd previously planned out to get to your water source. The lake in the valley, yeah? I left it right there in my car for everyone to see, with my hiking plan, the date and time, emergency contacts in case I didn't come back when I said I was planning to come back. I had it all covered. All the bases. I didn't miss anything, and still, we're here, and no one showed up. I even told the owner of the bed and breakfast I was staying at that I was coming out here. She knew. I'd talked to a living person about it. You'd think someone could've figured it out."

"*I* did," Rip muttered.

"I know. And thank you. But ... well, look where *that* got you."

Rip laughed again before it turned into another coughing fit he quickly tried to stifle.

"I left my car on the turnoff, too," Kody added. "Right at the end of your directions. Someone should've found that, at least."

"Your car wasn't there."

She slowly lifted her head to look up at him in the thick darkness, and somehow, she could still see the deepening frown he sent her way.

"Yes, it was," she said.

Rip shook his head. "The assholes who put you down here put me down here too. My bet is they found your car and moved it before anyone else noticed a thing. So no one ever had a clue as to where you were. Plus, I'm the only one who knew where I'd told you to go in the first place."

"Okay, but then someone has to know where *you* went, right?" Her voice trembled again, and she pressed her lips tightly together to hopefully get her emotions back under control. "Rip, please tell me you told someone you were coming up here to look for me."

"Yep. I told someone I was going out to the lake. I was

supposed to meet someone else up there too, who was looking for *you*, no less. But then I got cocky."

"What does that mean?"

With another heavy sigh, he dropped his head forward and muttered, "It means I changed plans last minute. My men knew exactly where I was planning on ending up eventually, but I took a little detour. Deviated from our normal route everyone knows, because that's how we get to and from the lake."

"So you got lost?"

"Hell no," he said with another cough that might also have been a laugh. "Let me tell you something, kid, there's no one in these mountains who knows this area of land better than I do, because it's mine. I knew exactly where I was going. I knew exactly where I wanted to look for you. Problem was I didn't know there were a pair of assholes camped out on my land, waiting to clock me a good one on the side of the head and throw me into a pit."

"Makes sense." She nodded, then stopped abruptly. "Wait."

"Huh?"

Kody looked up at him again, ignoring the stiff ache in the side of her neck from having stood like this for so long. "What do you mean you deviated from the route?"

"Pretty self-explanatory, don't you think?"

"No. You shouldn't have found me if you went off-route," she said. "I followed your directions exactly, Rip. At first, I thought maybe you'd gotten it wrong or that you were just trying to screw with me and lead me somewhere else, but I found everything you told me to look for, and I ended up *here*. So how did you—"

"Goddamnit! I *told* you this is how it's going to be, and I don't wanna hear another fucking thing about it!"

The furious voice blasted through the cave and down

435

toward Kody and Rip in their foot of water filling the bottom of the pit. They both looked up at the pit's edge, but that only revealed darkness and more darkness while the argument up above continued.

"This isn't right. You *know* that. We can't just—"

"We can do whatever the hell I say we can do, and that *makes* it right. You've been here with me this whole time. You knew what was coming. You knew the risks. And now we get to lie in our damn bed, 'cause there's no going back now. You understand?"

"But we *could*. There's still time, if we just—"

A heavy, smacking thump followed by a grunt and a quick scuffle across the cave floor cut the conversation short.

After that, Kody could only hear someone's heavy breathing from up above. She had a feeling it came from the younger man, the son, the only one with a conscience who clearly didn't want to keep her and Rip down here long enough for them to drown or freeze to death or both.

Then the cave was silent again, punctured by another wheezing cough from Rip and Kody's chattering teeth she could no longer silence no matter how hard she tried.

"I thought I taught you better than that," the older man grumbled.

Rip jerked his head up at the sound and hissed out his next breath. "Mattie? Is that you?"

Kody almost stepped out from under his arm to look at him, then remembered she was the only reason the guy was still standing.

"You know these men," she whispered.

"Hush. Let me handle this." Rip cleared his throat to shout this time, "Damnit, Mattie! Now I *know* it's you. What the hell do you think you're doing, huh? You get your ass over here and let us out this goddamn minute, or so help me, I'll—"

Another violent fit of coughing cut him short, and he pressed a fist to his mouth while the wheezing hacks echoed up out of the pit. When he reeled where he stood, Kody shimmied closer against his body to hopefully keep him from collapsing right there.

She wasn't sure she'd be able to get him back to his feet otherwise.

Then a few plunking splashes rose from the opposite side of the pit. When she looked up, Kody found the older man with the long gray hair, presumably Mattie, peeking his head out over the edge and staring down at them.

Holy shit, he does *look just like Rip.*

They had to be brothers. Or cousins, at the very least.

Breathing deeply now that the coughing fit had ended, Rip looked up as well and scowled at their captor.

One side of Mattie's nose wrinkled into a sneer.

"Yeah, I know you heard me," Rip growled. "Get us the fuck out of here. What are you *doing*?"

"Sorry, Rip," Mattie replied with as much emotion as he'd shown Kody since the beginning. "Can't do that."

"The hell you can't," Rip shouted. "You're the one who put us in this mess, but *both* of you are gonna go down for this if something happens to us. You know that, right?"

"A risk I'm willing to take," Mattie said with a slow shake of his head. "Too bad for all of us. Wasn't part of the plan for that dam to go up in smoke the way it did. But nothing to do about it now. That there hole's gonna fill right up, and yeah, unfortunately, it's gonna take you and the girl with it. It's inevitable at this point, Rip. Breaks my heart. Really does. But that's just how it's gotta be."

"Christ, you always were the biggest idiot I ever met,"

Rip shot back. "What the fuck were you two doing up here in my caves, anyway?"

Mattie raised his thinning eyebrows, looked like he might have been on the verge of answering, then pushed himself up out of his squat at the edge of the pit and walked away.

"You stupid sonofabitch!" Rip roared. "Get back here! You want murder on your hands too now, is that it? Hey! I'm still talking to you! Get the fuck back here!"

Kody didn't have the heart to tell him shouting like that just wasn't going to work.

FORTY-FIVE

Sam

By the time Sam finally returned to Birdsong Park, and her trailer, and her tiny twin-sized bed smashed into the end of it, she was exhausted. Not just physically but mentally as well. And, yes, if she forced herself to really think about it, she supposed a level of emotional exhaustion also existed.

It all came crashing down on her the second she landed backwards on her bed, her arms spread wide as she stared at the Deville's ceiling.

For the first time today, she felt like she actually had time to think about everything going on within her personal life and within this case, and more specifically, trying to help Brad and Denise find their daughter. So far, since the day Brad showed up and told her why he was here, Sam thought she'd been doing a pretty damn fine job at keeping the worst of her negative emotions at bay.

She hadn't freaked out. She hadn't gone off the deep end. She hadn't tempted fate by playing dangerously on the edge of a seriously bad decision that would only end up hurting her in both the near future and the long run.

She'd kept it together, kept a cool head, managed to control her emotions and at the same time separate them in an effective way from what she tried to focus on in the present moment.

But now?

Well, now she finally tried to relax in her own bed with nothing to distract her and no one else to keep her busy, and all the thoughts and feelings she'd handled so well came to pay her another little visit.

So many things about Kody's disappearance and trying to find the girl reminded Sam of the stretch of time from right before to long after she'd lost her Sophie. Hands-down the absolute worst chapter of her life by far, which technically hadn't even quite come to an end until recently — until Sam had finally realized she could mourn her own daughter, continue to love her Sophie the way she would never stop loving her, and find a way to move on with her life all at the same time without becoming a complete and utter mess along the way.

That was something Sam hadn't thought remotely possible until now.

Until the moment Brad had first mentioned Sophie a few days ago in a fit of pissed-off mouthiness. She was sure he'd spouted off with the intention to get his hooks in and make her hurt just like him. Maybe even to take her down to his level of anger-management issues. But Sam had surprisingly remained calm and relatively unaffected through all of it.

Tonight, though, it didn't quite seem like that was where this was headed.

Tonight, all these thoughts and feelings, the parallels she could so easily draw between what Brad and Denise were going through right now and what Sam had experienced herself with Sophie so many years ago, were almost too much.

She just didn't have the energy to sit with them, to look at each of them and decide how she felt, and then to tell herself it was okay to feel whatever the hell came up because she was a grown-ass adult and could get herself through moments like this, right?

Not tonight.

She spent the next fifteen minutes lying on her bed, trying to push down the bubbling emotions that clearly wanted some time in the spotlight.

Not tonight. I just can't handle this shit tonight.

In the morning, though? Sure. That was always a possibility.

Before she could get any further with that personal intention, though — and before she found out whether these new tactics of hers were sustainably effective — her phone rang.

At first, Sam was grateful for the distraction. Then she looked at her phone and saw it was Zach calling her.

What did he want?

He'd lied to her about his relationship with Kody, then he'd still given her inaccurate information about the argument with his mom. Sam did not have the patience for this guy. Not right now.

She silenced the call and let it go to voicemail.

Now that she thought about it, she might even prefer thinking about Sophie to thinking about Zach or anything else involved with Kody and this current case.

Her phone rang again.

With a frustrated grunt, Sam picked it up off her night-stand and rolled her eyes.

Zach again.

"Nope," she muttered, then silenced the call and let it ring.

When the guy clearly just couldn't take a hint and dialed her a third time, she almost lost it.

She snatched her phone off the nightstand, accepted the call, and practically shouted into it, "What?"

"Sam? It's Zach Turner."

"Uh-huh," she said dully.

"Listen, I'm sorry to bother you so late, but uh... My dad's gone missing."

Sam bolted up. "What?"

"I know, it's weird as hell. I'm not quite sure myself how something like that happens."

"Walk me through it."

"I talked to my mom earlier. She told me you'd stopped by and asked a few questions. Said Dad got all riled up after you left. Then I guess sometime after that, he just ... I don't know. Walked right out of the house. I mean, I can't really say he *escaped* from his own home, but that's kinda what it feels like right now."

"I can imagine," she muttered.

"I know it's not your problem, Sam. I just... Well, you and my mom were the two people who saw him last, and she's pretty upset right now, so it's hard to get her to say much of anything at the moment. I was wondering if maybe my dad mentioned anything to you about where he might be headed. Or if maybe you saw something that hinted at a potential place I could look for him."

For a moment, Sam just stared at her phone and couldn't think of anything appropriate to say, because her current thoughts weren't exactly comforting for someone who'd called her to inadvertently request her help in finding his missing father with dementia.

What the fuck is happening to this town? Everyone's

going missing. Next thing you know, I'm gonna wake up one morning, and this whole damn place is gonna be completely empty.

"Sam?" he asked. "Are you still there?"

She quickly shook her head and cleared her throat. "Yeah. I'm still here. Sorry, Zach. Listen, I wish I could tell you I knew where your dad might be, but I have no idea. The only thing he said while I was over there… Well, it didn't really make sense. He seemed pretty upset to hear your mom and me talking about Kody, and then he got even more upset when *he* started talking about Kody being in the oven."

"The oven?"

It was a natural response to hearing something so inarguably strange, but something about the way Zach said the word instantly put Sam on high alert.

His voice had changed.

He knew something.

"I can tell that one struck a nerve," she told him. "What does that mean to you?"

"It could be nothing. Maybe I'm just overreacting, but … I mean, my dad has never cooked a meal in his life, you know? The only time I ever heard him mention an oven at all was when he talked about work. It's what he used to call the boiler in the office building where our dental practice is."

Sam sat up even straighter in her bed and blinked across the Deville. "He called it the oven?"

"Yep. If he was going on about the oven at home before just walking out, I'd probably think he meant to stop by the office building, but that still doesn't make any sense. I don't know why he'd have any reason to go to the basement of his old workplace. Or why he'd be talking about *Kody* being in there. It just doesn't…"

Sam missed whatever he'd said next as she leapt off her bed and stabbed her phone's speaker button so she could keep up the conversation as she moved about her trailer.

"Then that's where we need to go," she called out, hurrying around the tiny space and pulling on a black long-sleeve shirt and a pair of dark jeans. "I'll meet you there at your office building in fifteen minutes, okay?"

"Sure. And Sam? Thank you."

"No problem. Just meet me there in fifteen. We'll figure this out."

She ended the call, shoved her feet back into her sneakers, then raced across the Deville and paused only to pull the old pistol Syc had given her out of the tiny side table's single drawer.

Then she raced out of the trailer, the screen door clacking shut behind her, and jogged across the dew-studded grass, past the crackling firepit and a marginally curious Dog lying on his side. He merely lifted his head at her passing but didn't bark and didn't get up.

Wherever Syc was, it wasn't in his normal seat by the fire, but she didn't have time to find him first. She had to get her ass out to that old building as soon as possible, preferably ten minutes ago.

THIS TIME, Sam parked her Jeep in front of one of Rush's oldest standing buildings, not wanting to waste time in parking somewhere else and walking the rest of the way.

Hers wasn't the only vehicle parked out front. She didn't recognize the other; it could have been Steven's, or it could have been someone else's, but she didn't have time to investigate.

After tucking the pistol into the back waistband of her

jeans, Sam hurried toward the building's front door, which had since been opened and entered and left ajar. Its glass window had been smashed in, leaving a trail of shattered shards spilling into the building's entrance along with a lingering trail of blood.

There was blood everywhere, she realized as she took in the scene.

It dripped down the front door, splattered all over the floor both inside and outside the building's entrance, and smeared across what little glass remained in the door's window, plus the doorknob itself.

Grimacing, Sam pulled out her phone and instantly dialed 9-1-1.

"9-1-1, what's your emergency?"

"Yeah, I'd like to report a B&E." Then Sam rattled off the address of the old office building, which was all the information she had. After that, she didn't stay on the phone long enough to give emergency dispatch her personal information or any other details. Partially because she didn't *have* any other details, but mostly because with this much blood and an older man with dementia running around in the basement of a building he used to rent for his own business, there wasn't a whole lot of time to waste.

So she ended the call despite dispatch's consistent requests for more details, pulled the pistol from the back waistband of her jeans, and shoved open the broken door before entering the building on her own.

FORTY-SIX

Sam

THE INSIDE OF THE OFFICE BUILDING WAS COMPLETELY dark, with no lights on anywhere, as far as she could see from the front entrance.

Sam had no idea where to go, and she didn't have a flashlight on her, either.

With a frustrated grunt, she stepped cautiously toward the wall and ran her hand up and down to search for the light. When she finally felt the switch beneath her fingers and flicked the light on, a soft, pale glow emanated from two dusty-looking sets of track lighting filling the ground floor's lobby. It wasn't intensely bright now, but it was enough to illuminate the alarmingly thick trail of blood splatter moving across the lobby toward a door at the far end of the hall in the back.

Sam gripped the pistol with both hands and inched forward, walking as quietly as possible while attempting to clear every dark corner of the building's front lobby as she made her way farther and farther back.

The open door at the end of the blood trail led her to a set of stairs heading almost straight down into the building's basement. Sam had no choice but to keep following the trail.

She moved step by step down the creaking staircase, which was also dimly lit by overhead lights. But when she reached the bottom, there was yet another door in front of her to be opened. This one wasn't latched, either, but it must have swung shut again behind whoever had opened it.

That meant whoever had come down here to the basement level had been in a hurry, all that blood notwithstanding, had failed to close up behind themselves.

With her forearm, Sam nudged the basement door open and crept inside.

The lights were on down here too, pale and dusty from lack of use. She didn't see anything immediately condemning, no sign of someone else down here, but the echoes of banging and clanging and angry growls and shouts easily made their way across the basement.

So Sam inched forward, step by step, trying to follow the sounds without making too much noise of her own.

When the basement got too dim to see much of anything around her, she looked for more light switches but couldn't find any. Apparently, she'd passed them by at the foot of the stairs, so as she continued, the basement only grew darker.

Then it was too dark to safely continue. Sam had to make do with the flashlight app on her phone, which made for an awkward grip when holding it beneath her gun the way she'd been trained to do with a real flashlight.

But now she could see where she was going.

There was a lot more in the basement than she'd first assumed.

The yelling and banging and scuffling sounds continued.

"Hello?" Sam called out. "Anyone here?"

"Yeah! Sam, over here."

It was Zach.

On one hand, that was great; he'd shown up. On the other hand, not so great, because she'd said she'd meet him here *not* so he could show up first and go blindly racing into a dark building after his dad when *anyone* could have broken in down here.

It was a lot easier to follow the sound of Zach's voice than the echoing grunts and noises of a struggle she didn't quite think had come from the dentist, either.

The more she moved through the basement, trying to follow Zach's voice, the more she realized it was a maze down here.

Almost everywhere she looked sat one kind of antique machine or another, most of which she had no idea what they were or what their functions had been back in the day.

More frustrating than that was these obstacles' tendency to make visibility even worse. Sam was forced to move around them one by one just to get to the other side of the basement, all without knowing what waited on the other side of the next machine or if she would soon come face to face with Zach just around the corner or with someone or something else instead.

"Zach?" she called again. "You still down here?"

"Yup! I'm just—"

He grunted, followed by another shout that didn't sound like it came from him, either.

"Lights?" Sam asked.

She didn't get an immediate response, which could have gone either way, but a brief moment later, a loud pop echoed through the basement before the overhead lights burst on all at once.

Sam hissed and lifted an arm to shield her eyes against

449

the instant glare flooding the basement. So bright, in fact, that her eyes burned as if she'd just looked into the sun on purpose.

"Jesus," she muttered.

She finally stopped blinking against the light, and most of the spots in her vision disappeared. She could now see across the rest of the basement in front of her against the far wall.

Then she could see the rest of the basement.

She also clearly saw Zach and Steven. The older Dr. Turner held a huge, heavy-looking monkey wrench in one hand, and Sam caught the tail end of him swinging it back over his shoulder before he brought it sailing down in front of him toward his intended target.

The wrench clanged against something metal with a reverberating echo like a cheaply imitated gong. Something groaned and shrieked. Then Steven drew his arm back with the wrench for another crippling blow.

Delivered to what looked a whole lot like the door of an old boiler.

"Zach?" Sam called again as she headed forward.

Steven didn't seem to hear her or notice her presence in the basement; he just kept banging away at the door.

"I'm here," Zach replied.

She turned left toward his voice and saw the man leaning against the left-hand wall, one hand extended to prop himself up while the other prodded gingerly at the side of his head.

That was definitely more blood.

Sam hurried toward him, diverting only slightly from what would have been a straight-shot path to Steven and the boiler.

For the moment, it seemed slightly more important to tend to the far more lucid man with all his wits about him and a new head wound than the old, retired dentist who'd lost his mind and now thought Rush's newest missing person was inside the defunct boiler in his old office building.

"What happened?" Sam asked, heading toward Zach.

Steven surprised everyone by whirling away from the boiler and brandishing his wrench right at Sam's face. "Back off!"

"Whoa, hey. Okay." Sam lifted both hands in concession, trying to act like the pistol didn't still hang from her grip, because what kind of a threat could an old man banging around with a wrench really be?

The least she could do was to play along and keep both her and Zach from sustaining any further injuries, however unlikely.

"I'll stay back, Steven," she said. "Sure. You wanna tell me what you're doing over there?"

The old man grunted in frustration, then spun back around to face the boiler door and lifted the wrench high above his head again. "I'm gonna do it," he muttered. "I'm gonna get the girl out. Just wait."

Sam turned to fix Zach with a wide-eyed look.

The younger man just shook his head and puffed out a sigh. "I have no idea what he's talking about, Sam."

She believed him.

She also had the distinct impression that Steven knew exactly what he was talking about. Or at least he believed he did, and that belief had clearly already put his own son in harm's way.

"You tried to stop him anyway?" Sam asked Zach over another clang and rattle of Steven smashing the wrench against the boiler's metal door.

"It wasn't on purpose," Zach explained. He took a deep breath, finally stepped away from the wall to prove to himself that his balance remained, and headed towards Sam.

His dad just kept banging away.

"I shouldn't have snuck up on him from behind the way I did," he confessed. "I knew that was a bad idea. I mean, it's a bad idea with *anyone*, but someone with dementia? Stupid. My fault completely."

"He still hit you."

"Pretty sure I just startled him. He swung around when he realized someone was there, and it's not like his arm strength is what it used to be."

Sam grimaced as she studied the gash on the side of Zach's head. "Clearly."

"By accident. Not on purpose."

"You aren't bleeding from anywhere else?" she asked. "I know head wounds bleed a lot, but that one doesn't look like there was very much. There's a whole lot more blood upstairs, though."

"It's his arm." Zach nodded toward his father again, and only now that it had been pointed out to her did Sam see Steven's left arm had, in fact, been cut open to bleed freely all over the broken glass of the door upstairs and the floor in the lobby and hallway.

It was still bleeding, though not as freely now; maybe all the heavy lifting with the wrench had gotten it to stop.

"What did he do?" she asked. "Just punched through the glass window?"

"That's my guess too," Zach said with a shrug. "I couldn't stop him. I don't know what he's doing, but it's obviously a big deal to him. I guess we could just let him finish, right?"

Sam was about to agree with him; it didn't seem like there was any viable reason not to. But then the faraway blaring of sirens growing steadily closer made its way into the basement over all the banging and clanging and heavy breathing from Steven's attempts to get into "the oven."

Zach turned toward Sam with wide eyes.

"Yeah, I called it in," she said. "Didn't wanna take any chances, but now we know."

"That'll be fun."

"We'll see." Sam set a hand on Zach's shoulder and gently led him away from the boiler and his father bashing away at it.

Steven seemed to no longer notice the other two people down here with him; only the boiler and his wrench existed, apparently.

"Let's see what we can do about this cut on your head," she said.

"I think there's a first-aid kit up on the wall somewhere over there."

Sam left him to investigate and found a first-aid kit almost exactly where he'd pointed. She brought it back with her to work under the brightest light on this end of the basement so she could simultaneously keep an eye on Steven for the moment as well. Dr. Turner the elder still seemed rather harmless again to everyone and everything but the boiler, but there was always a chance that might change, and she wanted to be prepared.

The first-aid kit turned out to be disappointingly low on stocked supplies, but she did manage to find a few wads of thick cotton padding to use as a compress pressed against Zach's head. The bleeding wasn't terrible, but it hadn't stopped completely yet.

Almost as soon as she finished with the compress, thundering footsteps and few shouted commands made their way down from upstairs as the police followed the blood trail into the basement just like Sam had. The next thing she knew, four officers rounded the corner of a final unidentifiable old machine in the back before stumbling upon Steven banging away at the boiler door with his wrench. Then they found Sam and Zach crouching together on the floor a few yards away with the first-aid kit open and the dentist pressing a ball of wadded-up cotton pads against the side of his head.

Decent response time for the Rush PD, Sam had to admit. She was honestly a little impressed.

But that faded the second she realized one of the four officers down here wasn't truly an officer but Rush's Chief of Police instead.

"Shit," she whispered.

At the same moment, Colton completed his visual assessment of the scene, and his gaze landed directly on Sam's face before his dangerously bitter scowl returned.

"Damn it, Salazar," he growled. "That's it. You're done."

FORTY-SEVEN

Sam

THE POLICE HAD FORTUNATELY ARRIVED ON THE SCENE with an ambulance, which made getting both Zach and Steven emergency medical attention that much faster and easier. The paramedics loaded Steven up into the back of the ambulance first. The man seemed to have forgotten halfway through his beating of the boiler what he was doing there and why he'd been tightly gripping a monkey wrench.

Fortunately, he hadn't remembered hitting his son in the head with it, so at least he didn't have to deal with the guilt of that as well.

Once they'd finished loading the older man, it was Zach's turn, but he pulled Sam aside first for a quick private conversation. "Thank you, Sam. For all your help."

"Of course. I'm glad you called, actually. So I could help. And I don't say that very often."

He laughed. "I had a feeling. Excuse me. I'm gonna call my mom now. I know she's worried out of her mind. Just wanna put her at ease about this whole thing."

"No problem." Sam stepped aside, gesturing for him to make that call, then looked around the parking lot.

She had a little time to let her brain do its thing and put together a whole bunch of different, seemingly random and unconnected details together before it revealed some kind of coherent shape. She'd had a feeling this was coming. She'd known something wasn't quite right about this whole situation earlier today, but she hadn't been able to pinpoint it.

Now, she thought she might just be a little closer to seeing that big picture as the end result, but she needed a few more details first to make that happen.

With the paramedics' and officers' attention all centered on the building itself and the father-son dentist pair being looked over and briefly questioned for their statements, Sam slipped out of the parking lot, hopped right up into her Jeep parked right there in front, and get the hell out before anything else got in her way.

She tried calling Brad multiple times on her drive to the hotel, but he didn't answer.

At this point, she was already close and in town anyway. So instead of passing the hotel on her way home, she stopped and decided to pay him an in-person visit.

This just felt too important to leave until the morning.

SHE BOOKED it down the ground-floor hallway toward Room 8 and knocked furiously.

If he'd fallen asleep already and missed all her calls, at least banging away like this would wake him up.

When the door finally opened, Sam didn't even give Brad a chance to say hello or invite her inside before she barged right in.

"Sam..." he started.

"Yeah, I know it's late. I get it. I'll be out of your hair in just a second, but I—"

She stopped when her gaze fell on Denise sitting upright on the room's single bed. The woman was fully clothed, fortunately, but the bed was unmade, and Denise's hair looked particularly disheveled, even for this time of night.

Sam pressed her lips together and froze. "Shit. I'm sorry, I didn't realize—"

"No, it's all right," Brad said. "I mean, I came to the door."

"Should've known you'd be sharing a room." Shaking her head, Sam headed back toward the door. She couldn't look Denise in the eye but had to say something anything. "Denise, I'm sorry. I shouldn't have burst in like this. I just need some information from Brad, and then I'll disappear."

"Did you find something?" Denise asked, ignoring all the awkwardness only Sam seemed intent on feeling right now and choosing instead to focus on the reason they were all here together for the first time in over fifteen years — something Sam never in her life would have believed possible if she weren't standing right here experiencing it.

"I'm not sure yet," she said. "Brad, I really just need Charles' number. That's it. I gotta check into something, but I don't have any way to get a hold of the guy."

"Sure." Brad hurried across the hotel room to grab his phone and quickly texted her the information she'd requested. "You gonna say anything about what you're thinking here, Salazar?" he asked as he set his phone back down on the built-in desk.

"Not quite yet. I might have something. Can't tell you one way or the other right now, but when I know, so will you."

457

"Fuck that," Brad said, heading after her and folding his arms. "You're here now. If you have an idea, if you think you're onto something, stay. It's something you can ask Charles and get a pretty concrete yes or no answer about, right?"

Sam's gaze darted around the room, briefly landing everywhere but on the faces of the other two occupants, both of whom seemed perfectly content now to be sharing the same hotel room with only one bed.

That much was immensely clear from the sight of Denise's closed suitcase resting on the floor next to Brad's open duffel bag, most of its contents overflowing from the unzipped top and spilling out across the floor.

Sam cleared her throat. "Yeah, pretty much. I just don't wanna overstay my welcome. Or whatever."

"Make the call, Sam," Brad said.

She nodded, pulled out her phone, and opened his text so she could get Charles' number, then called the guy herself.

"Hello?"

"Charles. It's Sam Salazar. Listen, I have to make this quick, but I've got some questions for you. Most importantly, did any of the missing women you've been looking into have dental appointments in town around the time they disappeared?"

"Huh. That's ... interesting." The sound of papers shuffling around and fluttering on top of each other came from the other end of the line. Then Charles sucked in a sharp breath. "Yeah, one of them did."

"What about Rose? Did she have an appointment set around that time with Dr. Steven Turner? He would've been the resident dentist in town at the time."

"No," Charles replied almost immediately. "No, Rose had a different dentist in another town. She'd drive an hour and a half away just to get out there to him. One of those things she was really picky about. She'd set an appointment with her dentist for, I think, about a week after the night she disappeared. Something about fixing a cracked tooth."

"You have those dates in front of you right now, or can you quickly get them in front of you?" Sam paced across the hotel room, no longer anywhere near as painfully aware of Denise and Brad watching her every move and hanging on her every word.

"Yeah, I know the exact dates," Charles said.

"I need you to look up the day Rose disappeared," Sam continued. "Maybe even the day she was scheduled to have her appointment with her regular dentist too."

"Sam, I don't have any records of an appointment she'd scheduled and never actually had. Why does that—"

"Okay, forget her scheduled appointment then, Charles. Did Rose go missing on a Friday?"

She was met with nothing but silence on the other end of the line for what seemed like a painfully long time.

Then Charles softly murmured, "Yeah. I'd stayed late at work getting ready for that weekend's editorial piece to go out the next day. It *was* a Friday. How did you—"

"Thank you so much," Sam interrupted, then instantly hung up on the man and figured she could make it up to him later.

"And?" Brad asked, spreading his arms as Sam paced one more time across the room.

"What was all that about?" Denise asked.

"I'm not a hundred percent on this yet," Sam said, rubbing her forehead. "But I think I might've just figured out what happened to Rose. Charles' wife." She grimaced, stopped, and turned to look back and forth between Kody's parents. "I just need to figure out how the hell it's connected to your daughter."

Before she could even begin, a harsh, alarmingly official-sounding knock pounded on the outside of the hotel room door.

Sam frowned at the door and gestured toward it. "Do you guys mind if I—"

"Go ahead." Brad waved for her to answer it.

Sam definitely didn't miss the wordless look of silent understanding passing between Brad and his ex-wife as Sam herself headed to the door. But when she opened that door and looked up at the man standing there on the other side of it, all thoughts of anyone else instantly fled her mind.

"Samantha Salazar?" asked the grim-faced Rush police officer.

"Yeah."

"You're under arrest for unlawfully interfering with an active police investigation. Turn around and place your hands behind your back."

Sam gaped at him. "You've gotta be fucking kidding me."

460

FORTY-EIGHT

Charles
_____

AFTER SUCH A STRANGE AND UNEXPECTED PHONE CALL like the one he'd just gotten from Sam Salazar, Charles set his phone back down on the nightstand, turned over in bed, and tried to go back to sleep.

But now he couldn't.

For the next thirty minutes, he tossed and turned, unable to shut off his brain because it kept going over and over the questions Sam had asked him and the possible implications of his answers.

Finally, it was just too much.

He tossed aside the covers, all but threw himself out of bed, and hurried downstairs to go look at his wall in the living room.

There were all the Missing posters for all six women who'd disappeared in or around Rush in the last thirty years, including his Rose — and Kody Anderson.

What had Sam been onto?

Charles had no idea how long he'd been standing in front of his wall, nor had he heard anything else within the house until his son was standing right beside him, frowning at the same posters.

Charles blinked groggily at the boy, though he didn't actually feel tired in the slightest. "Frankie, what are you doing down here?"

"Same thing you're doing down here," his son replied with a shrug. "Staring at your wall."

"It's late, son. You need to get back in bed, and this isn't something you need to worry about right now, okay?"

"I don't really care about the pictures," Frankie said. "I heard you running down the stairs, so I wanted to see what was going on." The boy slowly turned his head to look up at his father's profile. "Should I call Patty?"

Charles forced himself to hold back a laugh. "No, Frankie. Quick thinking, but no, I'm all right. Listen, you have school in the morning, and I wouldn't be doing either of us any favors if I didn't make it clear you need to get back upstairs right now and go to bed. You need your sleep. And school is what?"

"More important than everything," Frankie droned after the countless times his dad had fervently drilled the saying into him.

"That's right. That's my boy. Come here." Charles threw an arm around Frankie's shoulders and tugged him close in a sideways hug. The boy looked up at his father in wide-eyed surprise, and Charles could only laugh.

"Okay..." Frankie said, which surprised them both. "I'll go back to bed. Love you, Dad."

"Love you too, kid."

If he'd had enough time and energy to think about it, he would have realized the look of utter shock on his son's face for what it was — silent proof that neither of them could remember the last time Charles had said those words to anyone, even his own child.

Right now, though, Charles was otherwise occupied by the new thoughts swirling around in his head. Which meant he could only laugh at the baffled expression on Frankie's face before he bent over and planted a kiss right on the center of the top of the boy's dark curls. "Now get back upstairs and go to sleep. Understand?"

Frankie slipped out from under his dad's arm and did as he was told, stopping only once to look back over his shoulder at his father before slipping silently back up to his room again.

Charles didn't notice, though.

He was too busy scanning the women's faces in those Missing posters and mulling over the strangely hurried conversation he'd had with Sam.

Then he moved back to the kitchen table, where all his papers and notes and snippets of case files and various statements were still spread out in an organized pattern of his own design.

Charles sat down at the table to review everything he'd collected on these women. It didn't take him long to find what he was looking for.

The report from the third missing woman sixteen years ago, with a short statement referring to the dental appointment she'd made the week of her disappearance. On a Friday. The woman had told one of her co-workers she needed her shift covered because she'd made an appointment at a free clinic where she could get her teeth fixed, but it had to be *that* day.

Beyond that single woman, though, none of the other victims' friends or families had mentioned anything about teeth. The woman who'd disappeared before Rose, however, had seemed to complain an awful lot about jaw pain right before she went missing.

Scowling at the papers, Charles went back through all

the information to first double-check every single date of each woman's disappearance.

They were all five years apart, yes, but all of them had gone missing at different times of year. That had been part of the pattern he'd tried to pull out that just didn't add up, but now he knew about the days of the week.

Friday.

Charles checked, then double- and triple-checked until there was no doubt he'd gotten the dates right and had looked them up correctly.

Each one of these women had gone missing on a Friday.

With trembling hands, he sifted through the papers to go back over the records of Rose's disappearance and the ensuing investigation that had led to absolutely nothing. There was the police report, the official statement of the Rush PD accepting defeat and naming this an unsolved case.

He pulled out the photocopy of a picture taken of the inside of his wife's car the night she disappeared. That brown paper bag of hard candy sitting on the front seat. The candy his wife had loved so much that she bought some for herself every day and brought some home for their son every Friday so he could enjoy some too.

What if Rose had been eating that candy on her way home from work? What if the cracked tooth she'd already complained of had broken even further when she thought she'd have just a quick little treat at the end of the day?

She'd been on her way to pick up Charles from work that day, just like every day before they went together to pick Frankie up from Juana Aguayo's.

But what if on her way to pick her up husband from work, Rose had run into Steven Anderson on his way to or from work himself?

The newspaper's headquarters and Rush's single dental practice were only a few blocks apart. Rose and Steven had probably run into each other several times before then. Charles himself had seen the man walking along Rush's downtown sidewalks at all different hours just enjoying himself and the decent weather.

What if Rose had said something to their resident dentist about her cracked tooth? Maybe she'd complained about the pain, mentioned she'd made an appointment for the following week with her own personal dentist almost two hours away.

If Steven was the one with the free clinic giving out pro bono dental work on Fridays, that would fit.

Charles grabbed his phone and went right back to the last voicemail his wife ever left him.

He listened to it four times over, from beginning to end, no longer hanging on his wife's every word and trying to decipher the meaning of some things he couldn't understand or wondering why she'd sounded so funny.

Now he was just trying to make the pieces fit to double-check his theory.

And only now, six years later, did he realize this was an actual possibility.

What if Rose's mouth had been numbed by some sort of medication after receiving last-minute dental care from Steven Anderson? That would absolutely have explained why she sounded so odd in that voicemail, like her lips were made of pillows and she was talking around a mouthful of cotton.

Pressing a fist to his mouth, Charles knew exactly who he wanted to call next, exactly who he wanted to question to get the last bit of information he needed.

But it was late. He didn't want to bother anyone. He didn't want to ruffle any feathers, cause a big scene, do anything to make people start talking about him behind his back again, thinking Charles Putnam had finally lost what remained of his sanity.

Then he remembered he wasn't the only one who would benefit from discovering the truth. That girl Kody was still out there somewhere, lost and waiting to be found.

Maybe it wasn't too late.

It had been too late for his Rose, but it still might not be too late for Kody.

So he dropped all sense of decorum and neighborly politeness and dove into his research again to find a number for Susan Hooper, Steven Turner's wife, who hadn't taken her husband's name when they'd married but who now cared for the man in his later years.

Even with Steven's dementia, she ran a B&B out of their home.

Lucky for him, Susan had recently had a website created to draw more guests to her place, and her phone number was clearly listed right there among the contact information.

Charles made the call.

"Hello?" The woman sounded surprisingly awake, chipper, and downright peppy for almost 10:00 p.m.

"Susan?" he said, realizing how tired he sounded in comparison. "It's Charles Putnam with *The Daily Rush*."

"Charles! What a surprise to be hearing from you. How are you?"

"Just fine. I'm sorry about the late call."

"Nonsense! I don't get much sleep these days, anyway. Tell you what, that's just what getting old does to you."

"I'm starting to understand some of that myself, yeah."

"What can I help you with?"

Charles cleared his throat and steeled himself to get

this done. He had to at least ask, no matter what the answer turned out to be. Until he asked, he couldn't move forward. "I was just looking over some information, and a few ideas occurred to me. I was wondering, back when your husband was still doing dental work and ran his practice downtown, do you know if he ever offered free dental services out of his office?"

"I *do*. And yes, he did. My husband left one afternoon slot open every single Friday for as long as he worked. It was normally reserved for emergencies, just in case one presented itself, but when there wasn't, he opened up the time to provide dental work for the less well-off in and around town. Steven was always a huge proponent of giving back to the community, you understand. He did everything he could possibly think of to—"

Charles ended the call. He hadn't meant to; he hadn't even thought about doing it, but as he'd listened to Susan talk, he realized he just couldn't handle the sound of her voice anymore.

He sat there at the kitchen table, fully erect, his eyes incredibly wide as he stared blankly across the kitchen.

His breath quickened, his pulse raced through his veins, and everything about Charles' world and what had become of his life was once more shifting.

He knew exactly what had happened to Rose.

FORTY-NINE

Sam

SAM PACED ACROSS THE INSANELY TINY SPACE WITHIN THE holding cell in the back of Rush's police station. Every five steps, she had to turn around and head in the opposite direction. No matter how late it was, sitting still, biding her time, and waiting for someone to come speak to her just wasn't an option.

The last officer she'd had contact with refused to be of any help at all, but he was the one making the rounds tonight, so he was the one she had to talk to.

"Officer!" she shouted, raising her voice as loud as possible without completely ruining it. "Officer Cooley? I need to speak with you. Get over here!"

There wasn't any response at first. There never was, especially when a newly incarcerated defendant kept making as much noise as Sam did. But she wasn't some obnoxious local, or a drunk, or a belligerent asshole refusing to see the signs of her own shortcomings.

This was a matter of life and death, and she really needed to get to work so she could ensure it remained a matter of life and nothing else.

Sam stopped in front of the cell bars, wishing she'd had something hard to throw at them, and resorted to banging against the bars and rattling the literal cage in both hands. The metal wobbled in her grip, clanging the cell door against its setting, and she kept at it.

"Cooley! Officer Cooley, I need to speak to you. Where are you? This is seriously important! I need to talk to Chief Colton *right now*. Cooley!"

She'd been at it like this for who knew how long. Her arresting officer had confiscated her phone and watch and all other personal effects before processing her and sticking her back in here. All standard protocol.

Except nothing about tonight was standard or normal.

Sam *had* to let someone know.

"Hello?" she yelled, banging around nonstop. "Is anyone even in this fucking station? Hello? I need to speak to you!"

The echo of a heavy metal door creaking open and slamming shut again somewhere farther down the hall made her stop. Then in strode the same tall, lanky officer who'd shown up outside Brad and Denise's hotel room to place Sam under arrest.

"Hey, hey!" Sam shook the cell bars again. "Officer Cooley! Hey, Officer Cooley, I really need to talk to the chief."

"This isn't happy hour, ma'am," he grumbled. The man's footsteps preceded him around the corner, then Sam's arresting officer came into view and stopped six feet away from the front of her cell, folding his arms. "You're making too much noise back here. So your choices are—"

"Yeah, yeah, I know what's on the menu for regular inmates, okay?" Sam blurted with a scoff. "Just listen to me, Cooley."

"It's Cowley," he growled, his scowl darkening even more.

This guy must've taken lessons in the same expression from Chief Colton.

Sam squinted at him, pressed her forehead against the cell bars, then tilted her head. "Cowley. Huh. Sorry about that. Couldn't see the W. Listen—"

"That's not how this works, ma'am. *You* listen. If I have to come back here again—"

"I shouldn't have to ask again, either," Sam interrupted, her exasperation bordering now on unbridled rage because this was serious. She renewed her desperate grip on the cell bars. "Listen to me, Cowley. There's something going down tonight. There's a missing young woman out there. That Kody girl. Rip Graham's out there with her too, and they need our help. This is a matter of life or death. I'm not trying to get myself out of a cell. I just need to talk to Colton."

"Not gonna happen," Cowley replied.

"Damnit, you need to listen to me!" she shouted. "I know you're trying to be a badass and do your job, but there's no time for that. Just tell Colton that I—"

"You need to sit down, shut your mouth, and quit being such a pain in my ass," Cowley barked.

It seemed he'd taken some lessons from Colton in how to speak to Sam Salazar in particular as well, though he wasn't nearly as successful with it as he was with imitating Colton's perpetual scowl.

Then the man spun around and marched back toward the door.

"No, no, no!" Sam shouted after him. "Wait, I'm serious! *This* is serious. If you don't get Colton in here right now, innocent people are going to die! Is that what you want, Cowley? Cowley!"

Sam jerked on the cell bars again, just trying to make as much noise as possible. "You want both their deaths on your conscience? Because that's what's gonna happen if I don't speak to your chief. You hear me, Cowley?"

The heavy door slammed shut again, marking the officer's exit.

She glowered in that direction, then hissed and threw herself away from the cell bars. "Fuck!"

She was so close to figuring out exactly what had happened to Kody and where she'd find the woman. She was only missing a few small pieces, and she would have been able to put them all together tonight if Colton hadn't been so adamant about keeping his fucking promise.

She continued pacing for who knew how long, then the door into the holding room squealed open again. The second it did, Sam was back at the cell bars, both hands squeezing them tight as she pressed her face forward as far as possible.

"Listen, Cowley," she started again. "I know you don't like me making noise back here, but until I talk to Colton, I'm not gonna stop. You'll have to knock me unconscious otherwise, because this is something I can't afford to let you ignore."

Slow, echoing footsteps approached, then a figure appeared around the corner to stop in front of her cell.

But it wasn't Officer Cowley.

"Tempting. To knock you unconscious, I mean."

It was Colton.

"Finally," Sam blurted. "Thank fuck."

"If it's so important, Salazar, you need to start talking. Now."

"Colton, listen. I found out how it's all connected, okay? You and your men came to that old office building, and I know the scene you found there was a little odd, but it all comes back to Steven, right? Steven Turner."

"The man's got dementia," Colton murmured. "Pretty bad, from what I hear."

"Yeah, well, this isn't about what he's doing *now*. It's about what he's *already* done," Sam blurted. "Listen, the man was convinced Kody was in that old boiler in the basement. That all he had to do was open the door and get her out of there. That's not just the ravings of an old man, Colton, okay? We've been talking about Kody, and he knows Kody's in danger, but I don't think he was looking for Kody. Not specifically."

Colton raised an eyebrow. "You got dementia too? Because this sounds like rambling bullshit to me."

"No, just *listen*!" Sam jerked on the cell bars to rattle them again.

Colton's hand moved toward the grip of his service pistol holstered at his hip but just to rest there.

She took a deep breath.

Pull your shit together and make it fast. He's already run out of patience.

"Okay, look," she tried again. "Yes, Steven lost it a little, and he went to that basement saying he was looking for Kody. But what if he wasn't looking for *Kody*? That's just the name that's been on everyone's lips, so he picked it up. What if he was there looking for other women instead?"

Colton sucked on his teeth, clearly unconvinced. "Other women just randomly shoved into an old-school boiler?"

"What? Random — Jesus Christ. No. The other *missing* women. The other five Charles Putnam's been looking into. Including his late wife, Rose. What if Steven went looking for Kody in there because *she's* missing, and in his mind, he connected one currently missing woman to all the others that had at one point in time *been* in the boiler? Get where I'm going with this?"

Colton looked her up and down and slowly shook his head. "Not really."

"Oh, come on. What if that was where he'd previously hidden the bodies of his five other victims?" After delivering this last piece of what she hoped was thought-provoking information, she spread her arms and waited. "Come on, Colton. Say something."

"What if, huh? That would be a hell of a coincidence. Too bad it sounds like a whole load of conjecture and not a hell of a lot else."

Sam growled through her clenched teeth and forced herself not to start calling him names because he just wasn't getting it.

"It's not, Chief," she said stiffly. "I can promise you that, okay? I know it's not. You can go back through all those unsolved case files yourself, yeah? You'll find it all right there in the reports, just like I did. Just little snippets, but every missing woman had complained at some point right before they disappeared that they had a problem with their teeth."

"Huh." With a sniff, Colton picked invisible lint off his uniform shirt and flicked it toward the ground. "So now you're trying to tell me the Tooth Fairy's involved too?"

Now he was just screwing with her.

Of course he was.

The man had her in a cell for what he thought was interfering with an investigation. Of course he'd want to get in a few good ones first.

But she had to ignore it.

"Two things," she continued. "One woman with a sore jaw, and even Rose was having dental problems when she disappeared. She had an appointment already scheduled in a different town for a week out from the day she went missing. And oh, hey, look at that. *Steven Turner* was Rush's only available dentist at the time."

Colton slightly lifted his chin. "Keep going."

Sam wanted nothing more than to sigh in relief and take a moment to collect herself again, but there still wasn't time for a luxury like that.

"And look at where Rose's car was found," she continued. "Yeah, in the parking lot of the old bus terminal, right? It wasn't shut down back then, so everyone assumed she'd hopped on a bus. But that terminal is literally on the other side of the street from the Turner Dental offices. It's wide-open parking, and it's free. Hell, I had a cavity filled just the other day, and *I* parked in that empty lot because it was a hell of a lot easier than trying to find a spot in front of the old building. It doesn't have its own lot, okay?

"So Rose parked at the bus station and went in to see Steven for a last-minute appointment on Friday, the day she disappeared, because back then, Dr. Turner left an open slot in the afternoon every single Friday for last-minute emergency dental work if something showed up."

"That's a whole lot to take in," Colton said.

"Well, take it in fast, Chief. Go back to the office building. Go open the door to that boiler. I wouldn't be surprised at all if you found human remains in there, okay? *That's* what you're looking for."

The chief's scowl softened a little, though his skepticism was still remarkably palpable even with the bars of a jail cell between them.

"To go do all that," he said, "I need permission first."

"And you'll get it," Sam said. "Trust me. Go talk to Zach, Steven's son. He's the one running the practice now.

And I'll bet he'd give you his permission just like that. No questions asked, okay? We gotta get this done."

Colton studied her a moment longer, then nodded. "So that's what you've been yelling about in here this whole time?"

"Come on. I wasn't gonna trust Cowley with all this. *You're* the one who needs to hear it. You're the one who needs to go check it out. So go check it out, Chief. Don't worry about me. I'm not going anywhere."

Colton didn't say a word before he turned and walked out of the holding area.

Now that she'd finally told him everything she'd been desperate to tell the man since her arrest, a massive wave of exhaustion washed over Sam with a heavy sigh. She staggered backward away from the cell bars and plopped down onto the hard concrete bench built into the cell's back wall. Then she closed her eyes, took several deep, rhythmic breaths, and hoped none of this had come too late.

IT COULDN'T HAVE BEEN MORE than twenty minutes before Colton reappeared in front of her cell.

Sam perked up a little when she saw it was him, but she didn't bother to get to her feet again. "That was fast."

Colton folded his arms. "Let me tell you why. I called Zach Turner. Asked him about the boiler. You know what he told me? When they switched from boiler to electric heating, that old piece of junk was cleaned out. Sprayed down with a hose. Washed out, dried up, vacuumed damn near spotless before they sealed it back up again for safety. And the building's tenants put together a cute little time capsule to stick in there behind the sealed door. Pretty sure that time capsule doesn't include bones and teeth from the old dentist's victims."

No. That doesn't make any sense…

Then Sam's surprise and confusion quickly melted away into something else when she put the pieces together in her mind.

A heavy, sinking weight like disgust and guilt and the humiliation of not having realized sooner.

"Shit," she muttered.

"Yeah, you're telling me," Colton grumbled.

"Not in the boiler. Chief, in the dental offices on that building's second floor, there's an antique curio cabinet with a pretty gruesome display. You should confiscate that display, then go check the DNA of the teeth you'll find there against the DNA of those missing women. Five of them, anyway. I'm really hoping to hell right now Kody hasn't made it to the trophy case yet."

Yes, it was one hell of a macabre thing to say. And yes, it sounded crazy as hell.

To his credit, Colton didn't say a thing about it, which would have only stated the obvious at this point. Instead, he merely stood there with his arms folded and stared at her.

Sam stood and spread her arms. "Listen, just do it. Go run the DNA from all those teeth in the cabinet. If I'm wrong about this, Colton, I will leave town the second you let me out of here. And I will *never* come back. I'll be out of your hair for good. You'll never see me again."

It felt like it took the man forever to finally give her an answer.

"Well, it won't be the second I let you out of here," he said as the harsh jingle of a heavy keyring echoed around the holding area. "Let's just settle on you keeping your word the second I get in touch. If you're wrong about this."

"I'm banking my entire life in this town on not being wrong about it, Chief."

"Yes, you are."

He found the appropriate key for unlocking her individual cell, opened the door, and gestured for Sam to follow him out of the station.

THE OTHER OFFICERS on duty tonight stared after Sam and Colton as if their Chief of Police were leading a three-armed, green-skinned extraterrestrial through the station.

Sam's release was processed with astounding speed for how long she expected the officers to take, and she was returned her personal effects with a curt nod from Colton to get the hell out of there. "Either way, Salazar, you'll be hearing from me soon."

"Yeah, I'm counting on it."

She hurried out to her car, both aware of and unaffected by the late hour. Not so late that Sam was too exhausted to do what had to be done, but getting in touch with certain people she really needed to talk to would be more difficult.

There still wasn't any time to waste.

There wasn't even time to sit and think about how miraculously unexpected it was for Colton to have taken her seriously and turned her loose because of it.

Sam could worry about all that later.

Right now, pulling her Jeep out of the station's parking lot without breaking all the traffic laws and getting herself popped again — this time for public endangerment and high-fine traffic infractions — was all she could manage.

She definitely wasn't going home.

The next time she got out of her Jeep, she'd parked it in front of Charles' house. The lights inside were still on, thankfully, at least on the main level. The second story was dark, but Sam did already know Charles had a young son who was most likely in bed asleep right now.

She hoped it stayed that way.

Sam knocked on the door, shifted uncomfortably from foot to foot, and gazed around the residential block. There was no one else out here. Didn't even seem like anyone else was awake, which was all for the best.

The conversation she was about to have with Charles was the kind definitely better had in person.

But when the door opened, Sam found herself staring not at Charles but at a woman Sam didn't know or even recognize.

"Uh … sorry to bother you. I'm looking for Charles."

The woman's eyes widened. "Who are you?"

"Sam Salazar. I've been working with Charles the last few days. Helping the family of the missing girl."

"Oh." The woman's eyes widened even more, and in the low light spilling from the softly glowing bulb on the porch, Sam noted the instant shift from surprise to dread, helped along by the new shimmer in the woman's eyes.

"Please," the woman said, "come inside."

They didn't make it any farther past the front entryway.

"Where is he?" Sam asked.

The woman shook her head. "He's gone."

"What do you mean, gone? And, I'm sorry, who are *you*?"

"I'm Patty. Patty Bellhurst. I've worked with Chuck at *The Daily Rush* for years."

"And you're answering his front door because…"

Patty sighed and tucked her shoulder-length hair

behind one ear. "Chuck and I have been dating for the last few years."

Sam glanced around the inside of the home and nodded. "Do you know where he went?"

"No." Patty's voice broke, and Sam was sure the woman would burst into tears at any second.

Somehow, though, she didn't.

"No, he's not here," Patty continued. "He called me about an hour ago, I think. He was hysterical. It sounded that way on the phone. I couldn't make out half of what he said, but he was going on and on about how he knew what had happened to Rose and he was going after the person who did it. To get justice for his wife's death. To make it right."

"Where did he call you from?" Sam asked.

"From here, I'm assuming. I was at home when he called, and he didn't sound like himself, you know? I was worried. When he hung up on me, I came over here as fast as I could, but he was already gone. And he — God, I can't believe this is happening again. He left the house unlocked and his son here, sleeping upstairs in his room all by himself, with no one else around. He didn't call me to ask if I would watch Frankie. Honestly, I don't know *why* he called, but he's out there somewhere, doing God knows what, and I'm just trying to hold things together here while—"

"Patty?" The small, groggy-sounding voice made both women turn in the foyer to see Frankie standing there at the base of the stairs, his eyes wide with concern as he looked back and forth between them. Then the fear in his expression only deepened before he asked, "Is Dad okay?"

"Go back up to your room," Patty said, clearly fighting to keep her voice neutral around the kid.

"And he didn't tell you at all where he was headed?" Sam asked.

Patty shook her head. "The only specific thing he mentioned that actually made any sense was that he'd just gotten off the phone with *you*. And that now he knew what had happened to Rose. I just assumed…"

If Sam hadn't been behind bars at the time, Patty would have assumed correctly. Sam would have been with the man already.

Now Charles had gone off without any idea what he was getting himself into.

And the rest of the time Sam had hoped she'd left had just completely run out.

"Shit."

FIFTY

Charles
_____

CHARLES REALIZED HE WAS POUNDING ON THE FRONT door. In the back of his mind, he knew this was coming on too strong, that he was making a scene already and he hadn't even looked the man in the eye yet.

But he couldn't contain himself.

It didn't matter at this point anyway. Charles was here for one thing and one thing only, and he'd be damned if he let himself be cowed by social niceties before he'd seized his moment to set the record straight.

To make things right.

It felt like he'd been pounding on the door forever, so it startled him when the door finally opened and he found himself staring at the woman who lived here. "Susan."

"Charles?" She blinked groggily, frowned at him, then squinted into the night with a brief investigation up and down the street. "My goodness, Charles. What's going on? Do you know what time it is?"

"I need to speak to Steven."

"It's incredibly late. Why don't you tell me what—"

Charles muscled his way past the old woman and

stomped into the house — something he never would have done before. But now, apparently, it was his first instinct. "Where is he, Susan? I need to speak to your husband."

She shook her head as she shut the front door behind them and followed him across the entryway. "He's not here. They drove him out to a different hospital after they picked him up at the office building. What's this about?"

"Susan," he said, spinning quickly around to face her. "I know. About all of it."

"What's that, now?"

"Everything. There's no hiding it anymore. I know all about what Steven was doing at his practice. That he killed my Rose. That he lured her in—" His breath caught in his throat, voice breaking. Charles turned away from the woman.

For being disturbed this late at night by a highly emotional man accusing her husband of murdering his wife, Susan remained amazingly calm. She fixed Charles with an empathetic frown and gently took his hand in both of hers before patting the back of it. "Everything's going to be all right. You're clearly excited, Charles, I see that. Come inside. Come sit down. I'll make us some tea, and we can talk."

He took a deep breath, oddly calmed in his moment of fury by this woman's friendliness and willingness to actually sit and talk with him. "All right."

"Good. Please. Come on in."

She led him through the enormous home and into the sitting room before gesturing toward one of the couches. "I'll just go put the tea on. Make yourself at home. There's no one else here. All the guest rooms are empty. Just take a few deep breaths, and I'll be back before you know it."

Both surprised by how effective the woman's calm composure was in settling him and admittedly frustrated by it, Charles meandered across the enormous sitting room toward the collection of couches and chairs on the far side by the fireplace. It took him a moment to feel fully comfortable dropping down onto one of those couches, but when he did, the cushions were so incredibly soft beneath him, he felt as if he'd just unloaded a massive weight.

Pull yourself together. You stormed in here accusing this woman's husband, and he's not even home. You didn't come here to scare her, man. Get a hold of yourself.

For the next several minutes, Charles sat on the couch, listening first to the slightly off-putting silence filling the old house around him, removed just far enough away from downtown that the regular sounds of Rush's nightlife didn't reach them out here.

That silence made it impossible to ignore the sound of Susan bustling around in her own kitchen and filling a tea kettle, which he assumed was electric because he never heard the shrill scream of a regular steam kettle before Susan joined him in the sitting room again.

The large serving tray clinked and jingled as she carried it toward him in both hands. The tray and teacups, saucers, and all the usual accessories for tea settled down onto the coffee table before Susan grabbed a teacup for herself, which she had already filled. As she sat down on the couch opposite him, she nodded toward the second teacup, full and steaming and filling the air with a slightly fruity aroma with hidden notes Charles couldn't quite place but which he found surprisingly calming already.

"That one's yours," Susan said. "Go ahead. Have some tea, Charles, then tell me why you're here looking so desperately for my husband."

Ten minutes ago, Charles had been unable to sit still or to get a hold of himself. He'd been revved up and ready to do whatever it took to see his Rose's murderer brought to justice.

And now here he sat on a couch with that murderer's wife, drinking tea.

Was this really what he wanted?

Was the alternative really what he wanted either, though?

Susan nodded at him again. "Take your time. I'm not going anywhere."

Charles took a deep breath and nodded. "I figured it all out. In the days before Rose disappeared, she said she'd cracked a tooth. It was bothering her so much."

"Of course it was. That's incredibly painful."

"She'd made an appointment for the following week with her regular dentist, but I think … I think she went to see your husband instead."

Susan's frown deepened as she cocked her head. "But Rose was never a patient of his."

"No, she wasn't. I think the day she disappeared, she ran into your husband that afternoon, chatted to him. You know, as we all do here in town when everybody knows practically everyone else."

The woman slowly sipped her tea, holding the saucer delicately beneath the cup raised to her lips. Once she swallowed, she murmured, "Go on."

No longer thinking about the specifics of where he was or what he was doing, Charles lifted his own cup to his lips, blew on the steaming tea a few times, and took a quick sip. He didn't taste it as it went down, but the warmth spreading through him definitely seemed to help.

"I think they talked that afternoon," he continued. "I think Rose mentioned her broken tooth. And I think your husband offered to fix it for her that day, because he always left appointment times open in the afternoon on Fridays for last-minute emergencies or free dental work."

Smiling softly, Susan nodded. "Yes, he did. Most of the time, those open appointment slots filled at the last second."

Charles took another sip of tea. "I think she went with him to his office. And then I think your husband killed her. He murdered her right there in his office, and then he disposed of her body and left me and my son alone. Clueless. While the rest of the world tried to convince us the mother of my child had just woken up one day and decided to abandon her family without a word."

Susan didn't immediately respond, which instantly made Charles feel even more self-conscious, not to mention frustrated by the whole situation.

Then she sipped her tea and nodded. "Charles, I absolutely understand how you might come to a conclusion like this. I understand how hard it must be for you. Not knowing for certain what happened to Rose that night. I'm not angry with you for telling me. And I don't think any less of you, first of all."

Charles looked up at her with wide eyes. "Really?"

"Of course not. This is a difficult situation. I do have to say, though, that I still don't understand why my husband would have done this if it happened the way you say it did. If this really were true, why? Why would he do that? As far as I know, they hardly knew each other more than in passing. Same as you and me."

"I know, Susan. I know. And I can't figure that part out, either. But when I look at the bigger picture, everything together as a whole, it just … it makes sense. Rose wasn't the only one of these missing women who'd had dental issues or who'd mentioned tooth aches or sore jaws or having dental issues that needed to be addressed. But it all fits perfectly together when you think about it. Each of these women got into your husband's chair. He sedated them. When they felt safe and trusted him to help them. And then he killed them."

"Without rhyme or reason, though? Just like that?" Susan slowly shook her head. "That's the part I can't wrap my mind around."

He looked down into his teacup, which was still mostly full. The tea was good, yes, but he hadn't come here for tea.

The surface of the liquid shimmered.

Charles blinked.

Then blinked again, harshly this time.

The teacup blurred in his vision, the brightness of its white china dimming with alarming speed.

He was losing it. Wasn't he?

"It just…" He breathed deeply through his nose. "It just … makes … sense. And I…"

Charles blinked heavily again, slightly more concerned now because he couldn't remember what he'd just been about to say.

"Yes?" Susan leaned forward toward him.

"I just…"

The teacup rattle against its matching saucer in his hands. Charles blinked again, his breath moving rapidly in and out of his lungs now.

Something wasn't right.

"Susan?"

A wave of dizziness overwhelmed him, and he groaned against it, clenching his eyes tightly shut.

"I'm here," she said.

The next second, Charles could hardly feel the teacup and saucer in his hand. He was vaguely aware of something hot splashing against his thigh before something else shattered close by. When he opened his eyes again, his vision wobbled and blurred, like he'd been out on an all-night bender instead of sipping tea with Susan Hooper.

"I…"

Whatever he'd been about to say swirled through his head, mixing with the fog and the numbness pouring into all his senses and overtaking everything.

The next thing he knew, Charles found himself staring at the side of the couch's armrest a mere two inches away from his face.

He was lying on his side.

He couldn't move.

He tried to ask the woman what was happening to him, but the only sound he could manage was a low, gurgling moan.

Susan slowly placed her teacup and saucer back down on the coffee table with a gentle clink. "It's all right, Charles."

He heard her moving, was still aware of her presence with him in the sitting room, but he couldn't see her with the couch's armrest right up against his face.

He still couldn't move.

A shadow fell across him, and a soft, cool hand settled gently on his shoulder before Susan shushed him again.

"It's all going to be okay. Soon, Charles, all the pain will be over. I promise."

Charles tried to scream. He tried to push himself up off the couch. He tried to move, failed to accomplish any of it, then everything went black.

FIFTY-ONE

Sam

SAM BROUGHT HER JEEP TO A SQUEALING STOP AT THE curb in front of Susan and Steven's B&B.

The next second, she recognized Charles' sedan in the driveway and hoped like hell she wasn't too late for this one too.

Moving quickly, she headed up the walkway cutting through the manicured front lawn, stepped onto the porch, and approached the front door to give it a loud, hearty, official-sounding knock.

There was no reply. No sound of any movement from inside.

But that didn't necessarily mean anything, did it?

Lifting the old pistol in her hand, Sam gave the front doorknob a quick jerk before pushing the door open the rest of the way with her shoulder. She waited a second longer, then stepped quickly inside, firearm raised and at the ready.

At almost 11:30 p.m., the inside of Susan and Steven's house was as bright as day. All the lights in the entryway were switched on, as well as in the smaller living room at the front of the house, continuing all the way back.

Sam moved quickly and quietly through the home, clearing every small room and corner in the space behind open doors as she went. There was no sign of movement. No sound.

Then she reached the enormous sitting room at the back of the house, which was also empty.

Until she caught sight of the pair of legs hanging over the couch cushions without a body sitting upright to match.

Weapon still raised, she hurried across the living room and rounded the corner to see Charles lying there on the couch, eyes closed, one arm drooping over the side of the cushions.

"Shit."

She reached down to feel for a pulse at his neck.

It was faint and slow but definitely still there.

Not dead, then. Just drugged.

For now, it was safe enough to leave him here.

"Charles," she whispered, leaning down toward him. "Charles, can you hear me? It's Sam."

There was no change in his breathing. No response that showed he heard her. Only a new sound coming not from the sitting room but from down the hallway at the back of the house.

Rising again, Sam turned in that direction, lifted her pistol, and headed toward the noise.

The first two rooms she passed were empty, but the third was clearly the source of all the rumbling, banging, and hurried footsteps.

Sam nudged the door open with the back of her hand and let it swing aside into the room on silent well-oiled hinges.

Susan bustled around the room, grabbing various items

of clothing from the closet and dresser drawers before haphazardly tossing them into an open suitcase on the bed. She didn't notice Sam's presence until she spun away from the closet again.

When she finally saw her newest guest, the woman didn't start or jump in fright. She merely slowed, looked Sam over from head to toe, and said, "Sam. This is certainly a surprise."

"For both of us." Sam nodded toward the open, half-packed suitcase on the bed. "Where are you headed?"

"They took Steven to a regional hospital outside town after that fiasco at the office building." The woman tossed the newest item of clothing into the suitcase, then went straight for the dresser again to search for more. "So I'm just putting a few things together to go join him. He needs his wife."

Sam wrinkled her nose. "He might have. But I'm not convinced that's the case anymore."

"You're allowed to think whatever you like, Sam," Susan said. Still, she didn't stop packing.

"You know what I really think, though?" Sam continued. "I think you haven't been honest with me, Susan. That looks like an awful lot of packing for a few days' stay in the hospital. It's only a couple hours' drive."

"You never know what you're going to need when you're that far from home," the woman retorted.

"See, though, something tells me you're not going to take care of your husband. Looks more like you're trying to leave town. Like you're running away from something."

Susan merely shrugged.

A weak but unmistakable groan came from the main sitting room at the far end of the hall.

Susan froze, and when she spun around to look quickly up at Sam again, Sam had the pistol raised once more.

This time trained on Susan.

"Yep," Sam said. "I found Charles. Anything you wanna tell me about that?"

"I didn't hurt him, if that's what you want to know. I had no reason to hurt the man. I just needed him out of the way."

"Sure," Sam said. "But you had plenty of reason to hurt other people, right?"

Susan's eyes widened as she gestured in the direction of the sitting room. "That man came waltzing into my home almost in the middle of the night, accusing Steven of murdering those missing women. Can you believe that? As if Steven could have actually accomplished such a thing. I can't just sit here and wait around for those kinds of rumors to start."

"Is it the rumors you're worried about? Or the truth?"

That made Susan pause again, and despite having a loaded weapon aimed directly at her, she didn't look in the least bit afraid of the younger woman holding that weapon.

"The truth," she muttered. "What do you know about the truth?"

"I think Charles thought *he* knew," Sam replied. "But I think he's wrong. I don't think your husband attacked or killed any of those women. I don't think he's ever been anything more than an experienced dentist with a big heart. Truth is, the way I see it, *you're* the one who killed them."

Susan stared back at her with an almost convincing cluelessness before she scoffed and let out a high-pitched chuckle. "That certainly makes for an interesting story, doesn't it?"

The woman resumed her packing, but then the sound of multiple pairs of footsteps echoing toward them from the other side of the house made her stop again.

"Interesting idea," Sam said. "Yeah. And convincing

enough to make a few other people just as curious as I am."

The door to the bedroom swung open again, and Chief Colton stepped into the room.

Sam was aware of the low conversation taking place in the sitting room down the hall, muttering voices and more footsteps moving quickly. It definitely felt good to have some backup for once. Hopefully, Colton's other officers could get Charles out of here quickly and safely.

"Chief Colton!" Susan exclaimed. "Well, my B&B finally seems to be a popular spot."

"It won't be when this is over," Colton replied. "You won't be here either, Susan."

"You can't take me anywhere. My husband needs me. You wouldn't condemn a good man like Steven to that kind of fate, would you, Chief?"

"Funny thing about your husband, actually," Colton said, his scowl twitching at the corners. "Turns out all he needed was a little time away from *you*. A few hours of not being constantly drugged by his wife and, hey, miracle of all miracles, the man opens his mouth and starts spilling his guts, just like that."

Susan froze again, but this time, her eyes were wide and bright, glistening with that kind of fear carried by a deer caught in the headlights or a young child caught with their hand in the cookie jar.

"Boy, did your husband have a hell of a lot to say about you, specifically," Colton added. "About what you've done over the last thirty years to at least five women in this town. And those are just the ones we know about."

"So far," Sam added.

Susan looked quickly back and forth between them, then sucked on her teeth with an agitated clicking sound.

"Well, this night turned out quite a bit differently than I thought it would."

"You'll have plenty of time to think about it behind bars," Sam said.

The other woman sighed and gestured down the hall again. "You have to know I really didn't hurt Charles at all. It'll wear off in a few hours. I just couldn't let him get in the way. He came barging in here, thought he'd figured it all out. He was almost right, wasn't he?"

"He just had the wrong spouse," Colton said.

"But it wasn't Steven." Susan scoffed. "Oh no, he could *never*. That man doesn't have a violent bone in his body. And, oddly enough, the hardest part was getting him to drag the bodies down to the boiler in the first place. But it had to be done."

Sam tightened her grip on the pistol, gritting her teeth. "Why? Why those women, Susan?"

She met Sam's gaze with such convincing incredulity that it sent an unnatural shiver tingling down Sam's spine.

"Something had to be done about it," Susan replied with a bitter laugh. "Steven wouldn't hurt a fly, sure, nor would he ever risk hurting someone's feelings by turning them down. My husband has always been *so weak* when it comes to standing up for himself. And those women, each and every one of them, knew it. Oh, they knew so well what they were doing. They all knew my husband wouldn't lift a finger against it or utter a single word to stop them. So *I* had to."

"Stop them from what?" Colton asked.

"Trying to take him from me." Susan's smile disappeared. "Oh, I knew every single one of them wanted what I had. They wanted Steven, especially. It was so easy to tell which ones, too. He'd see them once in or around the office, or maybe he'd bring them in from the street. The man was a dentist, yes. It was his calling. But there was something else there too. Whenever he admired another woman's teeth? *That's* what I knew. That was the key to seeing that each one of them was trying to take him away from me."

Susan shook a finger in Sam and Colton's direction, as if her husband were standing right there beside them as well. "I *knew*. You can't leave a thing like that untended. Oh no. It has to be cleaned out. So that's exactly what I did. I cleaned out the *rot*. I *purged* my marriage. I made sure I was the only woman my husband would ever need, and if anyone felt differently and thought they could do better, I proved them wrong, didn't I?"

"Is that what you did with Kody too?" Sam asked. "You really thought a twenty-five-year-old grad student was hitting on your husband? A man in his late seventies who *you* poisoned to the point of convincing everyone he had dementia?"

Susan turned slowly to more fully face Sam and sank down onto the edge of the mattress behind her, moving her hands behind her back to prop herself up.

"Kody?" A surprised laugh escaped her. "I haven't done a thing to Kody. I wasn't lying when I told you how much I enjoyed her company here. That young woman is extraordinary. I really did like the girl, you know. I do hope you find her."

"When we do, you can read all about it in the paper." Colton stepped forward with his cuffs in hand. "From the inside of a cell."

"No," Susan said sweetly, batting her lashes. The woman looked entirely unaffected by the prospect of being taken under arrest for the murder of five different women, potentially six. "No, I think I'll take my chances else-where, thank you."

The instant smile flashing across her lips made Sam's stomach drop.

Then she noticed Susan pulling one hand out from behind her back.

Between the woman's fingers, the thin sliver of a silver syringe needle winked in the bedroom light.

"Shit!" Colton spat, lunging forward.

Susan jabbed the needle into the side of her neck, depressed the plunger, and raised her eyebrows with another remarkably calm smile before every hint of expression disappeared from her face.

Her eyes rolled back in her head, the syringe fell from her fingers to clatter to the floor, and the woman slumped sideways onto the mattress.

At that exact moment, Colton reached her and instantly snatched up her body again. "Susan, no!"

He shook her gently by the shoulders, but there was no response.

Grimacing and breathing heavily, he checked for a pulse at the woman's neck, waited for what felt like an agonizingly long time, and finally pulled his hand away with a heavy sigh before gently laying her back down on the mattress.

"Chief?" Sam asked.

He turned around to face her, his lips pressed together in a painfully tight line, and shook his head. "She's gone."

FIFTY-TWO

Kody

SHE WOULD NEVER GIVE UP, AS LONG AS SHE WAS STILL breathing and could move her body.

But there was no telling how much longer that would be.

The water level at the bottom of the pit had now risen dangerously high and was up to her waist, slightly above Rip's hips where he stood beside her. It was only going to get worse from here. She knew the water wasn't going to stop flooding in anytime soon, especially when this cave was naturally underwater in the first place. Short of some unlikely miracle, neither of them would make it out of here before either the mud filling up the pit sucked them under and suffocated them or the cave filled to its ceiling with water and they drowned.

Neither possibility seemed particularly preferable to the other.

The hardest thing to do right now was just trying to keep themselves warm. Kody had attempted several more times to climb up the walls of the pit, thinking maybe the change in the mud and water might also change her ability to escape. Every time, she kept sliding back down the walls, which broke away beneath her hands with increasing frequency and in increasingly larger amounts.

Then she eventually had to stop trying, not because it was pointless but because Rip's condition was only worsening, not improving.

For both of them, it was almost impossible now to get warm, and for Rip, it was almost impossible to stay awake. At least four different times now, Kody had been forced to leap into action away from trying to climb the walls of the pit and back toward Rip because the man's legs had buckled, and he would have dropped to the floor of the pit if it hadn't been filled with water.

The man could drown just as easily if he lost consciousness now and disappeared beneath the steadily rising surface of muddy, silty, frigid water.

The mud was thick and heavy, and every time more chunks of it collapsed into the pit with them, Kody thought of wet cement.

Now she was afraid to let go of Rip for more than two seconds at a time because he was having serious trouble staying on his feet. Worse than that, she was having serious trouble keeping his head above water.

Especially now that that water was up to the center of her chest.

And it only continued to rise with ever-increasing speed, as if someone had turned on an enormous invisible cave faucet and left it on to fill the place to the brim.

Rip murmured something beside her. His eyes rolled back in his head before his legs gave out again and he started to drop into the freezing water.

With a cry of alarm, Kody hugged him tighter against her with her arm wrapped around his middle and, straining, stood fully upright again to lift both their weight out of the water as far as she could.

That was the only positive of slowly being overtaken by a pit filling with water. The higher the water rose, the less of Rip's bodyweight she had to support on her own.

That wouldn't mean shit, though, if the pit flooded and the soggy earthen walls caved in and the last thing she and Rip heard, saw, felt, tasted, breathed was all this thick, heavy mud.

If they were even able to feel anything at all anymore when it got to that point.

She could hardly feel her legs beneath her keeping her upright on a piled mound of silt and soil that kept slipping away beneath her with the rising water levels. Her arms ached from holding Rip up beside her, but she was pretty sure she wouldn't be able to feel that for much longer either.

And still, she kept thinking about her parents and how they would never know what had happened to her. They would never know where she'd gone or why, how hard she'd tried to escape or get word to them.

How she'd died.

They probably wouldn't ever even know that in the end, she hadn't died alone. That in the end, someone had tried to help her. That a man like Rip had been with her through the worst of it. That they'd supported each other and warmed each other all the way up to their last breath.

Assuming he didn't die before she did.

I have to make sure they know.

That thought repeated over and over in her mind while the water just kept filling the pit until Kody had to act on it.

She couldn't do *nothing*.

Even if it was too late for her and Rip, she had to face

the end of this knowing she'd done everything she could to ensure even a small chance of her parents eventually discovering what had really happened.

Her last gift to them.

Everyone deserved the truth.

She would have used her own phone if she hadn't crushed it days ago.

Rip still had his cell, though. She knew she'd given it back to him when he'd regained consciousness, once it seemed shitty to keep a man's phone when he was trapped in the same death pit.

She looked for it now.

She remembered watching him slip the phone into an inside pocket of his thick button-down shirt that was more like a jacket. Struggling to both hold him upright above the water and search his person for the phone, Kody fumbled with the top buttons of his shirt.

Her numb fingers failed her.

Rip let out another groan, and his eyelids fluttered. "What?"

"Phone," she replied quickly. "Where's your phone?"

His eyes rolled back in his head despite how hard he tried to keep them open. "Inside…"

Yeah, she already knew that. No big help there.

Kody could only double down on her efforts to quickly open his thick shirt and get to his cell phone.

She almost lost Rip once beneath the rising water, then finally got his phone out of the inside pocket and turned it on.

Of course, it had a lock screen.

With the man beside her still mostly unconscious, Kody grunted and shifted, trying to keep holding him up while also getting a good grip on his right sleeve so she could tug his arm above the water and get to his hand.

It took an aggravatingly long time to get Rip's index finger toward the phone's screen and the fingerprint-reader just to unlock the thing. She could hardly feel what she was doing, making the entire task awkward and fumbling and infuriating all at once. It didn't help that she was trying to move as quickly as possible.

Something told her they didn't have nearly as much time left as she otherwise would have thought at this point.

She almost let herself smile when she finally got Rip's finger against the fingerprint-reader, but the damn thing just wouldn't open.

"Shit," she whispered urgently, then looked down at his limp hand in hers.

Water. It was the fucking water making his hands swollen and misshapen from how long they'd been in here. Plus the cold and whatever other factors she couldn't control. Of course it couldn't read his fingerprint.

What else?

"Rip," she said. "Rip, I need you to wake up."

Without an extra free hand, she ended up gently smacking the side of his face with the side of his own cell phone to try rousing him. "Rip. This is important. I need you to pay attention. Answer me."

"Huh?" His eyes kept rolling back in his head, though Kody thought she could feel a lightening of his weight in her arms as he tried to bring himself back. "What?"

"I need the password to your phone," she said. "We have to at least try to get a message out. Right now. Come on. Think about it. Password to your phone, Rip."

He sighed heavily, offered an unintelligible grumble, then sucked in a sharp, startled breath when she jostled him again. For a moment, it looked like he was going to open his eyes and settle his gaze on her face with instant clarity, but then they rolled back in his head again and he muttered off a string of four numbers.

Kody punched in his phone's passcode, cursing at herself when her numb, bumbling fingers hit the wrong number too quickly and she had to start all over again. Then she finally got the phone unlocked.

"Yes!" Her lips felt like they were splitting open in her numb face when she broke into a grin. Then she remembered that this was only a small victory, a tiny win she was letting herself enjoy now because she'd already accepted the fact that they weren't going to get out of here.

Nothing really to be all that excited about, but at least she could do this last thing. She could get her parents a message, hopefully, if this last-ditch plan worked and someone eventually found Rip's phone somewhere out there on the mountain he owned.

That was all she had now.

"What are you..." he mumbled.

"I got your phone open," she told him.

He couldn't even successfully shake his head. "No service."

"I know," she replied, scrolling through the apps on each screen. "It doesn't matter anymore. This is for everyone else."

Whether he was too out of it to care or didn't need any further explanation, Rip didn't ask who everyone else was. She was pretty sure that was perfectly clear.

She opened the first voice-recording app she found and started a new audio recording, painfully aware of how violently her teeth chattered as she spoke.

"This is Kody Anderson," she said, "recording this message in a cave on a mountain just outside Rush, California. A mountain that belongs to a man named Rip Graham. The man who tried to save my life. He's with me now, and unfortunately, we couldn't save each other. We tried.

"We're trapped in the cave. It's filling up with water. I'm pretty sure neither one of us is getting out of here, but to anyone who finds this phone, hears this message, please pass it along to my parents, Brad Anderson and Denise Hansen.

"Mom. Dad. I'm so sorry I worried you. So sorry you spent all that time not knowing where I was. I tried to reach you. It just wasn't possible out here. I want you both to know that I love you. You've been here with me the whole time, keeping me strong, your words and all the things you taught me—"

Her breath caught in her throat, and she swallowed thickly before forcing herself to continue.

"That's what kept me going. Hearing both of you. Knowing I had two of the best parents anyone could ever ask for, despite everything. Mom, thank you for all the hard choices you had to make for me. Dad, I'm so glad you finally answered those annoying phone calls from an unknown number. I love you both. Don't forget that."

She was barely able to get the final word out without bursting into tears, but somehow, she got through it. When her message was over, she left the recording on.

"Rip? You wanna say anything to anybody?"

He grumbled something, then seemed to draw from some previously hidden reserve of strength to speak into the recording. He never opened his eyes, but his words came out with more clarity then Kody had heard in his voice since she'd realized he wasn't dead.

"Meredith. My daughter. Girl, I haven't always said it, but I want you to know that every second, through all the bullshit and the fighting and your old man's stubbornness, I always loved you. And I'm proud of you for everything you've done. For putting your life back together when everyone else figured it was damn near over, including me. Just keep on keeping on, even if they never find me. It was Mattie who put us down here, kid. I know he's family, but if I had my way, I'd make sure you never talk to that sonofabitch again."

Kody had no idea why she thought it was so funny, but she couldn't suppress a shivering chuckle at that.

"Anyway, this is me saying... Oh, hell. Saying I love you. You've been a good kid, all things considered. I've been an ass, all things considered, but I did my best. And for Christ's sake, Meredith, if you gotta sell the farm, just don't fucking sell it to Whit Carlyle. That fucking amateur. My last words and dying wish. So don't forget that."

With his eyes still closed, Rip nodded and coughed a few times. "Yeah, that's it."

Kody stopped the recording, saved it on the phone, and changed the file name to: "Emergency Rush PD." It was the only thing she could think of to grab someone else's attention, whoever happened to find this.

Rip's legs gave out again, and they both struggled together until they got their footing beneath them and his arms situated again across Kody's shoulders. The man's breath was dangerously shallow and ragged now, and his head kept lolling to the side to rest against the side of hers.

"Now how..." He had to stop to catch his breath again before continuing. "How the hell are we gonna know anyone will actually get this? This cave floods, we get stuck in here, that's a whole lotta waterlogged phone."

"Shit," she muttered. "I didn't — Oh, wait."

Once again trying to maneuver at all with a large man like Rip slung halfway over her shoulders and resting his weight against her and a phone in one hand was particularly difficult, not to mention the freeze of the water had now soaked her through completely and she couldn't feel anything. She could barely even move.

Somehow, though, Kody finally got her hand into the pocket of her light windbreaker, shoved it down, and heard the crinkle she'd been waiting for.

When she drew out her hand, the plastic Ziploc baggie she'd loaded up with granola before setting out up the mountain dripped with freezing water, but it was there.

She shook it out a few times in front of them, then moved slowly and deliberately, taking great care not to drop the phone into the water instead before she ever had a chance to seal it up in the plastic bag.

Then the phone slipped inside, pulling itself down between the sticky sides of the plastic with its own weight. Kody went over the Ziploc opening several times, pinching it between her fingers over and over to ensure that it had, in fact, sealed.

"There," she said, her teeth chattering more than ever now. "All sealed up and ready to go."

She stared at the Ziploc bag with his phone in it, then looked down at Rip beside her and tried to smile.

The man nodded solemnly, unable to keep his own eyes open. "Good enough."

Her tight, numb smile faded. She studied the side of his face, her breath hitching in her throat because the water was almost up to her collarbones now, making it hard to draw breath in the freezing temperatures. She couldn't do anything to get out of it.

This is it. This is really it. We're gonna die here. This is the end, and I barely even started doing what I wanted in this world…

"Got any regrets, girl?" Rip asked.

She blinked at him. "What?"

"Regrets."

"I don't know… Not making it out of my twenties."

Rip chuckled, but even that seemed too much for him before he was coughing and wheezing and fighting for breath again. "That's all right. You're not missing much. I only got the one."

"One what?"

"One regret," he said, moving with agonizing slowness that for some reason terrified her even more. Rip turned his head toward her and tried to open his eyes. His lashes fluttered, and Kody caught a hint of the whites beneath them, but that was it.

His head bobbed toward her, but then he quickly picked it back up again and managed a crooked smile, weak and fading but definitely there. "I'm just sorry it had to be like this. Last words in this shitty-ass cave on my mountain. Always thought a yacht would be a better place to go."

The man chuckled at his own words. There wasn't much energy to the sound or the intention behind it.

Kody tightened her arm around his waist. Or at least she thought she had. She couldn't feel anything anymore.

She knew Rip was just trying to make her laugh, to bring something positive to the last few minutes of both their lives because that was the kind of man he was. She'd learned that quickly enough.

Even knowing this, though, she couldn't think about forcing herself to smile. Tears burned in her eyes instead, and when they welled up to spill over and course down her cheeks, she couldn't even feel their heat.

FIFTY-THREE

Sam

FLASHING LIGHTS FROM FOUR SQUAD CARS AND AN
ambulance lit up the front drive of the bed and breakfast
like an early Christmas.

After giving her statement and politely reminding
every officer she spoke to that they still had work to do,
preferably tonight, Sam finally had a moment to head
toward the ambulance where Charles received necessary
medical attention.

Fortunately, he was conscious now and didn't seem the
worse for wear after whatever Susan had slipped into his
tea. The man was still a little groggy, though, which made
Sam smile when she approached the open rear of the
ambulance to check on him.

"Sam!" he exclaimed, reaching toward her with a weak
hand that only made it slightly out of the gurney on which
he lay.

She approached him with a tired smile and nodded.
"Next time a conversation with me gives you some kind of
epiphany, Chuck, promise me you'll run it by me first."

"You got my word," he said. "Though I'm pretty sure

I'm done with solving crimes. At least for a little while. I'm good with just writing about them."

She chuckled. "Good idea. Stick with your day job."

She took his hand and squeezed it as the man smiled weakly up at her.

"Thank you, Sam. For everything. I wouldn't have been able to do any of this without you."

"You mean make stupid decisions and confront a jealous-wife serial killer all on your own?" Sam snorted. "You know what? I'll let it go this time. You don't have to thank me for that at all."

This time when he laughed, the energy returning to his voice was vibrant and clear. "But I couldn't have done it without you. In all seriousness, you helped me find Rose. You can't imagine what that means to me, even after all this time."

"Trust me, Chuck," she said. "It's easier than you think."

A car pulled up on the curb along the opposite side of the street. Two doors opened and slammed shut in quick succession. Then two forms in the distance raced through the darkness.

"Where is he? Where is he? I'm looking for Charles. Charles?"

"Over here," Sam called, raising a hand for Patty to see her within all the flashing lights and the hubbub of police and first responders and detectives scurrying around the scene.

Patty darted into a jog, then turned back to grab Frankie by the hand and pull him along with her.

Charles shifted on the gurney and winced before closing his eyes. "One more question."

Sam turned back toward him. "Sure."

"You really think the police are gonna find her there? Her…"

"Her teeth?" Sam asked, finishing for him. It was weird enough to think about, let alone say out loud, especially when they were talking about his wife.

He looked up at her with a pinched expression. "Yeah. You think she's really there?"

"I don't know who else it could have been, Chuck, honestly. I specifically remember seeing a set of teeth with a bad crack along one of the … I don't know. Not the molars, but the next ones. Whatever they're called. That's Rose. You'll see."

He nodded solemnly, then Frankie and Patty reached the back of the ambulance.

Patty let out a cry of relief before flinging herself on top of Charles' chest and throwing her arms around him while he still lay on the gurney.

Then she tugged Frankie behind her so he stood in front of his father.

The boy looked Charles up and down with a sad, wary smile. "You okay?"

"I am now, bud," he said. "*We* are now. It's all gonna be okay."

Still, Frankie looked remarkably confused.

"What's the matter, bud?" Charles asked.

The boy looked embarrassed, but with several nods of reassurance from all the adults, he licked his lips and finally blurted, "Did you get shot?"

Sam and Charles both laughed. Patty tried to fix them with a disapproving scowl, but she failed and ended up smiling with them.

"Nope." Charles reached out to set a hand on his son's shoulder and give it a squeeze. "No guns involved, fortunately. Just some really strong tea."

511

Sam chuckled, shook her head, and turned away from the reuniting family to survey the rest of the front yard swarming with police and emergency response teams and various professionals of Rush all doing their jobs.

After Sam had admittedly done a significant portion of it for them, but still.

One mystery down, one more to go.

That was what still bothered her, that Kody and Rip were both still out there somewhere, still missing. And while Charles and Sam had uncovered the identity of a genuine serial killer right here in Rush, the other missing person's case still hadn't been solved.

The clock was still ticking on that one.

But for right now, Sam was just fresh out of ideas.

She hurried off toward her Jeep, not wanting to get caught up in the proceedings any more than she had to be, grateful that Colton had at least trusted her enough to believe what she'd told him and give her a chance.

The least she could do was get out of his hair before the man ever felt the need to tell her so.

The second she slumped behind the wheel and pulled the front driver's-side door shut, her phone rang.

It was Hector.

"Hey, Hector. You really—"

Sam stopped and grimaced when the shrill, curdling scream in the background kept her from even being able to hear her own thoughts.

"Hector? Hello? Are you there?"

"Sam." His voice was muffled through the unexpected static coming over the line. It sounded like he was physically struggling with something. "Sam, are you there?"

"Yeah, I hear you. What's going on? Who's that screaming?"

"About that. Well, I'm here — Oh, shit." Hector

grunted and took a deep breath. "I'm at the Community Center right now. With Meredith. She's been drinking and, you know, I'm starting to think it might not be enough to just have me here with her on her own. Sorry to cut into your night like this, but do you think you could—"

"I'll be there in ten minutes." Sam quickly ended the call, started up her Jeep, and took off in that direction.

FROM THE SECOND Sam stepped through the front doors of the Community Center, she knew it was bad.

She could hear Meredith screaming all the way from here, down several different hallways, the sound echoing in all directions. She quickly headed down the closest hallway toward the administrative wing but stopped when she passed the meeting room with its doors propped wide open.

Just in time to see Meredith swinging one of the folding metal chairs they used for meetings in both hands and aiming for Hector Aguayo's head.

"You can't stop me!" the woman shrieked. "I have to do this. I *have* to, Hector! You don't understand. My dad is out there, and I have to find him!"

"All right, just hold on now." Hector tried to approach her, both hands outstretched in supplication as he took short, staggering steps toward her. Reaching the woman or calming her down was made all the more difficult by the fact that even in her inebriated state, one swing from that chair in Meredith's hands would undoubtedly pack a serious punch.

Of course the man kept his distance.

Sam quickly entered the meeting room and didn't hesitate to approach Meredith from the side. "Meredith. Hey. I thought I might find you here."

That unexpected interruption caught Meredith off guard. She spun around to face Sam, swaying on her feet and blinking heavy eyelids before she lifted the chair in both hands again, this time threatening to swing it at Sam. "I'll do it! I will, I swear I will! Because no one else in this fucking town is gonna do it. *I'm* always the one who has to!"

"Yeah, you're right," Sam said, gesturing for Hector to stay where he was for now, with Meredith newly distracted. "You *do* have a lot riding on your shoulders, Meredith. You always have. I know that. Everybody in these rooms knows that, and that's why we look up to you, yeah? Not to say even *you* can't have your bad days, obviously. But right now, Hector and I are here to help. So why don't you let us help you."

"I don't need your help," Meredith shouted. "*Rip* needs your help. He needs *my* help. We have to do something! I have to go up the mountain. That's where he is. I know that's where he is!"

"Okay, whoa. Hold on, all right?" Sam inched closer. "Hey, why don't you set the chair down just for a second and tell me all about where you think your dad is, huh? Then I can help."

Meredith studied her with swollen, red-rimmed, glassy eyes. Then the chair dropped from both her hands and clanged to the ground before those hands went up to the woman's face and she sobbed into them.

"He needs help!" she cried.

Sam moved closer and managed to snake an arm around the other woman's shoulders. "You're right. And that's exactly what we want to do. We want to help Rip, just like you do. What do you know about where he went?"

"Up the mountain! That's where he said he was going.

He told everyone where he was going. He told me. I know him the best. I'm his daughter. I know he's up there. He always does what he says he's gonna do. Always! He said he'd be back... He never came back..."

"He went up to go look at the lake?" Sam asked. "The water supply, where he told Kody to go?"

Meredith sobbed into her hands again but nodding now as she did so.

"All right, you know what?" Sam said. "I'll go. I'll go look for him. And Meredith, I *will* find him."

"You *what*, now?" Hector asked before returning the dropped chair to the stack of them against the wall.

"I'm gonna go look for him."

"Sam, it's one o'clock in the morning."

"At first light, then. I'll head up there because Meredith's right. Someone needs to keep looking for Rip and Kody. I'm almost certain the two of them are together. And, you know, I promised Kody's parents I'd look into it again. I'm promising Meredith the same thing now, all right?"

He stared at her a moment, then grunted. "I'm coming with you."

"No, Hector. Stay with Meredith. Please. For the rest of the night and maybe even after. She needs someone with her. Someone to help take care of her."

"I can stay with her," he said slowly, "but you can't go up the side of that mountain on your own. I can't let you go up there on your own, Sam. Day or night."

"I won't be alone," she said. "I promise. I've got friends, and they'll come with me no problem, no questions asked. Meredith, I'm gonna go find Rip. I need you to give yourself a break, all right? Get some rest. Hector's here to help you. He'll drive you home, stay with you. Maybe even make a pot of coffee and cook you up a big-ass greasy breakfast. How does that sound?"

Meredith didn't remove her hands from her face and just kept sobbing, but at least she wasn't belligerent anymore. Nor did she vehemently disagree with the current plan.

"First light?" Hector asked as he approached and put an arm around Meredith's shoulders instead.

"First light." Sam nodded. "I'll pick up my friends who're coming with me, and I'll text you when we leave."

"I'll be waiting for it."

SAM KNEW it was a bad idea to go hiking up through the California wilderness, no matter whose land it was, no matter what time of day or night, without a full night of sleep behind her.

By the time she got back to Birdsong Park and her trailer, it was almost 2:30 a.m. No matter how tired she might have been or how important she knew sleep was, she just couldn't manage it.

So when her alarm went off at 4:45, she was up again and on her feet anyway, preparing to go talk to her friends who she knew would jump at the chance to come with her on the search. Especially if it meant being there when Sam found their daughter.

SAM HAD EXPECTED NEEDING to pound on Brad's hotel room door for ten minutes straight before it actually woke the guy and he got out of bed to answer.

But Brad was at the door almost immediately, answering it with wide, heavy-lidded eyes. "Sam?"

She took a quick step back in surprise, then sighed and looked him over. "Wow. Couldn't sleep, huh?"

"That obvious?"

"Yeah, me neither. Listen, I know it's early as hell, but I wanted to come by in person and ask you for a favor. Sort of."

"Who is it?" Denise called from farther inside the room — most likely from the bed, if Sam had to guess.

"It's Sam," Brad replied.

"What?"

Sam could hear the woman moving quickly around the room and getting dressed, but she focused on Brad instead. "I'm going back up the mountain this morning. To look for Rip. I bet you anything Kody's with him, and I don't know how much more time we have. We need to hurry. And I promised someone else I wouldn't go up there alone, so ... will you come with me?"

"Right *now*?" Brad squinted, then turned around to look at the windows of his room with darkness on the other side.

"Right now," Sam said. "By the time we get up there, the sun'll just be coming up, and that gives us plenty of daylight to work with. That's what I'm thinking."

"Okay." Brad glanced back into the room at Denise, then swung the door all the way open and gestured for Sam to come inside. "Just give me five minutes."

Sam slowly walked in, let the door swing shut behind her, and found herself looking at Denise. "Sorry to barge in on you like this..."

"You're going out to look for Kody?" Denise asked, now fully dressed but not quite looking fully awake yet.

Sam nodded. "I promised I'd look into it again. I promised both of you, and I also can't help feeling a little responsible for getting Rip caught up in all this too. I'm the one who called him about her, and I'm the one he was gonna take up the mountain in the first place. I'm gonna find her, Denise."

The other woman nodded solemnly, then Brad came bursting out of the bathroom.

"All right, let's get going." He stopped in front of Denise. "We'll be back … I don't know. Later. Might take all day."

"Fine by me." Denise grabbed her shoes and started to tug them on.

"Just Sam and me," he corrected her. "We don't know what we're walking into up there. It might be dangerous."

"Which means it can't hurt to have an extra pair of eyes with you," Denise retorted, brooking no argument. "I'm coming too."

"No, I need you to stay—"

"And *I* need to do something besides sitting in this hotel room all day, twiddling my thumbs and hoping someone else will do my job for me. I'm her mother, Brad. I'm coming."

They both turned to look at Sam then, as if she had the final say in this.

She almost burst out laughing but instead gestured behind her toward the hallway. "Jeep's got plenty of room. Let's go."

FIFTY-FOUR

Sam

SAM HAD IT IN HER MIND THAT SHE WOULD DRIVE THEM all the way back up to exactly where she, Brad, and Charles had pulled over off the road when they'd meant to meet Rip up here a few days ago. The sun hadn't quite risen yet, but the darkness of night had started to give way to the blue-gray glow of morning twilight. Not that she needed a whole lot of light to see where she was going up this frontage road. Her Jeep's headlights were more than bright enough, and Sam had driven this route plenty of times to know it very well.

Once they got up to Rip's farm off the frontage road, Sam started to really narrow in on exactly how she wanted to handle this search.

They would find Kody and Rip up on this mountain. That was the only thing that made sense.

She felt it in her bones.

It was just a matter of timing, and now Sam hoped she hadn't gotten it all desperately wrong.

Up the frontage road they continued, past Rip's farm, and the light in the sky steadily increased and intensified while Sam tried not to drive like a lunatic up the winding dirt.

"Oh, right there!" Denise jumped in her seat and pointed out the front passenger-side window, her nail clicking against the glass. "Sam, that's it right there. You just missed it."

Sam shot her a quick frown. "Missed what?"

"That's the cemetery," Denise replied. "You said the directions were to turn at the cemetery. You just missed it."

"No, that's the old cemetery," Sam replied. "It's not—"

A lightbulb exploded in her mind, and she reacted by slamming on the brakes.

The Jeep lurched to a stop, jolting both Brad and Denise in their seats to jam against their tightening seatbelts.

"What the hell, Sam?" Brad grumbled in the back seat.

Denise merely stared at her in concern. "What's going on?"

Sam gritted her teeth and stared through the front windshield. Then she turned toward Denise. "You can help me answer this. How would an outsider or a newcomer to town, for example, someone who didn't grow up here and didn't know the area, tell the difference between the old cemetery and the new cemetery?"

Denise blinked at her. "That one didn't have a sign."

"No, it didn't," Sam said.

"So I guess they *wouldn't* be able to tell the difference."

"Exactly." Instead of wasting time by turning around, Sam shifted into reverse and drove back the way they'd come, almost at the same speed.

Brad hissed in the back seat. "What the hell are you doing?"

"Recognizing the one giant mistake everyone in this

town made, simply because it's way too goddamn obvious."

She lurched to a stop again, right at the entrance to the old cemetery, and took a left off the highway to head down the road stretching up into the hills.

She didn't have to follow it very far until the road ended, and there was the narrow turnoff, almost completely hidden by trees. It was difficult to find, but now Sam was looking for it.

She pulled into the turnoff, parked, and circled her finger in the air to indicate the area around them. "This is the turnoff for going up into the mountain past the *old* cemetery, which only someone who knew about both cemeteries would have specified, because the *new* cemetery farther up the frontage road is just 'the cemetery' now. Nobody else would've known that unless they'd already been here a while. And look at this place. It's surrounded by trees. Hard enough to find unless you're looking for it."

Brad nodded slowly. "Uh-huh…"

"I'm guessing Rip had the same aha-moment I just did," Sam said. "It just took me a little longer, because *I'm* not the one who gave Kody directions up to the lake in the first place. He just told her 'the cemetery.' That's what the new cemetery's become now. But on the drive out here, the old cemetery is the first one you see. *Kody* would've seen it first too. She would've turned off *here*, thinking Rip's directions were off a little but thinking she could still follow them relatively well."

Neither of Kody's parents said a thing, so Sam spun around in the driver's seat to look at Brad head-on. "I'm also willing to bet the day we were supposed to meet Rip at that turnoff with Charles was the day he figured this out on his own. Realized Kody had probably pulled off right here instead and went looking for a lake that wasn't actually in this area at all."

A bitter laugh escaped her as everything else started to add up at lightning speeds. "Hell, Rip could've parked his truck right here under these trees while we were driving up to meet him, and we wouldn't have even seen it. It's so far off the road, you can't see anything through all the woods. Like it basically doesn't even exist."

"So she didn't follow directions perfectly," Brad muttered. "He just ... what? Forgot to differentiate between the current directions and the outdated ones?"

"Bingo." Sam unbuckled her seatbelt and all but leapt from the Jeep before opening the rear doors to grab a large pack she'd borrowed from Syc, plus some other materials doubling as hiking gear she'd brought along for a trek just like this one.

"This is where we're getting out to look for her?" Denise asked.

Brad opened his door as well. "Looks like it."

Sam took the lead down the trailhead, more convinced now than ever that she was finally on the right trail.

The trail *Kody* had taken, anyway.

Because Sam knew for a fact this particular path did not lead to the lake serving as the water source for Rip's farm. It was still part of the man's land, though.

She'd done her research on that once upon a time, when she first came to Rush.

Setting a fervent pace, Sam led the trio farther along the trail, Brad and Denise breathing heavily behind her.

About an hour and a half in, with the mountainside lighting up for the morning, Brad called out to her, "Sam! Hold up a sec—"

"We gotta keep going," she said. "There's not a lot of time here."

"Right, but this isn't a field exercise, and it kinda feels like you forgot we have a civilian with us."

Denise snorted, huffing and puffing up the trail after having already fallen behind them by quite a bit. "Civilian, my ass. I did my time being married to *you* for twelve years."

"So this is how you make up for it?" Brad spun around and glared at her. "By driving our daughter away so forcefully that she won't even tell you where she's going for her research?"

"Oh, so you're making it *my* fault now?"

"Of course it's your fault, Denise! If you heard *half* the things she told me about how much the two of you fight whenever she brings up what she wants to do after grad school."

"At least she and I *have* fights," Denise quipped. "You know why that is, Brad? Because *I* spent the last almost two decades raising our daughter by myself! Puts a lot of pressure on everybody. And yeah, there are going to be some fights. But you wouldn't know about that, would you?"

"Jesus," he murmured, shaking his head, "I don't know how many times I have to repeat myself. I made a mistake. I made a shit-ton of mistakes, Denise. But that doesn't mean—"

"Hey!" Sam shouted, spinning around to face the pair on the trail.

Both Denise and Brad turned toward her, their mouths open, each of them looking like they were ready to start bickering at Sam now, too.

Not a chance.

"Both of you need to shut the hell up and keep moving," she snapped. "Denise, I get it. I'm setting a fast pace. I'll slow it down a little. But I need you to keep going, and I need you to keep up. Brad, if you can't figure out how to speak to the mother of your child, then you should just not say a goddamn thing. I don't wanna hear any of this shit. And the *last* thing Kody needs when we find her is to see the two of you verbally kicking the shit out of each other. Actually, I'd prefer it if she saw *me physically* kicking the shit out of both of you. None of us want that. Understood?"

Denise stared back at her with wide eyes, more surprised by the fact that anyone would speak to her like that than the fact that it was Sam.

Brad gaped at her as well, but then he barked out a laugh and shook his head before continuing along the trail after Sam. "Yes, ma'am. Loud and clear."

Fortunately, Sam had made her point, which meant the only time Brad and Denise exchanged further words with each other was to either answer Sam's questions or point out something they'd noticed along the hike.

That included their observations when the trio reached the top of a rocky cliff Sam was sure overlooked a small valley down on the other side. When they reached the top, sure enough, she'd been right.

Now that they could see so much of what lay in front of them stretching across said small valley, she let Brad and Denise take a brief break to catch their breath, have some water, maybe eat a protein bar.

"We can't stay too long," she told them. "Just a few more minutes, got it?"

Kody's parents nodded, saying nothing, until it was time to go and they were on their feet.

Then Denise pointed to the left beyond the ridge. "Look at that. All those caves over there. Do you think…"

"If I were Kody coming up here, thinking I'd find a lake in this valley but then ended up finding nothing?"

Sam nodded. "Yeah, I'd probably see if I could go shelter in those caves. Let's check it out. At the very least, we can cross it off our list if we don't find anything."

There was no argument, so all three of them headed down the other side of the incline together and made their way toward the caves.

When they reached the closest one, Denise's first inclination was apparently to go rushing off ahead, running blindly into who the hell knew what.

Sam grabbed the other woman by the arm instead and hauled her back as gently as possible. "We don't know what's in there. Could be an animal. Could be people who aren't supposed to be there, or people we don't want to find. We just have to be smart about this."

Denise nodded vigorously. "Right. Sorry. Why don't you go ahead?"

Sam approached the mouth of the cave and listened for a moment before calling out, "Hello? Is anyone in there?"

There was no reply, but just once was never enough to get an accurate read of what they might be facing.

"*Hello?*" she called again into the cave's dark entrance, cupping both hands around her mouth. "Kody? Rip? Are you in there?"

Sam's voice echoed over and over for several seconds, but there was still no response. She scanned the darkness anyway, wanting to be perfectly sure there was absolutely nothing in here before they decided to move on.

She heard it at exactly the same time Denise did, but the other woman was faster to mention it.

"Wait." Denise flapped a hand in Sam's direction, as if that were the best way to get her attention. "Did you hear that?"

"Hear what?" Brad asked, stepping forward to join the women at the mouth of the cave.

"That's…"

"Running water," Brad finished frowning at the cave entrance.

"Yes, it is." Nodding, Sam turned slowly away from the cave entrance to look back at him.

Brad shook his head. "What?"

"The question now is what's *that*?" With a nod, Sam pointed at a relatively level shelf of rock jutting from the wall of the mountain just a few feet away from where Brad stood.

He turned around looking, for what she was talking about, and almost broke into a run toward it when he realized what it was. "That's a mug."

"A what?" Denise spun around to look for herself.

Brad closed his fingers around the tin mug for a few seconds, then released it again. "It's still warm too. Smells like coffee."

"Which means someone's definitely been here," Sam said. "Recently. If it's not Kody and Rip, then it might be someone who's seen them or who knows where they are."

"Or who kidnapped my daughter before dumping her car in a gorge," Denise seethed.

"Or that," Sam conceded. "We're gonna go in quiet from here, Denise, so Brad and I need you to stay out here. Wait for us to tell you it's safe. And hell, if you wanna be a lookout, that would be very much appreciated. Just shout to us while we're in there if you see someone coming."

"Stay here?" Denise folded her arms. "No. Absolutely not."

"Hey, it's all right." Brad put a hand on her shoulder and nodded. "Sam knows what she's doing. I know what I'm doing. When it comes to something like this, at least. Safest place for you right now is right here, and it *is* a massive help to have someone on lookout to warn us ahead of time if someone's coming. We won't be long."

With a heavy, defeated sigh, Denise thrust out her hip and watched Brad and Sam move in on the cave and whoever happened to currently occupy it. Which could have been anyone, for all they knew.

Brad switched on a lightweight flashlight he'd brought with him, which wasn't nearly as awkward as trying to use a flashlight app on a phone.

The cave wasn't all that deep. Though they couldn't see the back from where they stood, it didn't look like it had that much more space going on forever.

Then again, looks could be deceiving.

They stepped silently forward, searching the darkness. Shuffling step by step and waiting a moment to listen for sounds of another occupant before moving farther in.

Convinced no one was going to jump out from the shadows and get the drop on them, Sam decided she might as well risk making a little more noise.

"Kody?" she called. The name echoed a long time in the cave, but there was still no response. "Rip? Is anyone here? It's Sam."

Still nothing.

"Whoever had their morning coffee with that nice mountain view on the side left in a hurry," Brad said. "That's the only reason I see for leaving an unfinished cup of coffee behind. But from the looks of *this*, I'd say they're planning on coming back any time now."

"Looks of what?" Sam turned around and stared at the folding card table laid out at the side of the cave where Brad stood. She frowned at it. "That was just there the whole time?"

"Since we stepped inside, yeah. There's a couple of

tools here. Headlamp. Can of bear spray. That comes in handy in a cave, I suppose. And—"

"That's hers!" Denise's exclamation echoed even more violently through the cave, joined by her desperate footsteps as she abandoned her lookout post to join Sam and Brad inside. "She's here! She *has* to be here. That's *hers*!"

Sam noticed the woman's finger stabbing in one direction as she approached the table and joined Brad to go take a closer look. "What is?"

"That whistle. Right there!" Denise jabbed her finger at what Sam only now realized was, in fact, a whistle. At first sight, it looked more like one of those cheap Happy Meal toys loved so dearly by kids ages four to ten the world over.

"That's a whistle?"

"Yes, it's a whistle," Denise snapped. "Hello Kitty. I bought it for her years and years ago. You know, when she had a Hello Kitty phase."

"She did?" Brad asked.

His ex-wife scowled at him. "Yes. She did. She loved this whistle back then, and then she kept it as more of a joke than anything else."

"You're sure it's Kody's?" Sam asked.

"Look at this thing," Denise said. "How many of these do you think are out there floating around and just happen to belong to someone else on the same mountain where my daughter disappeared? Come on."

After a closer inspection of the whistle and reconfirming it was Kody's so there could be absolutely no doubt, Sam scanned what little she could see farther into the cave, then turned back toward Brad. "Flashlight."

"I can hold it for you and light the way just fine. Leave your hands free."

"The ground starts to give away over here," she said.

"It gets slippery. I wanna figure out what's going on. Give me the flashlight."

He glared back at her, silently challenging, but then the man noticed Denise's stare on him as well. So he quickly made the smarter decision by relenting to them both.

He slapped the flashlight down into Sam's open and waiting hand.

"You just stay right here," she said. "I'm not going far, but I wanna see what's over there. Stay within shouting distance so if anything happens, you know about it."

"I'm not moving an inch." Brad folded his arms and nodded.

Then Sam took off into the cave.

Her initial assessment turned out to be pretty damn accurate. The cave did not extend very deeply into the mountain, but past the main entrance, it dripped with water and smelled like it had been underwater for quite some time. Solid, rocky ground covered the cave floor; the farther she moved into the cave, the more that solid rock gave way to loose earth and shale, a whole bunch of pebbles, then packed earth, then damp dirt, then wet, squelching mud.

With her next step, the ground beneath her jolted and slid out from under her boot.

Sam backpedaled with a shout, her feet slipping in the mudslide now running at an incredibly steep angle away from her and disappearing over an edge that dropped into complete darkness.

"Sam!" Brad shouted from the entrance. "Talk to me."

"The ground's really giving away back here," she said. "It's wet. Like, *really* wet. I think there might be some kind of waterfall or maybe a leak in the cave walls. And there's ... I don't know. Like a pit back here. Wouldn't

surprise me if the floor just gave out all of a sudden.
Maybe Rip and Kody are—"

"Caught in the landslide down there somewhere?"
Denise shouted, almost shrieking now. "Fuck this! We
have to find her. Kody!"

Sam turned around with the flashlight to see Denise
hurrying toward her. The woman's eyes were wild with a
combination of fear and hope, and Sam hated to draw all
that to a close when she stepped into Denise's path to stop
her from going any farther.

"No, no. Whoa. It's not safe here—"

"I don't give a shit! My *daughter's* down there. I know
she's somewhere in this cave, and we're going to find her.
Kody? Do you hear me?"

No answer.

Sam looked back at Brad, who had slowly made his
way toward them now.

"If she's anywhere, Sam," he muttered, "it's here."

She pursed her lips for a moment, then nodded. "Well
then let's make sure we search every goddamn inch of this
cave."

FIFTY-FIVE

Kody

THE ONLY REASON KODY KNEW SHE WAS DREAMING WAS because she actually felt warm.

She'd been so cold and so uncomfortable for so long that no longer freezing, no longer feeling every ache and pain and tight muscle and numbness in her entire body, no longer being exhausted to her bones was the most unnatural thing in the world.

Okay, well maybe she was still exhausted in this dream too.

But it was the warm, cozy, comfortable, melt-into-a-soft-blanket-of-clouds kind of exhausted.

The kind that beckoned her to just snuggle in close and let her worries float away and stop trying so hard because this really wasn't all that bad after all.

In her dream, she had no idea where she was. Somewhere dark. Somewhere with a gentle burble of a fountain or a small stream.

Kody couldn't see any of it in her dream, but the sound comforted her.

The darkness somehow was equally as comforting, and

she realized all she wanted to do was just close her eyes and drift off.

How nice would that be?

She wasn't particularly thinking about either of her parents, so when she heard her mother's voice calling her name, it made the dream that much sweeter.

Yes, she would have loved to see her mom again. To hug her close. To thank her for everything she'd done in raising her. For everything Kody had turned out to be.

She would have loved to wrap her arms around the woman who had birthed her, with the chance to tell her mom she loved her one last time before she went.

Now that voice was here with her, calling her name, beckoning her away from the suffering and the pain and the fear Kody knew had existed but could no longer fully remember.

A smile bloomed across her lips anyway.

"Kody..."

Death wouldn't be so bad after all. In fact, it might even be okay with this warm, supportive darkness, the cozy comfort, and the sense of settled rightness she felt now, joined by her mother's voice.

That seemed pretty all right. Preferable, even, to where she'd been before.

Everything would be okay, no matter what happened, because her mom was here.

Her mom would take care of her.

"Kody..."

Kody's smile widened, and she let out a contented little hum of a sigh. "Mom..."

FIFTY-SIX

Sam

"Mom…"

"Shh!" Denise skidded to a stop on the loose cave floor and held an arm out for Sam and Brad to stop as well. "Did you hear that?"

"Sounded like a voice," Brad said.

"A weak voice," Sam said. "Did it just say, 'Mom'?"

"Oh my god, Kody!" Denise scrambled forward, slipping and sliding down the loose earth and coating the backs of her legs and jeans and shirt in mud and sloshing water. "Kody, baby, I'm coming! We're here!"

"Denise, stop! Hey!" Sam lunged forward to snatch Denise's wrist and jerk her backward a second before the ground gave way beneath Denise's boot.

A huge chunk of it toppled away into the blackness below, like a sinkhole opening up right there.

The echoing whisper of mud and earth sloughing off and falling cut through the cave, followed by plopping splashes as it hit water below and, surprisingly, a low moan as well.

Denise fought to catch her breath as she lay on her

back now, having scrambled backwards to safety, thanks to Sam's grip on her arm.

Sam reached toward the woman. "You all right?"

"Yeah. I think so."

"Hang back." Sam pointed behind them both, then raised her voice and shouted, "Brad! I'm sending Denise back to you."

"But I can—"

"This isn't a discussion, Denise," Sam interrupted. "For *all* our safety, I need you back there at the cave's entrance. Right now. Let's go."

The woman looked like she was about to burst out crying, but she did as Sam said, which was smart on her part.

Denise's footsteps echoed across the cave, then Brad called out, "What do you see?"

"A shitload of nothing right now," Sam replied. "Can you find something I can prop up against the edge of this pit over here? Anything. Just whatever you can find. Whoever's been in this cave here was probably camping out for a while. There's gotta be something."

"Yeah, give me a second."

Sam tried to slide on her backside around the edge of the pit in front of her. The more she moved, the more the earth gave way beneath her. So she held perfectly still and waited.

That didn't make aiming the flashlight directly down into the darkness any easier.

Grunts and heavy metallic scraping echoed behind her. She didn't dare turn around to look and risk even more of the floor caving in.

"Think this'll work?" Brad grunted again, then there was another clang much closer behind Sam, followed by sliding crunches.

She looked to the side and saw the bottom of a metal ladder sliding forward beside her, inch by inch, until it hung past the edge of the pit by several inches.

"A ladder?"

"Yeah, they legit had one in here," Brad replied. "Nice stroke of luck, huh? Can you get that down there on your own?"

"Yep. Take this." Sam tossed him the flashlight, which he then aimed for her so she could see what she was doing when further lowering the bottom end of the ladder down into the pit.

She moved slowly, carefully, not wanting to bang the legs against the muddy walls or end up hitting something down below that could have gone quite a bit longer without being hit.

Like more unstable earth, an old landmine everyone had forgotten about, or a person...

Finally, the ladder's legs thunked down onto something relatively solid. Sam set the top of the ladder against the edge of the pit. It stuck up only two feet above the edge, and she positioned her feet on the rungs before spinning around to now climb down it.

Brad handed her the flashlight again without needing to be asked, then Sam started her descent.

She stopped after three rungs and aimed the flashlight down into the pit, where she realized in an instant where the running water was coming from. Somewhere in the pit's wall, water rushed from a leak or the beginnings of a flood. The pit was quickly filling with cold water and lots and lots of mud.

"See anything?" Brad shouted.

"I don't think so," Sam replied, slowly circling the flashlight around the pit's perimeter. "This is where the water's coming from, though. It's just a lot of mud. Like a giant — Oh shit!"

"Sam?" Denise called from farther back.

"Brad, get over here," Sam snapped. "I need you to steady the top of the ladder, and I need you to hold it and the flashlight."

"What is it?" he asked.

She looked back up at him with wide eyes. "It's your daughter."

"Kody!" Denise screamed. "Kody, honey, it's Mom! I'm here!"

"And Dad," Brad shouted. "We found you! Everything's gonna be okay. Sam's coming down to get you."

Sam was, of course, already on her way to do just that, with the narrow, lightweight flashlight clamped between her teeth as she carefully stepped down each rung and lowered herself with her hands.

There were *two* people down here. One she knew was Kody because the girl's head was slumped back against the pit wall, her eyes closed and a small smile on her lips. The water was all the way up to her neck.

The second person down here, whoever he was, leaned against the young woman, his face buried in the side of her head. He didn't move.

"Kody?" Sam gently reached away from the ladder and had to step down lower until her legs were submerged in the frigid water all the way up to the backs of her knees. Then her hand finally came down on the girl's shoulder, and she was able to jostle her a little in the water. "Kody? Kody, I need you to wake up now. Can you hear me? Hey."

The girl's eyes flew open, and she sucked in a halting, searing gasp that couldn't quite draw in all the way.

No wonder. It's fucking freezing down here.

"Hey, hey, hey..." Sam got as close as she could and tried to shine a little more light on herself as well without completely startling the girl. "Kody, my name is Sam. I'm here with your parents, okay? We're here to get you out."

The girl's gaze finally settled on Sam. She opened her mouth to say something, but all that came out was a long, concerning stutter and a weak moan.

"It's okay," Sam said. "You don't have to say anything. Just come with me. Let's get you out of here."

Kody finally started to move, and as she did, the figure leaning up against her shifted. She cried out, shaking her head. "I can't! I can't. He needs..."

"It's all right," Sam reassured her. "I'm here. Look. Come on over here. Just let him go, Kody, and come over here to the ladder."

"He won't..."

"Kody, who is that?" Sam asked.

"It's Rip," said another voice from above.

Sam flashed her light upward and couldn't reconcile what she saw with what she knew about the locals in town or how anyone she recognized could be involved in something like this. "Christian? What in—"

"Sam, is she okay?" Brad called.

"She's okay," she replied, frowning at Christian looking down at her from the other side of the pit. "She's here. She's all right. I'm just gonna try and get her up the ladder."

"I can help." Christian sidled toward her, stepping carefully around the loose earth that kept giving way to slosh down into the freezing pit. Then he too climbed down.

Together, they freed Kody from where she'd been standing, somehow strong enough to hold Rip's head above the rising water.

Whether it was adrenaline, excitement, relief, or simply the healthy body of a young woman in her mid-twenties, Kody came out of her frozen stupor with surprising speed and managed to climb the majority of the ladder up to dry ground.

As soon as Sam heard Brad and Denise both crying over their daughter now safely in their arms, she hopped back down into the pit and took over as the anchor keeping Rip Graham from drowning.

Then Christian descended all the way, and together, they got the old farmer up out of the water and out of the pit, rung by rung.

Rip flopped over the side of the pit first, and Brad was there a second later to help pull the man back onto more steady ground inside the cave.

Sam hauled herself up, sopping wet and already shivering. She hurried toward Rip lying on the floor and felt him for a pulse. It was still there, but just barely as she knelt beside him on the ground.

She heard the sound of metal scraping against earth and stone and looked quickly over her shoulder. "Brad?"

"Hey!" Christian shouted. "What the hell're you doin, pal? I'm still down here."

"You've been in this cave the whole fucking time!" Brad bellowed. With one final upward jerk, he pulled the ladder out of Christian's reach, then hefted it to the side and let it fall to the cave floor with a resounding clang.

"You can't just leave me down here," Christian said, his voice rising in volume and urgency as he splashed about in the cold water. "Hey, listen. I came back to *help* them. That's why I'm still here. Couldn't just leave 'em, either. I didn't want no part of this—"

"Should've thought of that before you threw my

daughter into a fucking death pit, asshole!" Brad hocked and spat over the side of the pit.

"Hey!" Sam leapt to her feet and headed toward him, wanting to move faster but uncertain as to how long the ground beneath her feet would hold even here. "Put the ladder back down."

Brad glared at her. "No."

"Right now. That pit's filling up, and it's filling up fast."

"You gotta be fucking kidding me, Salazar," he snarled. "This piece of shit is the one who threw Kody down there in the first place. And that other guy too, probably. He deserves everything he's about to get down there and then some."

"Brad, I know this man."

"I don't give a shit."

"His name is Christian DeRoune. He's lived in Rush all his life. He's a local. Spends nearly every day at the bar where I work."

"Sam!" Christian shouted from below. "Come on, Sam, please! You know me. This was never supposed to happen. No one was supposed to know. If I knew anyone was gonna get hurt, I never would've—"

"Shut your fucking mouth!" Brad roared.

"Put the ladder back," Sam repeated.

He glared at her in disgust. "You're gonna vouch for this piece of shit?"

"For some things? Yeah. I sure as hell am *not* gonna jump to conclusions right now, though, one way or the other. You know why? Because it's not our *job* to decide what happens to him after this. Not here. Not this way. You understand?"

For a moment, it looked like the guy was just going to ignore everything she'd said and storm back out of the cave or do whatever he could to stop Sam from putting the ladder back.

Finally, though, Brad sighed and headed toward the ladder he'd tossed across the cave. "You better be right about him, Sam. But I swear to Christ, if he tries to pull anything, he's going right back down there, and I won't stop at just pushing him in. You understand that?"

"Fair." Sam nodded. "Did you hear that, Christian?"

"Loud and clear." He sounded terrified. "Please just let me back up."

Before returning her attention to Rip, Sam watched Brad walk back toward the ladder. "Anderson."

He stopped with a heavy sigh and turned to meet her gaze.

"Thank you," she said.

He offered no reply but picked up the ladder and returned it to the edge of the pit, where he quickly muttered, "Watch yourself," and let the ladder's legs fall dangerously fast into the black hole.

There was a splash of water, a shout of surprise, then a disgruntled grumble before more splashing water as Christian climbed his way back up.

With a contemptuous snarl, Brad turned away from the edge of the pit.

At that exact second, Sam saw movement from the corner of her eye, which instantly put her on alert.

Brad was the only other person in the cave with her. Christian hadn't reached the top of the ladder, and Kody and Denise were outside.

So who—

She turned toward the movement and reacted with a warning cry of, "Brad!"

But it was too late.

The newcomer's fist connected with the side of Brad's

face just as Brad started to turn Sam's way. The blow sent the guy reeling backward, but he righted himself before he would have fallen into the pit.

"Stop!" Sam shouted at the man stalking toward Brad still. "Hey, asshole! Did you hear me? I said stop. Right now!"

Sam's hand went to the back waistband of her jeans, but no, she hadn't thought to bring the pistol with her on a day-long rescue hike.

Now Brad and this new man with long, stringy gray hair were at each other's throats.

No one said a thing. They didn't have to.

Brad swung at the older man's face, missed, and staggered past him, leaving himself wide open for his assailant to sock a fist into Brad's kidney on the way past. Brad cried out, stumbled again, and spun around in time to block another blow. Then he kicked out and caught the older man on the side of the shin.

Snarls and growls and grunts echoed throughout the cave, clashing against the sound of running water and of Denise shouting from outside, "What's going on in there?"

"Denise, stay where you are!" Sam hollered. "Keep Kody safe with you. Christian!"

"I know, I know!" Huffing and puffing, Christian finally pulled himself up over the top of the ladder and almost collapsed there on the cave floor, sopping wet and shivering and blowing sprays of muddy water off his lips as it kept pouring from his hair and over his face. Grimacing, he pushed himself up onto one foot, then the other, and staggered toward Brad and the older man, who had taken each other to the ground and now spent more time wrestling and rolling around together than actually fighting.

There was slick mud and freezing water everywhere, making it impossible to get any good footing.

"Christian, stop him!" Sam shouted.

If she hadn't been kneeling at Rip's side, trying to rub some warmth back into the man's arms and shoulders while simultaneously attempting every few seconds to drag him farther from the pit and toward the cave's exit, she might have jumped into the fray herself.

Then again, she'd left her newly gifted firearm in the Jeep, she was laughably small compared to every man here, and getting between two hot-headed morons the size of Brad and the older man trying to fight each other to the death was just asking to get banged up in the process.

"Christian!" she shouted again. "Right now! We don't have a lot of time."

Christian said nothing but stumbled across the floor of the cave toward Brad and Mattie hissing and spitting at each other, snarling and landing half-assed punches wherever they could in the slippery muck. "Hey, hey, hey! That's enough. Come on. Cut it out. We don't need any of this shit, huh? It's over."

Growling like a cornered animal, Mattie hauled himself to his feet, delivered a quick kick to Brad's ribs, then spun around on his son and whaled on Christian instead.

His first and only hit landed squarely on the side of Christian's jaw and sent the man spinning sideways before he collapsed. "Mind your fucking place," Mattie hissed, then spat at his son's feet and turned back toward Brad.

But Brad had already picked himself back up. When Mattie spun to face him again, gazing at the ground because he'd expected his opponent to still be there, he found himself staring at Brad's boots instead.

Sam's old Army buddy sent a vicious uppercut into the

underside of Mattie's jaw with a sickening crunch and echoing clack.

The blow almost swept Mattie off his feet.

It didn't matter where his feet were anymore, though, because as he staggered backward, the floor of the cave no more than a foot away from the pit's edge crumbled beneath him, sliding and breaking away before it just disappeared.

And Mattie disappeared with it.

The man shouted in surprise, the sound cut short by a violent splash as he hit the water below.

"Hey!" Holding his jaw, Christian headed toward the edge of the pit. "Damnit. Come on. Help me out. We gotta get him up here."

"Brad! Help me," Sam shouted as she tried moving Rip toward the cave entrance.

A gasping breath and spray of water came from the bottom of the pit, followed by a furious roar. "I swear to Christ, boy! Get your ass over here, or you'll be begging me to—"

"Look out!" Brad lunged for Christian, who was already on his way toward the pit. He barreled right into the other man, this time actually swiping his target off his feet and diving with him to the ground toward the front of the cave.

The second they hit the floor, the rest of the sodden, muddy, slippery, loose soil around the edge of the pit crumbled and kept crumbling and didn't stop.

It happened all at once, like a great, gaping maw opening up in the floor of the cave before turning inward on itself.

Water splashed up at the impact. The soft earth collapsed farther and farther out from the edge of the pit until it hit the walls of the cave, and then even more of the floor farther back into the mountainside fell upon itself with a rumbling roar.

It happened in less than three seconds. Practically all at once.

When it stopped, the three conscious people surrounding one unconscious farmer in the cave all stared in mute shock at the result.

The pit had collapsed on itself, burying both the ladder and Mattie beneath it.

"No!" Christian leapt toward the mess of mud and pebbles and icy sludge. He dropped to his knees and started digging with his hands, but whatever hole he made instantly filled in with more mud. "No, no, no, no…"

"Christian." Sam glanced briefly back at Brad, then pointed toward Rip still lying on his back.

Brad got to his feet again with a grunt, shot a quick look at the desperately digging Christian over his shoulder, then stooped to prop Rip over his back and shoulder before carrying the man out of the cave.

Then Sam went for Christian.

"Come on, Christian. Hey. Stop."

"He's in there! Right down there! I have to—"

"There's nothing you can do." She brought a hand down on his shoulder. "He's gone, Christian. I'm sorry. There's no way for us to get him out of here. That's just how it is now. But the cave won't hold up much longer, okay? We need to get out of here, get Kody and Rip medical attention, and then… Well, then we'll work through whatever happens next. But we can't do that if we don't leave *right now*."

Swaying on his knees, Christian sighed heavily. A sob caught in his throat, but he forced it back, gritted his teeth, and pushed himself to his feet again.

Sam patted his upper back one more time. "Time to move."

The sound of running water, wherever it was coming from, continued in the cave as if nothing had changed.

Outside the cave, Brad walked around, climbing halfway up the rock walls and waving his phone in the air until he finally shouted, "I got it! I got a signal!"

"Then make the call," Sam said, not quite feeling as cold as she knew she was. She stripped off her light canvas jacket, dropped it to the ground, then went to go check on Rip again.

The man was still unconscious, with a dangerously blue tint to his face. His pulse was still there when she checked for it, though. For now, he was still hanging on.

"How is he?" Christian asked.

"Still here," Sam replied. "Stubborn bastard. Denise, how's Kody?"

"She's freezing." Denise cradled her daughter in her arms as if Kody were still a very young child, vigorously rubbing the young woman's arms and rocking her back and forth. "Hypothermia. We need to get her warm. We need to get them both out of here. Now. Otherwise—"

"Hello?" Brad shouted into his phone. "Hello? Yes! We need emergency medical attention. Up on the mountain just east of mile marker twenty-one…"

All conversation ceased so Brad could finish making the call and providing the appropriate information. Once he finished, all they could do was wait for emergency response all the way out here. Most likely, that would come in the form of a rescue helicopter to get both Kody and Rip Medivac-ed to the closest hospital.

While they all waited together outside the cave, no one knew quite what to say until finally Christian sidled up next to Sam. She stood beneath a wide ray of what little direct sunlight existed in this part of the mountains at this time of day.

Leaning back against the stone cliff face, she let her head rest against the warm rock behind her while the sun poured down on her face. It didn't immediately dry her, and it wasn't hot, but it was better than being soaked to the bone with water that felt like it had just melted from a block of ice the size of her trailer.

"Sam?" Christian murmured.

"Whatever you have to say," she said, "better save it for the authorities. You don't have to tell me a damn thing."

"I know that. But I want to. I want you to know this whole thing ... this was all my dad. It was never supposed to involve anyone else. No civilians. No one from town. Just the two of us. I wanted to let the girl go, but my old man? He ... had other ideas."

"Like what?" Sam muttered, her eyes still closed. "Was he just biding his time for the right moment to ransom? Thought keeping a young woman in a freezing hole like that would give him some kinda superpower? What the fuck would make someone do something like this?"

Christian cleared his throat and paused, then, "She already knew Rip. He saw them together in town one day. Figured they were close enough friends that if we let her go, she'd go straight to Rip and tell him what she'd found."

Sam finally opened her eyes and slowly rolled her head across the rock wall behind her. "And what exactly did she find? Besides the closest brush with death this young woman's ever had or will probably ever survive?"

The man shoved his hands into the pockets of his frozen, sopping jeans. "Gold."

"Fuck."

"On Rip's property." Christian nodded. "We found a few veins and had to stop the water flow so we could get into that cave and tap into 'em. Dam up the lake. Empty out the tunnels. That cave is one of 'em leading right out to Rip's farm. We had ourselves a whole lotta work to do. When my old man first told me, I didn't want a thing to do with it. But then, I mean ... hell, with all the cutbacks at the sawmill and having shit else to do? Damnit, Sam, he made it sound like a good plan. A decent plan, where nobody got hurt. And then it just ... I didn't want to..."

"I get it," she told him. "I hope for your sake that Chief Colton gets it too, man. I really do. But if it's any reassurance at all, probably not, but still, I'm happy to give my statement." She nodded toward Brad, who had finished his emergency call and was now huddled with Kody and Denise. "You saved that man's life today. And Rip's. And that young woman's. That counts for something."

Christian gazed out over the valley stretching out below them and sighed. "I hope so."

FIFTY-SEVEN

Sam

A FEW DAYS LATER

SAM WAS ALREADY on her way out for the day, just about to hop into her Jeep, when the rumble of a loud engine made her look toward the entrance of Birdsong Park.

She laughed when she recognized the enormous, gas-guzzling SUV with ridiculously dark-tinted windows and stepped slightly away from her Jeep, arms folded to await that vehicle's driver.

The SUV came to a rumbling halt in front of her. The engine shut off. Then both the front driver's-side and passenger-side doors opened at the same time, and two people exited the vehicle when she'd only expected to see one.

The first was Brad, and that made sense.

The second was Denise.

That also made sense, but it still came as a bit of a surprise.

"Well look at that." Sam smiled as the couple rounded

the front of the SUV and approached her. "Looks like you can find your way around these frontage roads after all. Guess I'm out of a job as your chauffeur then, huh?"

Brad shot her that gleaming grin and shrugged. "It's for the best. You probably won't even miss it."

"Yeah, the pay was shit."

"Sam." Denise approached from Sam's other side with her arms spread open in an oncoming invitation for a hug.

Sam tried to ignore the hug part while also trying to smile. "Denise. Good to see you."

And *there* was the hug.

The other woman pulled Sam in for a tight embrace and stood there, hands pressed against the center of Sam's back, for an awkwardly long moment until Sam finally lifted a hand to pat Denise's back a few times in return.

She was greatly relieved when the other woman finally released her, but before she could get away, Denise took both Sam's hands in hers and nodded without letting go. Tears shimmered in her eyes. "I want to thank you, from the bottom of my heart, for saving my baby."

"You're very welcome," Sam said.

"From one mother to another."

Sam's mouth popped open, and she shot a quick glance at Brad, who now leaned back against the hood of his SUV and shrugged.

"He told me about Sophie," Denise continued.

A lump formed in Sam's throat, but there were no tears. She didn't try to bury the emotion in a sudden upswell of rage, nor did she try to snatch her hands out of the other woman's grasp.

In this moment, she could actually stand there, accept the thanks, and hear what was being said.

Somehow.

"It means so much," Denise continued, "that after

everything you went through personally, with your own family, you would risk yourself the way you did to help bring my daughter back. And we hardly even know each other."

"It's what anyone would do, Denise," Sam said.

The woman chuckled softly, tears still swimming in her eyes, still holding onto Sam's hands. "Given our ... unique history, the three of us, that's not even remotely true, and you know it. I just wanted to thank you. I want you to know how much it means to me, and how grateful I am to you, and that I'm sorry for the way I reacted. To a lot of things."

Sam dipped her head and wanted nothing more than to disappear.

Instead, the next words coming out of her mouth seemed like they belonged to someone else. "All water under the bridge."

Brad pushed himself off the front of his SUV and approached them now that the private moment had ended. "We get to pick Kody up from the hospital in a couple days. And then, believe it or not, the *three* of us are heading home. Together."

No longer holding Sam's hands hostage, Denise stepped up to her ex-husband, who was now her boyfriend — or however the fuck that worked — and slipped her arm around his waist.

"If you're ever in the area, Sam," she said, "call us. We'd love to see you. And I know Kody would always appreciate spending time with the woman who saved her life. Absolutely whenever, you hear me? Our door's always open."

Sam could only nod slowly like a limp puppet. "Got it."

Then the conversation ended, and the general air

among the three of them started to lean toward the slightly awkward before Brad slapped a hand down on the hood of his car. "All right. We got shit to do. I'm sure Salazar does too, so we'll get outta your hair. Good to see ya."

Sam barked out a laugh. "Yeah, you too. Drive safe, huh? And don't ever stalk me again, no matter what town I happen to be living in. Got it?"

"You call it stalking. I call it looking for a friend."

Sam waited until the enormous SUV had disappeared down the frontage road before rolling her eyes and letting herself laugh at how damn weird the last fifteen minutes had been.

Weird. But not in the worst way.

After that, she hopped up in her Jeep and headed into town.

She had two more stops for the day — the first to pick up a quick gift she'd recently learned could mean all kinds of things, and the second to deliver that gift to a friend.

As SAM WALKED up the front porch steps of Charles' home, the front door opened, and out stepped Chief Colton.

They both froze when they saw each other. Sam pressed her lips together, sighed through her nose, and continued across the walkway toward the porch.

Colton pulled the door gently shut behind him and met her at the bottom of the steps. He looked her up and down, glanced at the gift in her hand, and cocked his head. "Something tells me those flowers aren't for me."

"Very astute of you, Chief," she said with a wide grin. "I don't care what anyone says, you keep that wit nice and sharp, you hear me? Have a good one."

She tried to step around him, but he blocked her path.

Then he cleared his throat and hooked his thumbs through his belt loops.

Sam slowly looked up at him. "Is there something else?"

"I suppose you'll be wanting all the credit for bagging Susan the other night."

It wasn't a question, but he posed it as one. At least, she thought he had.

She couldn't help but laugh. "Not at all, Chief. I don't give a shit about who gets credit for what. Honestly, I'm just glad Charles got the opportunity to finally put his wife to rest."

"Yeah." Colton sniffed. "That's worth something too."

"Right."

What did this guy *want* with her?

He looked like he'd just swallowed a giant beetle.

"Well, have a good one, Chief. I'm just gonna—"

He blocked her again, removed his thumbs from his belt loops, and tugged at the buttoned-up collar of his uniform shirt before clearing his throat again. "Listen, Salazar."

"It's all good. Honestly. I'm *not* gonna come bugging you for credit, all right? It's fine."

"That's not what I'm trying to say."

"It's totally fine." She tried to step around him again.

"Stop. Let me say this. It's important."

"No, I'd really rather—"

"Sam, *please*."

She stopped. It wasn't a desperate plea, it wasn't an authoritative shout, and he didn't sound like he was panicking.

In fact, it was calm, straight to the point, and surprising as hell because the Chief of Police never called her by her first name, and as far as she knew, he didn't say please.

Sam backed up two steps and looked him in the eye again. "Yes?"

His scowl returned with full force, which didn't leave her with that much confidence in where this conversation was going, but she waited anyway.

"Thank you," he said.

Damn. Please and *thank you?*

She fought back the urge to look up in the sky and ask when the pigs were about to fly over.

"I, uh…" Sam huffed out a laugh. "I honestly don't know what to say."

"Then don't fucking say anything and just listen," he said. "No, I'm not your biggest fan, and you're certainly not mine. I get that. But you were an invaluable resource in this last case, and we couldn't have solved any of them without your involvement over the last week and change. Managed to wrap up five just like that, and then you snagged the sixth less than twelve hours later. I wanted to acknowledge that in person. And I wanted to thank you."

She nodded. "Message received. And, you know, in the future, feel free to consider me something a little higher up the food chain than just your local pain in the ass. I *am* good for something, sometimes."

"Don't push your luck." Colton snorted, then finally stepped aside so she could head up the front porch steps while he walked out to his squad car at the curb.

Sam felt herself wearing that shit-eating grin she normally reserved for flashing at the chief whenever she knew he'd be pissed off to see her, but this time, she didn't bother turning around to make sure he saw it.

She stopped at Charles' front door and knocked before readjusting the bouquet of flowers settled in the crook of her arm.

The knob turned. The door creaked slowly open. Sam

had to lower her gaze by at least a foot to look her host in the eye. "Hey, Frankie."

"Sam!" The boy grinned. "Wanna come in?"

"That was the plan, yeah."

He stepped aside to let her through, then eagerly shut the door behind her before racing off through the house. "Dad? Dad! It's Sam!"

"We're in the living room," Patty called.

Sam made her way there, and when she entered, she saw both Charles and Patty sitting on the couch together.

Patty stood with a knowing smile and quickly wiped the corners of her eyes. "It's good to see you, Sam."

"You too. I hope this isn't a bad time."

"It's never a bad time for *you*," Charles said before turning around on the couch to face her.

He'd clearly been crying as well — his eyes puffy and red-rimmed, the tip of his nose just a darker shade of red, and his hair was streaked back away from his forehead but still sticking up at an odd angle where he'd run his hands through it repeatedly.

Oddly enough, the sight of a grown man crying in front of his son and girlfriend didn't make Sam feel like she'd just stepped into an episode of *The Twilight Zone*.

Instead, she stepped farther into their living room and rounded the couch to offer the flowers directly to Charles himself.

Stunned at first, he blinked in surprise at the bouquet before glancing up at her. "What are these for?"

"Compassion and empathy," she said. "To show you I know a little about what you're going through. To show you you're not alone. That's what somebody told me a while back, anyway. Beyond that, though, the flowers are to say I know what it's like to lose someone important to you, to experience their death over and over again just because you're trying so hard to keep the memory of them alive. They mean, 'I understand.' And if you're up to it, Chuck, I'd love to hear about Rose."

The man gaped at her, stunned and speechless, until Patty finally stepped forward and gingerly took the bouquet from Sam's hands.

"I'll go find a vase for these. They're beautiful, Sam. Thank you. And then I'll make some tea."

"Coffee," Charles quickly corrected with a sheepish smile.

Sam choked back a snorting laugh.

Patty's smile just widened. "Right. Coffee from here on out. Gotcha. I'll be right back. Frankie, come help me with these."

As Patty and Frankie left for the kitchen, Sam sat down on the couch beside Charles, leaving plenty of room for personal space but still close enough to show she wasn't completely freaked out by this period of renewed mourning.

"You really want to hear about her?" he asked.

"If you wanna tell me. Absolutely."

"Okay, then." Charles stood, walked across the living room toward one of the bookshelves, then pulled out a large, leather-bound volume to bring back with him. He returned to his seat on the couch with a heavy but contented sigh.

The spine of the large book creaked loudly when he opened the front cover to reveal the first page of his family's photo album. There, right up top, large and perfectly centered, was a gorgeous photo of Rose that had to have been taken at least twenty years ago, judging by the slightly faded color of the print and how young and insanely happy she looked.

Sam recognized it as the photo Charles had offered the

police six years ago to use on his wife's Missing poster. Only *this* version was the original.

"I took this picture of her two weeks after we met," he said.

Sam shot him a sidelong look and a gentle smile. "It's a good one. Show me more."

The End

About The Author

Lauren Street has always loved a mystery. As a kid growing up in bible belt country she devoured every whodunit book she could get her sticky little hands on and secretly investigated all of her (seemingly) normal boring neighbors. Sometimes their pets and farm animals too. All grown up now and living in the UK with her thoroughly unsuspicious (and often unsuspecting) husband, she writes domestic psychological thrillers about families torn apart by secrets and lies. And she sometimes still peers over garden walls to check up on the neighbors.

Also By Lauren Street

The Bishop Smoky Mountain Thrillers

Hide Me Away

Fuel To The Flame

Closer By The Hour

A Gamble Either Way

Calling My Children Home

Too Far Gone

Here You Come Again

A Friend Like You

Replaced with Nolon King

Replaced

In Her Place

Irreplaceable

The Salzar Redwood Forest Thrillers

The Girl Who Couldn't Stop Dying

The Girl Who Couldn't Get Out

The Girl Who Couldn't Be Found